Viet Nam Body Count

By

MUSHROOM MONTOYA

ISBN-10: 1484132823:
ISBN-13: 978-1484132821

DEDICATION

This book is dedicated to all the parents who's sons and daughters died in Viet Nam, be they South or North Vietnamese, Hmong, American, Chinese or Russian. This book is also dedicated to all those who died or were harmed in Viet Nam, be they soldiers or civilians, children or the elderly.

Contents

ACKNOWLEDGMENTS ii

1 – DISCHARGE HEARING 2

2 – DAY ONE, THEY'RE JUST TARGETS 6

3 – FIRST LETTER HOME...14

4 – POOP DECK 20

5 – IVAN FALLS IN THE MESS DECKS............................26

6 – THE DREAM WEAVER'S OMEN 30

7 – PAYDAY 34

8 – GETTING TO KNOW THE CHIEF..............................40

9 – CLASS LEADER 46

10 – JAFFE'S NIGGERS...51

11- MAIL CALL 56

12 – REQUEST FOR COOKING OIL................................64

13 – HOTDOG PROTOCOL 68

14 – ONE OF OUR FIFTY IS MISSING 72

15 – SAINT JANE 78

16 - WHISPERING 84

17 – NEGLIGEE AND DIAMONDS 88

18 – IN THE EYES OF THE BEHOLDER 91

19 - PISTOL..96

20 – REFUSAL TO FIRE THE ROCKETS 106

21 – WHITE FLARES 113

22 – BITTEN FINGERS 119

23 – VIET NAM MEDITATION 124

24 – SEA FAIRIES 130

25 – BODY COUNT 134

26 – STANDING INSPECTION 140

27 – MIG ATTACK..146

28 – BUTTON EYES 158

29 – TALKING ABOUT GIRLS WITH FREDDY 166

30 – BREAD AND THE CHURCH.......................................172

31 – SETTLING ON A SOLUTION 177

32 – FIXING THE HATCH 182

33 – THE KNOCK..190

34 – SNEAKING UP TO THE HELO DECK.....................194

35 – FORCED SILENCE...200

37 – MAKING AMENDS WITH FREDDY..........................204

36 - NO! NOT JEREMY! 210

38 – THREE DAYS OF SILENCE 218

39 – DISPELLING THE LEGEND 228

40 – IT LURKS...236

41 – PHONING HOME 244

42 - NIS COMES CALLING 250

43 – FIRE DRILL..260

44 - USS WARRINGTON DD 843 264

45 – BATTLE STATION GRUNT 268

46 - GREED 272

47 – REARDON"S PLEA 276

48 – DEATH IN THE FAMILY 282

49 – THOUGHTS OF HOME 286

50 – SHE HAD MY EYES 290

51 – WOULD FREDDY REALLY SHOOT HIM?.................296

52 – THE DECISION 304

53 – LETTER T FOR TRUTH IS TREASON 308

54 – ANOTHER PAIR OF PANTS 314

55 – MATTY'S REVELATION...320

56 – JAFFE'S RESCUE 328

57 – BLUE DAMSELS 336

58 – THE FINAL DECISION 342

Viet Nam Body Count

ACKNOWLEDGMENTS

I want to thank the people that I served with in Viet Nam aboard the USS John Trippe DE1075. A special thank you goes out to Matty, Gary "Krack" Krackenberger, and Norman Poulin who's courage I continue to be grateful for.

Thank you to my writers group: John Stacy, Nancy Mary, Daal Praderas, Barbara Eknoian, and Vonda Pelto for the many hours they spent reviewing my chapters, offering suggestions and for their encouragement.

Thank you to Kathy and Kiss who were my lifeline to sanity when I was in Viet Nam.

Thank you to Denise, my loving spouse, for being understanding when I went through depressing moods while calling forth long hidden memories to write this book. She spent countless hours reading my chapters and encouraging me to seek help from the VA PTSD counselors.

I want to thank the VA Medical Center, Long Beach for the work they do to help veterans.

Thank you to my adult children, Celeste, Bonnie and Orlando, who encouraged me to write about what I have kept painfully hidden all these years.

Thank you to Chief Jaffe (not his real name) for the opportunities to practice forgiveness and standing up for myself.

Thank you to my little sister, Mary Montoya, a Navy veteran, for her expertise in how to cuss like a true #%*&# sailor, goddammit!

Some of the names and time frames have been changed to protect the guilty and incriminate the innocent.

Viet Nam Body Count

1 – DISCHARGE HEARING

"Are you sure you want to go through with this?" my father asked as he walked from the kitchen and put his newspaper on the dining room table. The headline story for April 5, 1975 showed a photo of a plane crash and a story about the Vietnamese baby lift. He took a slow sip from his coffee cup. His brow furrowed as his eyes looked inward. The clock ticked louder than usual. "I wish you'd reconsider filing," he said. "This could ruin your life."

"My life will never be as screwed up as the Vietnamese children who we maimed with our bombs and rockets or turned into orphans like those kids in the paper."

My father squinched his eyes and asked, "What if they give you less than an honorable discharge?"

"We've gone over this, Dad. I know you were proud to be in the Navy during World War Two. Viet Nam is nothing to be proud of." I looked at my reflection in the wood framed mirror that hung on the wall behind the couch as I retied my black Navy neckerchief. "Too many innocent people got killed and maimed. One of my shipmates came home in a body bag."

Denise stood beside me, wearing her light blue mini skirt. She put her arm around my waist and hugged me saying, "We were always afraid that you might be killed."

My mother came out of the bathroom wearing her burgundy

Sunday dress, holding a lint roller in her right hand. She stood behind me and ran it along the back of my navy blues. "Every night, after the evening news announced the number of casualties, we prayed for their parents and for God to keep you safe."

"That's why I have to do this, Mom. No parent should have to worry about their children being killed in war. I wish Dad understood."

"Your dad really is behind you on this, even if he doesn't sound like it," she said, as she rolled the lint remover down my arms. "We are both proud of you. He just hopes that you aren't ruining your chances for a good job in the future by doing this."

"What good is a well-paying job, if I can't look at myself in the mirror because a coward looks back at me?"

"You always make things so dramatic," my mother said, as she bent down to roll the lint remover down my wool bell bottoms. "It's hard to believe your pants pick up so much lint and dog hair."

"You did two tours in Viet Nam," Denise said. "That shows that you're not a coward."

My mother stood up, looked into my eyes and shook the lint roller at me. "We prayed for you every day that you were there. We went to Mass every Sunday."

"You and Dad never miss going to church on Sunday."

"You know what I mean," she said. "We were worried about you. Your letters scared me. I cried every time one came through the front door mail slot."

My dad walked over to the electric clock mounted on the wall above the kitchen door. He synchronized his watch and then turned to us. "We have to go or we'll be late. Your hearing is at eight, right?"

I nodded affirmatively.

"Are you sure that they won't retaliate?" he asked.

I looked at my dad, let out a big sigh and bent down on one knee to polish a smudge off my black shoes. My father was concerned about the Navy's propensity for retaliation against minorities. That had been his experience in WWII.

"If the hearing goes well, I will be out of the Navy with an honorable discharge and they won't be able to touch me," I said. Denise and I walked out the front door with my parents following close behind. I looked back at my dad. "If it doesn't, I'll have hell to pay for the next six months. I can handle it."

I opened the passenger side door of my parents 1969 blue Chevrolet Impala, gave the keys back to my father, and held the door for Denise. I admired her long legs in her little blue skirt as she scooted into the back seat. I squeezed in next to her. My mother got in, pulled a little mirror out of her purse and checked her lipstick. My father pushed his foot on the clutch, inserted the key in the ignition and turned it to the right.

The car radio came on with the end of the news broadcast, "Yesterday, a judge released Lt. Calley, the convicted war criminal, on bail. More on the hour." That was immediately followed by a commercial for a new 1974 Chevy Blazer, "It never forgets it's a tough truck."

"I can't believe that they released that murderer," my father said, slamming his hand on the steering wheel, as he drove. "He disgraced America and stained our flag."

"Riders on the Storm" by the Doors played its low rumbling rhythm next. My dad leaned over and turned it off. No one spoke. When we drove over the bridge onto Terminal Island toward the Navy base, my stomach tightened with apprehension. A marine guard stopped us at the gate and checked our IDs. My hands were already sweating.

Dad parked to the side of the old concrete administration building, in front of a visitor parking sign. My mother got out and held the car door for Denise and me. A cool salt breeze blew in my face, making me shiver. I reached into my pants pocket and pulled out a piece of paper with directions to the hearing room.

"It's on the second floor," I said. "Room 202."

Two palm trees flanked the sidewalk leading to the entrance and cast long winter shadows across the road. We walked up five steps and met a marine guard, standing at attention at the front door. He directed us to the stairway in the middle of the corridor. The building was cold, even though I felt the heat coming out of the old steam radiators along the walls as I walked by. We climbed the Spanish tile stairs and walked down an eight foot wide hallway. The sound of our shoes striking the tile floor echoed loudly. The dark wooden door to room 202 was open at the end of the hallway. The room was dim, lit only by the north facing windows. We walked in and stood just inside the door. The off-white walls had a four foot tall mahogany wainscot. A long highly polished mahogany table rested at one end of the room. Three leather and wood chairs were positioned on one side of the table. A lone wooden chair sat on the opposite side. Four rows of wooden chairs filled the rest of the room.

A Navy chief entered behind us and flipped on the lights. We all turned. My stomach did a somersault. He wore perfectly pressed khakis and sported a flat top haircut. He held a manila envelope under his arm.

"You must be here for the hearing, right?" he asked. "Are these your parents and your wife?" Without waiting for an answer, he turned to them and pointed to the rows of chairs saying, "You can sit back there." When they went to take their seats, he pointed to the lone chair. "You sit there and wait until the hearing officers get here."

When my mother went to take her seat, she gave me a supportive wink. For a split second, her eyes reminded me of the vision of the Vietnamese lady who visited me in my meditation sessions so often in Viet Nam. A chill electrified my spine.

The chief put the manila folder on the table in front of the middle leather and wood chair. When I saw my name on the tab, my bladder and my stomach began competing for attention. As I pulled the lone chair away from the table to sit, I wanted to ask the chief where the restroom was located and if there would be enough time.

The chief must have read my thoughts. "If you need to use the head, go down the hallway past the stairs you came up. The men's is on the right and the women's is on the left. You have about fifteen minutes before we start."

I jumped up quickly and walked to the men's room. I stood in front of the old white porcelain urinal and slowly unfastened the thirteen buttons on my dress blues. My stomach tensed as I wished that this hearing didn't have to happen. Two weeks ago I had filled out all the required forms, attached letters of support from the parish priest, neighbors, and longtime friends. I hoped they were convincing. I worried about the questions they would ask at the hearing.

"This hearing is going to be a battle," I said to myself. "It's one I have to win." As I walked out of the men's room and back down the hallway to room 202, the clacking of my heels against the cold tile floor propelled my thoughts back to my first day in battle in the Tonkin Gulf.

2 – DAY ONE, THEY'RE JUST TARGETS

Three years earlier, the clacking of my heels echoed off the steel bulkhead of the U.S.S. Jon Trippe as I hurried along the passageway on my way to the helo deck for a special announcement from the ship's captain. "Now hear this, now hear this. All hands on deck," came over the ship's intercom as I took my position with the other members of the repair gang. The dial on my brand new orange Seiko watch pointed to 17:00 and its date box showed 7-2-72. We were dressed in our work uniforms; bell bottom dungarees and white cotton T-shirts. The officers and chiefs wore khakis. My boss, Chief Jaffe, stood on deck facing the open helo hangar door. As always, his shirt and pants were perfectly pressed and starched.

Otis, an eighteen year old electricians mate, stood next to me and said, "You're wearing the .45 caliber pistol. Where's the sounding tape and clipboard?"

"I left them inside, next to the hangar door," I said. "Why do you want to know?"

"If we get to Viet Nam tonight, I want to be wearing that gun. I hope the captain tells us when we're going to get there. I have the next sounding and security watch at 20:00."

We came to attention when Captain Reardon walked into the hangar and stood behind a wooden podium. He turned his ear to listen for the thumpity thump when he tapped the microphone

6

with his finger. He cleared his throat.

"Tomorrow morning, at 08:00, we go into battle," he said. "We will earn our combat ribbons as we fight the Viet Cong. Communism is a threat to America and to the world. We are here to drive out the communists and make Viet Nam safe for democracy." He looked down at his notes. "We will be firing our Mk-42 cannon, our M60 machine guns, and our rockets. We not only expect enemy fire, we welcome those commi-gooks to try to blow us out of the water…."

I don't remember what he said after that. The rumbling of the ship's engines grew louder. The winds changed direction, blowing the diesel exhaust fumes into our faces. I felt queasy and my hands began to sweat. I understood my role to drive out the communists from Viet Nam. It was my duty to serve my country with honor, as my father did in the Navy in World War Two. I tried to swallow, but all the moisture had disappeared from my mouth. I looked out over the water. The Viet Nam shoreline and the threat of death waited for us beyond the horizon.

When the captain finished speaking, each chief made an about face and addressed his men. Chief Jaffe put his arms at his sides and screamed out, "A-ten-SHUN!" Then, in an unusually somber voice, he said, "Gentlemen, tomorrow we go into battle. This might be the last time I ever talk to you."

He had never referred to us as gentlemen before. Maggots, pussies, wimps, sorry ass excuses for something only slightly more intelligent than a sea slug, these were our common titles. His demeanor took on an air of patriotic pride. He pulled out a clipboard that he had tucked into the back of his pants and read our names with our assigned battle stations. He told us that the following morning we would join the battle on the gun line in the Gulf of Tonkin, Viet Nam.

"Stay alert and be aware of where you are and where your fellow sailors are at all times," he said, "Make your country proud. Dismissed."

We broke ranks and went to our stations. I resumed my sounding and security watch, making my rounds throughout the ship. I looked at the pistol hanging on my hip and rubbed my hand over the holster. I wondered if I could really kill someone and shuddered. After I entered the bridge at 20:00, I gave my final report to the officer on deck. Otis stood next to the helmsman, watching me remove the clip from the gun and inspect the pistol's barrel to ensure that it was clear. I replaced the clip and handed Otis the gun.

"We're safe until tomorrow," I said. "I'm going to hit the sack and try to get some sleep. We need to be rested and ready for tomorrow's battle."

I ambled my way to the berthing compartment that I shared with twenty-one other shipmates. The space was cramped; measuring fifteen feet deep by eighteen feet wide, with racks stacked three high. It was dark, except for a dim red light near the steel entry door. I stripped down to my underwear, put my clothes in my locker, and climbed to the top of three racks to get to my bed. I pulled the thin white sheet over me and laid my head on my pillow. My muscles would not relax enough for me to fall easily into much needed slumber. I turned over on my stomach, closed my eyes and tried to go to sleep, but the captain's words, "Tomorrow we go into battle," repeatedly dove into the pit of my stomach, setting off miniature grenades, making me twitch involuntarily until sleep took over.

"Mushroom, wake up," Otis said, shaking my shoulder.

I pulled my sheet away and climbed down from my top rack. The captain's words revisited me as I turned the combination and opened my locker.

"Come on." Otis said, rubbing his stomach. "I'm starving. Let's hurry and get some breakfast before they call morning muster."

The scrambled eggs tasted as if they had been cooked in last night's fish pan. The milk's texture seemed thicker than normal. The smell of cigarette smoke made me want to gag. Everything seemed out of kilter. "Now hear this, now hear this. All hands on deck!" came over the ship's intercom.

"We'd better not be late," Otis said, his eyes opened wide. "Not today. Not on our first day on the gun line."

We put our food trays into the dishwasher's window, then ran out of the mess decks, along the exterior passageway, passed the life boat and up the ladder to the helo deck to join ranks with the other members of "R"gang, the ship's repair crew. My stomach felt as if a swarm of anchovies were flopping around inside, making everything below my bellybutton twitch.

Chief Jaffe stood at the back of the helo deck waiting for us to take our places at muster. Otis and I stood in the back row. Our pants fluttered in the wind to the same vibration of the ship's rumbling. My abdomen squeezed when up ahead, I saw hills rising out of the horizon, our destination: Viet Nam.

"A-ten-shun!" the chief yelled. "You were assigned your battle stations last night. In a few minutes we will join the other ships in the gun line. This is our finest hour. Make your country proud. Dismissed."

I had been assigned to an alternate battle station as a spotter. My job entailed looking through the big eyes to identify our targets and verify our hits. The big eyes were huge gray binoculars, about a full arm's length that were mounted on a heavy steel tripod. I was a second pair of eyes for the Mk-42's gunners mate. This was my first glimpse of "real war"; no more simulations, no more trial runs, no more practice.

I leaned over the side of the ship as we approached the shore. I could see the sand on the bottom. The white sandy beach had a back drop of lush green jungle behind it. The aromas of salt spray, diesel exhaust, and jungle musk filled the air. I had never seen a beach that pristine or trees that vibrantly green, even along the Southern California coast. Its beauty held me in awe.

The gunner, with his pudgy freckled face and carrot colored hair, yelled out, "Keep a sharp lookout," as he ran past me, still tying his helmet straps. He reminded me of the boys in the Norman Rockwell paintings. He stopped, turned around, wide-eyed, excited. "I'm gonna blow the fuck out of those gooks. Watch me."

He made an about face then ran to the gun mount, opened the side door, and climbed into the big gray bubble that sat on the ship's bow, hiding all but the Mk-42 cannon's twenty-two foot long barrel inside. We called the cannon our five-inch gun because that was the diameter of the barrel.

The ship made a hard turn to port. The water was so clear and clean, I could almost count the grains of sand on the bottom. I worried that we were getting much too close to shore and would run aground. If that were to occur, we'd be like freshly caught fish, waiting for the Viet Cong to pull in their nets and fry us.

I jumped when I heard the blasts from our other ships which were ahead of us. Fear jumped into my belly making it squeeze tight. The smell of gun powder mixed with the ocean spray and the musty scent of the jungle. Exhilaration joined my fear in the mix. My kneecaps shook as all the muscles in my back tightened. I put on the head phones. The barrel of our Mk-42 cannon turned to starboard aiming at the beach.

I peered into the big eyes. As I adjusted the lenses, the beach, sand, and bushes came into focus. Three young boys, barely teenagers, came into view. They carried a heavy, slatted, two foot square wooden box over a small sand dune. The handles looked like they were made out of rope. I tried to identify what they were carrying in the box. Watching them run with the box reminded me of when I was twelve, and my best friend and I found a trunk that resembled a treasure chest in an alley. We ran home with it, hoping to find money or jewels inside. We found nothing. My mother told us that we had stolen it and made us take it back.

The Vietnamese boys wore civilian clothes. The one in the front wore green slacks and a white t-shirt. He caught my attention because he looked like Otis, our young Japanese-American electrician's mate. He ran slightly ahead of the two other boys who were carrying the box.

BAM! The boys carrying the box disappeared into the smoke along with the box. Direct hit! Screams, smoke, and body parts. An electric jolt shocked me just below my navel, making me almost puke.

"Wait! Wait!" I screamed into the microphone, waving my hand for the gunner to stop.

The boy wearing green slacks got up and ran as fast as he could. My abdomen vibrated, tightened and vibrated again. I found myself hoping that the kid could run faster.

BAM! Again. No screams, just smoke and a green lump lying on the sand.

My whole body trembled. So much sweat poured out of my hands that I couldn't turn the focus adjustments on the big eyes. I dried my hands on my pants.

The gunner climbed out of the gun mount and ran over to me, smiling wildly. He removed his helmet and wiped off the sweat from his brow with his forearm. "Did you see that!" he yelled, "Three kills with only two shots!"

"What are you talking about?!" I screamed. "I told you to stop! You don't know who they were. You never gave me a chance to identify them. They were young boys, civilians."

"Fuck you!" he shouted back. His lips were redder than normal, accentuated by his freckled face and his flat top haircut. "Why did you have to go and spoil it? That's a better than perfect hit on a moving target."

"Spoil it? Spoil what? They were just boys!" I yelled. The hairs on the back of my head felt as if they were standing straight out.

"They're not boys!" he shrieked, his cheeks turning red. "They're not people, they are just targets! Damn it! I couldn't do my job if they were people." He spit on the deck and turned around to climb back inside the five inch gun mount. Just before he entered he called over his shoulder, " You're such an asshole! They are just targets!"

My knees trembled uncontrollably as my feet began to sweat. The Trippe had sailed too far away from our first kill for me to see if anyone was trying to rescue their bodies or the box. I did not want to look through the big eyes anymore. I did not want to see any more flying body parts from any more people that looked like my cousins running for their lives on the beach. The gunner's ears were closed to my screams to make him stop. My fingers wrapped around the big eyes as I leaned my head against the rubber gasket on the lens.

"Why did I ever join the Navy?" I cried out, but the blasts from the gun drowned out my voice.

No amount of training had prepared my heart for going into battle. I knew my job inside out. I had rehearsed putting out fires, fixing broken pipes, patching big holes in the ship's side. But no one had taught me how to calm my nerves or keep my feet from sweating when I heard the gun blasts. No one had given me training on how to keep my heart from getting into my head and telling me that we had just blown up children.

Up ahead of me, our five inch gun, along with those of the other ships on the gun line, blasted away into the jungle beyond the beach. I was caught between being in awe at how beautiful the beach and jungle were, and the horror of blowing up paradise and boys. Not even fish were safe. The Captain's percussion grenades brought them floating to the surface as we slithered to and fro on the gun line. I endured the next five hours looking through the big eyes seeing death and beauty side by side. I didn't say anything to the gunner. He wasn't listening, anyway. I could feel my spirit trying to run away because I didn't have the power to stop; to stop the senseless killing.

The gunner climbed out of the gun mount when our battle station watch finally ended. Sweat dripped down the sides of his head. He walked past me, glared, and said, "You're no good to me as a spotter. I'm getting you replaced, asshole!"

Getting replaced would be a welcome relief. I didn't want to see our guns kill any more people. The gunner could call them targets if he wanted, but they were still flesh and blood. His first three targets were just kids.

The U.S.S. Trippe stopped bombing the shore and headed out to the open sea at 16:00 to replenish our supply of arms. After the ammo ship sailed away, I trudged toward the galley to eat dinner. The captain and the XO (executive officer) stood in the passageway, blocking my way. I waited.

"Get me the name of the gunners mate," the captain said, turning to the XO. "The one who manned the five inch gun when we joined the gun line this morning,"

"What's up? Will I need to be involved?" the XO asked.

The executive officer is responsible for all personnel matters.

"I want to congratulate him," the captain said.

Why would the captain want to congratulate him? I had assumed that the gunner would be in trouble for not giving me the time to verify our target before he fired and killed those three young civilians.

"Is he the one who had three kills with only two shots?" the XO asked.

"Yes," said the captain, beaming with a proud smile, as if he had done the shooting himself. "I bet no other ship has done that within their first few minutes on the gun line."

"We can stick that feather in our cap," the XO said.

"I can't believe how lucky we were today," said the ship's captain. "My body count started as soon as we sailed onto the gun line."

Body count? He can't be serious. How can he be happy about killing boys? My whole body stiffened and my breathing accelerated.

"If we can keep this up," he said, "I'll advance from the rank of commander to captain before we leave Viet Nam."

I stood, frozen. The ship swayed as it slid over the ocean's swells. The captain and the XO continued through the passageway without acknowledging me.

I couldn't believe the conversation that I had just heard. *We're lucky?* I thought. *Body count? Killing people to make rank? Is this what body count is all about? Making rank? Oh, my god! We killed people today. I saw it. I'm part of it. I certainly don't feel lucky. I feel like I did something immoral and that I need to fix it, but can't. Doesn't anyone else feel this way?*

I wobbled through the passageway and into the galley. I stood in line, grabbed a tray and some utensils. I passed through the chow line, oblivious to the aromas from roast beef, reconstituted mashed potatoes, and canned corn that the cook plopped into my tray. I sat alone, unable to speak. The captain's words ricocheted in my head, "lucky…body count…earning rank." Those words may have made more sense last night. But that was before we killed three young boys.

I couldn't taste the food. Unable to finish more than a couple of bites, I stood up and dumped my food into the garbage. I felt nauseous. The mess deck was stuffy and hot. I headed outside for some air. I needed to run, to scream.

I climbed the ladder to the next deck. Seeing the ship's single smokestack, I ran toward it. My arms and legs took on a life of their own as I ran. I circled the smokestack and I let out a scream. I couldn't stop. I didn't want to stop. I went on screaming and running around the smokestack until my throat had drained of all its sound. Sweat slid down my neck and into my shirt. I exhausted myself. I couldn't catch my breath until I slumped to the deck, leaning my back against the smokestack.

I felt eyes penetrating me. I looked across to the helo deck. Chief Jaffe held onto the lifeline, his hands white knuckled. His stone cold eyes glared at me.

3 – FIRST LETTER HOME

The sun began its nightly descent. The warm air embraced me, giving me a salty kiss on my lips. Salt covered everything. A layer of gray gooey salt obscured my glasses. As I wiped them off with my shirt, I wondered if the salt would scratch them. Norman, the rocket launcher from Leominster, Massachusetts, came up to me, cleaning his glasses as well.

"They'ah gonna think you ah crazy, ya know," he said, in his Boston like accent. "You almost crashed into me when you ran to the smokestack, screaming. At first, I thought something had happened to you. I started to come over to see what was wrong. Then, I don't know why, I waited and watched you run around and around. Why were you doing that?"

My stomach tightened into a ball. Why did I scream? I didn't know how to answer him. I wanted to tell him that I felt as if something had taken over my body. My legs buzzed and my knees twitched and the scream came from deep inside me. I just stood there, staring, waiting for the words to come out. Finally, I said, "The U.S.S. Trippe tripped up big time. She has fallen from grace."

"What the hell are you talking about?"

"We came here to kill communists."

"Yeah, so?"

"The U.S.S. Trippe is a new Knox class destroyer escort on her first combat mission. Her first kill, ever, was not a Viet Cong soldier; it was a group of three young boys, civilians."

"How do you know that?"

"I saw the whole mess, looking through the big eyes. We murdered three boys with our first two shots on the gun line. I don't remember how many more we killed after that. We're tainted with the blood of innocent civilians. We've lost our innocence."

"Don't go and get too philosophical on me," Norman said. He stood motionless for a moment. The sea breeze fanned his enormous red beard that flowed half way down his chest. Stroking his beard while clearing his throat, he said, "I heard the radiomen talking in the galley. We're getting into some heavy shit tonight."

"Nighttime shore bombardment?" I asked. "More killing. Shit!"

I inhaled deeply, waited a few seconds and let it out slowly. Then I asked, "How will we know where to aim our guns?"

"Computers." Norman said will all seriousness, "We've got some pretty sophisticated computers on board that allow us to hit just about anything we want within our range. Remember, I'm a Fire Control Technician, trained to work the computers that fire and guide the rockets. So don't plan on getting any sleep tonight."

Night flew in from the east by the time I gathered my wits enough to stand my battle station watch. At 19:50, I stopped at my berthing compartment on the way to my battle station. I grabbed my purple stationary and purple pen that brought a little piece of home into my hands. Their purple color made me feel artistic and non-military. Sailing close to shore gave us a better firing range, but it also made us vulnerable. Expecting our ship to get hit racked my nerves. I needed a distraction. Since each battle station watch lasted five hours, I had plenty of time to write a letter. I took a clip board out of the repair locker so that I could have a hard surface upon which to write. Sitting on the deck, I began my letter.

Otis came over, sat beside me. He was a young 18 year old, who looked one hundred percent Japanese, like his mother. His dad's family had lived in the backwoods of Kentucky for generations. The only obvious Kentucky things about Otis were his name and his accent. Otis usually succeeded in hiding his accent, but when it sneaked out, I always grinned.

"What'cha doing?" Otis asked.

"I'm almost finished with this letter I'm writing to my little brother, it's his birthday."

"Really? What's it say so far? Can you read it to me? Maybe it'll give me some ideas to write to my momma."

"Happy Birthday, John, your turning seventeen makes me feel old, even though I'm barely twenty-two. The USS Trippe killed her first North Vietnamese today. Somebody's mother's child is dead and, unfortunately, I was part of that. It makes me sick just to think about it. Vietnamese mothers are going to be crying tonight, just like Aunt Tima did when she found out that her son got killed over here. I can't tell you much though `cause mom's ears and eyes would hurt. And the censors won't send my letter on if I say too much. Don't tell mom or dad, they'll only worry."

Otis interrupted, "I couldn't write and tell my momma that. She'd tell my poppa and they'd both be worrying like a couple of hogs at the slaughter house. I thought our first shots killed those three boys. Aren't you gonna tell your brother about that?"

"I left that out because the censors will block it and I might get in trouble."

"I didn't think about the censors," he said. "What can we write about then?"

"If you let me continue, I wrote about what we do, meaning what our jobs are. Ready to listen?"

"Yeah, that's a good idea," he said, "I could tell my momma that."

"Then listen up." Continuing with the letter I read aloud, "By the time I get back home, you'll be eighteen and you could hook me up with some girls. Are you practicing on that guitar I bought for you? When you get the chance, send me some cassette tapes, the new Peter, Paul and Mary album or the Moody Blues would be great."

Otis piped in, "Why don't you ask for Dolly Parton? I really like her music."

"I don't really care for country music, Otis. I'm pretty thoroughly Californicated, although, I do like some Dolly Parton, and I like Poco. Why don't you write to your mom and ask her to send you some Dolly Parton cassettes."

"Naw, my momma don't like Dolly Parton on account of her big boobs. My momma says that God didn't make boobs just to have men gawk at 'em. And Dolly Parton obviously made her boobs really big so men could gawk."

"Let me finish reading my letter to you, so that I can finish writing it and send it home."

"Don't let me stop ya," Otis said, grinning too widely.

"My boss, Chief Jaffe, gave us our semi-annual evaluations this week. I got all fives. That's like getting all "As" on a report card. But he added that I was a "Peace-nik" in the comments section."

Otis's eyes grew wide as he asked, "You got all fives? But he doesn't even like you."

"Exactly!" I said, "But, since I do more than what I'm required to do, and whenever, he sends me out to fix the plumbing or to weld something back together, I make sure that I do it right so that he can't send me back to do it over. When I get assigned to compartment cleaner, I make our compartment so clean that you could eat off of the floor. I make him obey his own rules when I do a better job than anyone else."

"You do that just to get fives on your evaluations?"

"No, Otis. I do that to make sure that he can't take away my liberty when we're in port."

"You're smarter than you look, Mushroom. What else does your letter say?"

"Let me see. Oh yeah, here's where I left off," I said. "I'm in R-Gang. The R stands for repair. Our job is to fix anything that breaks. And, when we get attacked, our job is to keep the ship from sinking. I remember you asking me why I don't know more about knots and rope. There are two groups in the Navy: the deck apes or swabbies and the snipes. The deck apes are the sailors who do things with the ropes and swab the deck. They are the guys who drive the ship and tie it up when we get to port. They also paint the ship. There is so much salt in the ocean that those guys are always painting to keep the ship from rusting. I found out that everything above the main deck is made out of aluminum. And the steel below is only a quarter of an inch thick. That's scary because even a small blast could poke a big hole and sink us. Don't tell mom or dad that part. Dad was in WWII and those battle ships had hulls that were a foot thick. Let dad think that I'm on a thick skinned ship.

I'm a snipe. I'm part of the engineering group. We make sure the ship runs smoothly. We fix the plumbing, we fix and maintain the engines, and we get dirty with oil. My primary job is a fire fighter. I'm in charge of training part of the crew to rescue the helicopters in case they crash or catch on fire. Don't tell mom and dad that either. Just tell them that I am a plumber and a welder.

We're on the gun line. That means that our ship gets in line with a few other ships and we bomb the hell out of the Viet Cong near the shore. Our five-inch gun can shoot seventy pound bombs fourteen miles inland. And we can shoot twenty-eight of those bombs a minute. I'm surprised that I'm not deaf already. It's ironic that they call our MK-42 cannon a five-inch gun. It's huge. The barrel is over twenty-two feet long. Actually they call it a five-inch gun because that is the diameter of the barrel. I think that they should call it a twenty-two foot gun or a sixty ton gun. Did I mention how loud it is?

Please send me Jeremy's shoe size. Take out a ruler and measure his feet. I'm going to buy him some shoes when we get to port.

Tell everyone that I miss them, especially, Jeremy.

Love Mushroom"

"That's a good letter, Mushroom, but who's Jeremy?"

"I have a two year old son. My parents are taking care of him while I'm in the Navy."

Otis stood up and stretched. Looking down at me he said, "Well, you'd better make sure that you don't get killed or your son will be a war orphan."

4 – POOP DECK

"Who's the asshole who shit on the deck?!? That's fucking gross!"

I heard the gunner yell as I made my way toward the bow on my rounds on Sounding and Security watch. My nose twitched, fighting to sort out the combined scent of brine, diesel fumes and something that smelled like poop. The sun had not yet come up to paint the morning clouds, attempting to erase the war that waged a few hundred yards off our starboard side. The light from the moon and stars did not expose my presence to the gunner who trudged around the five-inch gun, holding his head down, eyes focused on the deck. He continued yelling obscenities, his arms flailing, his neck muscles bulging as he scanned the deck around the forward cannon. He reminded me of an angry Donald Duck, dressed in his sailor outfit, throwing a fit.

"What's gross?" I asked. The gunner's ranting blocked my words.

"I'm going to kill that cock sucking asshole when I find out who he is."

"What are you yelling about? Who?" I asked.

"I don't know who," he said finally acknowledging my

presence. "But when I find out who shit next to this gun, I'm going to kill him. God damn peace-nick!" he yelled as he spit over the side.

"What are you talking about?"

"I know it's dark, but not that fuckin dark. Look!" he said, pointing to a brown lump on the deck. "Some mother fucker took a crap right there, next to my god damn five-inch gun. Right where I climb down."

"Holy shit! Does whoever took a crap know that this is not the poop deck?" I asked, smiling at my own cleverness.

"Fuck off, Mushroom. I'm in no mood for your jokes. You were on watch last night; didn't you see who did this?"

"No, I didn't see anyone. I can't stand poop guard over the five-inch gun all night long." I said as a chuckle escaped through my throat.

"You're such an asshole!" he said, "Don't laugh. This isn't fucking funny. I have to clean that shit up."

"What's the big deal?"

"My god damn shoes, that's what! I stepped in it when I got down from the gun."

My shoulders began shaking, as I worked hard to suppress a burst of laughter. "At least it is not as bad as stepping into my shoes and finding warm vomit," I said.

"Oh, that is gross. When did that happen?"

"The last time we were in Subic, the first class Hull Tech came back drunk one night and up chucked on the floor and into my shoe."

"Yeah, that might be grosser, but shitting on the deck is just plain sick!" he said.

The ship turned, propelling the scent of poop to my nostrils. "Holy shit! That stinks!" I said.

My smile made his teeth clench as he blurted out, "You're a fucking asshole. This isn't funny!"

"Just get a hose and you can wash off your shoes and the deck." I offered.

Removing his left shoe, he stormed off, saying, "Don't go anywhere, I still want to talk to you. Just wait here, while I get the hose."

While he walked off, Norman came by and asked me if I knew who was causing all the ruckus. When I told him that someone shit in front of the entry door to the five-inch gun and that the gunner stepped in it when he dismounted, Normal burst out laughing, and then stopped abruptly. He scanned the horizon, as if searching for words in the hills to the west, to explain how he felt.

"It serves the asshole right," he said. "It pisses me off knowing how much he enjoys talking about his kills."

"I don't like it either," I said. "He's been that way since the first day on the gun line. He threw a fit and got me kicked off spotter duty because I yelled at him for killing the three boys before I could identify who they were."

Norman grabbed my arm and pulled me closer to him. I could feel his enormous beard on my cheek as he whispered, "Ever since our body count turned sour from our killing too many civilians and especially our own people, a lot of the guys have been talking about how they hate this war and how they think it's fucking wrong."

"I'm not surprised," I said. "It's too bad that it took killing all those innocent people to wake them up to the truth."

"You woke them up."

"How did I do that?"

"When you started screaming around that big dick of a smoke stack, they couldn't pretend that what we're doing here is the right."

"My screaming can't have that much of an impact, can it?"

"The hell it doesn't," he said, turning back to look at me, "Every time we get news that we overshot our target and killed innocent villagers, the guys on the ship work harder trying to bluff their way through this war. They pretend that they are protecting America from communists. But not you. You run around that smokestack every night after dinner and scream. You tell us all that we're a bunch of fucking killers."

"No I don't!" I said. "I don't say anything when I scream. And I never use the F word."

"Well, you should, you'd get some fucking sympathy if you did."

"I'm not looking for fu ... Hell, I can't even say it. I'm not looking for fucking sympathy. Boy, that sounds weird coming out of my mouth!"

Norman's eyes smiled as his teeth beamed through his beard. "I'm beginning to believe that you really did go to school to study to be a Catholic priest."

"I did. I went to Our Lady Queen of the Angels seminary in California."

Norman turned to look at the shore and pointed above the western hills. The sunrise cast a hint of pink over the sand as its reflection sparkled across the water.

"Look at those clouds," Norman said. "They don't make a fucking impact like you do. They make me feel good. They help me forget the war. They look like sticks of pink cotton candy."

The fragrance from the cinnamon on Norman's apron brought me memories of Indian Fry bread at the New Mexico State Fair.

"Damn I wish I was home," Norman said. "Right about now the county fair is in full swing. If I were there, I'd take my girlfriend."

Bam! We both turned toward the shore. Norman's eyes dropped.

"That blast spoiled my fuckin fantasy. I wonder who fired it. Look! There's black smoke rising over in that jungle to the right of that hill. Shit. I hope it's the Viet Cong and not our guys."

As the gunner stomped back to the bow carrying a coiled hose on his shoulder, he asked, "Where the fuck am I suppose to connect this?"

Norman rolled his eyes. "I gotta go," he said. He patted me on the shoulder and whispered, "Good luck with him."

I helped the gunner connect the hose to a water pipe. His shoulders drooped. His earlier tirade had blown the fury out of his face. His voice sank low, barely audible over the ship's engine.

"It's not fair, you know," he said. "I'm a damn good gunner. That's my job. I don't pick my fuckin targets. I just do what I'm told."

"You say that, but you're totally thrilled whenever you have a kill. You rave about it."

The gunner turned on the hose, picked up his shoe off the deck and turned it over. Placing his thumb over the end of the hose, he washed off his shoe. As he squirted the poop into the ocean, he cocked his head toward me.

"Everyone knows you're a god damn peace-nick. With your name being Mushroom, it's so obvious. But me, I'm just a fucking whore, just faking it. I have to look like I'm enjoying my job. But I don't."

"Why do you do it then?" I asked.

He didn't answer me. His eyes wandered away, searching for a way to respond. We both turned when we heard the machine gun fire from the helicopters on shore.

"See those choppers. If I wasn't such a fuckin good gunner, they'd get shot out of the sky by those gooks."

"I understand that. But you get so excited whenever you kill someone."

The gunner's cheeks flared bright red as he put his face inches away from mine. I could smell his breath of rotted onions as he yelled, "I don't kill anyone! I just hit targets. And I'm fucking good at it. We've already gone over this before. Remember what I told you? They can't be people, they have to be targets. Fuck off and leave me alone."

5 – IVAN FALLS IN THE MESS DECKS

"I can't believe someone actually took a shit by the five-inch gun last night," Otis said to Ivan as they ate lunch in the galley.

I sat a couple of tables away from them, but clearly within earshot. They didn't seem to notice me.

Ivan had manned the five-inch gun during the previous night's bombardment.

"Didn't you see anyone when you were on the gun last night?" Otis asked.

"Once we're inside the gun mount," Ivan said, "we're completely blind to anything around the gun. So there's no fucking way that the other gunner could've seen who shit on the deck."

"I wonder who did it?" Otis asked. "Who would know where the gunner would place his foot when he got down from the gun mount?"

Ivan's face flushed red, as a shit eating grin sneaked up on his face.

"God, Ivan, did you do that? You did! Oh my god. Why?"

"That other gunner's an asshole and he freaks me totally out the way he keeps score of his kills. I can't enjoy it the way he does."

"What do ya mean, Ivan? You're a fucking gunner, too."

"Yeah, I am. And I'm a better shot than that asshole. But when we're ordered to blow up enemy targets, I listen to my spotters before I fire."

Turning around to see who might be listening, Ivan lowered his voice to a whisper, "And when the captain orders us to fire on the villagers, I purposely miss. I don't want innocent people's deaths on my conscience. Not when I can prevent it."

"You're momma would be proud of you for doing that."

"Thanks. Keep your mouth shut and don't you ever repeat what I told you." Slapping Otis on the back, he said, "I just wish I could've seen that asshole's face when he stepped in my shit."

As Otis and Ivan were finishing lunch, and laughing about the other gunner, Ivan ran his fingers along the table's aluminum lip that prevented the food trays from sliding off the table when the ship rocked. Ivan grabbed Otis' hand and ran it along the edge of the table as he said, "Lookie here, Otis, Some idiot gouged a piece of metal off this lip. It's sharp. Someone could get hurt."

"Ouch! I'm gonna hurt you, if you do that again!" Otis said as he inspected the tip of his finger.

"Ya know, Otis, that flack jacket I wear when it's my turn to man the machine gun, don't come anywhere near long enough to cover my balls. Shit, if one of them Gooks shoots me from his boat, he's gonna blow my nuts off."

"Then you can become a soprano in the church choir."

"Fuck you, Otis."

"What are you complaining about? You'll be surrounded by all those choir girls."

"And what girl is gonna wanna date a dude who can't make her a baby?"

Although very different from each other, Otis and Ivan enjoyed the fact that they grew up in the same Kentucky neighborhood. Ivan reached into his pocket and pulled out a letter from his mother.

"Hey lookie here, Otis, I got a letter from Momma. I forgot to open it last night 'cause of that damn bombardment."

"Open it up and read it to me. I didn't get any mail at yesterday's mail call. Did your momma mention anything about my mom?"

"Keep your pants on, I just told you that I haven't read it yet."

Ivan scanned the letter quickly to make sure that his mom didn't write anything that would embarrass him. His smile morphed into a scowl as he read aloud, "I'm sorry to tell you that your brother, Frankie, wrecked your motorcycle. He only bruised his knee, thank the Lord." Ivan's eyebrows scrunched together, looking like two motorcycles crashing into each other. "I'm gonna kill my little brother when I get back home."

"Hey, Ivan, at least your brother's OK."

Ivan looked at his watch and told Otis that he needed to get to his battle station. He still had a scowl on his face when he picked up his metal food tray and stood up. He glared at Otis and said, "Stop ruining my mad."

Laughter broke out on the mess decks. Ivan rolled his eyes. He turned around to leave and lost his sea legs as the ship heaved to the side. With both of his hands still holding onto the food tray, Ivan began his comical descent onto the floor. Laughter erupted again. Bam! His head hit the corner of one of the tables as he tumbled to the floor. We were still laughing as some of us got up from our tables to help him.

Otis flew from his side of the table, being the first one to reach Ivan.

"Hey, Ivan, you are such a klutz. Here let me help you. Ivan, are you OK? Ivan?" Looking up to those that were gathering around, he said, "I think he knocked himself out."

More laughter erupted.

Otis refocused his attention back to Ivan. Worry lines wrinkled his face. The palms of his hands glistened with sweat. His voice shaking, he said, "Hey, he's not waking up."

Someone called out, "Check his pulse."

Otis knelt down next to Ivan and grabbed his wrist.

"I can't find his pulse," Otis said. "Quick, call the corpsman."

He shook Ivan violently. His fingers dug deep, leaving imprints on Ivan's exposed arms. "Answer me! Answer me!" he yelled. Darting his head from one side of the mess decks to the other, searching for help from the faces of those around him, he yelled, "He's not breathing!"

"Did he choke on something when he fell?" someone asked.

Otis's voice became shrill. "Ivan. Wake up! Ivan! Damn it! Where the hell's the fucking corpsman?" Turning back to Ivan, Otis's voice softened, "Ivan, I didn't mean to upset you. Please wake up. Please quit goofing around and answer me!"

Legs and feet, crowding all around him, were all that Otis could see as he knelt next to Ivan on the floor of the mess decks. Sweat dripped down his back, soaking his shirt. He held Ivan's face close to his chest and then put him down and began CPR. Otis became oblivious to those around him. He talked to himself as he pumped Ivan's chest.

"Ivan has to wake up. What could I tell his parents? That he fell and hit his head? No. That's stupid. I can't do that. Ivan has to pull through or he'll die. I have to make him come out of this."

Otis was so caught up in the moment that he didn't notice when the corpsman arrived. The hospital corpsman knelt down next to Ivan and put on his stethoscope and searched for a heartbeat.

Otis's words faltered when he observed the stethoscope, "Is, is, is he going to be OK?"

"I'm sorry, Otis," the corpsman said, "Ivan's dead."

Otis, tears streaming down his face, said, "God, what am I gonna tell his momma? He's our first Viet Nam casualty. Who's gonna be next?"

6 – THE DREAM WEAVER'S OMEN

The combination of daytime and nighttime bombardments made the whole crew tired and irritable by the third day on the gun line. My battle station watch ended at 03:00. A quarter of the moon shone brightly above the horizon as I walked down to my berthing compartment. My ears were still ringing from the gun blasts as I took off my clothes and climbed into my top rack. Ivan's fall and death began replaying itself in my head as I laid my head on my pillow. I wondered who would be the next sailor to die. I felt restless, even though I was very tired. I rolled over on my side and looked toward the door. The red light by the door triggered memories of my grandfather's stories of the dream weaver, his Apache grandmother had taught him. He taught me that the dream weaver sends premonitions that we should not ignore. The rocking and rolling of the ship opened the door for my grandfather's dream weaver to enter my sleep.

In my dream, my mother shook me and said, "Wake up. Get up and get dressed. We don't want to be late for your cousin's funeral."

I threw on my suit jacket and climbed into the back seat of the family's 1959 yellow Chevy Biscayne, with its big winged trunk. It wasn't long before we pulled into the church parking lot. A white Cadillac hearse, with a Navy captain sitting in the driver's seat, waited outside the church's entry. As I walked past the hearse, a hot and humid breeze blew across my face. The captain polished his medals with a red handkerchief.

Inside the church, the smoke filled odor of frankincense permeated the air. People, dressed in black, were crying while they waited in line to file by the coffin. The women wore black lace veils over their heads and held white handkerchiefs in their black gloved hands. When we approached the coffin my mother fell on her knees, wailing, "Oh Dios mio! Why did you take my son?!!"

Her words startled me. I thought we were at my cousin's funeral. Which of my brothers was in the casket? My father grabbed my shoulder as I approached the coffin. His eyes were cast down.

His voice barely a whisper, he said, "Don't go."

I stared at my father trying to make sense out of his words. As I turned away from him, I noticed that we were now at the grave site. Everyone stood on the wet lawn around the coffin that was suspended over the empty grave. The captain, who I had seen in the hearse, now stood at the foot of the coffin happily polishing his metals. He looked familiar, but I couldn't place him. The sun shone so brightly that my eyes began to water. I shaded my eyes with my hand and stepped toward the grave. My mother held her hands to her face and wept along with my father who stood next to her. Oversize tear droplets ran down his cheeks when he turned to me and said, "We asked you not to go." I took a couple of steps forward and looked inside the coffin. I stopped breathing and froze. My brother was not in there. I was.

How was that possible? I shut my eyes. My breathing accelerated. When I opened my eyes again, I watched the captain of my ship close the coffin lid, with me inside. The coffin rocked as it was lowered into the grave. I tried to yell, but no words came out. I kicked and clawed at the inside of the coffin lid. I pounded it with my fists. The lid burst open and bright light returned to my eyes waking me up.

My heart pounded and sweat dripped down the back of my neck as I awoke. I pulled off the sheet and climbed down from my rack. I ran into the showers and let the water wash the nightmare down the drain.

I walked back into the berthing compartment holding a small white towel around my waist. Otis sat on the deck, wearing only his white briefs, as he pulled his shirt and pants out of the bottom locker. He looked up at me with his bloodshot eyes.

"You had a rough night, last night," he said. "You made noises and you were tangled in your sheets when the lights came on. Did you have a nightmare? "

"I did and it scared the hell out of me," I said as I turned the dial on my locker's combination lock and pulled out my clothes. "It started out about my cousin who got killed here in Viet Nam last year. His death really shook up the family."

"Sorry about that," he said and stood up, pulling his white tee-shirt over his head.

"It started with me going to my cousin's funeral," I said, closing my locker door and spinning the combination. "But it ended up the captain shutting the coffin's lid, with me inside, alive."

"Shit, that is a nightmare."

Yawning, I rubbed my eyes then looked at Otis. "The really scary part is that it might be an omen."

7 – PAYDAY

I walked down into the mess decks to get paid and heard Otis behind me, "Hey Mushroom, wait for me."

"How are you doing, Otis? It's been three weeks and I still can't believe that Ivan is dead."

"Ah kyan't ee tha," he said in his backwoods Kentucky accent. "I've been trying to write a letter to his momma. But every time I try, I get choked up. Now I'm starting to feel guilty 'cause I haven't written to his momma."

I changed the subject when his eyes pooled and he was about to cry. Creating a playfully authoritarian tone, I said, "Being out at sea on payday affords every sailor on the U.S.S. Trippe two options: Number One: Accept pay in cash. Number two: Leave it in the safety of the ship's safe. What's a young sailor, like you, with no where to spend any money going to do?"

A glimmer emerged from Otis's eyes. Following my lead, his voice mimicked mine, "A smart sailor would leave his money in the safe."

"Yes, that's what he would do," I said, "unless he wanted to buy popcorn or soda or some M & Ms."

"But there was only so much candy and soda a sailor can eat without making himself sick," he said while struggling hard to suppress a laugh.

"We can't let that happen. He must buy Kiwi shoe polish, lots of it. One can for each shoe."

"Of course," he said, "How else will we keep our shoes shiny enough to blind the enemy when they try to take over the ship?" His smile inflated his cheeks so much that they concealed his eyes as he burst into laughter.

"I'll never understand why they make us polish our shoes so often, especially in a war zone," I said.

Otis shook his head and asked, "So how much are you going to take, all of your pay or just a part of it?"

"I'll only take about $20.00," I said. "That should hold me until next payday."

Being an enlisted man, with less than a year of active duty, allowed for only a meager paycheck. I earned $275.00 a month, which was less than half what I made as a civilian making beer cans at the Reynolds Aluminum can plant. Even buying a soda for fifteen cents seemed expensive.

When we reached the front of the line, Otis turned around and said, "Oh shit. I forgot that we have to take those fucking malaria pills before they give us our pay."

Payday had been a day we all looked forward to until the U.S.S Trippe sailed into the Philippines. Viet Nam has mosquitoes that are infected with the malaria virus. In order to protect the sailors on the U.S.S Trippe Chief Shea, the hospital corpsmen, provided each crew member with large black malaria pills. Refusing to take the malaria pills was not an option. Every weekend, diarrhea, stomach aches and nausea paid a visit to each sailor who swallowed the required malaria pill.

Every Friday, whether at sea or in port, every member of the U.S.S. Trippe's crew lined up in the mess decks to receive his pay. It did not matter whether we intended to leave our money in the ship's safe or take it from the Disbursement Officer. All of us obeyed the order to line up. Chief Shea stationed himself in front of the pay line. As each sailor came forward, we added our signature next to our name on the corpsman's list. Placing the malaria pill into my left hand and a paper cup filled water into my right hand, Chief Shea watched to ensure that I swallowed the foul malaria pill. Then, just to make sure, he asked me to open my mouth lift my tongue, and open my hands. I really couldn't blame him, though. My buddies and I tried various schemes to avoid having to take the pills. I tried not showing up in the payroll line. He caught me while I was at battle station and gave me the pill. Hiding it in a large wad of gum I was chewing failed, as did eating an onion and hoping my breath would make him turn away. Chief Shea was determined to keep the crew malaria free, even if it killed us.

As each of us received our turn in front of the line, the Disbursement Officer asked, "Name?"

Irritation at having to take the malaria pill soured my mood. The officer knew very well who each one of us was, since only 250 sailors were sardined aboard the U.S.S. Trippe.

"You know who I am, Sir."

He kept his eyes down, pointing his finger to the line on which I need to sign.

"Name?" he asked again.

My eyes narrowed as I watched the Disbursement Officer pointing to my name, even before he asked for it. Realizing that I was holding up the line, I uttered the required reply, "Montoya. Sir."

"Do you want to receive your pay, today?"

I gritted my teeth, keeping myself from saying that so much of what the Navy made us do, seemed childish and a waste of my time. Waiting for the appropriate answer, he scanned the list on his clip board.

"Yes, Sir," I said. "I only need $20.00, Sir."

"Sign here," he said, pointing to a blank line adjacent to my name.

I looked up at the Disbursement Officer as I bent down to sign my name. "You know, Sir, if I intended to leave my money in your safe, I wouldn't be in line, now would I? Why do you have to ask those dumb questions?"

"Stop being a smart ass and holding up the line. Just write down how much you want, sign it and I will give you your cash."

Raising his left eyebrow he began counting out loud as if he were asking a question, "Five?, ten?, fifteen, twenty? Is that right? Or is that just a dumb question?" We both laughed.

I found Otis waiting for me outside. "Why do you have to hassle the Disbursement Officer?" he asked, "You know damn well the Navy ain't gonna change."

"You're right, Otis. It just irritates me. We are killing people. Up until we got here, I could never have imagined that I would be involved in killing people every single day. And they still want us to play these stupid little Navy formality games. I'll see you later; I have to go on watch in a few minutes."

Sounding and Security watch was almost enjoyable. It occupied my mind with distractions, both required and opportunistic. Taking over the Standing Sounding and Security watch, I remembered my first day on the U.S.S. Trippe. The First Class HT Petty Officer gave me instructions on standing watch.

"You are responsible to protect the ship, ensure it does not sink and to take care of any trouble makers," he said. "You are the ship's cop. You carry a gun. No one's gonna mess with you."

Standing watch required me to carry a .45 caliber semiautomatic pistol around my waist. The pistol weighs 3 pounds. It is awkward, if not impossible to carry through small hatches, along with a sounding tape and clipboard. Often, I would have to remove my holster, in order to crawl down a small hatch to reach a lower level in the ship. I remembered our gunnery instructor admonishing us, "Never forget, that this gun is for killing and for nothing else. Never load it and point it at someone unless you intend to kill them. You do not warn people with this gun. You do not wound people with this gun. You kill people with this gun. You must kill them. This is the only reason you would remove the gun from its holster and load it. Do you understand?"

Every time I took over Sounding and Security watch, I remembered the gunnery sergeant's words, "This gun is for killing and for nothing else."

I traversed the length and breadth of the ship from the flying bridge to the deepest hold, continually returning to the bridge at 30 minute intervals to announce, "Sounding and Security, all secure, Sir," to the Officer of the Deck. The only time the gun left its holster was when we inspected it at the change of the watch.

Along with the gun, I carried a sounding tape, which is a large tape measure with a pointed weight at the beginning of the tape. Throughout the ship there are sounding ports, pipes that reached to the bottom of the ship, that are strategically placed to identify water leaking into the ship. Stopping at each sounding port, I unscrewed the cap and lowered the sounding tape. I looked for evidence of water as I rewound the tape. If I found water, I recorded the amount, in inches, onto the Sounding Sheet on my clipboard. As long as the amount of water did not rise, the ship was safe and secure.

I walked in to the forward berthing compartment to take a sounding. The door opened as I was about to grab the handle. Otis came walking out, wearing a grin. He winked at me.

"That was the fastest fifty bucks I ever made," he said. "Only took me ten minutes."

"Is there a poker game going in there?" I asked. "How much have you lost altogether since you started playing?"

"I don't play often," he said. "Mostly, I just watch. But today, I felt lucky. It was a fast hand. The pot got to sixty bucks, including the ten that I put in. I had a royal flush. I took my money and left."

"If you were so lucky, how come you didn't continue playing?"

"I've got the next watch, so I coudn't've stayed anyway," he said. "Where are you headed now?"

"I'm heading for the bridge to meet my replacement, which I guess must be you."

"I got my winnings in my wallet," Otis beamed. "I might as well walk up to the bridge, with you."

He stepped back inside the forward compartment and I followed him, latching the door behind me. I found the sounding tube and lowered the tape. While I recorded the water level, Otis tapped my gun.

"Have you ever wondered if you could really kill anyone?" he asked. "I mean like someone you know, here on the ship? Could ya?"

"That is a hard one, Otis. We've been trained to kill. But our training hasn't changed who we are inside."

"I've thought about it a lot," he said. "I might could kill a Viet Cong who was trying to get on the ship. But, I don't think I could kill someone I know."

"I don't know if I could either," I said. "When we were standing in line waiting to get paid, I was wondering. Are we really fighting communism or are we just paid killers?"

"I don't think we're really here to stop communism," Otis said. "And I don't want to think that we're paid killers. I just won't really know until I come face to face to someone I might have to kill."

"Oh, shit! I'm going to be late for battle station," I said, looking at my watch. "I've got two minutes to get down there. I've got to go."

Otis pointed to the fishermen in their boats and said, "When I see those gooks, who look like me and you, ah kyan't help but feel that we really are just paid killers. And I don't much like it."

8 – GETTING TO KNOW THE CHIEF

Bruce, one of my fellow hull maintenance technicians, waddled down the passageway, stepped into the repair locker behind us, and grabbed his battle helmet. He walked out and stopped in front of Barry and me as we sat with our legs outstretched on the deck. He stood six feet tall, with broad shoulders. The overhead fluorescent lights reflected off his brightly polished black boots. "What are you two clowns still doing here? It's my turn to take over the battle station."

We removed our battle gear, stowed it in the repair locker then ran topside to get some fresh air. The smell of salt spray from the warm breeze filled my lungs. Taking in a deep breath I said, "Damn, am I glad to be out of that hole."

"This hole, as you call it, is like sitting on a floor of a fancy hotel compared to the river boat that I was assigned to before I arrived on the Trippe. Hell, I became a communications technician hoping that a job like that would keep me on the bigger ships or on land. When I got promoted to petty officer, third class, they sent my ass into the Mekong Delta on a river boat."

I didn't know how to respond. I looked away from Barry and

cast my sight over the water. The sun shone brightly overhead. The clear blue ocean mesmerized me into daydreaming about what it would feel like to float along the Mekong Delta in a river boat.

"That new guy, Bruce, is going to be a lifer." Barry said, as he leaned on the lifeline and ran his fingers through his curly red hair.

"What makes you think that?" I asked. "His polished boots?"

"He told me that he had wanted to go to the Naval Academy," Barry said. "He couldn't because he had to marry the girl he knocked up. Now he wants to be a chief like his old man was."

Bam! Our forward gun's blast startled me. Barry grinned and slapped me on the back.

"We never get used to it. So don't ya even try," he said with a hint of a Texan accent. Looking passed me he added, "Uh oh, I'm outta here."

He did a quick about face and disappeared into a doorway. I turned and saw Chief Jaffe walking toward me.

"You've just finished your battle station watch, haven't you?" Jaffe asked.

"Yes, and I have my sounding and security watch in an hour."

"Follow me then, you'll have time. One of the pipes is clogged in the forward head. It's backing up the pissers. Grab a couple of pipe wrenches from the forward repair locker while I stop at the R-Gang shop to get the plumbing snake. I'll meet you in the forward head."

I admired Jaffe for his knowledge and skill. Unlike some of the other chiefs, Jaffe didn't mind getting dirty. He liked teaching us how to fix things. Clearing a pipe in the forward head did not sound like fun, but Jaffe was all smiles.

The smell of urine and salt water permeated the air in the forward head. Jaffe came in and wrinkled his nose. "Pee you! I wonder how long these urinals have been clogged," Jaffe said. "If it was R -Gang's turn to clean the head, we would have never let it get this bad."

Pointing to the pipe that traversed the bottom of the urinals, he said, "Take that pipe wrench and slowly, and I do mean slowly, remove the cap from the end. Make sure the bucket is underneath."

"What happens if too much water comes out of the pipe and

overflows the bucket?" I asked.

He looked down at me and said, "That's why I told you to open the cap slowly. Let it fill the bucket, before you completely remove the cap. If the bucket gets full, tighten the cap and empty the bucket."

I didn't like his answer. If I had to tighten the cap while water and urine were squirting out, I would get urine all over my hands. He must have read my mind.

"If you leave the wrench on the cap, you won't get your hands dirty. And even if you did, we are right here with soap and water. And besides, urine is sterile."

The bucket filled up and, as I feared, urine squirted over my hands as I tightened the cap. I emptied the bucket and loosened the cap. When the pipe stopped dripping, I opened the cap. I inserted the snake that Jaffe handed to me into the pipe. When I pulled it out, what looked to me like a large wad of tobacco came with it. Jaffe took out a pocket knife and moved the wad around.

"Does that look like marijuana to you?"

I didn't know what to say. It was tobacco and I knew that. I felt that he was setting me up. If I said no, he would suspect that I was a dope smoker.

"I don't know, Chief."

"Don't give me that bullshit. Everyone knows. We all got training on not using dope and we were shown what it looks like. And no matter what you say, I know that you know about marijuana."

I shook my head and said, "It looks like someone shoved a whole pack of cigarettes into the urinal."

"Run the snake through again and see if anything else comes out. If nothing does, I'll flush the end pisser and let it flow into the bucket. If only water comes out, we're done."

Jaffe walked over to the bucket and watched the water come out. My stomach churned when I saw him stick his finger in the water as it poured into the bucket and taste it.

"If you don't taste urine, then it's OK," he said.

I stood there, dumbfounded.

He winked at me saying, "I told you, urine is sterile."

His wink ran circles around my gut giving me the feeling that he was fooling me with an illusion, making it look like he tasted the water. I suspected that he hoped I was stupid enough to taste the water myself. I had no intention of letting any of that foul liquid touch my tongue.

"Why do we call the bathroom the head?" I asked, trying to calm my stomach.

"It's an old navy term that comes from the sail boat days. They put the bathroom in the front, also called the head, of the ship. Can you think of the reason why?"

I thought about it as I replaced the cap. "Is it because the wind pushed the sails from the rear and that way the smell would be blown away from the ship?"

Jaffe smiled and said, "I guess you're pretty smart for a Mexican."

I started to say that I wasn't a Mexican, but realized that he was just trying to get my goat. I asked instead, "Why are you so hard on us?"

I was referring to the minorities that worked for him, but he didn't answer it that way.

Rather, he said, "I worked hard to make the R-Gang a top notch outfit. We are respected on this ship and I intend to keep it that way. I ride your asses so that we're the best. That way, when we want something, we can get it."

I scowled as I started to say, "Can't you do that by being sof ..."

He cut me off saying, "I don't have a soft side. I didn't earn my gold hash marks by being soft. My wife is the one with the heart and soul in my family. When I'm with her, I'm like a normal person. I couldn't live with myself without her."

I couldn't imagine who would want to marry the chief. If what they say is true, that we marry our opposites, the chief's wife must be a saint or a glutton for punishment. *When we get back to Rhode Island*, I thought, *I would like to meet his wife, if we don't get killed out here first.*

"General quarters! General quarters! This is not a drill," blasted out of the loudspeakers.

Jaffe patted me on the shoulder and said, "We finished just in time. I'll put these things away. You go to your battle station."

Donning my battle helmet, I began thinking about Chief Jaffe.

Barry joined me and asked, "What did the chief have ya'll do? I saw you two walking toward the forward head, earlier."

"He helped me clear out a clogged pipe," I said. "He doesn't seem like such a hard ass when I work with him, one on one."

"I kinda like him, most of the time," he said. "He doesn't

bother me much."

"He almost seemed human when we were unclogging the pipe."

"He knows what he wants and he know how to get it," Barry said. "He can be nice when he wants to."

"Yeah, I've seen the way he pampers the Anglos who work for him," I said. "But he rides everyone else's ass. He even yells at the junior officers when they need haircuts. They obey, even though Jaffe isn't even an officer."

Barry rolled his eyes. "Remember, they don't call him the Hulk because he is so nice. Commander Reardon may be the ship's captain, but we all know that Chief Jaffe runs the ship."

"Why do they let him get away with that? He's such a pain in the ass," I said.

"Because he's dyed in the wool navy. And because he believes that he has the right to," Barry said. He grabbed my face with both of his hands and looked intently into my eyes, "That man has a ton of personal power. Don't be a dumb fuck and get on his bad side."

9 – CLASS LEADER

"We may well be paid killers, but so are the Viet Cong," Barry said. "I heard you and Otis talking when ya'll were topside. We're all paid killers."

Barry squirmed in his pants as he sat next to me on the shiny linoleum deck at our battle station adjacent to the forward repair locker. He stood up, scratched his crotch and wrinkled his face.

"Right now, my crotch is killing me. That ointment the doc gave me ain't stopping this crotch rot from itching like crazy."

"Maybe you ought to consider changing your underwear more often." I said.

"Hell, I'm changing my shorts twice a day as it is. It's so fucking humid out here."

"How long have you had crotch rot?"

"The first time I got it I was on the riverboats. I thought the ointment they gave me cured it. But, shit. It's back. The doc told me to use lots of powder and to sleep naked. It'd be more fun sleeping naked with a girl instead of with you fuckers."

"I'm just glad you aren't sleeping next to me," I said. "I heard Bruce call you, tóc đỏ lee or something like that. What's that all about?

46

"That's a nickname I got on the riverboats. It's Vietnamese for windy redhead or some shit like that."

"Why did they give you that name?"

Pulling the crotch of his pants out to a point, he said, "cause of this big pecker."

"That little thing?"

"Nah, actually it was because I have red hair and because I was the communications guy. Ya know, I never really thought about it that much. Maybe I just liked the sound of it. Tóc đỏ lee.

How about you? How did you get your name?"

I got it when I was in "A" school.

"Really? I thought you got it because your teensy weensy pecker is like a teensy weensy mushroom," he said as he held out his thumb and finger in front of his squinting eyes as if he were measuring something very small.

"Do you want to know or not?"

"What "A" school did you go to?"

"Since the Navy merged Damage Control rate and the Shipfitter rate to make the Hull Maintenance Technician rate, a school didn't exist yet. The Navy sent me to Damage Control school in Treasure Island, in the San Francisco bay. I arrived there with shoulder length hair, in my uniform."

"With long hair, in uniform? Were you crazy?"

"I must have been, but not as crazy as they were. They made me get four haircuts before they processed me in."

"That doesn't sound so crazy," Barry said.

"That's not the crazy part. On the first day of school, we all met in a large classroom in Austin Hall, the Damage Control school. The officer in charge called out my name last, after taking role. He asked me to come to the front of the classroom."

"I bet you were going to get your ass whipped."

"That's what I thought, Barry. I was a nervous as hell. I figured that they were going to punish me and use me as an example to warn the rest of the sailors not to show up with long hair while wearing a Navy uniform."

"So what did they do to ya'll."

"To my surprise he shook my hand and said, 'You are the senior ranking enlisted man here. You are the class leader. These thirty-five sailors are your responsibility. Make sure that they perform well.' Now that's crazy."

"Get outta here! No shit? Hell, if I had done that they would have had me swabbing the fuckin decks for the whole time I was in school."

I told Barry that I since I was in charge I had to march my guys to the mess decks for breakfast and get them back to Austin Hall before 07:30. I hadn't marched for nearly three years. While I was trying to remember what commands I needed to say, the officer asked, "Who is your assistant?"

I had only met a few of the recruits the night before. I had no idea who to choose. Rick, a guy who shared my room, looked at me, with eyes that said, "Pick me, pick me." So I did.

"Was he any good?" Barry asked.

"Not really. Rick did a good job as an assistant, as long as I didn't leave him in charge of the other students. No one would listen to him. He didn't have enough personal power."

"When the officer finished with the orientation and walked out the door, I stood up and looked at the 35 young men that were now my responsibility. "Let's go eat breakfast." I said. They walked out of the classroom and assembled themselves, in formation, at the front entrance of the Austin Hall. They stood there waiting for me to call out the marching orders. I couldn't recall any marching commands."

"None?" Barry asked, his eyes opened wide. "Ya'll must've looked like a fuckin idiot."

"I felt like one. I could feel my cheeks getting hot. Looking over at Rick, I asked, "How do I get them started?" A big grin emerged on Rick's face. The same big grin emerged on everyone's face when they realized that I did not know any of the marching commands.

"Alright, you guys. I'm getting hungry. We have to march to the mess hall. So you will have to bear with me until I get a hang of this marching thing."

"But you're our leader, you are supposed to know how to march," one of the guys said.

I briefly explained that I had just re-enlisted after having been out of the Navy for two and a half years. Rick was still smiling broadly as he suggested, "Try, forward march."

I did. The entire class took about three steps toward me. "Stop!" I yelled and laughed. "OK, OK, let's try this again. Rick, how do I get them to turn?"

"Say, Right face. Then say 'Forward march' to get them

moving."

"Right face. Forward march!" They moved in unison. Coming to the next street, I needed them to turn left, so I yelled "Turn left!" The kept on marching and giggling. "Stop!" I yelled. They kept on marching. "Help me Rick." I felt like Lucille Ball in the candy factory episode."

Barry turned to look at me and rolled his eyes. "Ya'll have got to be making this up."

"Believe me," I said. "This stupid war and the noise from our guns have killed any ability I might have to make anything up."

Barry sat on the polished green and white checkered deck across the passageway from me and nodded his head for me to continue.

"If my new assistant's mouth opened any wider, his tonsils would have been showing. 'Tell them to halt. Then say, 'About face'. Then, 'Forward march.' When we get to the street, say 'Right Face.' One more thing, whenever you see a bollard, a trash can or any anything in our way, call out, 'Dempsy Dumpster, hut!' They'll march to the left or right avoiding whatever is in the way. That's not an official marching command, but it works.'

We marched to the mess hall, ate our breakfast and marched back to Austin Hall on time, albeit with a lot of giggling."

"What did ya'll learn in HT school, besides marching orders?" Barry asked.

"We spent the first week learning how to put out fires. One day, while I was holding the nozzle, the hose sprung a big leak and collapsed. A loud voice behind me yelled, "Hold on tight." They dragged me out of the smoke filled room on my butt."

"Was that a real fire?" Barry asked.

"Hell yeah! And it scared the hell out of us. That fire burned hot and the instructor placed me right in front, holding the fire hose. After a week's fire training, we had earned liberty. We went into San Francisco after class on Friday."

"Did ya'll go into town to get laid?" Barry asked, "When I was there, I sure did. Hoo Wee!"

"Let me finish my story. Before we could go on liberty we had to stand inspection. When the officer got to one of the guys, he said, "You look like you're wearing mascara, son, do a better job of washing your eyes after firefighting class." It was hard not to laugh. The day before, we were practicing putting out oil fires.

The soot clung to our skin like shoe polish adhered to our shoes. It refused to leave without a lot of soap and hard scrubbing. Eliminating the mascara look was as difficult as giving a cat a bath and almost as painful.

I marched my men back to the barracks after our last class. Having arrived at the barracks, I asked everyone to meet me in the lobby at 16:00 so that I could give them last minute instructions before we went into town. While we waited for the rest of the class to assemble, a few were already drinking beer from the beer machine down stairs. I gave them safety guidelines to follow while in San Francisco, reminding them that they were not allowed to get drunk. I told them that we were only given "Cinderella liberty" and they had to be back in the barracks no later than midnight.

'Why midnight?' one of them sarcastically asked. 'Will we turn into pumpkins?'

'No, but you will feel like Cinderella when you lose your liberty next weekend and have to spend your time cleaning Austin Hall.'

I turned and began walking away. One of my men wanted to ask me a question but he had forgotten my name. He looked at the tee-shirt I was wearing and yelled out what was written on the back.

'Magic Mushroom! Wait, I need to ask you question.'

The words, Magic Mushroom, made me turn around. That's how I got my name."

Barry grinned and said, "That's a good story. But I just can't help thinking that ya'll made the whole damn thing up."

"Oh, yeah, Barry, like I'm making up those gun blasts we're hearing."

10 – JAFFE'S NIGGERS

Chief Jaffe barged through the repair shop door. "You," he said, pointing to me. "Grab the arc welder, some tools and go down to the aft berthing compartment. One of the racks broke loose during last night's shelling. Fix it."

He handed me the work request. "This will tell you where the broken rack is located."

"Do you want me to do it after this morning's muster?" I asked, "Or can I do it after breakfast?"

"I want you to do it right now."

Irritation splashed the inside of my head, making my eyes squint, as I realized that I would miss out on breakfast. The chief didn't mention an urgency. I didn't understand why I needed to forgo breakfast to fix a rack. Meanwhile, a storm busied itself playing with our ship as if it were a slinky, sliding up and down the swells. I struggled to keep my balance while carrying the arc welder and welding tools up and down the ladders.

When I arrived at the aft berthing compartment, it appeared unoccupied. I read the small work request that I pulled out of my shirt pocket: 'Item: Broken rack support. Location: aft most rack, exterior bulkhead, port side.' At the far end of a row of racks,

Norman sat on the shiny green linoleum deck with his back against the bulkhead. He reminded me of a giant leprechaun as he stroked his red beard that hung half way down his chest.

His Boston accent removed the 'r's at the end of words as he said, "You look like a drunken saila carrying a keg of beeah."

"Beer? Don't you wish? Do you know where the broken rack is?"

"Yup. Ova daya," Norman said as he pointed to the far corner of the compartment.

I climbed over the middle rack because electronic equipment blocked my access from the bottom rack. Looking down, my heart sank when my eyes found what needed to be fixed. The angle iron that supported the corner of the three tiered rack had been broken and shoved out of place. I would need to get another piece of angle iron to reconnect it.

"When I climbed into my rack after I finished baking this morning," Norman said, "my whole rack wobbled with every roll the ship took. If we weren't sailing through a storm, I would've never noticed."

"How did this break?" I asked.

"It probably broke during last night's bombing."

"How is that possible? We didn't take any direct hits."

"How can you be so sure?" Norman asked. "The guys that sleep in here told me that just before they heard the announcement for general quarters last night, a blast shook them out of their racks."

I crawled out from the middle rack and scratched my head. "We fired a rocket last night. I can't imagine that we took a hit. We would've heard about it as soon as it happened."

"But what if we took a hit when we fired the rocket? Norman asked. "What if we hit a mine that only did minor damage? We aren't fuckin invincible ya know. This is still just a floating tin can."

I climbed back over the middle rack and looked along the exterior bulkhead.

"Oh shit," I said.

"See? I told you that we got hit last night," he said, with a wry smile.

"Norman, the bulkhead it fine. There's no evidence of getting hit."

"Then why did you say, 'Shit'?"

"There's no room for me to fix the rack support. I'm going to have to come in from the top. The only way I can do that is to hang upside down."

"Fuck is a better word than shit," Norman said as he crawled onto the middle rack to take a look for himself. "With the ship acting more like a roller coaster, you better be praying that you don't fall off the rack and break your neck."

"I'm not falling because you're going to hold my legs."

"This is something I don't wanna miss," Norman said. "I can't imagine how you are going to hang like a fuckin bat and weld that support back into place."

"They didn't teach us how to hang upside down in welding school," I said. "We learn that on the job. First, we need to remove the mattresses and anything else that might burn. Then I'm going to give you that fire extinguisher to use in case anything catches fire."

"Like your ass?"

"I'll be right back. I need to grab another piece of angle iron and some C-clamps from the repair shop."

Barry walked into the repair shop as I cut a twelve inch length of angle iron. "Aren't ya'll gonna eat breakfast?" he asked. "The cinnamon rolls are fresh and hot."

"I can't. Jaffe told me to fix a broken rack right away," I said. "Why does he want me to do it right now?"

"He likes to make his niggers do the shit jobs," Barry said as he winked at me.

"What!?"

"The whole ship knows that Jaffe has four niggers working for him: a black, a Jap, a Filipino and you."

The word, 'nigger' stung, reminding me of elementary school in California. I had attended a nearly all white school. There were no Black or Asian children at Saint Matthew's Catholic school. The seventh and eighth grade boys often picked on the younger Latin American kids, calling us niggers. I am still surprised that I have my teeth after having my face smashed against the drinking fountain and being told that niggers weren't allowed to drink from the white kids' fountain. A white kids' fountain didn't exist, of course. The boys were just being mean.

"I'm not being racist, Mushroom. I'm just telling ya what Jaffe calls ya'll behind ya'lls backs."

"I know you're not. I just wish that Jaffe wasn't such a piss ant."

"Damn, Mushroom. You're in the fucking Navy, for god's sake. Learn to say, 'mother fucker,' like a real sailor. Come on. Jaffe's a mother fucker. You can say it."

I shook my head and rolled my eyes. "You know that I spent 11 years in Catholic school. I feel guilty just saying, shit."

Barry patted me on the shoulder. "Ya'll are hopeless. I'll go back to the mess decks and get ya a mother fucking good cinnamon roll. And I do mean mother fucking good. Where is that rack your fixing?"

"In the aft berthing compartment," I said.

When I returned, I found Norman sleeping on the mattresses he had tossed onto the deck. He woke up when the C-clamps and angle iron clanked on the rack.

"You've got a hell of a frown on your face," he said. "What happened?"

"I just don't like being referred to as a nigger," I said.

"Fuck Jaffe," Norman said. "He's just an asshole anyway."

"You don't even work for him and you know that he refers to me and the other minorities as niggers?"

"Get your fucking head out of the sand, Mushroom."

We both climbed onto the top rack. Hanging upside down from my knees, I struggled to attach a couple of C-clamps to the angle iron that I placed alongside the broken rack support. The ship's rocking made me bang my head against the bulkhead with a painful thud.

"I heard that," Norman said. "You're gonna have one big fuckin lump on your head."

I reached up, grabbed the edge of the rack and heaved myself up. I rubbed my head and grimaced as I donned my welding helmet. That lump had grown bigger than I thought. Getting my bearings, I eyed the spot where I needed to place the welding rod. I waited until the ship rolled and felt stable. I shut my helmet and struck the angle iron with the rod. It stuck. I pulled off my helmet and pulled on the rod with my gloved hand. Beads of sweat rolled up my neck and into my ears as I hung upside down. I waited again for the ship to finish its roll.

Bam! I stopped welding. My stomach muscles tensed. I hung, listening for an announcement. My hands were soaked inside my leather gloves. Hearing nothing, I returned my attention to welding the rack support.

"I hate not knowing if those blasts are ours or if we're being attacked," Norman said.

I shut my helmet and struck the rod against the angle iron. I winced every time a piece of hot slag jumped onto my neck and chest. I didn't want to stop until I finished.

"You're burned," Norman said as he helped my back onto the top rack. "I'm glad I'm not a fuckin welder. I couldn't handle those sparks burning my neck."

"I wish they were just sparks. Slag is molten metal that flies off whatever I'm welding. It hurts like hell." I paused for a moment and added. "But not as much as being called a nigger."

Barry came in to the compartment as I collected my things saying, "Put that shit down and take a bite out of these mother fucking good cinnamon rolls."

"Thanks, Barry," Norman said. "I'm glad you like my mother fucking good cinnamon rolls. I made them while you mother fuckers were sleeping."

I bit into the pastry while looking at Barry. "Wow, these are mother fff-these are good."

While Barry and Norman laughed we didn't notice Jaffe walk in. I had no sooner taken a big bite out of the cinnamon roll than Jaffe said, "I told you to fix the rack before you had breakfast."

I jumped and almost choked. Jaffe stood with his hands on his hips.

Before I could react, Norman said, "He finished before Barry gave him one of my delicious cinnamon rolls. Did you have one this morning?"

Jaffe didn't answer. Keeping his attention on me, he said, "We're expecting a chopper to come in from the carrier sometime today. Don't be late."

"I've never been ... ." I started to say. He turned and walked out before I could finish my sentence.

Barry put both of his hands up and said, "See. Ya'll are just one of his...."

"Stop!" I yelled as I held my hand up. "Don't say it."

11- MAIL CALL

The whop, whop, whop preceded the intercom's announcement of a chopper's arrival. I ran up the ladder to meet my helicopter fire crew and assemble them at the helo deck. I opened the repair locker and distributed the firefighting and rescue equipment. My primary function was to be the ship's firefighter, the scene leader in charge, especially in the combat zone. That's what I had had been trained to do in Damage Control School. Even though I was a lower ranking enlisted man, I was in charge of the five men on fire rescue crew. I conducted weekly fire drills in the weeks prior to our arrival in preparation for combat duty in the Tonkin Gulf. I prayed every time a chopper landed that the training had paid off and that we were combat ready.

One of my men took the cabled glove that prevents static electricity arcing from the ship to the helicopter. He walked out to the middle of the helo deck and attached the metal cable from his glove to the electrical grounding clip in the middle of the helo pad. His shirt and pants flapped like flags in a wind storm. He sheltered his eyes from the blasts of air that the rotors generated while he waited for the helicopter to descend.

Otis donned the aluminum covered fire suit. He never complained about the awkwardness that he felt walking in the big pants and jacket. Nor did he complain about the difficulty seeing where he was going as he peered through the small glass panel in the fire hood, with sweat dripping into his eyes. He asked for the seat belt cutter, which looked like a hatchet with a metal ball in front of the blade. If the helicopter were to burst into flames, I had trained him to run into the fire, open the helicopter door, hit the pilot in the chest with the metal ball of the seat belt cutter, pull down hard and cut the seat belt. Having completed that initial task, he was to extricate the pilot by grabbing the pilot's arm and pulling him to safety.

During the first training exercise, he asked, "If I hit him hard, couldn't I break his ribs?"

"Yes, you could," I answered. "I'm sure he'd prefer you risk breaking his ribs, instead of letting him burn to death."

Two of the sailors grabbed the fire hose nozzles, while two others connected the hoses to the water lines and charged them. We were ready.

As the helicopter descended slowly onto the deck, one of the helicopter crewmen lowered the anti-static cable to the sailor, who was wearing the cabled glove. Grabbing hold of the helicopter's cable, the sailor attached it to the ship's anti-static cable that was attached to his glove. Once safely connected, he removed his glove from the combined cables and ran over to where the rest of us who were standing. Permission was given to land. Whop, whop, whop, the helicopter blades slowed to a stop.

Only one of the chopper's crew jumped out onto the helo deck. The setting sun, behind him, allowed only his silhouette to be seen. He turned around and pulled out a large bag and placed it on the deck. It was the mail. I smiled, along with my entire fire rescue team, in anticipation of getting a letter from home. The ship's postman signed the release that the crewman had given him. He picked up the mail bag, threw it over his shoulder and, looking like a young Santa Claus in July, hobbled down to his office below decks to sort out the mail. When the chopper flew off, and we finished putting away our rescue gear, I hurried down to the galley and stood in the crowd of sailors waiting for the postman to arrive. It always seemed to take the postman a long time to sort the mail and take it up to the galley. And today was no different. While we waited, we talked about past letters that we received from girlfriends and our parents and wondered if the questions that we had asked in previous letters would get answered.

All eyes were glued on the postman when he entered the galley, carrying a large box with letters and a few packages. Taking a handful of letters in his hand he began calling out names. We waited like kids at an elementary school raffle. Those who weren't waiting in the mess decks were on watch or battle station. The postman would deliver their mail to their racks, later. But for now, those of us in the galley waited and hoped for our names to be called. As each sailor's name was called, he ran up grabbed his letter and ran out of the mess decks. My feet twitched at the announcement of each name. I wanted to grab the letters out of the postman's hand and search through his box. I hoped that the postman would call my name and that I would receive a letter from someone, anyone. When I ended up empty handed, I always looked enviously at anyone who received a letter from home. Mail call always felt like playing a slot machine; someone always won. And when it wasn't me, I felt forgotten and lonely.

Cigarette smoke billowed out of Matty's mouth when he said, "Damn, he's only got two letters left; I hope one of them is mine."

"Montoya! You got a letter, a post card and a package," called the postman.

"Wow! I hit the jackpot!" I yelled and I ran up to the front to get my prizes. A smile erupted on my face while Matty's eyes looked down, almost as if he were going to cry. I looked at the return addresses, a post card from a friend from firefighting school, a letter from my friend, Kathy, and the package from my parents. I had just passed through the galley door when Matty caught up with me. He was an eighteen year old radioman from the Bronx. He reminded me of my younger brother, only taller.

"What's ya got in the package?" he asked. "Cookies?"

"If we're in luck," I said. "Come with me to my berthing compartment and we'll see."

I took out a pair of scissors and cut open the brown paper bag wrapping and string. I pulled out the letter that was on top, and set it aside.

"What's in there? I wanna see," said Matty.

"Hold on to your horses. Wow! A bag of homemade tortillas

and venison jerky."

I pulled out the jerky and read the note. It said that my grandfather had gone hunting and he made some jerky. My fingers became uncoordinated with excitement as I struggled to remove the clear cellophane wrapping. I lifted out a piece of jerky. When its odor hit my nose, I said, "Oh shit!"

"Oh shit what?" Matty asked.

"The venison has mold on it. Hand me the letter. I want to see when my parents sent this to me." The date on the letter was three weeks ago. My heart sank. I felt cheated. "Damn humidity and damn this war. Well, so much for the jerky."

"Gee, that's too bad, Mushroom. What about those tortillas? They look thicker than what I usually see."

I took one of the tortillas out of the plastic bag and sniffed it. It didn't smell moldy. But when I took a bite, the sour taste made me spit it out. My eyes drooped and I hung my head down low. I wanted to cry.

"Isn't there anything else?" Matty pleaded. He looked as dejected as I did.

I pulled out some photographs. Under the photographs I felt cardboard, the bottom of my package, or so I thought at first. "We're in luck!" I exclaimed, pulling out a yellow and brown box. "Ginger snap cookies! My favorite. Here have one while I read my letter."

"I didn't get a letter," he said, his shoulders slumped. He took a bite out of the cookie and smiled. "Can you read yours to me?"

"Hola Hijo. Cómo estás?"

"Ah sucks," Matty said as his smile flattened. "I didn't think that your letter would be in Mexican."

"It's not in Mexican. Mexicans don't speak Mexican any more than Americans speak American. I'm just teasing, you Matty. It's written in English. There is not much too it. Here, you can read it.

It just says that they hope the food is still good when I get it and a couple of notes about my son.

While Matty read my letter, I looked at the photographs in the box. When I pulled out the third photo of my son, I slapped my thigh and said, "Hey, look at this photo of Jeremy. He's covered in flour. They wrote on the back that he wanted to help make tortillas for me."

Matty took a look at the photo and grinned. He said, "My

mom has a photo of me covered in flour too. I was helping her make my birthday cake when I was about 3, like your son. What's the other letter say?"

I placed the cookie in my mouth and enjoyed the crisp crack when I bit into it. "We're going to have to eat these soon, if we don't want the humidity to ruin these, too." I grabbed another ginger snap and held up the post card and letter. "Which one first, Matty?"

"The post card is easy," he said, "Let me see it. I'll read it to you that way I can pretend that it came to me. It has a picture of the San Diego zoo on it. It says, 'Dear Mushroom, I got transferred to a submarine tender in San Diego. Wish you were here. It is really just a floating dry dock. But the duty is great. I hope you survive out there. See if you can transfer to my ship. Your brother, Rick.' Is he your brother?"

"No. He's my best friend. He's like a brother to me."

"Oh. I forgot the P.S.," Matty said. "It says, 'Did you hear that the South Vietnamese Army wiped out the My Lai massacre survivors?'" Matty handed me the letter and asked, "What's he talking about?"

"That's horrible," I said. "Do you remember, a few years ago, an army company went into a village and killed a bunch of people who lived there, including kids?"

"I have a vague recollection," Matty said. "When did that happen?"

Scrunching my eyes and scratching the back of my head, I said, "In sixty-eight. I think."

"I was only fourteen years old," he said.

"The massacre at My Lai was on all the TV networks," I said. "Even where you lived, in the Bronx."

"Oh. Yeah, now I remember," he said. "But why would the South Vietnamese kill the My Lai survivors? And why now?"

"War sucks," I said. "Too many innocent people get caught in the middle. The South Vietnamese probably accused them of being communist sympathizers. Hell, I'd be a sympathizer too if American soldiers came in and killed nearly everyone in my town, including the kids."

Matty shook his head and put up his hand waving it to stop me. "Open the other letter already," he said. "Who's it from?"

"It's from my friend Kathy, I met her in art class in college."

"Is she your girlfriend?"

"No. I'd like her to be my girlfriend. But she already has a boyfriend, named Barry."

"Why would you let that stop you?"

"He's a friend of mine too. We're all good friends."

"That's cool. So what did she say in the letter, read it."

I opened the envelope then unfolded the letter. I found a magazine article, cut out of a Time Magazine. Looking at the title, THE MY LAI MASSACRE, Friday, Nov. 28, 1969, the hair on my arms stood up.

"Now this is not just a coincidence," I said. "This is weird."

I wondered why she sent an article that was two and half years old. I also found a newspaper clipping with a photo showing a young naked girl who had been bombed with napalm by the South Vietnamese. The bombing occurred on June 8th, just a couple of months ago. I recoiled at the photo.

"I can't believe what war does to people, Matty. Here, take a look at this newspaper clipping."

Matty read it and stared at the photo. We both sat in silence.

"She's only a little kid," he said. "God! All you see in this picture are kids and soldiers. Why were they attacking little kids with a chemical that burns off their flesh? What's that called? Oh yeah, napalm."

"The article says that they were Viet Cong sympathizers," I said. "My God! How could they use that as a justification? They're just kids. I hate this fucking war."

Matty took a deep breath and ran his fingers through his thick black hair. "I don't believe that those kids could be sympathizers, not really. God! That picture freaks me out." Handing the newspaper clipping back to me, he asked, "Why don't you read Kathy's letter?"

"Dear Mushroom," I read aloud. "How are you? Thanks for your last letter. Kriss, Janey, Barry and George say hi. Kriss, George and I formed a band. We already played a gig in one of those bars on 4th street in Long Beach. We only got thirty-five dollars and free beers, but that's a start."

"Your friends are in a band?" Matty asked. "That's cool. I want to learn to play the guitar real good so I could be in a band too. What else does she say?"

I was relieved that we weren't looking at the photo of the girl burned by napalm. I continued to read aloud.

"I know that a lot of the news you guys hear is censored. So I am sending you a couple of clippings. One is of the kids that got burned with napalm in June. Oh, Mushroom, I hope you guys aren't involved in any of that stuff. The other article is about the My Lai massacre. I cut it out of a magazine I found in my dad's garage. I heard on the radio that the camp where they sent the My Lai massacre survivors was destroyed by the South Vietnamese Army. That is why I am sending you the Time magazine article about the My Lai massacre. Please stay safe. Love, Kathy."

"Is that all there is?" Matty asked.

I didn't answer him. Reading the Time's article about the My Lai massacre consumed all of my attention. When I finished reading it, I stood up, looked around and kicked the bulkhead. Tears ran down my cheeks. My back muscles tightened. The smell of diesel wafted down into my berthing compartment. I inhaled deeply, spun around back to Matty and said, "If I had known that we were killing babies at point blank, I would've run off to Canada or filed as a conscientious objector."

"We did that?" he asked. "What does that article say?"

I started to hand him the clipping, but he raised his hand up to stop me. "If that article has any pictures of burning or dead kids I don't want to look at it. Just tell me what it says."

"Shit, Matty, I don't know if I can talk."

"That's why I don't want to read it. If it makes you cry, no way am I gonna read it. It has pictures, doesn't it?"

"Yes, it has pictures," I said.

"Don't tell me what you see in the pictures," he said. "Just tell me what the article says."

"It says that this is the worst atrocity committed by US soldiers in a war. Lieutenant Calley was in charge of C Company. He ordered his men to kill all of the villagers, even the babies and kids."

Matty's eyes were wide, his mouth open. He inhaled slowly and asked, "And his men followed his orders?"

"It says, two small children, maybe four or five years old. Holy shit! Wait a minute," I said. "I can't believe that Americans can actually do this." My fingers squeezed the letter tight. The words in the letter killed the moisture in my throat. "A guy with an M-16 fired at the first boy, and the older boy fell over to protect the smaller one. Then they fired six more shots. It was done very businesslike."

"Business like? What the hell?" Matty exclaimed. "Not even the mafia, back home in New York, would kill kids like that. Not five year olds."

My stomach began a nauseous rumble. "I never imagined that I would think that the mafia stood on a higher moral ground than American soldiers."

"Did all of Calley's men join in the killing?" Matty asked.

"No. It says that some of the men refused. One of the men even shot himself in the foot so he wouldn't have to kill the villagers."

I would've done the same thing, if I had to kill little kids," Matty said.

"What really sickens me," I said, "is that out of all the guys who took part, Lt. Calley was the only one convicted."

"Are you shittin me?" Matty said. "All those guys got off Scot-free? No way would I ever shoot an innocent villager. That's just wrong."

12 – REQUEST FOR COOKING OIL

I had been thinking about the My Lai massacre when an old, weathered and wrinkled Vietnamese fisherman attempted to bring his wooden boat alongside of the U.S.S. Trippe as we patrolled back and forth about a hundred yards from the shore. Standing in the hot midday sun, on the edge of his rickety boat, the fisherman pulled back his pointed straw hat and yelled up to those of us on the main deck. We couldn't understand what he we saying.

"Stay back! Get away from our ship!" someone yelled from the helo deck, above me.

Unfazed, the old man continued getting closer.

"What the hell does that gook think he's doing?" One of the gunners mates asked as he ran to the machine gun on the helo deck. "That fuckin Charlie better not be hiding a mine under his boat."

I put my hand on my pistol. Sweat ran down my back. The old man put both his hands up, asking for something, in Vietnamese. I stared at the boney, bare chested fisherman, wearing what looked like pajama bottoms. A team of butterflies began taking up residence in my belly. I pulled my pistol an inch out of its holster, hoping that he didn't have a mine or bomb hidden in his little old wooden boat.

Otis donned his flack jacket and took his position, manning the M60 machine gun on the bow. It was mounted on a tripod at the edge of the deck with an unobstructed view of the rickety wooden boat. Otis's hands were sweating. I could see them clearly. His palms glimmered with droplets. They were in contrast to his eyes that were frozen. His grip on the M60 machine gun was so tight it was making me sweat even more.

Barry was summoned over the intercom as the ship slowed to a stop. He knew how to speak a little Vietnamese, having spent a year on the riverboats before he arrived on our ship. I took a position next to him when he came on deck. He looked down at the fisherman and yelled something in Vietnamese that sounded like "Gone monkey." The fisherman yelled something that sounded like "jawl ahn."

"I asked him what he wanted," Barry said to us. "He told me that he wants cooking oil."

Barry turned to first class boatswains mate Keegan, who had been standing behind the helo deck and said, "Ya'll can have your deck apes lower the ladder. I'll be right back."

"Why are we giving that old man cooking oil?" I asked Keegan.

"We want to keep em happy and on our side," Keegan said as he shaded his eyes from the sun. "Ye wouldn't want them planting a fuckin bomb just 'cause we be too stingy to give em a wee bit of cooking oil, would ya now?"

I glanced over at Otis. He looked like a statue, stiff and rigid, his index finger frozen against the trigger. Sweat glistened in the afternoon sun off of Otis's forehead. The muscles on his forearm gave evidence that he held a death grip on the machine gun. I wondered what thoughts Otis might be entertaining. I worried that he might misinterpret a movement that the Charlie might make.

"Remember, Otis, this Charlie is friendly," I called out gently but with enough force to get his attention. "He only wants some cooking oil. Don't worry; I have my .45 loaded and ready. Just take it easy."

The deck apes lowered the ladder. Charlie tied his boat to it. He wore a forced smile, his teeth clenched, under his pointed straw hat. His elbows hugged his torso for protection. The veins in his hands bulged out as he gripped the ladder's railing. His dark brown feet climbed one slow rung at a time. He approached the top of a ladder the way a boy would approach a viciously barking dog. Otis's eyes peered down on him from behind the M60 machine gun. I was sure the Charlie could see Otis's glistening hands, giving evidence that death was a mere trigger squeeze away. Charlie did not come up all the way. He stopped about three rungs from the top and reached out his hand, palm up, trying to show that he meant no harm.

I turned away from Charlie to check on Otis. His eyes blinked rapidly as soon as Charlie set his foot on the third rung of the ship's ladder. Otis's hands were white, all the blood squeezed out with each step that Charlie had climbed.

It seemed as if we had been waiting for Barry to return for hours, even though my watch indicated that it had only been ten minutes. He finally walked over to the top of the ladder with Hank, one of the "deck apes" who was paying his dues by working in the galley. Hank carried a five gallon rectangular cooking oil container. He smiled at us with lips that parted wide enough to expose a gold canine tooth. Otis did not see Hank. He did not see Hank's gold tooth. Otis's gaze looked right through him, to Charlie waiting, three rungs down.

"Cảm ơn bạn, cảm ơn bạn (thank you)," Charlie said and bowed gratefully to Hank and Barry. Hank placed the can on the deck, next to the top of the ladder. Barry told him to pick it up. The old man looked up at Otis and bowed. He wrapped his boney fingers under the wire handle and lifted the can. He smiled.

"Di di mau. Beat it," Barry said, when the old man took the oil can and backed down the ladder. The can was heavy. The old man could only carry it down four rungs at a time before placing it down. He looked up at Otis each time. And each time he put the can down, the butterflies in my stomach did a little war dance. When Charlie reached the bottom, he stretched his left leg widely to pull his boat next to the ladder. He placed the can of cooking oil on the deck of his boat and let out a sigh of relief. He untied his boat from the ladder, pushed off, waved goodbye and bowed. Our ships screws began to rumble as we pulled away from his boat. He continued saying, "cảm ơn bạn, cảm ơn bạn" (thank you) until we were out of earshot.

Otis kept the machine gun trained on Charlie. "Otis!" I called out, to get his attention as Charlie's boat floated away. "Otis!" I called out again as I approached him. A smile came over his face and the muscles in his arms and shoulders slid down his bones and back into their normal position.

"I was ready." Otis said. "I was ready in case that Charlie did anything funny."

"I know you were. Let's go grab a Coke." I suggested.

"Can't. I'm on watch and can't leave my post."

"I'll bring you one." I yelled to him as I turned to leave.

"Wait!" he yelled back. Holding his arm outstretched, he motioned for me to come back. "I think I could've actually killed him. But I wouldn't like it." Winking at me he added, "Paid killers."

13 – HOTDOG PROTOCOL

The U.S.S. Trippe made an about face and sailed north, up the Gulf of Tonkin. Daily, we patrolled up and down the gulf firing on targets, some on the shore in plain sight, some hidden behind the verdant hills. The sun poised itself high in the western sky above the hills that we had just fired upon. I hated being blind to whom or what we were shooting. If I could see Viet Cong advancing against our troops, I could more easily justify our bombing them. But not knowing if we were firing on villages and killing innocent people made me feel shameful, sinful, as if we were the ones on the wrong side.

The beach, with its backdrop of varied green trees and bushes looked like a gorgeous place to have a picnic, drink beer, eat hamburgers and hotdogs, play volleyball and swim. We had been firing at targets all day. We would soon be turning eastward to replenish our arms and get a few supplies from the ammo ship. Before we turned away from the shore, we fired over the fishing boats. A Vietnamese man lifted his arms and shook both his hands for us to stop shooting. He looked like the fisherman we had given cooking oil to, earlier today. Why did we fire? I wondered. Was it just to scare the fishermen in their little wooden junks? I clenched my teeth. Why do we antagonize the fisherman? I thought we wanted them to be on our side. They are just trying to make a living while our ship shoots bombs and rockets over their heads.

When we finished re-arming and transferring supplies from the ammo ship, I noticed a couple of cartons of wieners, hotdog buns and sodas on the deck. I wished that we could go ashore and have a picnic on the beach. But not here. Not with all the shooting and bombing.

After eating a hot dog for dinner, I ran around the smoke stack, screaming out my frustration at not being able to stop this nightmare of a war. I wore myself out just as ensign Denny finished with his daily prayer group. He usually reminded me of a happy altar boy, but today he frowned. He turned his head toward me as if to say something, but didn't.

"Good evening, sir, you look upset," I said.

"It's nothing really. Our prayer group was praying for patience and understanding."

"Patience? Understanding for what? This inexplicable war?"

"Nothing as big as that. I was just upset with wardroom protocol and the captain's love of hotdogs."

"You're losing me, Sir."

"The wardroom is where the officers eat."

"Yes, I know that."

"I know that you know that. Just let me get to the point."

"OK."

"The captain's protocol requires that no one order a meal that is better than his when we eat together. He loves to eat hot dogs. And I hate hot dogs. They make me sick."

"How so? If I may ask?"

"When I was in high school, I took my girlfriend to the fair. After eating hot dogs, we went on the hammer ride. We both puked while we were going around and around. We had puke all over ourselves by the time the ride stopped. Now I can't even smell a hot dog without feeling nauseous." Looking up at me, he added, "I probably shouldn't have told you that."

I asked, "Did you order a hot dog or something else?"

"I really didn't have a choice," he said. "The captain eats like he's in a hot dog eating contest," he said. "He had half a dozen hot dogs on his plate and he consumed them all before I could force down one. He grossed me out."

"He's pretty weird, don't you think?"

"I shouldn't have told you about that," he said. "But the captain does some weird stuff. I guess we all do. That is why I pray for patience and understanding."

"Well, sir, as for me, I guess my screaming around the smokestack is pretty weird too. But I'll go completely nuts if I can't scream. I thought we were here to help the South Vietnamese fight communism. I don't believe that anymore."

"Then why don't you join my prayer group? I'm sure God has a plan for us in all of this. If we pray together, God might give us some insight."

Although I had spent four years in a seminary to become a priest, I couldn't imagine why God would want to be involved in any part of this war. Looking the ensign in the eye, I said, "If God has a divine plan that includes me killing innocent villagers, I don't want to pray to that God." I surprised myself with my reply.

"I don't think that God wants us to kill innocent villagers," he said. "I pray to understand why we are here."

"I wish you luck, sir. This war is eating us, the way the captain eats his hotdogs. Neither he nor the war will be satisfied until there is nothing left."

"Before I forget," he said, "the captain is going to hold a Minority Affairs Council meeting. Chief Jaffe will take you to the wardroom."

"Will they serve us hot dogs?"

"No," he said, with a smile sneaking out of his mouth.

14 – ONE OF OUR FIFTY IS MISSING

Chief Jaffe spotted me eating lunch in the mess decks and told me to meet him in the wardroom at 14:00 sharp. We were going to have our first Minority Affairs committee meeting and being the only Chicano on board, I was automatically on the committee.

Realizing a schedule conflict, I said, "Chief, I'll be on my underway watch at 14:00."

"I'm fully aware of that. I've already talked with Barry. He will relieve you at 13:50. When the meeting is over, find Barry and finish the remainder of your watch."

"Aye, aye, Chief."

Never having been inside the wardroom, I was a thrilled to be invited, even if being the only Chicano on board was the only reason. The wardroom was where the officers ate and had their own meetings. The only enlisted people who entered there on a routine basis were the stewards. They were almost always Filipinos or African Americans. They cooked and cleaned for the officers, like personal valets. I wondered if any of the stewards had been invited to be at this meeting, or if they would be relegated to serving us coffee and getting us something to eat.

When I entered the wardroom, I was struck by how different this compartment was from all of the others on the ship. No steel or exposed conduit could be seen on these bulkheads; rather, they were paneled in a dark rich mahogany whose grain matched the large mahogany table and chairs. Noticing Captain Reardon's photograph hanging side by side to that of President Nixon, I suspected that he was displaying his over inflated ego.

The Captain, a tall and slender man with a pointed nose, began the meeting by telling us that everyone aboard the U.S.S. Jon Trippe needed to get along. He wanted to know if the minorities on the ship had any specific needs. He surprised us all when he said, "I'm the ship's captain. I'm the one who makes decisions here. I'm the one who has the last say."

I began thinking that this meeting was going to be a waste of time.

One of the African Americans raised his hand. "Excuse me, Captain. I would like to know what Chief Jaffe is doing here. I'm not comfortable speaking openly with him in this meeting."

Squinting over his reading glasses, he looked over at Chief Jaffe. "This is a meeting for minorities, Chief. Why are you still here?"

"I'm a minority."

"You don't look like a minority. You look like an American to me. What makes you think you are a minority?"

"I'm a Jew."

I raised my hand and directed my question to Chief Jaffe, "How would anyone know that you are a Jew, unless you tell them? You look Irish. You don't wear a kippah. You wear a Navy uniform."

"That is irrelevant," he said as a scowl clouded his face. "Jews are minorities. Look at it this way: if you were blond and blue eyed, and your name was Ron Glenn, and your parents were Mexican, would you still be a minority?"

The captain, interjected, "He's right."

Although I understood the chief's point, I did not feel comfortable with Chief Jaffe in the room. I didn't trust his motives. I felt that he was using religion as an excuse to see what the minorities were up to. The Chief was known for treating minorities unfairly.

"Since this is our first meeting let's introduce ourselves. I'm Captain Reardon and this is my ship. I'm from Buffalo, New

York."

Addressing me, the Captain said, "Tell us who you are and where you are from."

"I'm Hull Maintenance Technician, Montoya. I'm a Chicano from Albuquerque, New Mexico."

"You are from New Mexico?

"Yes, Sir."

"Did you join the Navy to get American citizenship, like the Filipinos?"

"New Mexico is a state. It became a U.S. Territory in 1850 after the U.S. went to war with Mexico and stole more than half of that country. It became the 47th State in 1912."

"I wasn't asking you for a history lesson. I just want to know if you joined the Navy to become a U.S. citizen."

"No, captain, I was born a U.S. citizen."

"So, do your parents still live in Mexico?"

"No, captain, they live in California."

"Hmmm? Then how did you get your citizenship, if you were born in Mexico?"

"I was not born in Mexico. I was born in New Mexico."

I struggled to keep from rolling my eyes in disbelief in front of him.

The captain continued, "You said that you were born in New Mexico, but that doesn't explain how you got your citizenship."

"New Mexico is a state. My parents were living there when I was born."

"Oh, I see. Your parents are American citizens?"

"Yes, Sir."

"From California?"

"Yes, Sir."

"Who were living in New Mexico when you were born?"

"Yes, Sir."

"So, you get your citizenship from your parents, even though you were born in New Mexico?"

Realizing that the captain was not going to understand, I said, "Yes, Sir."

Chief Jaffe caught up with me after the meeting. He took hold of my arm as he led me down the passageway. "Don't ever tell the captain that he's wrong," Jaffe said. His grip on my arm grew tighter. "That will only cause trouble. I want the Repair Gang to stay in his good graces. I've worked hard to get us here and I don't want a little wise ass Mexican messing it up."

"I'm not a Mexican."

"Mexican or American, I don't care. Just don't make us look bad. The captain hates to be told that he's wrong, especially from someone who is just an enlisted man." Jaffe hesitated, then added, "What's this shit with you calling yourself, Mushroom?"

"That's my nickname."

"It's a stupid nickname. Shows you're a peace-nick or a doper or both and that makes us look bad. I worked hard to get to where I am and I'm not going to let a little Mexican peace-nick ruin it."

"I'm not ruining anything. I do my job, and I do it well. And you know it," I said. "I was eligible to take the advancement test when I arrived on the ship, but you told me that you needed to observe me for a year before you could recommend me."

"So?"

"So, Bruce arrived on the Trippe two weeks before the advancement test. He wasn't even eligible and you tried like the dickens to get him to take the test. Is that because he's white?"

"Shut up! It's my business who I recommend. You'd better keep your nose clean and don't make us look bad, or I'll be on your ass every minute."

Seeing the Chief's racism raise its ugly head immediately after the Minority Affairs committee made all of my muscle's tense up. His words, "I don't want a little wise ass Mexican messing it up," kept repeating themselves in my head. His blatant racism confirmed my mistrust of his motives for being in the committee meeting.

Otis, the Japanese/American at the committee meeting, ran after me as I started my search for Barry. "Hold on there," he said.

"What's up, Otis?" I said as we walked down the passageway together. "I have to find Barry and finish my underway watch."

"I just wanted to bounce something off of you. It pissed me off, the way the captain said that he has the last say no matter what the committee recommends."

"It pissed me off, too," I said. "That meeting was a waste of time."

Otis grabbed my shoulder, stopping me as he said, "I couldn't believe it when the captain said that he would have to think about it, when the African Americans asked him to allow them to order Jet magazine."

"I couldn't believe it, either. It's not like they are asking the captain to pay for a subscription out of his own pocket. The funds for magazines come out of the money we get from the vending machines."

"If he doesn't approve it, I'm going to write my congressman." The scowl on Otis's face brightened into a gleeful smile as he added, "Did you see the look on Jaffe's face when you asked him how anyone would know that he's a Jew? I almost wet my pants trying not to laugh."

"Yeah, the whole top of his bald head turned red. I didn't believe his explanation for one minute. He wasn't there because he is a minority, he was afraid that we'd tell the captain what a racist he really is."

"I don't think the captain gives a shit." Otis said. "And now you've got Jaffe pissed off at ya. You'd better watch your ass, for sure. I just passed him down the passageway. He was mumbling something about frying a little Mexican ass."

15 – SAINT JANE

"Guess what just came over the radio?" Matty asked as he roused me from a restless sleep.

My eyes felt like someone had squeezed petroleum jelly into them as I pried my eyelids apart to see who was talking to me. "What time is it?" I asked.

"It is about 06:00," he said.

I stretched my hands over my head and slowly lifted my head off my pillow. I swung my feet over the side of my rack and lifted my torso by pushing my left hand against the mattress and grabbing an overhead pipe with my right hand. Rubbing my eyes and yawning widely, I looked down at Matty. "What did you hear on the radio that's so exciting?"

"Jane Fonda," Matty said as his eyes grew big and round, "You know, she's the one who starred in "Barbarella". Wow, she was hot in that movie."

"Yeah, she was real bitchin. What about her? I know that you didn't wake me up just to tell me how hot she is."

"She's in Hanoi with her anti-war movement. She demanded that the Viet Cong stop the war, and she accused our generals of being war criminals."

"Are you serious?" His words blasted the cobwebs out of my sleepy head.

"Yeah, I just heard it on the ship's radio. It's being broadcast in the news back home, too."

"Wow. She's not only sexy," I said. "She has big huevos too."

"Big huevos? Are those big boobs?" he asked.

"Not big boobs," I said with a grin. "She has big balls. Huevos is slang in Spanish for balls. She has bigger balls than you and I put together."

"Bigger balls than we do? She accused our generals of being war criminals on TV and on the radio," Matty said. "That's just not right."

"They are war criminals when they blow up villages and kill children for a body count," I said. "Did Jane Fonda really fly into enemy territory and demand that the Viet Cong stop fighting?"

"Yeah. But she's just a girl," Matty said.

"That girl has balls. We didn't have the guts to ask the captain not to bomb entire villages just for his body count. We have no huevos, Matty."

"She has no business doing that. That's the military's job, a man's job."

"My mother would be proud of Jane Fonda for doing a man's job. Hell, I'm proud of her. If she can get the Viet Cong to stop fighting, I will write to the pope and ask him to make her a saint."

Matty shook his head and rolled his eyes as he blurted, "The pope won't make Jane Fonda a saint. She appeared naked in Barbarella."

"She'd be the sexiest saint ever." I said as I imagined her with a golden halo above her head, dressed in the skimpy outfit that she wore in the movie, Barbarella.

"She's a fucking traitor. I hope they shoot that bitch," Jaffe yelled as he entered the berthing compartment.

His ranting entry startled me. I sat up so quickly that I hit my head on the overhead pipes and gave myself a throbbing headache.

"Who does she think she is, calling our generals war criminals?" Jaffe yelled walking over to my rack. "They're saving the Vietnamese from being taken over by the communists. She's probably a communist sympathizer. And if she is, she's a fucking whore! What does she know about war? She's just a pampered

Hollywood starlet. It's a man's job to end wars, not a fucking girl's job. She has no right to get involved in a man's war!"

I scurried down from my rack. Matty and I stood with our mouths open, frozen in time.

Jaffe put his hands on his hips, his big bald head turning fury filled red. He leaned his face an inch from mine, gritted his teeth and said, "If you think she's a saint, then you are a traitor too."

He stomped out of the berthing compartment and slammed the door to the workroom behind him.

"What was that all about?" Matty asked as he drew his tongue back into his mouth.

"He's gung ho military," I said. "The idea of a girl asking the enemy to stop the war made him mad."

"But that mad?" Matty asked, "I thought he was going to drag your ass down from your rack and beat the shit out of you before you had a chance to get down."

"Funny you should say that. I was thinking the same thing. I'd better take a shower and get ready for watch before he comes out of the workroom." I wondered how long he had been listening to Matty and me. And I wondered why he got so riled up over what Jane Fonda was doing. Didn't he realize that she was trying to end the war so that we could all go home?

As I opened my locker, I saw Jaffe open the door and glare at me. He turned to the right and ran up the ladder. Matty's eyes followed the chief out of the compartment. Norman walked past the top of the stairs. Matty said goodbye and left to tell him what happened. Being alone, I took the opportunity to pull out a clean set of sheets from my locker and climb back up to my rack to change them. When I finished, I returned to my locker and pulled out my blue work uniform and placed it neatly on my rack. Removing my white Jockey briefs that I wore as pajamas, I wrapped a towel around my waist, inserted my feet into my flip flops and headed for the showers.

As I entered the shower room, I saw Barry standing by the door. He followed me into the shower room. He tapped my on the shoulder before I hung my towel on the bar across from the shower stalls.

"Man, oh, man, you've really pissed off Chief Jaffe," he said. "I overheard him talking to Chief Garfield about getting rid of your ass."

"What did he say?"

"I'm not really sure. It sounded like Jaffe said that he was going to figure out a way to get Shea, the chief corpsman, to say that you are doing dope and get that 'fucking screamer' out of his Navy."

"He called me a screamer?"

Barry laughed. "Yeah, a fucking screamer." His smile made the hair on my back stand at attention.

"When I got closer to 'em," Barry said, "I heard Jaffe tell Garfield that ya'll are a peace mongering hippie. And he'll do whatever it takes to get ya off this ship, even if he has to make something up." Walking out of the shower room, he looked back at me and whispered, "Ya'll didn't hear this from me. I don't want to get caught in the cross fire."

Jaffe liked Barry quite a bit and Barry enjoyed the perks of being in his good graces.

The freshly painted white bathroom was long and narrow with showers stalls on the bow side, sinks and mirrors in the middle and toilets along the bulkhead behind the wall of sinks. After hanging my towel on a hook adjacent to the sink I entered a middle shower stall and pulled the yellowed clear plastic shower curtain closed. The stainless steel shower stalls were barely wide and deep enough for a grown man to stand in. The water, splashing down my face and neck, renewed my sense of wellbeing as it sprayed away the sleepiness from my face.

I turned off the shower and rubbed off the excess water from my arms and legs. Pulling the curtain open, I stepped out to get my towel from the sink across the room. Before I finished my first step, Chief Jaffe and two other chiefs came into the shower room and blocked my path.

I felt very uncomfortable standing naked, in front of the three chiefs.

"What drugs are you taking?" Chief Shea asked.

"The only drugs I take are those malaria pills that give the whole ship diarrhea."

He continued asking questions, often repeating the same questions worded only slightly different from the first.

Feeling the air around my exposed genitals as the water began to evaporate made me want to jump back behind the shower curtain. I didn't want to be naked in front of the three chiefs. As I tried to make my way around them to get my towel, Jaffe jumped in front of me.

"Where do you think you're going?" he asked, clenching his fist. "We aren't through talking to you."

"I'm getting my towel. Do you mind?"

Chief Shea and Chief Garfield smiled sheepishly as they moved out of the way, while Jaffe's bald head regained its familiar fiery red hue.

"What are you trying to pull?" Jaffe yelled as I reached for my towel.

By now I was mad. No longer afraid of Jaffe, I yelled back, "What are you trying to pull?" I wrapped my towel around my waist. "Why did you bring two chiefs with you to yell at me while I was taking a shower?"

"You're doing drugs!" he growled.

"You're lying, and you know it," I shot back.

"Only someone who's crazy on drugs would run around the smokestack screaming every fucking night."

"Killing innocent people is driving me crazy. I have to scream."

"That's fucking bullshit. You're doing drugs."

I stuck my neck out and looked Jaffe right in the eyes. "When we had the last locker inspection, did you find any drugs?"

"No. You must be hiding them somewhere else."

"You didn't find drugs because I don't have any. I'm not stupid. You're the one who is trying to pull something."

Jaffe's neck muscles pushed out the tendons as his whole face became the color of rage. "You aren't doing your job!"

"I came in here to take a shower so that I could do my job, like I always do," I said.

Chief Garfield's lips contorted into a forced smile as he put his hand on Jaffe's shoulder telling him that his cause was lost.

If there had been no witnesses, I am sure that Jaffe's anger would have unleashed his fists and I would have had wounds that needed bandaging.

As the three chiefs walked out of the shower room, Jaffe turned around and said, "Jane Fonda is no saint. She's a fucking traitor and so are ... "

I did not hear the rest because Chief Garfield grabbed his shoulder, turned him back towards the door and said, "Leave it for another time."

16 - WHISPERING

"What the fuck are you doing with this book?" Matty asked. He had come down to my berthing compartment to invite me to join him for dinner as I was opening my locker to get dressed. I had just taken a shower. The book fell onto the deck, losing its plain brown paper book cover.

"I heard that *Johnny Got His Gun* is banned," he said as he reached down to pick it up.

I put my finger up to my lips and whispered, "I know it's banned. Please put the wrapper back on the book."

Matty looked around the berthing compartment and followed my lead to whisper. "Why did you get it?"

"My high school friend, George, told me about it. He's a conscientious objector. That's one of the reasons I bought it."

"You'd better not get caught with that book."

"Why not? This is a free country, isn't it?"

"Not here, in Viet Nam. Not on the U.S.S. Trippe," he said. "Your boss, Chief Jaffe, will fry your ass, if he catches you."

Barry slid down the ladder, his flip flops slamming on the

deck. He walked into the berthing compartment, removing his white towel from around his waist.

"You've got the whitest ass I've ever seen," I said.

Pulling his pink penis out of a bush of orange orangutan pubic hair, Barry said, "It makes it easier for the girls to find my pecker."

"With that little thing," Matty said, "they're gonna need all the help they can get,"

"Fuck you. At least they can find mine."

Turning his head down sideways, Barry put a corner of the towel in his ear and dried it.

"What're ya'll whispering about?" he asked. "I could hear ya'll whispering before I entered the compartment."

Matty put his finger to his lips as he passed the book over to Barry. Taking it with his free hand, Barry walked toward the repair shop door.

"Is anybody in there?" he asked. "If there is, they'll hear everything ya'll say, even if ya whisper." He peeked inside and said, "Hmm. No one's there."

Barry opened the book when he was satisfied that the coast was clear.

"I know this one," he said, a smile brightening his face. "It's about a soldier in World War One who gets blown up. He's not much more than a thinking piece of meat."

Matty's eyes scrunched together as he asked, "They banned a book about a slab of meat?"

"No, ya' dumb ass," Barry whispered. "The soldier has no arms or legs, he's blind and he can't talk because his face is blown off, too."

"I don't get it," Matty whispered, squinting his eyes and putting his finger over his mouth to remind Barry to be quieter. "Why is the book banned?"

"It's an anti-war book," I said. "The main character figured out how to communicate. He tells the nurse, through Morse code, that he can earn a living by being his own freak show."

"But how does that make it an anti-war book?"

"I'll tell you," Barry said.

"Have you read it, too?" Matty asked.

"Yeah. While I was on the river boats. It opened my eyes to

just how fuckin' stupid we all are for enlisting."

"Weren't you afraid of getting caught?"

"Who the fuck would've caught me? Our boat's captain gave me the book to read."

"No shit?" Matty asked.

Lowering my voice, I said. "I finished reading it last night while I was at battle station."

Matty's eyes darted back and forth. "You read it during your battle station? That's fucking crazy, with Jaffe snooping around. I wouldn't be surprised if he were around the corner listening to us."

"Screw Jaffe," Barry said. "Only the selling of it is banned on base. They can't keep you from reading whatever you damn well please."

"That may be true," Matty said in a soft tone, "But Jaffe will give Mushroom hell, if he catches him with this book."

"That's why I wrapped it in a brown paper book cover," I said.

"I'm still confused," Matty said. "Why would a story about a soldier who wants to be in a freak show be considered an anti-war book."

"Because he would be a living 'dead' person," I said. "The soldier, in the book, wants people to see how badly mangled he is. He wants them to see a soldier that is worse off than dead. He hopes that parents won't send any more of their boys to war."

"He wants the people who see him," Barry added, "to know that every soldier who dies in war dies in vain. Every death is a total fucking waste."

Barry handed the book to Matty, "Here, ya'll need to read this." Then he turned to me and said, "I'll buy ya'll another one, when and if we get back to Rhode Island."

"The hell you will," Jaffe said while pulling the book out of Matty's hand.

I jumped and my stomach tightened. Matty didn't move a muscle. Barry stood smiling.

"Wipe that shit eating grin off your face," Jaffe said as he glared at Barry. "I expected more from you."

Barry turned and walked to his rack to put some clothes on.

Jaffe put his hands on his hips and looked Matty in the eyes.

"Don't waste your time reading this communist shit," Jaffe said as he slapped his hand with the book.

Matty didn't utter a word. He couldn't move. His eyes were fixed on Jaffe.

"Don't you have somewhere to go?" Jaffe said.

Matty made an about face, ran out the door and up the ladder.

I reached into my locker and grabbed a pair of briefs, trying not to look at Jaffe as I put on my underwear.

He slithered up to me, put his face inches away from my ear and whispered, "I'm going to get you the fuck off my ship, no matter what it takes."

17 – NEGLIGEE AND DIAMONDS

Bruce walked into the mess decks and handed me a plain brown box, while I nibbled on a meager lunch of a single thin slice of roast beef. "Heah," he said, "This is for you. Open it."

"What is it, Bruce?"

"How am I supposed to know?" he asked, throwing both hands in the air. "The note has your name on it."

"Note? I don't see a note."

"It musta fallen off somewhere," he said, averting his eyes.

Taking my keys out of my pocket, I placed the box onto the table and cut the tape with the key's teeth. Bruce loomed over my shoulder as I pulled open the flaps exposing the contents. "What on earth is this?" I asked. Reaching into the box, my fingers enjoyed the soft and silky material. Pulling it all the way out of the box, and letting it fall to its full length, I realized that I was holding a black silk negligee. Turning around to look at Bruce, I said, "Oh Bruce, this will look so good on you."

"Fuck you!" he said.

"Oh, and diamond earrings to match," I said. "These must

have cost you a fortune. And you did this for me?"

Bruce's neck muscles tightened and his eyes narrowed. His voice grew progressively louder as he said, "I told you. I didn't get those for you. I'm no queer!"

Just then, Ensign Denny walked into the mess decks with Chief Jaffe behind him. Seeing me holding the diamond earrings, Chief Jaffe said, "See, Ensign Denny, I told you that he stole the gifts I bought for my wife."

Bruce and I turned toward the ensign when we heard what Jaffe said. Ensign Denny walked over to me, placed his hands on his hips and asked, "What do you have to say for yourself?"

As Bruce opened his mouth to say something, the chief interrupted him saying, "Ensign Denny is not talking to you. Since this is none of your concern, I want you to leave. Now!"

I was stunned that Bruce left without saying that he had given me the package. Invisible fingers squeezed my stomach, sending glue to my feet making it impossible for me to move. Watching the Chief order Bruce to leave, I knew that he was setting a trap for me. My voice was held prisoner and couldn't get out of my throat. Sweat slid down my back.

"Bruce gave me that box," I blurted.

"Don't go blaming someone else for what you did," the chief said. "You are the one holding the gifts I bought for my wife."

"Why did you send Bruce away?" I asked. "If you don't believe me, bring him back here and ask him."

Ensign Denny ran to the door and called for Bruce asking him to come back inside. Bruce's head hung down when I asked, "Bruce, didn't you give me that box?"

Looking at the chief, Bruce said, "I'm sorry Chief, I know you ordered me to leave, but Ensign Denny called me back."

Turning to Ensign Denny, he said, "The chief showed me the note that was on top of the box and kept it." Turning and pointing at me, he said, "Then the chief gave me the box, told me to give it to Mushroom and leave right away. I didn't know why."

The Chief's cheeks flushed bright red. He snatched the earrings out of my hand, stuffed the negligee back into the box and left without saying a word.

"The chief is really going be pissed at me now," Bruce said. Turning his hands out towards me, he said, "I am so sorry I gave you that box. I didn't know that the chief was setting you up. Honest."

Ensign Denny said, "Don't worry about the chief, Bruce. You did the right thing." The ensign scraped some crumbs off the table and asked me to sit down. Looking down while squinting his eyes, he said, "The chief really is a good sailor."

My head began to throb. I wondered what Ensign Denny really wanted to say. Saying that the chief was a good sailor was meaningless to me. His words only fed my mistrust. My stomach groaned as I asked, "Then why did he do that? This proves that he has it in for me."

"I wouldn't go that far," he said. "I will have to sort this out. I'll have a talk with him. In the meantime, keep your nose clean."

"Keep MY nose clean?" I asked, not expecting an answer. Getting up from the table, I was furious. The muscles in my forearms tightened as my hands transformed into fists. I wanted to punch the chief in the face. "Why can't you see the obvious?" I asked as I walked out of the mess deck.

Krack, a fire control technician, (rocket launcher) who overheard everything while eating his lunch, came up behind me and placed his hand on my shoulder. "Lifers always stick together," he said. "Hell. Your face is as red as the tips of our torpedoes. Let's go topside before you explode. You need some fresh air. And besides, I have something to tell you. "

18 – IN THE EYES OF THE BEHOLDER

Krack followed me as I trudged up to the helo deck after we finished loading rounds of ammo into the MK42's magazine. We were tired from passing the seventy pound shells from sailor to sailor into the magazine beneath the cannon. The sun shone brightly up on deck an hour before sunset. The water rippled with the sun's diamond like reflection. We sat on the deck, just outside the hangar door admiring the sun's sparkling art work. A couple of guys were playing basketball inside. One of them asked us to play.

"I'd rather play on a court that doesn't have a constantly moving basket," Krack said. "The ones back home in Buffalo don't sway.

"Anticipating the speed of the ship's rocking is what makes shooting baskets such a challenge," a player said as he dribbled the ball in front of him a couple of times.

"How about you?" he asked, as he turned to face me. "If you're any good, we could play two on one."

"Nah. The gunfire from the choppers is too distracting," I said. "I've got too many things on my mind."

"I don't want to hear any bull shit whining out of you," Krack said as he stood up and grabbed my arm. "We're stuck in this fuckin' war. It's going to continue whether we play basketball or not, and right now, you need to play because we will all be back on battle station in a couple of hours."

Krack and I took off our shirts. He tossed me the ball and I dribbled until I was blocked. I passed the ball to him. He jumped and threw the ball, too far to the left of the basket, or so it seemed. The ship swayed and the ball swished through the basket.

"Tell me that wasn't the most beautiful shot you've ever seen," Krack said.

We played for twenty minutes until one of the other guys had to leave to stand his watch. Krack and I stepped out of the hangar while putting our shirts back on our sweaty torsos. We resumed our previous positions, sitting just outside the hangar door. Looking west, over the hills beyond the battle, I watched the sun descend behind the hills.

"Look, Krack," I said, punching him in the shoulder. "The sun is cloud painting again. God, that's a gorgeous sunset."

"It's weird that we can be out here on the water," Krack said, "the war waging not more than two hundred yards off our port side, and you stop everything to point out a gorgeous fuckin' sunset."

"It's no weirder than playing basketball on a rocking ship while our five inch gun kills only God knows who."

"Yes, it is. Well, maybe not, now that I think about it. Basketball is a war, one team against another. And there could be beautiful cheerleaders to watch at a game."

"Cheerleaders? What the heck are you talking about? How did cheerleaders get into this conversation?"

"I don't mean on the ship. I mean, at a basketball game you could be admiring the cheerleaders while the basketball players run back and forth across the court."

"Let me see if I get this straight," I said. "Are you saying that even though there's a war going on, beauty goes on as well?"

"Yeah, sort of," Krack said. "It's hard to explain what I'm trying to say. You can choose to look at the fake war on the basketball court, and you can also look at the gorgeous cheerleaders."

"That's true," I said. "Beauty is all around us and it is up to us to behold what's always there, whether there's a war going on or not."

"Yeah. That's what I wanted to say," Krack said. "Now that we are alone, I can tell you about another little war that is going on. This one doesn't have any pretty cheerleaders."

"Is this what you were you going to tell me when we left the mess decks?"

Krack looked around to make sure no one else could hear and whispered, "Jaffe told some of the other chiefs that he wants them to catch you doing something that will get you in trouble."

"Like what?"

"I don't know," he said. "Just be careful. It's time for me to get back to work. I'll see ya later."

Night decorated the black sky with twinkling stars. The moon hid behind a lone cloud. I climbed up to the flying bridge and found a secluded place to meditate. The signalmen were nowhere in sight. I leaned my back against the steel bulkhead and slowed my breathing. After a few deep breaths my shoulders relaxed and I began my mantra. I floated into a meditation of me sitting on the beach with salt spray teasing my nose. The sunrise tinted the clouds pink, yellow and orange. Thunder boomed in the distance and someone gently touched my hand. A nude Vietnamese woman, about my age, sat next to me with her legs crossed, facing the water.

"Take in a deep breath and hold it," she said in Vietnamese, but I understood every word. "Let it out slowly; let your breath take away all your deaths. Now breathe in slowly, let the air spirit restore your soul, let it bring in beauty."

The rumbling of the ship threatened to pull me out of my meditative trance. I told myself to let it go. Refocus my attention back to the Vietnamese woman's words.

"How can I do that? There is no beauty here," I said. "There is only hate and death."

"There is no death unless you hold it." she said. "There is no hate unless you refuse to let it go."

"But people are dying, we are shooting them."

She stood up, stretched out her arms and twirled around. Standing up, I became aware of my own nudity, but not embarrassed by it. She put her arm around the small of my back as we walked along the water's edge.

"Beauty cannot be stopped, even amid ugliness and death," she said. "It can only be ignored."

She recited a poem in a sing song voice. The sound of her Vietnamese words illuminated everything around me.

"Beauty abounds. Just take a look.
I mean really look. Beauty abounds around you.
Under foot, overhead, side to side.
Awe.
Such splendor is gifted upon us. Beauty abounds.
See the fairy hiding in her wooden cloak.
"Look!" She shouts. "Down here, up there, everywhere.
Beauty abounds.
Ignore not the wondrous glory.
Open your eyes and see.
Beauty abounds all around you."

Boom! I jumped. Our five inch gun fired at a target beyond the shore. Opening my eyes, I saw Krack climbing onto the flying bridge toward me.

"I thought I'd find you here," he said. "One of the sinks is clogged in the forward head. I went down to the repair shop and asked the chief if he could send someone to fix it. He told me that you were the only one who wasn't on watch. He said you'd fix it."

"So much for meditating," I said taking his hand to lift myself up. "Let me get a couple of wrenches, and I'll meet you in the forward head."

As I climbed two levels down to the repair locker, I thought about the Vietnamese woman in my meditation. She seemed so real. I remembered the softness of her hands when she put her arm around my waist. I pulled the keys out of my pocket, inserted the key into the huge padlock and opened the heavy steel repair locker, wishing that it was a magic door leading to the same beach where I walked nude with the Vietnamese lady. The door squealed indicating that I would need to grease the hinges. I turned on the lights and grabbed a couple of pipe wrenches out of the tool box on the bottom shelf. Stepping over the threshold to leave, I thought, *'Beauty abounds all around you.'* Hmmm. *I'm going to have to work hard to find beauty in a clogged drain while we blow the hell out of paradise.*

19 - PISTOL

Barry followed me down to my berthing compartment after I unclogged a drain line in the forward head. Sludge and goo clung to my pants and I needed to change.

"Why do ya'll have two squirt guns in here?" Barry asked as he stood looking inside my open locker.

"It is much more fun to have someone else to play with," I said.

"These look pretty cheap to me."

Displaying a broad smile, I said, "They're made of the finest quality, authentic plastic, all the way from Japan. They cost me a fortune."

"A fortune?" Barry scrunched his nose and rolled his eyes.

"Yes, a heavy fortune in copper. They cost me twenty five pennies each."

Barry inspected my limited arsenal of two squirt guns and asked, "Who gets the pink one?"

Winking at him, I said, "You do, you big pussy."

"Shut up!" he said as he tossed me the pink gun. "If we play, you get the pink one, not me. Do these even work?" he said as he squeezed the trigger on the blue squirt gun.

"Like I said, they're made of the finest material twenty five cents can buy."

Lifting his right eyebrow, standing up and pulling his shoulders back, he asked, "Do ya'll follow strict procedures when ya inspect these guns?"

"Of course. Would you like me to show you? I just need to get some water first," I said, trying to look serious.

"Not unless you give me one of those guns, and not the pink one, to fill with water, too."

"Can't do that," I said

"Why not?"

"This is the middle of the workday, you know we can't play."

"Bummer," Barry said.

I took off my dirty dungarees and chucked them into our berthing compartment's laundry bag. Chief Jaffe's boots echoed as he stomped into the berthing compartment.

"Did you finish unclogging the drain in the forward head?" he asked.

Before I could utter a reply, he said, "Go find Bruce and finish his watch."

"Do you have any idea where he might be?" I asked.

He did not answer. He walked away and stopped in front of the repair shop door. Turning around he said, "Hurry up. I haven't got all day. Put your pants on and go find Bruce."

Jaffe shut the door to the repair shop. Barry said, "It looks like ya'll get to play with real guns now and pretend to be a real Texan like me."

"I'd rather play with the squirt guns. That would've been a blast. Too bad, I have to go stand watch."

As I inserted my leg into a clean pair of dungarees, I heard footsteps coming down the ladder. Barry and I looked to see who was coming. Bending down to lace up my shoe strings, I saw Bruce's steel toed boot hit the deck at the bottom of the ladder.

"Jaffe told me to come down here and have you take over my watch," he said. "I just started a half hour ago, at 20:00. You will have the watch until midnight."

Bruce handed me the clipboard and sounding tape before he

removed the holster. He took back the clipboard and sounding tape with his free hand and handed me the holster. When I finished buckling the holster around my waist, I took out the .45 caliber pistol, released the clip and inspected the barrel. Seeing that it was empty, I reloaded the clip and holstered the gun.

"You always follow strict procedures when it comes to taking over watch, don't you."

"I don't like guns," I said. "This is not a plastic squirt gun. This one is lethal."

"All guns are lethal," he said with a wry smile.

I didn't like his smile. I could feel the muscles in my legs and stomach coiling around me. I felt like a snake readying itself to strike.

"As I was saying, Bruce, this gun kills," I said, venom spewing out of my mouth, "If the chamber is loaded, it could go off and kill me when the holster flips up as I climb through the smaller hatches."

Bruce put his hand out flat in front of him, stopping my words, "Take it easy," he said. "I was only kidding. Jesus, you are in a foul mood."

"I'm sorry, Bruce. Jaffe pisses me off. He's being an a ... , he's being mean."

"To hell with Jaffe. He is only concerned with looking good. You're running around the smokestack every night makes him look bad."

"How does my screaming make him look bad?" I asked, "I'm the one running around the smokestack."

Bruce's presence annoyed me. I wanted him to finish giving me the watch report and leave.

But he didn't leave. He stood in front of me, holding the clipboard and sounding tape. My annoyance grew in direct proportion to how relaxed he became. His eyes looked up at the ceiling as if he were thinking of what he wanted to say. Speaking at an irritatingly slow pace, he said, "Chief Jaffe is the most powerful enlisted man on this ship."

With each word growing progressively louder, I said, "What does that have to do with anything?"

His reply was slow and deliberate, one word at a time, "You're one of his men and you are running amok. His boss is going to think that he can't keep his men under control."

My shoulders slumped forward. My head hung low as my anger dribbled onto the deck, leaving me feeling empty. My mind began to process Bruce's words. Jaffe doesn't care about me or the rest of his men, I thought. He is only concerned with how we make him look. It is so obvious. Why have I been so blind?

Pulling back my attention to the task at hand, Bruce told me that he had only taken one sounding to check that the ship was not taking on water. I asked him where he had taken that measurement.

"I wrote it down on the clipboard. It's my last entry in the sounding log. Right there. See?"

"In the engine room?" I asked, feeling my anger sneaking back. "Most people start the watch at the bow."

"I know," he said and smiled. "But I wanted to talk to my friend in the engine room. And since that's where he was, I checked the sounding tube in the engine room first. Are you headed for the bow?"

"Of course. I don't want to screw up and miss a sounding. If what you are saying about Jaffe is right, he'll do anything to get me busted and kicked off his ship, as he calls it."

Bruce gave me a mock salute, made an about face and left. Barry must have been listening to our conversation while he stood next to his locker, eating a Hershey bar. "Bruce is right, ya know. Ya'll make the chief look bad to his superiors. He likes the power that he wields on this ship. Even the junior officers do what he tells them, without question."

"How can I ruin his reputation? As the saying goes, Jaffe may not be the captain, but he runs the ship."

"That's the point that Bruce was trying to show ya. Ya'll are a threat to his ability to continue running the ship. I'd watch out if I were you. If he feels cornered, he'll strike out with a vengeance, like a cat."

Barry's comment made me feel uneasy. I didn't want to think that the chief would be vengeful.

"Isn't the chief supposed to help his men?" I asked.

"Ya'll are so fucking dense sometimes. Ya want the world to be rosy and ya want everyone to be nice."

"So what's wrong with that?"

"The fuckin Navy is not that way and Jaffe's already tried to get ya in trouble with the gifts for his wife."

The ship rolled, and I fell against Barry.

"Good grief! You're right," I said, looking up at him. "He is trying to get me kicked out."

"No shit, Sherlock."

"If I get kicked out of the Navy, I won't be able to get a decent job, my father, who was sailor in WWII, would be so pissed off. I wouldn't be able to go home. He'd never let me raise my own kid."

"Oh yeah, I almost forgot that ya have a kid. Your parents are watching him for ya, right?"

"Yes, they are. What the heck am I supposed to do? I do my jobs well."

"It's not how ya'll do your job that makes him look bad. It's your fucking screaming."

"But I need to scream. I'm not wired to kill people, no matter what the Navy calls them; gooks or whatever."

"It's probably already too late. Ya better watch your backside. Jaffe is out to get your ass. Mark my words."

Smiling back at him, I said, "With phrases like, 'mark my words,' you're starting to sound like my elementary school teacher, Sister Rose Eileen.

"I'm no cock sucking nun, just watch your back."

I took the clip board and sounding tape, climbed the ladder out of the compartment and headed to the bow. Opening the door from the forward most berthing compartment, I entered the chain locker, where the sounding tube took residence between the two sets of rusty chains that held the ship's anchors. The chain locker always smelled musty and felt damp. The stormy seas caused the ship to roll up and down more than normal, making my legs feel wobbly. A single light, high up on the overhead, gave the chain locker an eerie appearance. Seeing the coiled chains made me feel as if a sea serpent, camouflaged in varying shades of orange and black, laid in waiting for his victim to come by and be devoured. My imagination ran amok until the bow dipped beneath me and I fell forward, landing on the winch and scraping my knees on the chains.

I nearly jumped out of my own skin when I heard Jaffe say,

"That was stupid."

I could feel my ears getting hot and my face flushing red with embarrassment as I picked myself off the rusty chains. "What the hell is he doing here?" I whispered to myself. I asked Jaffe what he wanted.

"I'm here to make sure that you don't make any more stupid mistakes while you take a sounding," he said with a forked tongue. He had convinced himself that I was hiding dope and he was determined to find it.

"Explain to me what you're doing as you are doing it," he said.

He was treating me like a new recruit. I wanted to retaliate, but thought better of it.

"Tell me how you are going to give me an accurate measurement with the bow rising and dipping, like it is."

"I will take two measurements," I said. "One, when the ship heaves up to its highest point, and the other, when it dips to its lowest point. The average of the two measurements will give me the number we need."

"You aren't as dumb as you look," he said while steadying himself against the door.

I wished he'd fall backwards into the berthing compartment. I removed a rag out of my back pocket to wipe off the tape and plumb bob. Making sure he was watching, I lowered the plumb bob to the bottom of the sounding tube allowing the slack to be obvious. I wanted no doubt in his mind that I was doing this correctly. The ship's rising and dipping made it almost impossible for me to remain standing. I waited until the bow dipped a couple of times before I reeled the sounding tape back up. The dim light in the chain locker made it difficult to see the boundary between the wet and the dry on the sounding tape.

"What's the water level?" he asked.

"The sounding tape is dry at eighteen inches."

I wiped off the tape once more and held the plumb bob just inside the sounding tube. The bow took a fast dip and leaned too far to the port side, making me lose my balance and fall once again. My heart began beating faster, supplying the blood that rushed into my face. I hated looking like a klutz. Glancing back at Jaffe, I saw his shit eating grin. I got up and spread my legs out wider, this time. I repositioned the plum bob just inside the sounding tube. I waited until the bow began its rapid ascent to drop the plumb bob and reel it back up before we dipped again.

"The water on the tape stopped at eight inches," I said.

"So what does that get you?"

"Thirteen inches of water in the chain locker's bilge."

When I picked up the clipboard and pen, I realized that I would need to get out of the dimly lit chain locker in order to record the sounding. Jaffe left before I returned to the better lit forward berthing compartment. Reading the previous recordings of twelve inches and fourteen inches made me smile with satisfaction.

The ups and downs of the ship reflected how I was feeling. I felt good about succeeding in the chain locker, but my anger and frustration with Jaffe made me want to scream.

Krack, one of the rocket technicians, caught up to me as I was nearing the end of my watch. He stopped me as I began climbing the ladder to the bridge. "You'd better watch out," he said.

"What's up, Krack? You heard something, didn't you?"

"Yup. He's going to get you. Shhh," he whispered. He scanned our surroundings for anyone who might be in hearing range, put his finger to his lips and motioned me with his head, to follow him. We stood on an exterior passageway where the wind blew, flapping my shirt sleeves like miniature sails.

"I overheard Jaffe tell that seaman, Flynn, that he was going to set a trap for you to get you kicked out of the Navy or at least off this ship."

"What kind of trap?"

"Beats me," Krack said, shrugging his shoulders. "All I know is that he asked Flynn to help him. And that little bastard said that he would."

I thanked Krack as he lit his cigarette and marched toward the helo deck in a cloud of smoke. I resumed my climb up the ladder to the bridge. Why was Jaffe doing this? Jaffe had been hounding me ever since he caught me telling Matty that Jane Fonda was a saint. It had to be more than that. The clock in the bridge showed 11:50. Barry, my replacement, was talking with the helmsman asking him what it was it like to drive the ship. I didn't notice Flynn standing just inside the rear door of the bridge, talking with the quartermaster.

I walked up to Ensign Denny, the officer on the bridge and saluted. "Sounding and security, all secure, Sir," I said.

I turned and addressed Barry, "Since you're already here, I'll give you the sounding and security report, and hand over the watch. You have it next. Right?"

Barry rolled his eyes, saying, "Do ya'll think I'd be here if I didn't?"

I handed him the clipboard, telling him about the difficulty I'd had taking a sounding in the chain locker that morning.

"It won't be hard now that the seas have calmed down," he said. "I'll let ya know how accurate ya were."

"Carrying this gun is so stupid," I said. "It weighs a ton. It only has an accuracy range of about fifty feet. And we're never going to shoot anyone with it." I took the pistol out of its holster, pulled out the bullet clip and inspected the barrel. I replaced the clip, making sure that the safety was in position before handing the gun to Barry.

Seaman Flynn held out his arm, his finger pointing at me. "I saw that!" he yelled out.

"You saw what?" I asked.

"You pointed the gun at the helmsman. That's assault. I'm going to report you."

"I didn't point the gun at the helmsman. You're full of it."

As if on cue, Jaffe walked into the bridge. Flynn ran up to him. Grabbing Jaffe's shirt sleeve, he pointed at me.

"You just missed it," he said. "He pointed the gun at the helmsman and fired it at him. Lucky for the helmsman, the chamber was empty."

I tried to sort out what was really taking place as I watched Flynn accuse me of firing the gun at the helmsman. Chief Jaffe positioned himself between his boss, Ensign Denny, and me. He gritted his teeth and glared at me. The hair on the back of my neck stood up.

"I'm charging you with assault!" Jaffe yelled. His face flushed red as his whole body shook. "If I get my way, you'll spend the rest of your life in the brig."

I froze, standing in disbelief, watching Jaffe take over the bridge. The volume of his voice cranked up a couple of notches as he turned to face the helmsman.

"I want you to come with me to press charges against him for assault."

I inhaled quickly and held my breath.

The helmsman gripped the helm with both hands. Forcing a laugh, he said, "Ha. Flynn is so stupid. There was no assault; no one pointed a gun at me. I repeat: Flynn is so stupid that he can't tell when someone is inspecting the barrel to make sure the chamber is clear before transferring the gun."

Ensign Denny's eye brows scrunched together as he said, "He's right, chief. I saw the whole thing."

I let out a sigh of relief.

Chief Jaffe glared at Flynn and motioned to the exit door with his eyes. Flynn made an about face and left. Jaffe turned to Ensign Denny. "Well, I'm not taking any chances."

"What kind of chances? What are you getting so riled up about?" the ensign asked.

"Montoya could hurt somebody with that gun." Jaffe said.

I put my palms up and raised my eyebrows giving a confused look to Ensign Denny. He walked closer to Jaffe saying, "I watched him follow strict protocol when he handed over the gun to the next man on watch. He'll do fine."

"But he screams around the smokestack," Jaffe said.

"He's just blowing off steam," the ensign said. "Maybe you should do the same."

Chief petty officer Jaffe glared at his boss, Ensign, Denny. "With all due respect, Sir, I run my crew, my way."

Jaffe crossed his arms over his chest and turned to face me. His eyes shot bullets as he said, "I'm pulling you off Sounding and Security watch. I'm making you compartment cleaner."

"That's really not necessary, Chief." Ensign Denny said.

The chief did not turn around to acknowledge his boss.

Knowing that I would suffer Jaffe's wrath, if he didn't get his way, I said to Ensign Denny, "It's OK, Sir. I don't mind."

I turned and headed for the exit before Officer Denny could respond. Biting down on my lip, I made a mental note reminding myself to thank Barry, Krack and Bruce for warning me to watch out for Jaffe. I climbed down the ladder to the next level and burst out laughing.

"What's so funny?" Norman asked as he came wobbling by.

"Jaffe got so riled up on the bridge that, instead of punishing me, he accidentally made things easier for me by making me the compartment cleaner."

"Don't be so shooah," Norman said. "I think he's up to something."

20 – REFUSAL TO FIRE THE ROCKETS

The following morning, I entered the bridge to take over the 08:00 sounding and security watch. Otis handed me the gun and the clipboard, as he informed me that a Captain's Mast was just starting. He put his finger to his lips and whispered that I needed to be quiet, court was in session. Captain Reardon stood next to the helm, his hands on his hips, eyes glaring at the two sailors in front of him. They had their backs to me. One of them turned to the other sailor who has standing there. I recognized Krack and realized that Norman stood next to him. They were both Fire Control Technicians. Their job consisted of programming the computers that launched the rockets.

Captain Reardon's eyes searched the faces of the sailors before him. "Since both of you are being charged with the same thing, I'm going to address both of you. You are being charged with refusing to obey a direct order to launch the rockets. How do you plead?"

"Guilty, Sir" they said in unison.

"You two took an oath to defend the constitution and to obey orders," the captain said. "What's this nonsense about not wanting to perform your duties?"

Norman cleared his throat, sucked in air through his nostrils and said, "With all due respect, Sir, killing innocent villagers has nothing to do with defending the constitution."

"We aren't killing innocent villagers," the captain said. "We're killing North Vietnamese communists and communist sympathizers."

Krack piped in, "Sir, I don't understand how all of the villagers could be communists, certainly not toddlers and little kids?"

"You two are stupidly naïve. We have reports that show that young girls have walked up to our boys in uniform and handed them live grenades, blowing themselves up along with our boys. You can't trust em."

"I don't believe that those young girls, that you mentioned, had any real choice in the matter. They aren't old enough to make those types of choices," Krack said.

The captain's voice grew louder as he said, "Yes they are. They could refuse, just like you two are refusing."

"I'm sure that if those kids refused," Krack continued, "that they would get killed or that they were threatened with someone killing their family."

"You've been reading too many suspense novels," the captain said.

Norman stroked his long red beard and said, "Sir, I swore an oath to defend our country. And I will. I'll even give up my life if I have to defend our country. But I can't fire rockets on civilians."

The captain threw his hands out as he yelled, "And why not? They're the enemy! Are you defying a direct order? Do you know the penalty for that in war time?"

I stopped breathing. The ships engine vibrated through the deck. My mind raced, wondering what penalty the captain could give them. I shuddered at the thought of what punishments were allowed in war zones. *Would the captain throw them in the brig, have them court martialed or shot?*

Norman let his head drop, he looked from one side of the bridge to the other, then back to the captain. "You can believe what you want; Sir, but Krack and I will not fire any more rockets."

The captain directed his attention to Krack and asked, "Are you going to refuse to obey a direct order?"

"If that direct order is to fire rockets, yes sir. I will refuse."

The captain tilted his head toward the XO and whispered something I couldn't hear. He returned his attention to Norman and Krack. In a slow and deliberate voice, he said, "I am demoting both of you to the rate of seaman."

I let out a sigh and covered my mouth. *Thank God he's not ordering them to be hanged.*

The captain continued, "I'm assigning you two to the galley. You will stay there until I can get replacements for you and get you off my ship. Be warned, that if I can get you court martialed, and get you off my ship sooner, I will. Do you understand?"

They both replied, in unison, "Yes, Sir."

The captain pointed his finger out the door and said, "Report to the galley and get out of my sight."

I walked out the door and down to the main deck. Norman slid down the ladder on his hands. I heard his feet hit the deck right behind me.

Turning around, I said, "You two have bigger *huevos* than I thought."

Norman heaved a heavy sigh. "*Huevos?* Oh yeah, balls. Balls haven't got a fucking thing to do with it. Hell, I was scared shitless. I was expecting the captain to throw us in the brig and then have us court martialed."

We made our way down the passageway and into the galley. The ship rolled causing me to lose my balance and crash in to the bulkhead.

"You look like a drunken sailor," Krack said, following us in. "Losing your sea legs?"

I grimaced and asked, "What caused you two to refuse to fire the rockets?"

Norman pulled out the order of the day and said, "Hey man, did you read this shit? Krack and I were reading it last night and that's when we decided that we couldn't blow innocent people up anymore.

Krack said, "I may be German/American, but I'm no fucking Nazi, blindly following orders."

Norman pointed to the first line on the order of the day, "This is nothing but fucking bullshit. This is old news coupled with lies. Here, let me read this to you.

"Number fucking one. *Well done to all hands for the outstanding job on the ORI. As you know we worked hard to reach the proficiency we demonstrated in yesterday's inspection.*"

Norman interjected, "Well done? That's it? We busted our asses off for that Operational Readiness Inspection (ORI) and all we get is a well done? And as for yesterday's inspection, we had that inspection a week before we arrived in Viet Nam. He's such an asshole."

He continued reading aloud. "*However, our training and drills will continue to he held in order to improve ourselves even more and to maintain the proficiency which we presently have. At present it appears that our assignment in the Gulf of Tonkin will be in the North SAR (Search and Rescue) station. This is the northern most station in the Gulf. We will be there with another DLG* (Guided Missile Frigate). *Our purpose will primarily be to rescue downed aviators who ditch their planes after their strikes in Hanoi, Haiphong and other North Vietnamese targets.*"

"This is bullshit! We aren't rescuing downed aviators. We're blowing up whole villages. And they aren't going to ditch their planes unless they are being chased by MiG fighters. Do you know who their next target will be? Us."

Norman's forehead became furrowed, beads of sweat formed above his eyebrows as he continued reading. "He knows we're going to send this home for our folks to read, so he isn't about to write down what we're really doing. And there is no fucking DLG, not here, not with us. That's a fucking lie."

Looking back at the paper in his hands, he added, "OK, now here is something that is truthful." *North SAR Station is approximately 30 miles from Haiphong harbor and approximately four minutes flying time from the nearest MiG Base.*"

Norman's eyes widened as he said, "Four minutes flying time from the nearest MiG base is too fucking close. That asshole is going to get us killed." Slapping the Order of the Day with his free hand, he spewed, "This is nothing but fucking bullshit!"

"Let me get this straight," I said. "You refuse to obey orders because the Order of the Day is bullshit? Hell, this whole war is bullshit."

"No, no, no! We refused to obey orders because killing innocent villagers is wrong, period. That letter just made us mad enough to have the courage to refuse. And what the fuck is the captain up to anyway, volunteering us for North SAR station?"

"I talked to Matty, the radioman, when I made my rounds on watch last night," I said. "He told me that since Captain Reardon is only a Commander that he will do anything he can to earn the rank of Captain, even if it means putting all of us in harm's way. He is one maniacally ambitious asshole. "

"You can say that again," Norman replied.

I continued telling Norman what the radioman divulged to me, "Matty told me that the reason we don't have a DLG with us is because Captain Reardon volunteered the Jon Trippe to be a sitting duck as we patrol the harbor. He wants to be a hero and have a big gun fire on us."

"What the fuck is he doing that for?" Norman blurted out.

"Matty told me that once the big gun fires on us, we'll be able to identify its location and tell the carrier where it is," I said. "Then the carrier will launch a couple of jet fighters that'll cut the balls off that big gun so badly that you'll swear its big dick went limp."

Norman rolled his eyes, saying, "And just how are we supposed to tell the carrier where the big gun is if the Trippe is at the bottom of the ocean? Like I said, Reardon is a fucking asshole."

When Norman finished reading the order of the day, I traversed the ladders, two decks down, to my berthing compartment. Opening my locker, I took a pair of scissors and clipped out the section written by Captain Reardon. Using my purple felt pen, on the bottom of Reardon's note, I wrote, "Don't tell my parents please. They'll only worry." I stowed the clipping in the zippered black leather stationary case that my good friend Kathy had given me as a going away gift. I planned to include the section of Captain Reardon's note that I had cut out in a letter that I would write to Kathy later in the evening, when I would find an hour to myself, between battle station watch and my Sounding & Security watch.

* * * * * * * * * *

Dear Kath,

How are you? Thanks for your letter. When you see my buddy, George, tell him that I'm proud of him for filing as a conscientious objector. I wish that I had the *huevos* to do that. Talking about *huevos*, do you remember Norman, the guy with the heavy Boston accent and the huge red beard that I wrote to you about? He and his buddy, Krack, got busted from petty officer, third class down one rank to seaman. Now we are all at the same rank. We were all so relieved. They could've been thrown in the brig or court martialed. Since they won't be firing the rockets anymore, Norman will be working with the night baker and Krack will be the salad maker.

I wish I could write to you about the ladies of the night in Olongapo City. But we haven't been back yet. I know that you always write me back when I write about stuff like that. We are here in the Gulf of Tonkin blowing up people, all kinds of people, not just the Viet Cong. Our Mk-42 cannon can shoot ten miles inland. I don't know why they call it a five-inch gun. They should call it a twenty-two foot long cannon, because that is what it really is. The five inch refers to the diameter of the barrel. The rounds weigh seventy pounds. I know, because I help load them, sometimes. They do serious damage to whatever they hit. And our captain has us shooting villages that he considers communist sympathizers. I can't give you any details. I just hope that the censors don't stop this letter.

Matty said that he wants me to teach him how to play the guitar. There are some pretty talented people on this ship. The baker that Norman will be working for plays classical guitar and he's good. If we can find time, he'll give Matty and me lessons. I'm pretty sure that I wrote to you about Matty. He's a young kid from the Bronx. He's a smart kid. I forgot to tell you that when we hit our last storm, a bunch of us were in the helo hangar. We saw Matty come in the side door. It was so weird to see Matty levitate and float across the entire width of the hangar and fall down. What really happened is that the back end of the ship dropped suddenly and rolled to the side, leaving Matty momentarily suspended in midair. You should've seen the look on Matty's face. You would've died laughing.

I am including part of our Order of the Day. It tells you what we were doing. It is supposedly written by the captain. But I have my doubts. I think that one of the junior officers actually wrote it. The order tells you that we are with another ship, a DLG. But that's bullshit, we're here alone. And that bit about rescuing downed pilots is a big lie too. We're playing decoy trying to find a big cannon hidden in the hills. Pray for us that we don't get shot out of the water. Don't show the Order of the Day to my parents. I don't want them to worry.

Please stop by the house and take some photos of Jeremy and send them to me. I'll pay for the film. I really miss my two year old son.

Chief Jaffe, my boss, is still riding my butt. I don't know why he is always on my case. He tried to set me up to get in trouble. What the hell? Now I have two wars to fight.

Write back soon,

Love you,

Mushroom, Jeremy's Father

* * * * * * * * * *

21 – WHITE FLARES

At 16:00, I finished stowing the fire hose couplings that I had been greasing back into the repair locker. I climbed the ladder, unlatched the door and stepped into the blinding sunlight. I shielded my eyes until they adjusted to the brightness and walked to the port side of the helo deck. Looking across the water, a couple of hundred yards off the port side and toward the shore, I spied a lone fisherman pulling his nets into his skinny wooden boat. He hadn't caught many fish. His boat looked like a canoe that had been put together with scraps of wood. Cigarette smoke wafted into my nose. I turned toward the bow to see who was smoking. Barry was leaning against the safety lines that protected us from falling overboard. He tossed a smoldering cigarette butt over the side and turned toward me. He motioned with his hand for me to stand next to him.

Barry had spent a year working on the river boats on the Mekong River. He knew what dangers slithered along the shoreline. We stood together and admired the beauty of the shoreline jungle. Reading my thoughts, or so it seemed, he pointed to the gorgeous landscape before us.

"Sure looks beautiful, doesn't it?" Barry asked.

"Yes it does," I said. "And I'd enjoy it a whole lot more if the Trippe wasn't making itself easy prey for that big gun hiding out there."

The verdant shoreline jungle deceived our eyes with its beautiful hopea trees, vines, flowing shrubs and stands of bamboo coming right to the edge of the sand. The mixture of musk, salt spray, and flowering vegetation delighted my nose. It beckoned us to come and relax its white sandy paradise.

"I'd love to go over there, Barry. My son and I could have a picnic on that beach."

"Fucking A, Man, I'd go skinny dipping," Barry said. "I can't believe how crystal clear the water is as we cruise along the shore."

"You've got that right. The Vietnamese fishermen can see the fish and know when to pull up their nets." As I watched the fishermen, standing on their little wooden boats and casting their nets onto the water, I wished that Viet Nam were as peaceful as it looked.

Donning an exaggerated regal stance while tossing his head back, with his arms outstretched, Barry began, "Sonny Boy, that Viet Nam beach is giving you a sales pitch for a product it can't deliver. Lurking beneath that cool refreshing water, mines patiently await the arrival of their prey."

"That would be us," I said.

"Don't interrupt the professor," he said with a smirk. "The Grim Reaper is taking a temporary nap, comfortably snoozing in those mines. He's in no hurry, biding his time, anchored to the ocean floor, watching the fish swim by. He knows full well that his time will come. Hiding like crocodiles in the bushes at the water's edge, torpedoes are ready to take a thunderous bite out of the Jon Trippe's underbelly."

I applauded him and said, "That's a pretty good speech, Professor Barry."

A proud smile made his teeth glisten.

My eyebrows rose as I facetiously asked, "Are you telling me that if the sonarmen don't ping their magic sound waves fore and aft, that the Jon Trippe will likely meet up with one of those mines or torpedoes and be given an explosive invitation to Davey Jones' locker?"

"Fucking A, ya'll got that right," Barry said holding up his right thumb up and winking. He leaned down and pulled out a pack of Marlboros from his sock. He pulled out a cigarette and held it with his lips while he hunted in his pants pockets for his lighter. "Got a light?"

I pulled out a pen from my back pocket and showed it to him, shaking my head, no.

"I saw ya writing a letter, this morning. Is it to your girlfriend?" he asked after he found his lighter in his back pocket and lit his cigarette.

"I wish. It's for my good friend, Kathy and her twin sister, Kriss."

"Twins? Really? How did ya'll meet 'em?"

"I met Kathy and Kriss in my first beginning art class at Long Beach City College."

"Art class? That's cool," Barry said. His eyes flashed and his eyebrows stood at attention, as he asked, "Did ya ever take one of those classes where they draw live naked ladies? Did ya bring any drawings of them to show me?" Noticing the frown that crept over my face he said, "Sorry, I got carried away. Ya'll were saying?"

"I was going to answer your first question about how I met the twins."

"Go on, go on, I won't interrupt," he said.

"On the first day of my first art class, September 1969, I was listening to the other students talk about all of the art classes they had taken since they were children. When Kathy asked me about my art background, I told her I had never taken an art class before and that I was probably in the wrong class. The professor overheard and told me, in the presence of Kathy, Kriss and the other students, 'No, you are in the right class. In fact, you might be my best student, because you won't have any bad habits to unlearn.'"

"That's cool!" Barry said. "Now are ya'll going to answer my other question?"

"Damn, you are a horny bastard. Yes, I did take life drawing classes. But, you know, Barry, it's the fat people that are the most fun to draw."

"But they can't be much of a turn on, if they're fat."

"You're missing the point, Barry. I take art classes to learn to draw better, not to get a hard on."

"If I were taking, what did ya call it? Life drawing? I'd be doing both," he said, forming the shape of a woman with his hands. "I'd only draw the hot chicks."

"Barry, you're hopeless. To tell you the truth, I wish we were both taking a life drawing class together."

Barry nodded and said, "I'd rather be drawing naked ladies, even if they are fat, instead of wasting my time on this damn tin can."

I looked at my Seiko wrist watch. I only had twenty minutes before my next Sounding and Security watch. Barry and I went our separate ways. Topside sailors, eyes glued to their binoculars, searched the hills for signs of the big gun. Blending itself into the carpet of trees, whose leaves were so thick that no branch was visible, the big gun succeeded in eluding their eyes.

By the time I completed my watch and transferred the .45 caliber hand gun to the sailor replacing me, I barely had time to grab a bite to eat before the galley closed down. When I finished a thin slice of roast beef and a glass of milk, I went topside to catch some fresh air. Chasing the sun westward, over the hills to the west, the night announced a change in how war was waged. There were no city lights, no street lamps, and no neon signs to frighten away the darkness on the shores of Viet Nam. Exposing the enemy was the illuminating task of the white flares that were shot skyward, and floated down, ever so slowly, suspended from their nylon clouds.

Barry plopped next to me, while I sat on the deck with my back against the helo hangar. I stared westward to the beach and hills that had beckoned us to relax earlier in the day and saw streams of light that preceded automatic gun fire. "Wow! Did you see that?" I whispered excitedly.

"Yup," he replied, "Those are tracers. Every fifth round in those rifles glows red hot and allows the soldiers to see where they're shooting."

Fascinated by the scene before me, I replied, "I know that. But it looks like a ray gun from a science fiction movie, especially when they shoot from the helicopters."

We sat cross legged on the deck, our backs against the bulkhead, watching the black jungle light up like a college football field at night. The white flares effectively removed the night's black curtain defense, exposing human targets on both sides. I worried that the tracers were exposing our guys to the enemy.

"It really pisses me off knowing that we are mere pawns in Reardon's game of 'Who can make Captain first'," I said, staring out at the illuminated jungle. "He doesn't care if he exposes us like the flares do, so long as he reaches his ... "

Boom! We both jumped up.

"What the fuck was that?" Barry yelled.

We'd been hit. We ran to the safety lines, leaned over and searched the side of the ship for damage. Seeing none, I looked up towards the bridge and saw Captain Reardon's silhouette, in the moonlight, tossing something over the side of the ship. Another Boom!

Barry shook his head and said, "It's the fuckin captain playing warrior with his percussion grenades. He claims that he's making sure that no unseen Viet Cong divers put explosives under the ship. But he's just fucking around with his toys. Maybe, ya'll ought to go up to the captain and offer to teach him how to draw naked ladies instead of playing with grenades."

"Oh how I wish I could, Barry," I said as we sat back down. "Maybe he would see life differently."

"I bet he never took an art class and never drew naked ladies," he said. "An art class might've made him more like a real human being, respecting the beauty of life."

"His ambition has blinded him from beauty," I said. "Now he only sees body count numbers. And that scares me more than those guns firing in that jungle."

I stood up and looked at the water toward the bow. Barry wiggled himself up and stood next to me. The phosphorescence in the water made our wake glow in the dark. I yawned. Having been awake for 24 hours and knowing that I could only get 4 hours of sleep before my next battle station watch, I bade Barry goodnight and walked back inside the belly of the Trippe to my berthing compartment.

I took off my uniform, folded it neatly and put it into my

locker. Grabbing hold of the top rack's metal platform, I climbed into my rack and pulled a sheet over my shoulder. Before sleep slithered away with my sight, I yawned and repeated my nightly prayer, "Dear God, please let this war be a nightmare and let me wake up back at home, in my own bed in Long Beach."

Slumber hid all thoughts of war until I was yanked out of my sleep by another percussion grenade's blast from Captain Reardon's personal cache. My berthing compartment was located directly under the water line three decks beneath the bridge. The Captain threw a few more grenades from the bridge before slumber returned. I awoke disappointed a few hours later. The sound of the ship's engines made me realize that God had not answered my prayers. I began to wonder if God was unable to hear my prayers above the blasting of Captain Reardon's percussion grenades. Did God even care? Looking at the empty rack next to mine as I got out of bed, I remembered that a new crew member would be arriving soon, maybe tomorrow.

22 – BITTEN FINGERS

The water churned violently between our two ships as we transferred food and equipment from the supply ship to our own. The ships matched each other's speed, creating a welcome wind tunnel in the late afternoon heat. The men on the supply ship dragged a boatswain's chair across the deck to the cable that transported our supplies. The boatswain's chair was no more than a flimsy metal cage with a seat, barely big enough to hold a man. A sailor wearing his dress white uniform stood next to the boatswain's chair looked over the side of the supply ship and shook his head no. The supply chief pointed his finger toward our ship, apparently ordering him to get into the boatswain's chair. The wind blew hard making the new crew member's pants flutter, but I swear I could see his knees shaking. He struggled to get into it and he had difficulty buckling the safety belt. I wondered if today's transfer included the replacement for the short timer who flew home from the Philippines when we were in port three weeks earlier. After what seemed like a very long time, the deck apes from our ship began pulling the rope that was attached to a hook and pulley at the top of the boatswain's chair and brought him across. His knuckles were white, his teeth clenched and his eyes squinted as he held on to the metal frame that bobbled precariously above the raging water between our two ships. My own hands began to sweat as I watched them pull him across.

A low rumble caught my attention from behind. I turned and looked past the helo deck. Two dots appeared over the horizon and turned into two jet fighters that roared so fast over our two ships that I couldn't tell if they were American F14s or Russian MiGs. My stomach squeezed tight as I turned, ready to bolt to my battle station. The noise from their engines was deafening and the vibration shook the whole ship. The man in the boatswains chair shook its frame as he stared at the jets and opened his mouth, screaming words that no one could hear.

Chief Jaffe sauntered down the ladder into my berthing compartment about an hour after we finished resupplying our ship. Behind him lumbered a tall, skinny, light skinned young man with a zit in the middle of his protruding Adam's apple.

"This is HTFN Dawson," Jaffe said. "Help him get situated and introduce him to the rest of R-gang. He'll have the empty rack next to yours."

"Aye, aye, Chief," I said.

"One more thing; Dawson will have the Sounding and Security watch after you, Mushroom. Fill him in on those duties."

Dawson stood six feet, three inches tall. The racks we slept in were only six feet long. I suggested that we sleep head to head to allow his feet to hang freely over the end of his rack. I didn't want him kicking me in the head while he slept. I showed him his locker, across from his rack.

"That locker isn't very big and my sea bag is pretty full," he said.

"If you fold things tightly, you should be able to fit everything from your seabag into your locker," I said. "When you get things squared away, come and get me in the repair shop. It's right through that door."

Twenty minutes later, he poked his head through the repair shop door.

"Come on in," I said. I introduced him to the only members

120

of the R-Gang that were not on watch. Bruce was busy welding another bead on his home made barbells. He stopped, lifted his helmet, shook Dawson's hand and returned to his welding. Barry had his back against a pipe perusing a Playboy magazine. He smiled and extended his hand to Dawson.

"Is this your first time at sea?" I asked. He told us that he had recently graduated from Hull Maintenance Technician school and that he wished he had finished a month earlier so that he'd be eligible to take the HT test to advance in rank.

"So ya'll are the new HT replacement we've been waiting for. How old are ya?" Barry asked. "Ya'll look like you're in high school. I bet you're still a fuckin' virgin."

His face flushed red. "I'm eighteen."

"Did ya pee in your pants when we pulled your ass across in that basket?" Barry asked with a mischievous glint in his eyes. "I bet ya'll did when those jets flew over us."

"Jeez! Barry. Give the kid a break," I said.

"Damn, it scared the shit out of me," Dawson said. "I could hardly tighten the seat belt, I was shaking so bad. When they pushed me over the side in that tiny boatswain's chair, I almost pissed in my pants."

"Barry would have shit in his pants," I said.

"Fuck you," Barry said as he flipped me off. A huge smile emerged as he pulled on the crotch of his pants, pretending to pee. "I would've stood up and taken a leak while they pulled my ass across."

"It totally freaked me out," Dawson said. "I kept thinking that they were going to drop me until I saw the two jets barreling toward us. Then I thought we were being attacked and the two ships would come together and flatten me." He slapped his hands together and his eyes grew bigger. "I wanted to jump out and take my chances in the water. I kept screaming for the guys to hurry up and get me across before the jets shot me."

"Those two jets freaked me out, too," I said. "They came down much lower than normal when they flew by."

"I thought they were enemy jets," Dawson said. "My stomach is still upset."

"Make sure that you have food in your stomach until you earn your sea legs," I said. "You don't want to get sea sick while you're standing watch. If you feel like you're going to be sick, find a place to lie on your stomach and eat some crackers."

"The chief told me my first sounding and security watch is tomorrow morning at 08:00," Dawson said.

"Mine is right before yours from 04:00 to 08:00. Meet me on the bridge at 07:50."

"I lost my alarm clock," Dawson said. "Do you have one I can borrow?"

"You won't need one. I will wake you at 07:30," I said. "Try to get a good night's sleep. This will probably be the last time you'll get close to eight hours until we get back to the Philippines."

Later that evening, I stripped down to my Jockey briefs and pulled myself up into my rack, thankful that we had one more person who could stand watch. That meant more opportunities to get at least a full five hours of sleep between battle station watches. Dawson was already in his rack. He rolled over on his stomach with one of his feet sticking out beyond his blanket. I was amazed at how quickly he fell asleep. I rolled over on my back, put my head on my pillow and wondered if his feet would get cold, hanging over the end of his rack.

Before I knew it, the Dream Weaver came to visit me in my sleep. Bam! What was that? Oh shit! We're under attack! We've been hit! Water poured into our berthing compartment.

"Get out! Get out!" someone yelled.

I jumped down from my rack and flew up the ladder. I didn't have time to put any clothes on. I was still in my underwear. As I raced along the exterior passageway, something hit the top of my head. I must have been knocked out because I came to lying on the sand. The night obscured my vision. I heard voices. They were Vietnamese. They grew louder as they approached. I didn't know what they were saying. I couldn't see them, only hear them. One of them poked me in the ribs and mumbled something. When one of them ran his hand across my forehead to my mouth, I lunged forward, biting down hard. Feeling the bones and hearing him scream. Victory was mine.

"Ow, shit! What the hell! Let go!"

What? That's English. Whose voice is that?

The cobwebs of slumber withered away and I realized that I

was still on the ship. If my teeth hadn't chomped the fingers of a Viet Cong, who did they bite? I wondered if they were the fingers of the guy who had the current sounding and security watch and if he had been trying to scare me. Then my voice recognition kicked in. *Oh my god, it was Dawson's hand that crossed over my face!*

Laughing that I had been tricked by the Dream Weaver, and embarrassed, I whispered, "I am so sorry, Dawson."

"Why did you bite me?" he asked.

"I didn't realize that it was you," I said. "I had a nightmare. When you dragged your fingers across my face, I thought you were the enemy out to kill me. If you're lucky, my teeth marks will be the only war wounds you'll get."

23 – VIET NAM MEDITATION

Daily I hunted for both time and a place to meditate. I had just started sitting in meditation behind the aft winch when I heard the whop, whop, whop, of the helicopter. I felt as if it were a divine tease to let me start just when the chopper was about to arrive. I stood up, got my bearings and ran up the ladders to the helo deck to meet my fire rescue crew. When my crew had their gear in place, the antistatic cables were attached and permission was granted to land. The whop, whop, whop slowed and quieted to a stop.

The soldiers, who had been sitting on their helmets, removed their flack jackets and got out of the helicopter. I asked one of the machine gunners why he was sitting on his helmet, rather than wearing it on his head.

"The Viet Cong are shooting at us from down below," he said while grabbing hold of his crotch. "I want to return home with my balls intact."

Slapping him on his shoulder, I said, "You guys aren't as dumb as you look."

Relieved to be safely on the helo deck, away from the airspace above the Viet Nam jungle, he saluted me and began to relay his day's activity. "Holy shit, man, you should've seen what we did to that little village back there. I couldn't believe what I saw. After we secured the village, I saw one of the marines cut the heads off of three dead Viet Cong (VC) guys and stuck them up on stakes on the trail that led into the village. The Marine told me that doing that would freak the hell out of the VC. Shit! Man! It freaked the hell out of me. Can you believe that shit? It's going to give me nightmares, for sure, Man. Hey, can I use my 'funny money,' my MPCs in your ship's store?"

MPCs were Military Payment Certificates that were given in place of US dollars in an attempt to prevent US Dollars from getting into enemy hands.

He switched subjects so quickly that he pulled me off guard. I was still reeling from hearing his story of the three decapitated Viet Cong.

"Hey, Man, can I use my MPCs? Here, I'll show you." he asked again as if I had not heard.

"Yes, you can use those here," I said. "We'll take it, just like real money."

I hated listening to their stories. They gave me nightmares, too. How could Americans do this? How could anyone do this? I hated looking at their wild eyes because I knew that the horror that they witnessed needed to be released. I knew that I was helping to perpetuate this madness. Since those of us on the helo fire crew were the first people they saw after landing, we reluctantly took on the role of Father Confessor. There was no place to hide, nowhere to run. We patiently listened as they passed us on their way below decks to the ship's store and galley. They relayed their stories, their eyes searching for some remnant of home, away from the blood, the screams, the heat of war.

The helicopter crew would not stay long. We knew that they were there, more to take a break on a safe haven, a little distance off shore, than for any need to buy anything. My fire and rescue crew quietly awaited their return. The first to return was the machine gunner that I had spoken to earlier. He was calmer, more relaxed. The wildness that shot out of his eyes upon his arrival had disappeared.

Waving his hand to get my attention, he called out, "Hey, Man, any chance we can fuel up with some jet fuel? I hear you guys use it?"

"We have JP5, will that work for you?" I asked. I knew it would, even before he nodded his head in agreement.

While we waited for the chopper to drink its fill of JP5, the machine gunner extended his hand to shake and said, "I'm Freddy. You?"

"Just call me Mushroom."

"For real?" Freddy's eyebrows flared up and a warm smile followed. "Mushroom, tell me what your job is. It looks like you're in charge."

"I am. My job is to make sure that you and everybody on this ship is safe. Sometimes I look at it like playing a game of basketball aboard ship."

"How so?" he asked.

"I am the fire scene leader. Like a basketball team captain, I assess my opposition and direct my players to the best strategic locations. I tell my firefighters to advance forward, against a fiery foe, whether it is a burning helicopter or a fire in the engine room. They chase after the source of the fire. As the battle heats up, and the fire continues devouring all it can in front of it, we rush in, kicking aside anything in our way. When we capture the fire in a net of water, we win the game."

"You make it sound like fun. Speaking of fun, I saw a basketball hoop in the hangar. You don't play when you're out at sea, do you?"

"Of course we do. When we have more time, I'll challenge you to a game," I said.

The rest of the flight crew had climbed on board by the time Freddy and I finished refueling the helicopter. Having put the fuel hose away, the machine gunner joined his flight crew on board and they fired up the engine. Whop, whop, whop, the helicopter flew away.

Putting away the fire hoses and the rest of the equipment back into the repair locker gave me time to think about the horrible things that Freddy told me. How could American marines cut the heads off real people and think it was anything but total lunacy? My stomach began to churn at the thought. I felt confused, scattered and angry. This is not what I came here for. I didn't join the Navy to be part of this. I had a little bit of time before my next battle station watch. I needed to find a quiet place, a secluded place where I could mediate. Making my way to the fantail, I made myself comfortable once again, sitting on the canvas that covered the aft winch.

"Hey Man, are you meditating? Wow, that's cool, man. I've never seen anyone meditating before. Wow."

I didn't recognize the voice of the sailor who was asking me those questions. I didn't care. I did not want to break my meditation practice. I didn't answer my shipmate's query, allowing him to yank my awareness back to the nightmare of war. Meditating allowed me to escape its oppressive weight, if only for the twenty minutes that I could steal away. Meditating was my secret doorway to other worlds, to oblivion and beyond.

"Hey Man, are you meditating?" I heard the voice ask again. "Wow, that's cool, man. I'll leave ya alone. I've never seen anyone meditating before. Wow." He stood for a few moments before walking away.

We were on our way back to the replenishment station, to take on more arms, more bombs, and more destruction to throw at the Vietnamese. Daily, I would find a place, a secluded place, a safe place, where I could escape the ever present oppressive weight of killing. I sat on the fantail with my back against the base of the aft winch. Looking at the white churning water flowing from the back of the ship, I took a few deep breaths and started repeating my mantra in my head. Drifting away in meditation, my mind took me to well beyond 1972.

I found myself on a sun drenched Vietnamese beach, a few yards away from lush trees, of varied shades of green and pink flowering bushes. I sat on at the water's edge, the wavelets lapping at my feet. The salt spray blended with the fragrance of the flowers and the musty odor of the jungle.

A soft female voice sang from behind me, "1972 is only a thought away, only a glance away, only a sting away from today."

Turning around, I saw the same beautiful Vietnamese woman who visited me before in my meditation. She wore a shimmering green traditional Vietnamese ao dai and a high peaked straw hat. Her eyes sparkled as she walked across the sand in her bare feet.

She sat down beside me and took off her hat.

"Viet Nam beckons you to return. Viet Nam is at peace now," she said.

I started to ask how that was possible, but she put her finger to my lips, shushing me. Tired and confused, I wondered what tricks my mind was playing as I sat mesmerized by her voice.

"I forgive you," she whispered. "I will help you forgive yourself and help you regain your soul. Come, I await your return to how you should have come in the first place. Come, I have forgiven you."

My buttocks had fallen asleep and I readjusted my sitting position. As the tingling sensation dissipated, my buttocks felt the vibration of the ship's screws churning beneath the fantail. Struggling to return to my meditation, my mind searched again for a secluded place, away from the bombs, away from the killing, away from the cries. I slowed my breathing and repeated my mantra. The Vietnam beach scene returned. Tears welled. My throat tightened. I sat. Quiet. Quiet. Quiet.

The Vietnamese woman stood, holding my hand.

"Will you release me before the war ends?" I asked.

She kissed me on the cheek and let go of my hand. "You are the one who needs to release," she said, walking away from me toward the jungle.

"How can I release when the war rages in my heart?"

"I forgive you. I will help you forgive yourself," she called from the jungle's edge.

"I don't want to end up like my uncles, with their wartime ghosts haunting them forever," I said. "I feel like I've lost my soul."

Stretching out her arm, she beckoned with her fingers as she sang, "I have forgiven you. Come. I await your return, to how you should have come in the first place. Come. I have forgiven you."

24 – SEA FAIRIES

I stood on the helo deck after dinner, watching first class boatswains mate, Keegan, yell orders to his deck apes as they pulled supplies and ammunition from the ammo ship. His pants fluttered in the wind of the two ships speeding across the gulf. Diesel fuel permeated the salt air as the sun began its descent into the west. We'd have to work fast to get the ammo below decks before darkness blinded our ability to see. When the ammo ship finished replenishing our supply of rounds for our Mk-42 cannon, the two ships maneuvered closer together. This allowed the deck apes to safely release the tension lines that kept the U.S.S. Trippe and the ammo ship a safe distance apart while we transferred the ammo.

I walked down to the main deck to take my place in line to reload the five-inch gun's magazines. I stood behind Otis worrying that the three large wooden boxes, filled with seventy pound bombs, would require a lot of effort to empty before darkness came.

Turning around to face me, Otis asked, "I wonder if I would

be any safer on the ammo ship?"

"Not really," I said. "An American ammo ship would be a great target for a Vietnamese MiG fighter."

Standing in the line of sailors, we helped pass the bombs from one man to the next.

"Use yer fuckin thighs, not yer backs when passing them fucking rounds," Keegan yelled. "Don't ya go dropping them or we'll all be blown to bloody hell."

The bombs snaked their way across the deck and down the ladder to the magazine under our five-inch gun. It didn't take long for our arms to ache and our brows to sweat.

"I can't believe how heavy these rounds are," I said to Otis.

Keegan put his hand on his chin and asked, "Would I be havin two pussies in me line? Quit yer damn belly aching. The sun's goin down and we ain't got much time. Just get a move on."

When Keegan walked away, Otis said, "He's such a bloody bastard for an Irishman."

"It's just a facade," I said. "Watch how well he takes care of his deck apes. He just wants us to be safe."

When we finished, I hurried to get to my battle station. I looked inside the repair locker and took an inventory of the equipment, noting the location of the fire hoses, wrenches and pry bars, the most likely tools we would need, if we were to get hit.

As the second hand inched its way around my watch, I thought about my earlier meditation and what the Vietnamese woman meant when she said she had forgiven me and that 1972 was only a thought away. I wondered if the war would end soon. God, I hope so. Would I want to come back after the war? I would love to swim in these waters. The Vietnamese women are beautiful with their fine features, tanned skin and sing song voices. Would they want us to come back?

Our Mk-42 cannon, two decks above me, fired at a target. My back muscles tensed, my breathing sped up. After a few more shots, then silence. The second hand on my orange Seiko watch resumed its slow march around the dial. My five hour battle station watch ended at three in the morning. I had an hour before my sounding and security watch. My arms were sore from transferring the ammo. I wanted to sleep. But I knew that in forty minutes, the sailor who was currently standing watch would attempt to wake me and that would only piss me off. I tromped over to the beverage machine hoping that a Coke would help me stay awake. Sitting at a table in the empty galley, I was grateful that I could drink a cold Coca Cola despite the battle raging on. I loved the fizziness and taste of Coke. It was a liquid candy bar that reminded me of cokes I used to buy at the liquor store on the corner of Anaheim Street and Junipero Avenue back home in Long Beach. When I was a paperboy, I used to put peanuts into the coke bottle and watch the peanuts slide down as I drank it. On this night, I missed not having peanuts. When I finished drinking my coke, I tossed the Coca Cola can into the waste basket and went topside to get some fresh air.

The effort that I had to exert to open the door surprised me. I lifted my foot over the threshold and ducked my head through the doorway out into a blackness that drowned every glimmer of light under its wave. Extending my hand and searching for an obstruction, I took one step. Black, nothing. I put my hand out again and took another step. Still black, nothing. Something wet grabbed my hand. "SHIT! What the ... " I jumped and every muscle squeezed the beejesus out of me.

"Ha! You'rrre blind as a bloody bat, arren'tcha laddy. Hold on and trrry not to fall on yerrr face."

Who was this guy? Where was he taking me? I did not recall anyone with an Irish accent that flowed off his tongue like he'd been telling stories about banshees all his life. It took me a while to realize that it was Keegan, the old salty sailor, boatswain's mate first class. "Lighten yerrr step laddy, the deck is slipperier than a wet dick sliding into a warrrm cunt." He laughed, gurgling a hint of whiskey on his breath.

"Look over the side, Laddy. What da ya see?"

"Is that phosphorescence making the water glow as the ship cuts through?"

"Fuck no. Tis sea fairrries that light yourr way acrross the ocean at night. I never get tired of watching em. Never. Reminds me of fishing as a lad, with me old man."

"What is that really, Keegan?" I queried.

"I told ya. Tis sea fairies." Keegan was in an unusually kind and friendly mood, aided by the contents of his canteen, no doubt.

"There's no such thing as sea fairies," I said and immediately felt stupid for stating the obvious. I hoped that he would tell me a sea story about how the sea fairies came to be.

"If you are going to be a bloody bastard and ruin me love of the sea, then bumble and rrrumble yer way back inside."

"Come on, Keegan, I'm only trying to learn."

"You young college types arre all the same. No love of mysterry. Just the facts mam, Mr. Joe Friday! Dinoflagellate."

"Dino what?"

"Look it up in yourr fancy encyclopedia. Go. Leave me be with me sea fairies."

I didn't leave. I laid down, hanging my head over the bow of the ship, mesmerized by Keegan's sea fairies surfing the waves as the ship cut through the liquid blackness.

"Keegan, aren't you afraid that we might get blown up while we sail up and down the coast?"

"Aye laddy, I'd be crazy if I wasn't. But I ain't gonna let what I can't control stop me from enjoying me sea fairies. Ya see, laddy, only the good lord knows when he's gonna take the wind out of our bloody sails and bring us home. So tis a fuckin shame if ya waste yer time holding on to yer wee little dick for fear that it'll get blown off. Enjoy whatever the good lord gives ya and to bloody hell to what worries ya."

"Keegan, you're a sea faring philosopher," I said. He would have been a good chief, were it not for his drinking.

"Ain't it time fer ye to get up, laddy? Would ye be having a watch coming up?"

"I do. Thanks for telling me about the sea fairies."

"Ye better keep a sharp eye out tonight. Me sea fairies told me there's danger afoot. Be off with ye now."

25 – BODY COUNT

Matty's boots clunked on the deck as he ran to catch up with me. I had an hour left on my 20:00 to 24:00 sounding and security watch. Matty's bloodshot eyes drooped. His speech was slow.

"Mind if I walk with you for a bit?" Matty asked.

"Nah, I could use the company," I said. "What's up, Matty? You look upset. Did you hear what the fly boys told us today? Is that what's upsetting you? It upsets the hell out of me. The pilot jumped down from his chopper and came right up to me. He was pissed off. He asked me why we fired on the village. I didn't know what to say. I didn't know that we had bombed a village."

Matty put his head down, shook it and asked, "What did he tell you about the village?"

"He told me that we killed almost everyone. There were bodies everywhere. He kept telling me that there were little kids in that village, over and over again. Shit! He told me that one of our marines was in the village and they had to medivac him out of there."

134

I stood in front of the repair locker on the second deck, motionless. The ships engines vibrated under my feet. I let out a heavy sigh.

"The pilot told me that the marines gave our ship coordinates for an area about 100 yards to the left of the village," I said. "That's where they found tunnels. How could our computers be so far off? They didn't ask us to bomb the village."

Matty grabbed my shirt.

"Stop talking and listen," Matty said, "I have something to tell you. Promise me you won't tell anyone this."

"OK. I promise. What's up?"

Matty put his finger to his lips, motioning for me to be quiet. He asked me to open the door to the repair locker. I removed the pad lock, put it in my pocket and went inside and sat on a tool box. Matty followed me, closing the door behind him. He made himself comfortable on a stack of rolled fire hoses.

He leaned toward me and whispered, "I did hear about that, but not from the fly boys. I sat at my station listening to the ship's communication radio when I heard the captain order us to fire not only on the target but on the village."

"Holy shit!" I said. My hair stood up. Possible scenarios popped into my head. "Matty, did our sources tell us that the village was really a Viet Cong base?"

"No," he whispered.

"Did the marines find a cache of ammunition that they wanted us to blow up?"

"No."

"How about a contingent of Viet Cong generals hiding there?"

"No, no, none of that," he said as he shook his head and lowered his voice. "The captain wants a fucking body count."

"We blew up a village for a body count!?" I asked.

"Shh! Quiet!" he whispered, "Yes, he ordered us to kill the villagers for a fucking body count."

"Are you telling me that there was no real threat from the villagers?" I asked, as my toes scrunched inside my boots and my hands formed tight fists.

"They didn't teach us how to handle a captain who's gone nuts in radioman school," Matty said. "They just taught us to obey orders and to keep everything we heard, secret. But how can I keep THIS a secret?"

Patting Matty on the shoulder, I tried to reassure him, saying, "You can't Matty. If you try you will go crazy. I'm glad you can talk to me."

Actually, I wasn't glad. I was shocked. I did not want to believe what Matty had just told me. Trying to make sense of this, I asked, "Did the captain actually say that he wanted to blow up the village to get a body count?"

"Yes. Well, no, not like that. He said that he wanted to make sure that no Viet Cong escaped. He wanted the whole village destroyed with everyone in it. Then he said that he wanted to make sure the guys on the ground gave him the body count. When the chief tried to tell him that we didn't receive a request to blow up the village, he shot back that he was the captain, he knew what he was doing."

"What did the chief do?" I asked.

"He just threw his hands up and turned around and relayed the order to the gunners mate. The captain kept asking us to find out the body count. I could tell the chief was getting mad, but he didn't say anything."

The door opened. Startled, Matty must have jumped 2 feet off the deck.

"Hey, what ya'll doing in there?" Barry asked. "Better not let me catch ya smoking any weed. That is, unless ya'll are gonna share it with me."

"Shit! Barry! You scared the hell out of me," Matty said. "Didn't you ever hear of knocking?"

"Hell no! Not when the door is already open. That is just a welcome invitation to come in. What are ya'll doing in here anyway? Looking for a place to hide your stash?" Barry was in a good mood. In fact Barry was almost always in a good mood.

I gave Barry a look, trying to convey that this was a private conversation. He didn't care. Closing the door behind him, he sat down next to Matty on the fire hoses. Giving Matty a quick glance, then turning to me, he said, "Matty probably already knows this. We're starting a negative body count. Whenever we kill our own people or innocent people, we get a negative body count. The captain ordered us to bomb the village. I just finished talking with the fly boys."

"How do you know that?" Matty asked.

"I just told ya. The fly boys."

"Not that!" Matty retorted back. "How do you know the captain ordered us to bomb the village?"

"I know because we're incredibly accurate with our rockets. And when I talked to the fly boys, they told me that the marines only asked us to fire where the tunnels were. They would never ask us to fire where their own men were."

"But that doesn't tell you that the captain ordered it." Matty was trying so sort things out and trying to see what Barry really knew.

"Look, Matty, ya'll are just out of radioman school. You're as green as they come. How old are you? 18?"

Matty nodded affirmatively.

Barry continued, "I spent a year on the riverboats in the Mekong and other rivers here. I'm a short timer, I've only got six months left and I'm out of here. I know how this Navy works.

Those rockets are expensive. Only the captain can authorize their use. I know he ordered the village to be bombed. No one else could have. He may or may not have been into body counts before. But now that he has a negative body count, I guarantee that the captain will be into it now. He has to turn that number around. So watch out. We may be in for some ugly shit before we get outta here."

Matty and I sat, silent.

Barry turned to look at Matty. "Am I right or do ya'll know something different, Radioman?"

"No, nothing different. I just couldn't believe it. We were just talking about that when you scared the bejeesus out of me."

Matty turned to look at me as if he were about to ask me a question. But he didn't. Looking back to Barry while pointing to me he said, "I was telling him that when we got the body count over the radio and found out that we hit one of our marines, the captain looked at the chief and asked him how many Viet Cong do we need to kill to put us in the positive."

"See? I told ya. We're going be in for some ugly shit, for sure." Barry stood up, opened the door and walked out.

Matty and I were overwhelmed. Being at war was traumatic

enough without the weight of this information. We sat on the fire hoses trying to process what we just heard. Both of us came to the realization that probably everyone on the ship knew what we now knew. Hiding in the repair locker was ludicrous but we stayed anyway.

Matty fidgeted on the fire hoses. He stroked his black hair with his hand and took a big breath. "You told me that you wanted to be a priest and that you went to a seminary for four years, right?"

"Yes, Matty. What are you getting at?"

"Did the German soldiers who killed the Jews have to go to confession and tell the priests what they did?"

I thought about the question for a little while. "The simple answer is yes. If you know that you are doing something against God's will and you do it anyway, you have to go to confession."

"I know that already. What I want to know is, if there is nothing that I can do to stop it, do I still have to go to confession. Is it still a sin? Going back to my first question, if the German soldiers felt that there was no way to stop it. That they had to kill the Jews or they would be killed, would they need to go to confession for following orders?"

Those same questions had been patrolling my mind. "I wish that there was a simple answer, but there isn't. This is going to take time to work through, Matty."

"That question doesn't have an answer and that is why you scream around the smoke stack, isn't it. I wish I could do that. I wish I could scream." Matty stood up, opened the door and held it open for me. As I was locking it he said, "When you scream tonight, scream louder for me."

26 – STANDING INSPECTION

Barry and I were both sitting on the highly polished vinyl deck, with our backs against the repair locker, dressed in our battle gear. I adjusted the strap on my helmet and tried to make myself comfortable.

"Battle station on this ship is really boring," Barry said. "This passage way has no windows. I can't see what's going on. I feel trapped, hearing our guns blasting above us."

"We can't have windows here. We're below decks, below the waterline," I said.

"I shouldn't complain. It's a hell of a lot better than my last duty station on the river boats. I almost got my ass killed too many times. To be perfectly honest, I don't know how I survived."

"Glad you did, Barry."

"Can I ask you a personal question?" Barry asked, with a coyote twinkle in his eyes.

"Somehow I get the feeling that you're going to ask it no matter what I say."

"If it weren't for your beard," he said, "I'd say that your mom fucked a Chinese milkman."

"I knew it, I should've said no to you. I'm not Chinese, Japanese or Korean."

"Then why do you look like that?"

"It's the American Indian in me."

"No shit? You're really an American Indian? What tribe?"

"I'm only part American Indian, Apache and Puelbo."

Barry moved out of arm's reach and said, "I didn't know that Apache squaws fucked Chinese milkmen."

I swung at him, anyway.

When he stopped laughing, he said, "The hardest part about being on this ship is standing inspection," he said.

Standing up, I adjusted my helmet and asked, "What does standing inspection have to do with Chinese milkmen?"

"Absolutely nothing. I was just sitting here looking at how shiny my shoes are. I hate standing inspection and polishing my shoes. When the Viet Cong are shooting at you on a riverboat, you don't give a rat's ass about inspections."

"Before our first kill on the gun line, I thought we were here to keep communism from spreading. I'm not so sure anymore."

Barry stood up, putting his hands on his hips and staring down at me. Shaking his head, he said, "Get your head out of the sand. If you follow the money, you'll see that we're pouring it into the pockets of the cigar smoking fatties at Dow Chemical.

"You mean the guys who make the napalm?"

"Yeah, and the butt heads that build our ships and fighter planes."

"But I thought that America is here to keep the communists from taking over Asia."

Barry shook his head and said, "This has very little, if anything to do with stopping communism. Hell, if the communists offered to buy our airplanes, we'd be saying that communism is a good thing."

Listening to Barry, my ears became red hot, as the knot in my stomach became tighter. I didn't like what he has just said. The sole of my foot started to prickle, making me stand up. I wanted to leave, to hide, to run away. My mind began to wander. Ignorance is bliss, I thought.

"We're killing the Vietnamese so that American business can thrive?" I asked.

"Fucking right," Barry said. "And we'll be doing this tonight, tomorrow, and every fucking day. That's another reason why I hate inspections."

"They are pretty stupid in a war. Since we're going to be stuck here for five hours on battle station, let me tell you my favorite inspection story."

"Sure," he said as he turned around to face me.

"Since I had been the class leader in Damage Control school, I never stood inspection."

"How did you get out of that?" he asked.

"Although I had to prepare for inspection, like everyone else in the Damage Control school, I was never inspected by the officer in charge. That's because I walked behind him, taking notes, as he inspected all of the other guys, taking a very close look at each sailor's hair, uniform and shoes."

"Well that's slick," Barry said. "I had to stand inspection until I got assigned to the riverboats. Anyway, go ahead with your story."

"When I graduated from Damage Control school, I flew down to San Diego to attend welding school. I was no longer the class leader. That meant that I was about to be inspected for the first time. Standing at attention, in the first line of sailors, watching the chief inspect the line of sailors made me laugh."

"Are you serious?"

"Yeah. The closer the chief came to where I was standing, the harder it became for me to maintain my composure and suppress my laughter."

"You must've gotten busted," he said.

"That's what I expected. While the chief busied himself inspecting the sailor next to me, he turned to me and asked, "What is so funny?"

"Nothing Chief, I'm just in a good mood." is what I said.

"And he didn't bust your for that, or make you do pushups, or something?" Barry asked.

"No," I said. "He just did his inspection and continued on. It struck me as being ridiculous that a grown man felt it was important to inspect the cleanliness of another grown man. The irony is that the men being inspected felt that their standing inspection made sense. So many things in the Navy make no sense to me at all."

"I'm sure that I'm not the first to tell you," Barry said, "The Navy makes war not sense."

"There's more to the story," I said.

"Well, go on then."

"When the chief finished inspecting the sailors in welding class, he dismissed us. The rest of the class broke formation, returning to the barracks to change into their navy dungarees, in preparation for welding class. I continued to stand at attention. I stood in the same place, facing forward, not moving. When the chief noticed me, and was about to ask me if I had a question, I immediately turned and walked away. I did this every morning after inspection. Finally, in desperation, the chief yelled out, "What?! What do you want?!"

"I got what I wanted, Chief, thanks." I said as I turned and walked away feeling very proud of myself.

"You are one lucky bastard," Barry said. "If I had tried that shit, they would have made me do pushups, for sure."

"One thing that I've learned, Barry, is that the Navy can't stifle self-expression, no matter how hard it tries to make everything uniform."

Barry grabbed a hand full of his red hair with his left hand and pointed to it with his right, lifting his eyebrows, as if to ask a question.

"What?" I asked. "Are you telling me that you're an orangutan?"

"Fuck you! I was going to tell you that when I was being processed in boot camp, I stood in line talking to this guy behind me. After they cut off my beautiful red curls, this 'other' guy came up to me and started telling me about the guy that he met in line. The guy he met was me. He didn't recognize me. I wasn't me anymore. I was just another sailor."

"That's funny. That happened to me too," I said.

"That's the point I'm trying to make: we all look the same in our short hair, wearing the same fucking naval uniforms."

"But we're still all individuals. And some of us celebrate our individuality."

"You do know why they want to make us all look the same, don't you?" Barry asked.

"Yeah," I said, "so that when one of us dies, like Ivan did, we can be replaced by another clone, making it seem like no one got killed. When I'm gone, people are going to notice."

"Ha! You can say that again! But you better watch your ass. The lifers hate everyone who stands out as being non-military. They view it as being anti-navy. And in your case, they probably see you as a hippie."

"A hippie?"

"Yeah, and an anti-war protestor to boot!"

"But why would they see that in me?" I asked. "We all look alike, remember."

"Open your eyes!" Barry yelled as his eyes grew as big as cannon balls. Sitting down in a lotus position, he closed his eyes in a mimic trance and said in a monotone voice, "You do that hippie meditation shit."

"Hippies aren't the only ones who meditate. Hell, I learned to meditate when I was studying to be a Catholic priest."

Barry stood up and ran in tight circles, flaying his arms and opening his mouth wide, mimicking me running around the smokestack, screaming.

"You're probably right," I said.

"You're damn straight, I'm right."

"General Quarters! General Quarters! This is not a drill," came over the loudspeaker. An attack was imminent.

Running to our battle station, Barry said, "You'd better hope that we don't get blasted out of the water and have to be rescued. They'll leave your ass behind."

"Why would they leave me?"

"Cause your mother fucked the Chinese milkman and now you look like a fucking gook," Barry said, as he slapped me on the back and ran down to his battle station.

27 – MIG ATTACK

"General Quarters! General Quarters! This is not a drill," came over the loudspeaker again as I donned my helmet and life jacket. The hair on my arms stood straight up. My knees began to shake uncontrollably. I looked at Otis, his face much whiter than normal, and said, "For as often as they call General Quarters, you'd think we'd be used to it by now."

The ship shook as our Mk-42 cannon fired several rounds. The machine gun blasts were muffled in the interior of the ship. I had opened the damage control repair locker and busied myself looking inside, taking a mental inventory of the location of the emergency equipment we would most likely need.

"I hate this fuckin shit, waiting down here, not knowing what the fuck is going on topside," Otis said. "They never tell us a goddamn thing until it's over."

"All Clear," came over the loudspeaker. "Eight MiGs have been diverted. Our F14s are in pursuit. All Clear." The ship's crew returned to what we were doing before the MiGs flew over us. I returned to my underway watch.

146

Otis, stood, wide eyed, staring at the sounding log I had just handed him. His Japanese eyes did not move. He wasn't reading the notes I had written in the log. Looking up from the tablet, he said, "A MiG attack. Eight Viet Cong jet fighters were gunning for us. We ain't got no anti-aircraft guns that could've stopped 'em from doing some serious damage."

Grinning at his Kentucky accent, which seemed incongruous with his Japanese face, I said, "Can you say, Quack? Our job is to be a decoy. Remember?"

"Yeah. But for the big gun hiding in the jungle, not for Russian MiGs," he said, his eyes darting back and forth. "We're just sitting ducks. Those MiGs could've sunk our ship. How do we know that they ain't coming right back?"

"We don't. Being inside the ship sucks big time."

"I hate not knowing what the fuck is going on out there," Otis said.

"We all do, but the damage control locker is down here in the bowels of the ship, not topside where we can see the action. If those MiGs come back and fire on us, we're going to have to act fast, if we don't want the ship to sink."

"Why did the Viet Cong send eight MiGs after us? That's kinda like overkill, ain't it?"

"Maybe the captain volunteered us to be decoys for the MiGs as well," I said.

"He wouldn't a done that. Would he?"

"Otis, he wants to make Captain, he'll do anything."

"But I thought he only volunteered us to lure the big gun."

"Get real, Otis. If that gun, hiding in the jungle, is as big as they think, it will sink the ship as easily as the MiGs could."

"We're fucked," he said.

"That is why we need to know our job inside and out. We're the "R" Gang. "R" for repair. When we get hit, it is up to us to make sure that this tin can doesn't sink."

"We are really fucked," Otis said as he fidgeted with the holster's buckle. "Our crew ain't had enough training." His face was ashen, accentuating the red of his eyes. His cheeks looked like someone had chipped out too much when sculpting his face.

"If it makes you feel any better," I said, "The Viet Cong aren't going to risk losing valuable MiGs just to sink our little tin can.

That is why they turned around when our war birds showed up. They were probably just checking the carrier's response time."

"God, I hope you're right."

"Be sure to wear these goggles," I said, "Put them on at least twenty minutes before you go outside, otherwise you'll be blind as a bat out there."

"I know, I know. I ain't stupid."

I had forgotten that I was going to go outside after I finished my watch and I hadn't worn the goggles. I stepped through the door onto the weather decks into the velvet blackness that stole my ability to see anything, even my hands. Shifting my weight, I adjusted my gait to counter the ship's rocking and rolling. Laughing at myself, I marveled at how adept my legs had become at walking aboard this wobbly vessel; how it had become second nature to continually shift my weight. Keeping in step with the ship's dance across the water, over and around its swells, heaving up and sliding down the sea's slippery slopes had become a valuable skill.

When the sun took refuge behind the western hills, the night, wrapping a black blindfold over my eyes, invited me to join the ship's liquid dance. Stepping forward, hands outstretched, I accepted the night's invitation to tango in her expansive and secret ballroom. Twinkling star lights shimmered across the domed ceiling. Lifting my head skyward, then tossing it to and fro, I stepped to the rhythm of the sea's undulations.

The salt spray tickled my nostrils with its oceanic aroma, reminding me of earlier times, watching fireworks from the Long Beach pier. Unlike the battle, playing out a few hundred yards off our starboard side, the Fourth of July fireworks, back home, filled me with awe and gleeful excitement. I remember shouting to my little brothers, Rick and John, "Wow, look up there, you guys! That red one looks like a giant beach ball. It's really pretty." There were no pretty explosions here.

The explosions, across the short distance of liquid ooze, did not bear gifts of delight and wonder. These explosions ripped limbs away from little Vietnamese brothers and sisters. These banging drums, with their cold steel drumsticks, ripped the shirts and blouses of worried parents and beat and poked bloody holes into their hearts.

"Shi ... ", my stomach tightened so quickly that it squelched my voice, when I felt a hand grab my shoulder.

"Come with me," said the voice.

"Jesus! Couldn't you have said something before you grabbed my shoulder? I almost peed in my pants!"

"That's what we were hoping for." Norman said. I could barely make out his grinning teeth, as the black fog slowly lifted and my eyes adjusted to the darkness. A voice from behind the rocket launcher whispered loudly, "Sit down. You're walking like a drunken sailor."

"No, I'm not," I said, "I'm dancing with the sea."

"Hell, if you call that dancing, you need to work on your moves or you'll never get a girl on a real dance floor," a disembodied voice, said.

I sat down with my back against the rear rocket launcher's base and I crossed my legs. Norman sat next to me. Matty drew his face close to mine and whispered, "I've been waiting for you." The darkness obscured Matty's face and the others who were with him. The rocket launcher hid the moon and the stars overhead. Its size always amazed me. It took up as much floor space as a garage. It held eight rockets, each were as long as a car and weighed just as much. I sat quietly under the massive weapon, waiting for the others to speak, for clues revealing who they were. Someone coughed, releasing an invisible cloud of hemp smoke that teased my nostrils.

"Heah, take a hit off of this," Norman said, as he handed me a glowing ember of grass.

"Thanks, but I can't," I said, as I passed it over to Matty. "I have battle station in about thirty minutes."

Matty inhaled deeply before passing the joint to someone else. "Thanks."

I recognized Krack's voice as he took the glowing ember in his fingers.

"Today, I gave up on the Navy," Matty said and slowly let the smoke escape from his nose.

"Ha. Only now? It's taken you this long?" Krack asked as he punched Matty in the shoulder.

"Nah. I'm serious," Matty said, his voice growing louder.

Norman, was still holding his breath after inhaling slowly on the joint. He let smoke billow out between his mustache and lower lip and asked, "So why now? Why today?"

"Remember when they sounded general quarters today and those eight Viet Cong MiG fighters were gunning for us?"

"There were eight? Holy shit!" Norman's voice crackled as he coughed out the last hit of smoke from his lungs. "I heard it was only four."

"Holy shit nothing, Holy fuck! Is more like it," Krack piped in. "Four or eight, it would've made no difference. We would've been shaking hands with Davy Jones, for sure, even if only four MiGs got to us."

The guys, normally cynical about anything military preferred to talk about their girlfriends, their cars, and their aspirations for what they wanted to do when they got out. This evening, we all talked in huddled voices about the MiG attack.

"It's one thing to see Viet Cong mortars fall short into the water beside the ship, but eight missile loaded MiGs are going to blow us all to hell," I said. I lowered my voice, pointing to the shore, I continued, "Our mothers will join those Vietnamese mothers, over there, who cry and pray for their dead sons."

Norman stood up, walked around to face us and said, "I'm not as religious as I should be, certainly not as religious as my mother would like, but I got to tell you, as we were standing at GQ, waiting for the MiGs to arrive, I prayed to the Blessed Virgin."

"Of course, you'd pray to a virgin," Krack laughed and added, "You're such a horny bastard."

Norman ignored Krack's comment and continued, "In my mind's eye, I could see those MiGs flying in over the hills, darting down, getting close to the water's surface. They were flying with fire and smoke trailing behind them. I could see the fucking pilot squeezing the fire button. Then the missiles blasted giant holes into the side of the ship. Bodies, blood, guts everywhere. I prayed real hard.

"Fuck your mind's eye, Norman," Krack blurted

"Fuck yourself," Norman said, "You can't tell me that you weren't scared too."

"I was scared shitless, like everyone else. I ain't denying that. I didn't waste my time worrying about what might happen."

150

By this time, my eyes had fully acclimated to the night and I saw Krack stand up to face Norman.

"What did you do, then, Krack?" Norman asked, protruding his chest.

I jumped up ready to stop what looked like a fight about to erupt.

Krack's voice lowered to a whisper, "I pulled out my pen and pad and wrote a letter to my kid brother, in case we got killed."

Norman, relaxed, "I suppose you wrote it on a waterproof pad that floats with its own postage stamp?"

"Damn, I knew I was forgetting something." We all laughed.

Krack talked often about his brother and shared with us both the letters he received from him and wrote to him. Most of Krack's letters were about how much he hated the Navy and how lucky and smart his brother was for not enlisting. He continually complained to his brother about how working for people that had pea sized brains was driving him crazy.

Norman, Krack and I sat back down. Matty, who had been sitting quietly, asked me, what I was doing during General Quarters.

"I wasn't praying to horny virgins, although I might consider that, next time," I said.

"Fuck you!" Norman blurted as he coughed out another cloud of smoke.

"When the General Quarters alarm sounded, I ran to my assigned repair locker. I opened it and took a quick visual inventory of my equipment. I took note of the location of the chemical warfare drugs. As the other members of the team arrived, I gave them assignments and handed them tools based on their skill levels."

"That sounds like a bunch of bullshit," Krack said.

"Remember, Krack, this is what I am trained for. This is my primary job. No bullshit here. I wait until everyone is in their place, then I pray for horny virgins."

"You can pray for all the horny virgins you want, but out here, on the water, we're nothing but bait," Matty said. "We're just a big piece of cake waiting for the Viet Cong to take a big bite out of our ass."

"Cake?" Norman said. "Hmmm? I sure could go for a nice

piece of German chocolate cake with pistachio ice cream right now."

"Chocolate cake with pistachio ice cream? That's gross," Krack said.

"Screw the cake and ice cream," I said. "I want to hear what Matty was going to say."

Matty sucked long on the glowing ember of hemp and held his breath. Slowly letting the smoke escape through his nostrils, he handed the glowing joint to Krack. Our eyes focused on Matty.

Taking in a breath of fresh air, Matty said, "We got word, over our Link Four communication radio, that eight Viet Cong MiG fighters were bearing down on the USS Trippe."

"What the fuck?" Normal said, "Are you shittin me?"

"Hell no! I was praying that it wasn't true."

Matty's words captured all of our attention. I stopped breathing.

"Lucky for us," Matty continued, "the carrier already had F4 fighters deployed. When the MiGs caught site of our war birds, they aborted their mission and flew back to fuckin Hanoi. But not before we started firing at 'em."

"Matty, what does that have to do with your giving up on chocolate cake?" Norman asked, "Oops. I mean the Navy."

"Somebody better get Norman some cake," I said. We all laughed.

Matty continued, "When we got word that the MiGs turned around, I stopped sweating. I wanted to jump up and hug the chief. Then the captain said, "Shit. There goes our chance for a fight." The captain wanted a fucking fight. He doesn't give a rat's ass about us. All he wants is to be a fucking hero."

"We'd all be dead heroes if the MiGs had attacked," I said.

"That is why I gave up on the Navy," Matty said.

The sound of machine gun fire danced across the water, leaped onto the fantail, and echoed off the rocket launcher, squelching our conversation. Looking out across the water, we could tell that a couple more helicopters had entered the foray. Although we could not see them, we saw the tracers, like science fiction ray guns shooting downward in hot pursuit of their prey.

"I'm sure glad I'm not a Viet Cong," Matty said, "They don't stand a chance against our choppers."

"The Viet Cong are stronger than you think, Matty," I said, "For one thing, they've been fighting us for a long time and for another, the French couldn't beat them before we got here. They have the jungle to hide in. We're just sitting ducks."

Rumble, rumble, rumble, the fantail deck began to vibrate as the rocket launcher began to rotate.

"Holy shit! Let's get the fuck outta here!" Krack yelled.

My heart started racing as we all jumped up and scattered, running to the ladders leading to the helo deck. Krack grabbed the ladder's railing and pulled himself up as fast as his arms and feet could climb the rungs. His feet nearly kicked me in the face with me climbing so close behind him. When we all arrived inside the hangar, Krack and Norman were laughing. Matty and I were trying to catch our breath.

Norman said, "One more toke on that joint and I might have been too stoned to run."

"When that rocket launcher rotated, I about shit my pants," Krack said.

"Man, oh man! We would've been charred bacon, if they fired those rockets. I wish they had warning lights or something," Matty said.

"No way! Matty!" Krack said. "I like being invisible at night. Warning lights would give away our position. We're exposed as it is when the rockets blast out of their tubes, and we fire our guns."

All of us were keenly aware of our "bait" status, trying to entice the big gun, hiding somewhere in the jungle, to fire on us and expose its position. Sailing as close to shore as our sonar would allow, without having the ship run aground or run into a mine, was enough to give us ulcers.

"I wish we didn't have to play decoy on a full moon," I said.

"If that gun hits us now, in the dark, how the fuck are we supposed to know where it's hidden?" Norman asked. "This is really fuckin stupid duty, and we're all stupid asses to stay here."

"Ah. That's why we need to be invisible." Matty said.

"Fuckin A, you got that right," Krack said.

First Class Boatswain's mate, Keegan waddled into the hangar and with a slight hint of an Irish accent, asked, "Would anyone be out by the aft rocket launcher? We're about to fire on a fuckin target."

"It's all clear, now," I said, as I walked over and patted Keegan on the shoulder.

Keegan jumped back, brushing off his shoulder, his eyes squinting, his lips pursed and said, "Don't be touching me. I don't want no grass stains on me."

"What's wrong with smoking a little weed, Keegan?" Norman asked.

"Smoking dope will make you illiterate," Keegan spit on the deck. "All dope smokers are illiterate."

We all burst out laughing. Keegan's eyes nearly disappeared amid the wrinkles of his eyelids as he walked away saying, "It was a waste of me fuckin time to warn ya. Yer all a bunch of illiterate bastards."

Krack lowered his voice to a staged whisper, "Oh Fuck! I think I forgot how to read."

"I just so happen to have a remedy for that," Norman said. "My remedy will not only bring back your ability to read, it will cure our munchies as well."

Krack punched Norman in the shoulder and said, "Well, what the fuck are we standing here for? Let's get that remedy of yours. I'm starving."

Norman led us down the ladder to the main deck. He stopped at the door across from the lifeboat until were all together. The ocean breeze brushed against our cheeks. The crescent moon reflected on the water as the ship swayed to and fro. Choppers, shooting at the enemy in the night blackened jungle a few hundred yards off our starboard side, made us want to run inside. In order to prevent any visible light from escaping beyond the ship's interior and revealing the ship's location, the interior passageways that led to exterior doors were equipped with hidden dim red lights that gave just enough illumination to see the interior doors if one stood inside the doorway. The illumination from the red lights could only be seen by those very close by. Norman opened the steel exterior door into a small interior passageway. We hurried inside, as he held it for us. I waited for Norman to latch the exterior door before opening the interior door. Norman passed me, leading us to the galley. He ran into the kitchen and brought out cinnamon rolls.

"I made these for midrats," he said.

Matty and Krack chomped their teeth into their cinnamon rolls. Before picking mine up, I asked Krack, "Have you heard any news about what they are going to do with you and Norman?"

Norman and Krack simultaneously said, "Ya mean about when we quit?"

Matty asked, "Quit what?"

"Haven't you heard, Matty?" I asked, "Norman and Krack are both Fire Control Technicians. They are rocket launcher wizards. They refused to fire the rockets when we got here. That is why they both work in the galley."

Matty stroked his chin. Looking at Norman and Krack, he asked, "You guys really did that?"

"Yup." Norman said.

"What's going to happen to you? Are you going to stay in the galley forever?" Matty asked.

Norman sighed deeply and said, "We're awfully expensive kitchen help. The Navy spent a whole lot of fuckin money to train us. But there is no way that I'm going to purposely kill innocent people who aren't a threat to the US."

"I know this sounds stupid," Matty said, "but isn't refusing to obey orders during war time a big deal? I mean, couldn't they send you to the brig or something?"

"Fuck yeah." Norman said. "The captain told Krack and me that we could end up in the fucking brig, or get a dishonorable discharge. That scares the shit out of me. We did our jobs well until we got to Viet Nam. Now we're working in the god damn galley as the bread maker and salad maker. The captain sent us to work here until the Navy figures out what to do with us."

The captain and their chief had tried to get them back in the fire control room to fire the rockets. Both remained resolute in their decision. I was proud of both of them.

Matty said, "You two are either blooming idiots or you've got the biggest balls in the Navy."

Norman grabbed his crotch, grinned and said, "Big balls for shua!"

We were all laughing when BOOM! We all jumped. Gagging

our laughter, the rocket launcher sent off its steel encased thunderbolt to bring death and destruction to everything and everyone near its target. The rocket blast stunned and vibrated through every fiber in my body, making my teeth clank against each other. My feet flew off the deck and for several moments afterward, my uncontrollably trembling legs could barely support me. Even though we had all experienced the launching of the rockets many times before, the power of the blast always took us by surprise. The intensity made me wonder if we had taken a hit ourselves.

"How many more babies, how many more kids and mothers will that rocket kill?" I yelled, slamming my fist against the table and bouncing up my cinnamon roll.

"That damn cinnamon roll isn't gonna save anybody's ass when those MiGs come back," Krack said pointing to my untouched cinnamon roll. "If you aren't gonna eat, I will," he said, picking it up. "It might be my last meal."

28 – BUTTON EYES

I trudged below decks to my berthing compartment after completing my battle station watch at 21:00. My eyes were dry after having only five hours of sleep in the last two days. Thankfully the lights were off in the compartment. I unbuttoned my trousers, put them in my locker, and climbed up to the third rack. Pushing the play button on my stereo, I closed my eyes, rolled over on my back and put on my headphones. The Doobie Brothers sang *Listen to the Music* to the rhythm of the ship's rocking and rolling. Their music unfastened my last remnants of wakefulness.

"Hey Dude. Wake up. A chopper is coming in. Wake up," announced a voice that was attached to the hand that shook me awake. It was Otis.

Roused from my music-filled slumber, I removed my head phones, rolled over and pulled back my blanket. My toes searched for the edge of the rack below me, making sure my feet did not step on my shipmates who were sleeping in the two lower racks. While I hurried to button my pants, the lights came on in the berthing compartment letting me know that reveille was at hand. Everyone would be waking up. Wanting to avoid the clash of stirring bodies, I ran out of the berthing compartment and up the ladders to the helo deck. The members of my fire crew were taking their places when I arrived at my station. "Whop, whop, whop," announced the helicopter as we prepared for its landing. The force of the wind from the chopper's blades made us shield our eyes.

Once safely on deck, the chopper's marine crew disembarked their helicopter. Freddie Garcia, the gunner I met on our first helo operation, came over to me. "It's so good to see you again. I'm sure glad you guys are here. I hate picking up our dead."

"What?" I asked as his words dive bombed into the pit of my stomach. "You brought them here?"

"No, I dropped them off at the base camp morgue earlier."

"Good, we have no place to keep dead bodies on the ship."

Freddie's brow wrinkled and his eyes squinted as he blurted, "I was just saying that it always freaks me out. It is the ants, man. It's the ants that freak me out the most."

"Ants? What are you talking about, Freddie?"

"The ants know immediately when somebody dies. They swarm around the eyes first. They make the eyes look like buttons, buttons that move as you get closer."

"Buttons? You're starting to give me a headache trying to follow you. What do you mean, buttons?"

"I mean that they look like button eyes on a teddy bear. The eyes are all black, no whites. It is just so weird. It freaks me out."

I looked down at his feet. A dead ant was stuck in the dry mud on his boots. My stomach began to get queasy.

Freddie scanned the coastline, as he grabbed onto the safety lines with both hands. Turning his head toward me, he continued, "The first time I saw the ants do that, I vomited my guts out. The sarge told me I'd get used to it, but I can't. Hell, now every time I see black buttons, I see ants eating out eye balls. I'll never be able to look at black buttons again."

"Why don't you run down below to the mess deck and get yourself something to eat." I said.

Freddy lifted his eyebrows as a big smile stretched across his face. "I can do that?"

"Sure! You're here in time for breakfast."

"Great! Once we fuel up, we need to leave, though. But we should have time to eat something. What are they feeding you guys down there?"

Grabbing hold of my eye lashes with my thumb and finger, I said, "Scrambled ants."

"God, you're a sick fucker."

We both laughed as he let go of the safety lines and walked away.

"Hey Freddie!" I called out, "Since you're going down to eat, tell your pilot that I am sending my fire crew to eat breakfast. You guys can fly out of here when we're done eating."

"Will do. Aren't you going to join me for breakfast?"

"I will when I secure my equipment up here."

Having made sure that the fire equipment was secure, I ran down to the mess decks. Grabbing a metal tray, I got in line behind Freddie, who had been waiting for me. He turned around to face me.

"Wow. You guys have it good, here," he said, wide eyed. "Fresh eggs, bacon, toast. And even a fresh milk machine. You guys are lucky."

"The only thing missing is chorizo and frijoles, eh Freddie? I know that you don't just eat K rations."

"Yeah we do, unless we are at a real base. When we are out on maneuvers, or on rescue detail, K rations is all we get. So, getting fresh eggs, real milk, and toast, even without the chorizo and frijoles is cool."

We sat across from each other at a table by ourselves. Freddie ran his fingers along the edge of the table, swallowed a piece of bacon then asked, "How come these tables have this one inch metal lip around the edge?"

"When the seas are rough, we don't want our food sliding off the table."

"Huh." He took his butter knife and slid it across the table until it came to a stop at the lip. "You sailor boys aren't as dumb as you look," he said with a wide grin.

"I wish I could say the same for you fly boys. You might as well carry a big sign on your chopper's belly that says, 'Shoot me here'."

"What? You didn't see it? Did it fall off?" He slapped his knee and we both laughed.

I continued to laugh but Freddie grew suddenly serious. His eyes were bloodshot, as though he had been in a cloud of smoke. "You know, Vato," he said. "I don't like what we are doing here."

"Who does? Killing people and getting shot at aren't fun."

"No! Man, when I look down from our chopper I see our gente, our people."

"What do you mean our people?"

"These Vietnamese are brown like us," Freddie said as he put his forearm against mine. "They are like the farm workers back home, like my Uncle Juan in Salinas, just farmers trying to make a decent living." He lowered his voice and looked around the mess deck to see who was within earshot. "What the hell are *we* doing here?"

"I ask myself that same question. They told us that we were fighting communists."

"No!" Freddie's voice boomed. He cupped his mouth with his hand and whispered, "When I said we, I meant you and me! *Us Chicanos.* The people I see running on the ground while our chopper flies overhead loaded with machine guns—those people are just farmers, man, like my Uncle Juan. That could be Salinas down there and we're blowin' it up."

"But this isn't Salinas. They keep telling us that Vietnam is a commie domino. If we fail they will add another step in their path to world domination. At first, I wanted to believe them."

"Yeah. They fed us that shit but I can't believe it. When I fly overhead I'm so close I can see them washing their babies outside their hootches."

"I know what you mean, man. I can't see any hootches from the deck of the Trippe. But I do see people fishing from their old rickety boats. I see old grandmothers babysitting their grandkids, making sure they don't fall into the water. It doesn't look like world domination to me."

Freddy looked up from the table, pointed with his eyes behind me and asked me who had entered. I turned around.

"He's the ship's captain, talking to one of the chiefs. He doesn't eat with us. He's just passing through."

161

Freddie put his head down and waited for the captain to pass our table. He followed the captain with his gaze, watched him ignore the sailors wolfing down their scrambled eggs and bacon. He saw him catch his balance as the ship rolled and observed him simultaneously duck and step over the threshold as he left the mess decks.

"I bet all you guys could've been eating breakfast naked and your captain wouldn't have noticed. Is he always like that?"

"Yes, I bet he didn't see you and your chopper crew. And he sure as hell isn't going to notice the grandmothers and babies on the fishing boats."

Freddie patted his chest and said, "Those farmers and fishermen are us."

"Yes, I agree," I said. "The Vietnamese look too much like our families back home."

Freddie took a drink of milk and ate a forkful of eggs. He sat motionless for a moment, his eyes focused inward, while I nibbled on my scrambled eggs without tasting them.

"Those white *viejos*, those old farts in the Pentagon, don't care about these farm workers any more than they care about the farm workers back home," Freddie said. "They don't give a fuck that they're making us kill our own people."

"I hate thinking about it that way," I said and sat quiet for a moment, taking in his words. Freddie articulated what I had been feeling since our first day on the gun line when we shot those three boys. They were brown and short like us. "You're right, Freddie. We are killing our gente, our own people."

"Damn straight, we are," he said as he took the last swig of milk and slammed it down on the table. He looked at his watch and told me he needed to go. He thanked me for breakfast as we left the table and put our trays and forks in the scullery.

I called out to the fire rescue crew, who were enjoying the short respite at breakfast, "The chopper's going to leave. Finish eating and get to the helo hangar."

As Freddie and I walked out of the mess decks, his voice quieted to almost a whisper, "They're talking about your ship having a high negative body count, back at base camp."

"Yeah, we do. It went negative when we started killing villagers and our own guys."

"Why would you do that?"

"Our captain is only a commander. He wants to be a hero so that he can earn the rank of Captain. If he hopes to make captain, he needs to turn his negative body count back on the positive side. That's why he's willing to risk killing civilians and sometimes even our own guys."

"That's crazy, Man," he said shaking his head.

"He's nuts and it scares me," I said throwing up my hands. "He doesn't see that we are killing real people. They are just numbers to him. Numbers like points in a game. If his positive numbers are high enough, he wins and gets promoted to the rank of captain."

"It's a good thing he ain't a marine. One of us would frag him, for sure. Someone would make sure that a grenade" … Freddy made quotation marks with his fingers … "accidently went off under his cot."

"Well, lucky for him, he isn't a marine. And there's nothing to frag him with."

I imagined one of our gunners mates putting one of the captain's own percussion grenades under his bed. I shuddered. The idea of killing our captain felt immoral, regardless of how crazy or bad he might be. I wanted to change the subject.

I blurted out, "We have rockets." I didn't know what made me bring up the rockets.

"No shit? Really? How far can they go?"

"They can almost but not quite reach Hanoi," I said. "They're accurate for 25 miles."

Freddie scrunched his eyes together. "If they're so goddamn accurate, why do you shoot the friendlies and our guys?"

"Believe me, Freddie, it is only the captain who takes those risks. He doesn't care about anything, except making rank."

"If he kills anymore friendlies, our colonel is going to ask headquarters to get him and your ship out of here."

"Why wait? Do that now. I want out of here, too." I lamented being an enlisted man with no authority or the means to report our captain.

"Easier said than done, *Vato*." He climbed aboard his helicopter and sat on his helmet. "Ha. You got it easy here, sailor boy. You get scrambled eggs, without ants."

163

29 – TALKING ABOUT GIRLS WITH FREDDY

"The dawn is the sun's early morning erection," Norman said.

BAM!

I nearly jumped out of my skin as much from hearing Norman's voice as I did when I heard the blast from our MK-42 cannon.

"That blast woke ya up, didn't it!" Norman said with his Bostonian accent. "Ya must've jumped two feet in the air. You'd betta check to make shuah ya didn't shit in your pants."

"I think it was you who scared the crap out of me," I said. "I didn't see you. I was caught up in the sunrise. Geez, it was beautiful. Did you see it?"

"Yup. I watched it come up," he said, smiling through his big red Santa Claus beard. "I also watched the gunner climb into the MK-42 gun mount. When I saw you gazing off into la la land, I knew you wouldn't be expecting the five inch gun to fire off."

"You could have warned me, Norman."

"Hell no! What fun would that have been? I got to see the sunrise and see you almost shit in your pants. You became my morning's entertainment. What were you doing in la la land?"

"I was thinking about how erotic the dawn can be."

"You've been out at sea too long if the dawn makes you

horny."

The ship turned around and headed back along the shoreline. The MK-42 gun mount turned 180 degrees and began firing into the jungle. As it turned about again, the ship slowed down. The gun mount turned forward and the five-inch gun took a rest.

"Ever notice how the five-inch gun looks like a skinny dick with a hard on?" Norman said, as he pulled the fly of his pants to a point.

"I'm not the only one who's been out at sea too long, but now that you mention it, it does."

"And it's fuckin the shit out of Nam," Norman said.

"What we're doing here is obscene," I said. "This place is a paradise. It's beautiful. We aren't fighting communism. We're raping Nam and then stabbing her when we're done."

Norman used his thumb and index finger to separate his mustache and sighed. "That's why Krack and I refused to fire the rockets."

I pointed westward into the sky. "I betcha that dot above the hills is a helicopter coming our way," I said.

"How do ya know for shuah?" Norman asked.

"I watched a chopper fly back and forth on this side of that hill. The sky was barely light enough to see a silhouette. Tracers came out of its machine guns right before the sun came up."

"Yeah. Those tracers make it look like a ray gun," he said.

"After the helicopter went back and forth for a while, it flew over that hill and disappeared. That dot is coming from behind that same hill."

"Heah it comes," Norman said.

"Chopper incoming," came over the loudspeakers informing me and the helicopter rescue crew to prepare for its landing.

Feigning a Boston accent, I said, "Ah gotta go, Nohman."

I took my place with the fire rescue team on the starboard side of the helo deck. We sheltered our eyes from the wind of the rotors. Barry donned the cable and glove and then attached it to the ground in the center of the landing pad. The chopper hovered and lowered a cable. Barry grabbed hold of its grounding cable and attached it to the cable on his glove. He took his hand out of the glove and ran to join us. When the helicopter descended, Freddy jumped out and hurried over to me.

"Hey, can you give me a hand getting some fuel?" he asked.

"Do I look like a gas station attendant?" I said.

"If you had a star on your shirt, you could be the Texaco man."

Freddy walked into the helo hangar and dragged out the fuel hose. While the helicopter drank its fill, Freddy opened his wallet. "Look what I got in the mail, yesterday; a photo of my girlfriend, back home."

"She's hot, Freddy. Why would she settle for someone as ugly as you?"

He grabbed his crotch, winked and said, "Cuz I got what she likes."

His girlfriend was a gorgeous olive skinned Chicana. She stood on the beach wearing a yellow bikini. I stared at the photo longer than he expected.

"Are you gonna stare at my girlfriend forever?" he asked. "Gimme that. Where's yours?"

"She's in New Mexico."

"So where is her picture?" he asked.

I reached into my front pants pocket, pulled out my mushroom embossed brown leather wallet, opened it and flipped through the photographs.

"Her name is Yvonne," I said, showing him her photo. "She's from Bernalillo, a small town north of Albuquerque."

"She looks like a Chicana, too."

"She is. I've known her since we were little kids. She's the daughter of my dad's best friend."

"You're alright, man. I like that you're not like the Chicanos who only date white girls."

"Brown is beautiful," I said. "Tell me about your girlfriend, Freddy. What's her name?"

"Her name is Imelda. I met her at my sister's birthday party last year when I was home on leave. Man, she looked so fine. She was wearing one of those. Hmmm? You know: those things that look like bikini tops."

"A halter top?" I offered.

"Yeah, that's it. When she came walking into the party, wearing that tiny halter top, she had the most beautiful *chichis* I ever saw. I'd never seen boobs that hot."

"I can see that from your photo."

"Yeah, man, my sister smacked me on the head, and told me to put my eyes back in their sockets."

We both laughed.

"Here, look at this one," Freddy said, as he took another photo out of his wallet. "It's her high school graduation photo."

"When was this taken?"

"Last year. She's only two years younger than me. Freddy closed his eyes and breathed in slowly. "Oh, if I could be back home with her now."

"Me too."

"Hey, get your own girlfriend," Freddy said as he punched me in the shoulder.

"Yvonne is who I want to be with," I said. "You can have your Imelda, even if she is too good looking for you."

Freddy smiled as he gave me the middle finger salute then turned and looked at the fuel gauge.

"Shit," he said as he squinted and puckered his lips. "We must've been flying on fumes."

"Seriously?" I asked. "Why would you guys shoot your wad like that?"

Freddy walked around the chopper and ran his hand under the fuel tanks. He sucked air through his nose several times

"The tanks didn't take a hit, but I smell fuel. I can't tell if it's from your fuel hose or from a leak."

"You better have your mechanic check it out when you get back," I said.

"Yeah, I will. When you asked me why we would shoot our wad it reminded me of the last time I was with Imelda." Freddy looked from side to side. "I've never told this to anyone before," Freddy blushed. "Imelda and I were making out at the park under a tree. We were just kissing at first. But I wanted more."

"You can't do much more if you're at a park," I said.

"It was after dark and there was no one around," he said as his eyes sparkled with the reflection of the water. "I unbuttoned her blouse and slid my hand over her boob. Oh man, that got me so excited."

"Yeah. I know what you mean, Freddy. I remember the first time I felt my ex-wife's boobs. But, at least we were in a car, at night."

"You have an ex-wife?" he asked.

"Yeah, I was married for eighteen months. We have a kid together. He's two years old."

"No shit?" he said.

"It's a long story. I like yours better. Go on with what you were telling me."

"She must've felt how hard my pecker was, because she put her hands on my hips and started rubbing her pussy on my dick," he said smiling and looking to both sides to see if anyone might be listening.

"You took your clothes off in the park?" I asked.

"No, no. We kept our clothes on. While I felt her up she swayed her hips like she was dancing. Gawd, it felt so good."

"I bet it did."

Freddy's eyes grew wide as he said, "Then, before I knew it, I shot my wad."

"In your pants?"

"Yeah. And I didn't care. It was dark and I was with her, and I wasn't here in fuckin Nam."

"What did she say? She had to have noticed."

"Wow. It got better because she said, 'Now it's my turn,' and she put my hand down her pants."

"Well, at least you won't get her pregnant that way."

"Hell no. If I did, not only would her old man kill me, my dad would kill me, too."

He gazed up at the sky. "Ha. Look over there to the north. Doesn't that look like the clouds are fuckin each other?"

"Yes, Freddy, I guess that even the clouds in Viet Nam get horny."

"But, we're not making love to Nam," he said, his smile faded. "We're raping her."

"I think the clouds are telling us the same thing that the antiwar protesters, back home have been telling us: make love, not war."

I'm really glad I can talk you, Mushroom. I'm the only Chicano in my unit. The guys in my unit don't see things the way you and I do. They don't see that we're killing farmers who are like our family back home.

"I'm the only Chicano on this ship," I said. "I need someone I can relate to."

"Look at those hills to the west. Something big got hit," Freddy said. "The smoke is black. They'll want us to investigate."

"What do you think that is?" I asked.

"Hopefully a Viet Cong fuel tank. I hope it's not your captain fuckin another innocent village with that MK-42 cannon of his."

30 – BREAD AND THE CHURCH

"I need to talk to you. Shhh. Meet me on the mess decks at a little after 05:00," Radioman Matty whispered as I made my rounds through Command Information Central (CIC) on my Sounding and Security watch. Matty's face looked like an over exposed photograph, overly white and lacking definition. When I tried to ask him what it was about, he shooed me away with his hand, pretending that he was receiving a message. Noticing the ensign, I got the hint and continued my rounds.

As I meandered through the mess decks, Norman stepped out from the galley, carrying a large baking sheet. The dim after hours lighting in the mess decks and the dusting of flour in his beard, gave him a ghostly appearance.

"Come here and taste this bread," he said, wagging his head from side to side. He carried the baking sheet to a table, turned to me and smiled. "It's still hot. I just made it."

Its yeast aroma wafted into my nostrils, reminding me of the times my mother baked homemade bread.

The hands on the clock ticked past 05:00, reminding me that I had already been up for over 24 hours. My eyes were as dry as overdone toast and the ship's rocking made my legs feel like they were filled with soggy corn flakes. And yet, my whole body vibrated, like a car's engine that is badly out of tune. When I picked up a slice of the bread and held it to my nose, my mouth watered.

Norman sat down at a table and grabbed a slice of bread for himself. His flour dusted red beard had grown half way down his chest.

"When you get old," I said, "you could be a Macy's Santa Claus, albeit, a little creepy."

"A little creepy? Bullshit! I'd be a crazed Santa with the blood of Vietnamese villagers in my eyes," he said, his eyes opening wide as he leaned across the table putting his face inches from mine.

"Are you going to just stand there holding the bread or are you going to eat it?" he asked. "Sit down. You look like shit."

"Thanks. You're not so good looking yourself," I said, taking a seat across the table from him. "That flour in your beard, your white apron and white T-shirt make you look like a ghost. By the way, have you seen Matty?"

"The radioman?"

"You know damn well, who I mean. We only have one Matty on board, for God's sake."

"Man, you are grumm ... py this morning. Here, have some more bread. So what's up with Matty?"

"I don't know. When I walked past him up in CIC, he asked me to meet him here at after five."

"Do you know what he wants to talk about?"

"Not really. I suspect that he heard some news over the ship's radio that disturbed him and he needs someone to talk to."

Norman looked up from the table. His eye brows went up as he produced a mischievous grin. Waving a piece of bread above his head, he said, "Hey, Matty, want some freshly baked bread?"

"Sure. Thanks. I'm starting to get used to all that nutmeg you've been putting into it. You do realize that you won't be able to put enough nutmeg into the bread to get us stoned, don't you?"

Norman had read somewhere that nutmeg could produce

hallucinations if taken in large quantities. He had been adding increasing amounts of nutmeg to the bread recipe for about a month. He had been adding the nutmeg so gradually that I had not noticed a difference in taste until Matty made his comment.

"I know that you didn't want to meet me up here to talk about how Norman is trying to get the whole ship stoned on his bread," I said. "So what's up?"

Matty turned toward Norman. Norman just sat there waiting for Matty to say something. Matty squinted his eyes, pursed his lips in anticipation of saying something. But he didn't. He looked down at his feet, and then looked up at me with eyes opening wide. He moved his eyebrows up as he tilted his head indicating that he wanted Norman to leave. Norman sat there, grinning. Matty finally turned to Norman. "Don't you have to get back and check on your bread?"

"Look Matty, I know that you are here to talk to Mushroom about the shit that the captain is doing. News travels fast. Bad news travels faster."

Matty scrunched up his shoulders up to his ears. He looked to both sides of the mess decks making sure no one else would hear what he wanted to tell me. He lowered his voice. "We received orders to blow up a church tomorrow night after the sun goes down. Tomorrow is Friday, right?"

"Yes, tomorrow is Friday," I said. "A church? What kind of church? And why a church?" The hair on the back of my neck stood up. Since I had grown up in a devout Catholic family and studied for the priesthood, I felt that blowing up a church, any church was immoral.

"Yes, we received orders to blow up a church. It's a Catholic church, I think. We received word from our informants that the Viet Cong are hiding ammunition under the floor boards."

My stomach tightened into a knot as I wondered if this could really be true. "Would the Viet Cong really hide ammunition under a church, a Catholic church?" I asked. "The priest would never allow that. Would he?"

"Probably not, unless he was forced to," Norman said.

"Are you sure that's correct, Matty?" I asked grabbing his wrist. "Could the code have been mistranslated? Could your guys have misunderstood the orders?"

"No. We got the orders right. We always verify. But that's not what I want to talk about."

"What is it that you want to talk about?" I asked. Fatigue crept over me, making me yawn.

"It's bad enough that we got orders to blow up the church on a Friday night," Matty said. He looked around the mess decks again, breathed in through his nose and whispered, "The captain won't be obeying orders, not exactly."

"Get to the point, Matty," I said.

"The captain's going to hold off until Sunday morning, then he'll blow up the church."

"That's just crazy, Matty. The church will probably be filled with people going to Sunday mass."

"And that's exactly what the captain wants." Matty's head went down and Norman's eyes went up.

My body began vibrating faster, along with my breathing. The muscles in my back tightened as I asked, "What for? He can't be thinking that the Viet Cong are going to go to church on Sunday morning? Wait."

I put both of my hands over my mouth, as in prayer. I was trying to make some sense out of what Matty was telling us. I could feel the sweat dripping down the back of my neck.

Slowly, with his Boston accent, Norman said, "That mutha fuckah is waiting so he can get a lahdge body count." His eyes narrowed.

Matty lost all color in his face. His fist clenched so tight that the bread oozed out between his fingers. He said, "You got that right. And it is driving me crazy because I can't legally tell anyone. Not even you. But I have to tell someone."

I stood up, looked around and sat down again. My legs wanted to run away on their own. I couldn't sit still. I stood up again. I looked down at Matty.

"Isn't anyone up there trying to stop him?"

Matty shook his head. "No."

Norman stroked his big red beard, stood up, leaned across the table and peered up into my eyes. "Reardon is the captain," he said. "This is war. And didn't you tell me that he said he has the last say? He already has a negative body count."

"We know that," I said. "Why would he risk killing innocent

people, again?"

"War makes people do crazy things," Norman said. "He's probably thinking that if he kills all those people in church, he'll be a hero and his body count will turn positive."

"Norman is right." Matty said. "I've seen the captain talk to the officers and chiefs in CIC, telling them that they have to turn his negative body count around no matter what it takes."

"But why don't they protest about this shit?" I asked.

"My chief is fed up with what the captain is doing," Matty said. "I heard him talking with one of the other chiefs about needing to do something."

The ship's engines rumbled in tune with my hearts pounding.

"Keep your ears peeled, Matty, I said. "Hopefully someone will talk some sense into the captain before Sunday."

"Go wash up, Matty," Norman said. You've got bread guts all over your hand."

Matty didn't laugh. No one did.

I sat back down and grabbed another slice of bread. I tried to think of a way I could warn those people not to go to church on Sunday. Could someone warn the priest to hold mass somewhere else this Sunday? But who? And how without getting off the ship. Maybe the fly boys will show up. Maybe I could talk Freddy into warning the priest.

"I wish I could do something," I said. "Got any ideas, Norman?"

Norman shook his head and walked back into the galley. He banged on the counter with the nutmeg container, smiled and said, "This is all I have to fight this craziness with."

31 – SETTLING ON A SOLUTION

The My Lai massacre occupied my thoughts as I sat at the table contemplating the USS Trippe blowing up a church full of Sunday morning worshipers. My mouth lost its moisture. I got up and walked over to the juice dispenser. As I watched the red bug juice pour into my clear plastic glass, my imagination turned it into blood. I groaned. Would I be as guilty as Lt. Calley's men, if I did nothing to stop the killings?

Matty stood at the table waiting for me to return to my seat across from Norman. When I sat down, he put both of his hands on the table and looked at both of us.

"Promise me," Matty said, lowering his voice to a whisper. "Promise me that you two won't tell anyone that I told you about the Captain's decision to blow up the church on Sunday morning. Promise?"

"Yes, I promise," Norman and I said in unison.

Norman returned to the kitchen to prepare breakfast. Matty mentioned that he forgot his notebook in CIC then darted out of the mess decks. I made my way to the helo deck to find a place to think. The salt air danced into my nostrils along with the jungle musk reminding me of what will happen in three days time. The ocean breeze ran her jittery fingers through my beard. Dawn began her preparations for the sun's arrival by spreading out her wispy fingers, attempting to shape a crown for the sun king. The night sky began withdrawing her dark starlit cloak from the Vietnamese jungle, as the moon kissed the dawn farewell while descending into the western mountains. Painting the clouds shades of pink, then erasing that color in favor of orange, the sun announced that a new day had begun. Why would God bring us such beauty when he knows that we are going to blow up his church?

While I admired the sun's artwork and pondered God's rationale, someone patted me on the shoulder. I jerked my head around. The flour dust in the furrows of Norman's forehead made him look like an actor with overdone ghost makeup.

"Something is going on today," he said.

"What do you mean, Norman?

"I don't know for sure. I just overheard a couple of the officers talking."

"What did they say?"

"I couldn't hear any of the details. I only caught a few words about the ship going somewhere. I got as close as I could without being obvious. But once the officers noticed me, they left."

My leg began to twitch and my voice grew louder, "Where are we going?"

"I don't know. They said that we will be moving into position."

"Position for what?" I swallowed and looked across the water to the shore. I imagined a small Catholic church with a thatched roof and wooden floors hidden beyond the trees. "Do you think that the officers talked the Captain into blowing up the church tonight instead of Sunday morning?"

"Maybe. I didn't hear them mention the church," Norman's voice softened. "So we can only hope."

He patted me on the shoulder and told me to go eat breakfast before they called morning muster. Breakfast consisted of powdered eggs, greasy bacon and Norman's nutmeg laden bread. At morning muster, Chief Jaffe told Dawson and me to stay put after he dismissed the crew.

"I want you two to fix the forward hatch after we connect with the supply ship," he said.

"Is that the one in front of the five-inch gun?" I asked. "What's wrong with it?"

"Yes. It's leaking. Apparently the recoiling of the forward gun is warping the hatch and causing leaks when water comes over the bow."

"When are we connecting with the supply ship, Chief?" Dawson asked.

"We'll meet up with her around 14:00. The captain wants a full supply of ammo for Sunday morning's attack."

My neck muscles tightened, suppressing a scream that was trying to crawl out of my throat.

"Sunday morning's attack?"

"Yes, but that is none of your concern. Your only concern is to make sure that hatch doesn't leak," he said, as he turned and walked away.

"Sunday morning's attack," reverberated in my head. Norman didn't hear what position we were moving into. Did the officers mean that we were moving into position to take on more arms from the ammo ship? As the Trippe slid over a swell, I moved my foot sideways to catch my balance.

"What are we going to do?" I asked myself aloud.

Dawson had no clue that my question referred to stopping the captain from bombing the church.

"You know," Dawson said. "We'll get the chalk to mark the rubber gasket out of the repair locker. I've never fixed a hatch. I was out sick the day they taught us how to do it in HT school. But I read how to do it in our HT book. I had to so I could pass the test. Haven't you fixed a hatch before? If you haven't, we'll figure it out together."

"Sorry," I said, shaking my head. "I was thinking about something else when I asked the question. I've repaired a dozen hatches."

Wanting to be alone to sort things out, I asked Dawson to meet me in the forward repair locker at 13:00 and we would go over the procedures for repairing the hatch.

My mind engaged itself in a race with my breathing as I ran up to next level. I found a secluded spot behind the smokestack and sat with my back against it. I hadn't slept for nearly thirty hours and my body vibrated with a shaking that begged for a bed.

"What am I going to do?" I asked again. Stroking my beard, I searched the sky and prayed, "Dear God help me save your church."

I decided to get up, find Norman or Krack and ask them for help. I scurried up to the helo deck, where Krack had set up his stereo equipment. The helo deck was empty. I wondered if Norman had found a place to hide and sleep for a few hours. No one I spoke to had seen him recently. I searched all of the obvious places. I gave up my search when it was time to take over the sounding and security watch.

At 13:00 the ship veered away from the Vietnamese shoreline, away from the targets, away from the shelling. The ocean's swells lifted the ship's bow and let it fall, rattling my already wobbly legs, forcing me to grab the lifelines. I finished my watch, turned over the gun and sounding log to Otis and returned to my hunting for Norman or Krack.

When I found Norman on the fantail, I let out a long low sigh. He was watching the ship's wake as we steamed away from the shoreline. Norman puffed on a cigarette, his eyes were bloodshot. A hint of hashish wisped in the air around him.

"I have an idea that might save the priest and the villagers," I said when he turned to look at me.

He moved his mustache away from his lips with his thumb and looked behind us to make sure no one could hear. His red bushy eyebrows scrunched together as he asked, "How do ya intend to get off this ship and warn em?"

"I don't need to," I said. "When I went looking for you in the helo hangar I thought about the fly boys. Maybe I could talk Freddy into warning the villagers."

"Nah, he won't do that," he said. "I don't think we have a prayer. That would be way too risky for him."

"How could that be too risky?" I pointed to the hills across the water. "He flies into those villages all the time."

Norman took another puff on his cigarette and blew out the smoke. "It's treason."

His words dive bombed into the pit of my stomach.

"What if we tell Freddy to warn the priest?" I asked. "That wouldn't be treason, would it? I'm pretty sure that he's Catholic."

"That might work," Norman said, his eyes sparkling. "He wouldn't let a priest die. Not just for a body count."

I breathed a sigh of relief and patted Norman on the back. I turned and ran up the ladder to meet Dawson at the forward repair locker. While we gathered the tools we needed to fix the hatch, I prayed that Freddy would arrive on the next chopper.

32 – FIXING THE HATCH

Dawson and I clung to the lifelines and braced our feet on the helo deck as the Trippe rendezvoused with the ammo ship, far enough out in choppy seas to avoid an attack from North Vietnamese MiGs. I hated knowing that we were re-arming in preparation for Sunday morning's massacre. Norman closed the helo hangar's side door with a bang, as the Trippe lunged to one side.

"I thought you two were going to fix the forward hatch," Norman said.

"We have to wait until they secure the lines with the ammo ship," I said. "Then we won't be in anybody's way."

The Trippe lurched and rolled over the green ocean swells of the Tonkin Gulf. The sky blazed brilliantly blue with a warm sun overhead, despite the wind. Norman latched on to the lifeline about a yard downwind from me. He motioned with his head, indicating that I should move closer. The wind battered his beard and flapped the sleeves of his white T-shirt and the legs of his bell bottom dungaree

"Aren't these seas too rough to transfer ammo?" Dawson asked.

"The ships will stabilize when we pick up enough speed," I said and turned toward Norman.

He pulled out his lighter, and motioned with his arm for me to get closer to him to block the wind while he crouched down in front of me and lit a cigarette.

"Look at the line of deck apes on the ammo ship facing that boatswains mate who's holding his hands behind his back." he said pointing with his cigarette. "They're lined up like a firing squad."

His words punched me in the stomach. The only things missing were their rifles.

"I've been thinking about your buddy on the chopper," he said.

"Do you mean Freddy?"

He nodded. "I don't think you should talk to him. Just forget it," he said and lowered his voice, barely audible over the rumble of the ship. "It's treason and he might turn us in."

"He wouldn't do that," I said.

"How do you know? We're at war and the penalty for treason is death," he said and blew out a big puff of smoke. "Think about it."

"They wouldn't really execute us for telling a priest to hold mass somewhere else, would they?" I asked, my stomach churning.

Norman turned and looked to make sure no one could hear us downwind. He whispered, "Our captain could set up a firing squad right here on the helo deck and have us fuckin shot."

I swallowed and exhaled hard. "He'd do that because we cheated him out of a body count, wouldn't he?"

Norman nodded in agreement as he flicked the stub of his cigarette over the side.

I looked across the water at the ammo ship and imagined bodies of children and grandparents strewn over the pallets as if they were parts of the blown up church. "I couldn't live with myself, if I didn't try," I said.

The two ships nosed together and raced through the swells at about 20 knots. They came within 25 yards of each other, so close I could see the faces of the ammo ship's crew. One boatswain's mate positioned himself on the ammo ship's prow. When his ship matched our speed, he raised his hand and gave a thumbs up. First Class Boatswain's mate Keegan gave the signal to connect.

The ammo ship's boatswain's mate lifted his musket and fired. It made a loud "pop" and my stomach tensed. A dirty white tennis ball arched over the water and fell, bouncing onto our deck, attached to a thin white cord. One of our sailors chased the ball, dove onto the steel deck and snatched the cord before the ball fell into the water. Our deck apes formed a line and began pulling the cord and then the rope that was attached to it. The same procedure was followed amidships and then aft.

The bright orange dial on my Seiko watch showed 13:30.

"We'll be back patrolling the shoreline this afternoon giving easy access for helicopters to land," I said, not realizing that Norman had left.

"Are you expecting something?" Dawson asked.

I was surprised that Dawson heard me. "I'm hoping we get mail from home," I lied. I worried about what else he may have overheard.

"Look how taut those ropes are," Dawson said.

The ropes were as tight as the knots in my stomach. The ships turned a few degrees away from each other. The ropes between them strained.

"They look flimsy enough to snap," he said. "I bet they'd cut somebody's leg clean off."

"Don't worry," I said. "The ropes are pretty strong."

The deck apes removed the lifeline behind the five-inch gun and formed a line across the deck. The ammo ship sailors wrapped pallets, filled with supplies and ammunition, in netting and attached them to pulleys. As each one was hooked, our deck apes pulled them over the water to our ship. The swaying of the pallets made me think about the helicopters and I wondered when Freddy's chopper might arrive. He was our only hope for saving the villagers.

"Look! Over there on the ammo ship," Dawson yelled as he grabbed my shirt and pointed. "That guy is stealing our cokes."

"What's the big deal?" I asked, irritation slithering out of my throat. "He's not blowing up a church."

"What?" he asked. "I didn't say anything about a church; I said he's stealing our cokes?"

"Don't worry about it," I said, relieved that he didn't pursue my mentioning the church. "He only took one and he's drinking it. Our supply chief will only sign off for what we get."

"Someone should report him," he said.

"Why don't you hop back into a boatswain's chair and go over and report him?"

"No way!" he said waving his palms in front of me. "I never want to ride across to another ship hanging from those skinny ropes. Hell, I almost peed in my pants the last time I did."

I laughed and looked at my watch. "It's getting late. It's already 14:00. Let's take our tools and fix that hatch before the sea gets any rougher."

We climbed down one level to the main deck and went inside the ship. We wobbled to the forward berthing compartment under the leaking hatch. Dawson placed a new rubber gasket and the bag of tools on the green linoleum deck, next a bucket and wet towel that had been left there. He grabbed a stick of white chalk and a wrench and handed them to me to put them in my back pockets. I climbed the ladder, reached up and turned the hatch's wheel.

Dawson pointed to a metal wedge attached to the wheel that opens the hatch. "Why do we call them dogs?"

"Beats me. Maybe that old salty sailor, Keegan, knows. Go ask him when we get done."

Dawson pulled a set of headphones out of the tool bag and put them on, connecting us directly with the bridge so that we could be warned of any danger and our need to abort our repair task. I took another step up the ladder and struggled to lift the steel hatch to its full upright position. It was heavy, even though it had a large spring to assist in lifting. Dawson locked the release lever in place. We climbed out of the hatch and inspected the 28 inch wide by four feet long steel door. Dawson ran his fingers along the four inch tall knife edge of the hatch opening. I inspected the black rubber gasket feeling for resiliency, tears or breaks.

"One of the dogs must be out of alignment," I said. "I'll rub some chalk on the knife edge and we'll lock down the hatch to see if we find any gaps on rubber gasket."

"That'll tell us which dog is out of alignment, won't it?" Dawson asked.

"Yes. We can't afford to have any leaks. If our electrical lines, below, get wet, we could be dead in the water, literally."

When Dawson climbed down inside, I lowered the hatch and tightened down the wheel. He aimed his flashlight at the dogs to see if they were all working properly. I turned the wheel clockwise to lock the hatch in place and put pressure on the rubber gasket that rested on the steel rim. When the wheel stopped, Dawson turned it counter clockwise, from the inside of the ship. We raised the hatch to its full vertical position and inspected the black rubber gasket. It had a four inch gap in the chalk line. I took my wrench and tightened the dogs closest to the chalk gap. Dawson re-chalked the steel rim, while I cleaned the rubber gasket. He began his descent down the ladder so that we could dog down the hatch again.

The ship heaved over a swell, making Dawson lose his footing. Reaching up to grab anything to keep himself from falling, he pulled the hatch release. The hatch slammed shut, knocking me to the deck with a blow to my head.

I saw stars as I grabbed hold of my head.

Dawson opened the hatch. "I'm sorry. I fell d ... Oh my god! You're bleeding."

"What?" My head pounded.

"You need to get over to sickbay! You're bleeding like crazy!"

"Damn it!" I brushed the blood from my face and sleeve of my white tee shirt. "I'll never be able to wash this blood out."

"You need to get the blood stopped," Dawson yelled. "Go see the corpsman."

I put my hand against my head to stop the bleeding. My legs wobbled as I struggled to stand up. I couldn't focus. I made my way under the barrel of the five-inch gun, passed pallets of cokes, flour and lettuce and into the path of an incoming four foot pallet of ammo shells that would be used to blow up the church.

"Get the hell out of the way!" a boatswain's mate yelled.

Norman sat on a bollard, watching the transfer of supplies and ammo. "Holy shit! What happened to you?" he asked when I walked passed him on my way to sick bay.

"A dog hit me on the head," I said.

"A dog bit you?" He slapped his thigh, rolled his head back and roared a belly laugh.

"No! A dog hit me," I said, blood streaming down the side of my face.

When I reached sick bay, I knocked and waited, balancing myself against the door. My head began to spin. I sat on the deck and leaned against the bulkhead. Waiting for a hospital corpsman to show up, I wondered when the helicopters would arrive. Would Freddy be on one? Could I convince him to warning the priest?

A trickle of blood slithered its way down my arm and oozed its escape from my fingers onto the deck. It pulled me out of my thoughts.

"Place the palm of your left hand over the wound and apply pressure," A woman's voice said.

I obeyed and looked up but saw no one. The metallic taste of blood ran from my cheek into my mouth, waking me up. I jerked.

"I'm really sorry it took me nearly an hour to get here," third class hospital corpsman, Powell, said. "If I had known how badly you were hurt, I would have come right away."

I must have passed out while waiting. It seemed as if the corpsman arrived at sickbay five minutes after I did. "I've been here for a whole hour?"

"Yeah. Chief Jaffe saw you walking to sickbay. When I started to follow you, he told me to stay in case someone got hurt. He said that you only had a scratch. Hell, I'm going to have to stitch you up to stop the bleeding. Can you get up? You'll need to get on the table once we get you inside."

I lost my balance when I stood up. I felt groggy.

"Don't turn white on me," Powell said as he grabbed my arm and helped me get into sickbay and onto the exam table. He grabbed some gauze and told me to hold it against my head. The pervasive odor of rubbing alcohol filled my nostrils. I wanted to ask him if he had been the one who told me to put pressure on my head, but his voice was too low and he hadn't shown up yet. Or had he?

He tried to get my full attention by shining a small flashlight into my eyes. He raised his eye brows to the top of his forehead and moved the flashlight from one eye to the other.

"Your eyes don't look right," he said. "I'm going to have to ask the chief about this."

My head pounded as if someone were punching it rhythmically. The rumbling of the ship seemed louder than usual. The overhead fluorescent light glared too brightly.

"I'm going to have to cut your hair so that I can see where I'm sewing you up," the corpsman said.

"No, please. Don't cut my hair." Tears began to flow. "Please don't cut it. It is already too short." I heard myself say. I felt odd to hear myself, as if I were another person.

I imagined being not only completely bald, but completely naked and hairless. I couldn't keep the tears from flowing.

"I'm only going to cut the hair that's in my way," he said softly. He held my head with his left hand and used the steel clippers in his right hand. My eyelids became heavy and I closed them.

"Draw the healing from his hands," a woman's voice whispered in my ear. "Feel their caring warmth." It was the same voice I had heard earlier when I saw the vision of the Vietnamese woman.

When Powell finished clipping and then shaving the hair around my wound he said, "This Lidocaine is going to sting a bit."

My muscles tightened and my teeth clenched when he pushed the syringe into my scalp. A miniature Viet Cong burned my head with a blow torch.

Someone knocked on the door. Powell turned his head toward it and yelled, "I'll be with you in a minute." He put the syringe away and said, "Lie here and be quiet while the Lidocaine takes effect. I'm going to see who's at the door."

I heard him open the top half of the door. He stayed there a short while, then closed it and walked back to me. "There was nobody there. Whoever it was must have gotten tired of waiting and left."

"You don't need to lie to me," I said.

"What makes you think I'm lying?"

"I heard Keegan's Irish accent. He told you not to tell me that he was checking to make sure that I'm OK."

"Yeah, Keegan is a pretty decent guy, for a lifer." The corpsman tied off the last stitch. "That is one nasty bump you got there. I hope no one else is hurt. Transferring supplies at sea is dangerous."

33 – THE KNOCK

We heard another knock at the door while I was lying on the sickbay table.

"Who do you suppose that is?" Powell asked.

The knock at the door became more insistent. Powell tapped me on my chest. "Stay put while I go see who is at the door."

The ghosts of the three boys we killed on the first day were standing on the table, taking turns, kicking my head to the beat of their own funeral dirge. Powell opened the top half of the sickbay door. I tried to turn my head to see who was at the door, but I stopped when I heard my boss, Chief Jaffe.

"You aren't going to put him on bed rest, are you?" he asked. "I need him to stand his watch. I can't go around changing my schedule every time someone gets a scratch."

"Mushroom has a concussion," Powell said. "It's the chief corpsman's call whether he goes back on duty or not."

"Well, he better be able to stand his watch."

My hands tighten into fists and my face heated up, causing my head to sting.

"I don't want him slacking off over a little bump on the head," Jaffe said.

"Your chief is a fucking asshole," Powell said when he closed the door. "I guarantee you won't be standing watch. We're sending you to bed for a while."

"What are you talking about?" I asked. I didn't mind being pulled off one watch. But I needed to be back on duty when the helicopters arrived. I needed to be able to contact Freddy. "You heard Jaffe. He wants me back on watch. He'll make my life miserable if you don't let me stand watch."

"Ivan died of a head injury less than two weeks ago," Powell said as he placed his hand on my shoulder, brought his face close to mine and lowered his voice, "We aren't going to risk another fatality just so that chief of yours won't have to readjust his duty schedule." Standing to his full height, he added, "God, he is such a dickhead."

Chief corpsman Shea sauntered into sickbay, blowing out the last vapors from his cigarette that he must have flicked over the side of the ship. He picked up the flashlight and looked at my eyes while Powell told him what he had done and about the encounter with Jaffe.

"You're right, Powell, his left pupil is larger than his right. It's not reacting to light like the other one. That worries me."

I had no idea what they were talking about. My head hurt and I wanted an aspirin.

"I'm pulling you off all of your watches," Shea said. "We're going to keep you in sickbay for a couple more hours. Then you're to go to bed and stay there until Powell or I say you can get up. Do you understand?"

"How long do I have to stay in bed? I have work to do. Chief Jaffe wa…"

"I'll take care of Jaffe," Shea said. "You are in no shape to stand watch. We already had one fatality from a head injury. You are not going to be the next."

"When I send you to bed, you stay there. That's a direct order."

Shea gave me a pain pill. Powell strapped two seat belts around me to ensure that I didn't roll off the examination table. He asked me if I minded listening to some music as he popped a Beatles cassette into his player. *'Let It Be'* along with the rocking and rolling of the ship lulled me to sleep. I awoke after a couple

191

of hours to the sound of Ringo Starr singing 'It don't come easy'. I tried to focus but my eyes kept pulling their eyelid blanket back down, resisting all desire to awaken. When I finally managed to keep my eyes open, the sickbay lights slowly came into focus, along with the exposed pipes and conduit.

"Are you awake?" Powell asked.

"Barely. What time is it?"

"It's 17:30. If you feel up to it, I'll let you go to your berthing compartment. But remember, you have to stay there."

I left sickbay, trying to regain my sea legs. Chief Jaffe's words, "I don't want him slacking off over a little scratch," slammed against the interior walls of my head. I stumbled down the passageway clutching the exposed pipes and electrical cables for balance. What have I ever done to make Jaffe think that I would be slacking off? I work my butt off. I'm the only one who gets 'Atta Boys' for the work I do. My shoulders tightened as my wobbly pace picked up speed. "I'm no slacker," I said out loud.

I spotted Bruce walking toward me, wearing the gun and carrying the sounding tape. I blocked Bruce's passage.

"Give me the gun and sounding tape," I demanded, holding out my hand. "I'm taking back my watch."

"Are you sure? You don't look very good. The chief told me to replace you."

My knees shook. I sucked in air through my clenched teeth.

"I'm not going to let a white honky chief say that I can't carry my own load," I said. "Now give me the gun. This is my watch."

Bruce handed it over, shook his head and hurriedly left, in the direction of the chiefs' quarters. I hadn't gotten very far, when he returned with the chief. Jaffe blocked my passage, spreading his legs across the walkway and putting his hands on his hips.

He bellowed, "What the hell do you think you're doing?"

A seaman banged the electric floor buffer from side to side, behind Jaffe. I wanted it to bang into him.

"I'm standing my watch!" I inhaled hard. "Isn't that what you want? Just so you won't have to change your schedule?"

"I'm ordering you to give me the gun right now!" he shouted. The ligaments on his neck bulged as his face turned red and beads of sweat erupted on his forehead. "I'm taking you off watch. Go back to your rack like Shea told you. That's a direct order!"

I clenched my teeth, removed the belt and holster and handed it to him. My eyes shot bullets at Jaffe while his eyes retaliated with fire.

"Now!" he yelled, pointing behind me in the direction of my berthing compartment.

34 – SNEAKING UP TO THE HELO DECK

My shoulders slumped forward. My chest slid down onto my stomach wanting to bury my defeat. Norman walked toward me, with his brow furrowed, turning off the music of my personal pity party. "I heard that you got hurt," he said. "Whoa, that is some bandage you got on your head. Are you OK?"

"No. A miniature Viet Cong got trapped inside my head and he is trying to dig his way out with a pick ax."

"Ha, ha. Well at least you've got your sense of humor. Where are you headed?"

"I've been ordered to bed."

"Some people have all the luck. Wait. Did you say that you've been ordered to bed?"

"Chief Shea did."

"Any idiot knows that you don't let a man with a head injury go to bed. Hell, I learned that as a boy scout."

"So much for naval intelligence," I said as rolled my eyes back into my head.

His smile faded, as he began tugging at his beard. "Will you be able to do helo ops?"

"Not unless they let me out of bed before Freddy's chopper arrives."

"When is he scheduled to fly in?"

"Unfortunately the choppers aren't on a schedule. They come when they need fuel or they just need a break."

"How often is that?"

"Norman. Where have you been? You hear the whop, whop, whop of the choppers when they fly in, don't you?"

"Yup, I do. But I don't pay any attention to how many times they fly in. I'm not on the helo fire rescue team like you are. Give me a break."

"They fly in two or three times a day on the average. Some days we get no choppers. Some days we get four or five. We can only hope that Freddy's chopper will fly here tonight."

"But if you are ordered to bed, how are you going to get to the helo deck?"

"I don't know, yet. I have to figure out a way to get back on duty status so that I can take my place on helo fire rescue team. Follow me to my berthing compartment before the Hulk catches me."

"What's up with your chief?"

"He's pissed off at me right now. Chief Shea pulled rank on him and pulled me off duty status. I got into it with Jaffe just a few minutes ago when I put myself back on watch. He gave me a direct order to get to bed. Now I have two direct orders making me go to bed."

"That's gonna screw things up. Oh, I forgot to tell you Matty heard about your accident on the ship's radio. He told me to come find you and see if you're OK. He is really worried about getting caught. He said it was treason."

"He's right. Aiding the enemy is grounds for treason."

"But Catholics going to mass aren't the enemy."

"Norman. Were you out sick when they taught us about treason in boot camp? Don't you remember Article 104[1] of the

---

[1] Uniform Code of Military Justice - 904. Article 104. Aiding the Enemy - 10. Punitive Articles
Any person who-

Uniform Code of Military Justice? Good Grief. They drilled that into us."

"Well, I didn't go to the same boot camp as you," he said, looking down at the deck.

"Part of Article 104 states that any person who knowingly gives intelligence to or communicates with the enemy, either directly or indirectly; shall suffer death. Heck, we're at war. The captain could legally have me executed if he caught me trying to tell Freddy to warn the villagers."

"But Catholics going to mass aren't the enemy. And we aren't warning the villagers, we're warning the priest."

"If they think that the priest is hiding ammunition under his church, then he is the enemy. This conversation is giving me a headache. I'm going to have to sit down." We sat with our backs against the bulkhead in an exterior passageway. I worried that the Hulk would get to my berthing compartment and not find me there. Norman and I began tossing ideas, rapid fire, back and forth. He proposed that he find Freddy. I told him that he would not be allowed on the helo deck when a chopper was arriving. If the chopper only came for fuel, he would not get the chance. And, on top of all that, he did not know who Freddy was. Among Norman, Matty and me, I was the only one authorized to be on the helo deck. The urgency of the situation made our plight all that much more troublesome.

"I'll have to risk disobeying a direct order. I have an obligation to humanity and to the Church to save the villagers."

"But how, if you are ordered to stay in bed?"

"This is a horrible dilemma. I'm damned if I do and I'm damned if I don't."

Pointing skyward, Norman said, "Look, there is a chopper headed our way."

The sun shone so brightly against the blue sky that my eyes refused to focus, choosing to shed tears instead. I could feel my

---

(1) aids or attempts to aid, with arms, ammunition, supplies, money, or other things, or

(2) without proper authority, knowingly harbors or protects or gives intelligence to or communicates or corresponds with or holds any intercourse with the enemy, either directly or indirectly; shall suffer death or other such punishment as a court martial or military commission may direct.

196

palms getting sweaty. My heart took the down elevator and began pumping on top of my stomach, making me feel queasy.

"This is the moment of truth, Norman. I have to go up to the helo decks and hope that the Hulk won't spot me before I get to Freddy. I just hope that he is on board."

Leaving Norman, my head began to sweat, racing my palms to see who could produce the most liquid. My back joined the race as I felt sweat sliding down my back. I stopped at the bottom of the ladder leading to the helo deck. The air felt thicker, and the smell of the diesel fumes was far more pungent than usual. Whop, whop, whop, came the sound of the helicopter blades. Running up the ladder, I passed the point of no return. I stood at the top of the ladder not far from my usual station. No one seemed to notice. Their attention was focused on the incoming chopper. I kept turning around, looking out for the Hulk and for the hospital corpsman.

When the helicopter blades came to a rest, and one of the crew secured one of the blades with a tie to the deck, my heart pumped as loudly as the whop, whop, whop of the helicopter blades. I strained to see if Freddy was in the chopper.

"What is taking them so long to get out of the chopper," I said, not expecting an answer.

My heart nearly jumped out of my throat when I heard a voice say, "Wow, that is one big bandage you've got." It was one of my fire crew. "Are you OK?"

"I'll be alright for now. You just pay attention to your job."

My heart hopped back to its rightful place, albeit at a rabbit's pace. A helicopter crewman stood on the other side of the chopper. It looked like it could be Freddy, but I couldn't be sure. But what I was sure about was that the longer I stayed on the helo deck, the greater likelihood that I would be caught. Whereas it was normal for me to stand behind the fire crew to give direction, it was not normal for me to walk out onto the flight deck. My job on the rescue team situated me behind the scenes directing the action. I felt like a cornered cat, the hackles on my back standing at attention. I inhaled deeply and walked around the front of the chopper. The helicopter crewman that I spotted earlier, walked around the back of the chopper at the same time. I saw his feet as he disappeared around the chopper.

I felt exposed and my body began to vibrate uncontrollably. I picked up my pace as I rounded the back of the chopper in pursuit of the crewman. I couldn't run without drawing unwanted attention to myself. Coming around I saw Freddy dragging the fuel hose over to the chopper. I looked from side to side. Just as I was about to approach Freddy, I noticed Shea. "What is he doing here," I whispered to myself. I froze and slowly turned back toward the other side of the chopper. I could feel the breath leaving my nostrils the way it did in the New England winter, as if it were carrying a heavy load of vapor. I hid behind the chopper until Shea passed by. I heard him asking for the pilot. Someone told him that he went down to the ship's store. When Shea left, I rounded the helicopter and walked towards Freddy. When I said, "Hey Freddy, I need to ask you something." The crewman turned around and replied, "I'm not Freddy. I'm Pete. What's ya need?"

I froze. "Uh, nothing. Freddy is a friend and I just wanted to chat."

"Freddy's on one of the other choppers," he said. "He likes coming here. He'll probably show up later."

"Thanks," I said as I turned and wobbled my way down the ladder.

35 – FORCED SILENCE

The disappointment of mistaken identity weighed on my shoulders like the sacks of dried potatoes that we carried on board to make fake French fries. The French fries looked real, they just didn't taste right. Realizing that the helicopter crewman was not Freddy greatly disappointed and worried me. I didn't know if I would get another chance to get back on the helo deck if and when Freddy actually arrived.

At that moment, I had to get back to the berthing compartment and into bed before either Chief Jaffe or Chief Shea caught me. As I walked back to my berthing compartment, Leo and Spook stopped me and asked to see my stitches. I could feel my neck muscles tighten as I snapped back at them saying, "Mind your own business. I'm not going to be a circus for anyone!" Leaving them with their mouths open, I wondered, "Where did that come from? Did I really say that to them?"

My pace began to slow down. The ship became silent, quiet. The passageway grew dimmer than normal. I felt like I was walking through the water. My forward motion halted when I arrived at the ladder leading down to my berthing compartment. I stared forward, not looking at anything. The sound of the ships engines rumbled into a buzz that did not allow another sound to enter the openings in my head.

"Are you OK?" Bruce asked when he saw me standing, motionless, holding on to an electrical conduit. I could not break the thump imposed silence. "You look pretty weird," he said as he walked away, continuing his sounding & security watch.

About 30 minutes later, he found me stuck in the same place. "Ensign Denny wanted to see you in the log room, but I told him that you were ordered to your rack. Why are you still here? Are you OK?"

I could not answer. I pushed through the blubbery air, one foot in front of the other, down the ladder towards my berthing compartment. By the time I reached the bottom step, I felt as if my legs were tangled in seaweed. I had come to a full stop at the fire hose. "What is happening to me?" My thoughts began to race, "Why are the lights so dim in here? Why can't I move? Everything is slow, too slow." My heart beat slowed its rhythm to a turtle's pace.

The first class Hull Tech flew down the ladder. After asking me several questions to which I made no response, he turned and ran up the ladder. It seemed as if he had turned around at the top of the ladder and brought a gang to stare at me.

I grabbed hold of a pipe to steady myself. My entire body tingled as if all the muscles had fallen asleep and were beginning to awaken. My stomach started to cramp. I opened my eyes wide trying to see where I was headed. Everything had become dark, hot and damp. When the first class Hull Tech grabbed my arm, I screamed, "Don't touch me!" The sound of my own voice gave me a jolt. A million pin pricks stabbed me where he grabbed my arm.

Chief Corpsman, Shea, pulled me off the pipe and onto the deck. I felt him putting something around my arm. I heard Chief Jaffe's voice, oozing napalm, as he yelled down the ladder, "Is he faking it?"

"Not with a blood pressure of 185 over 110." Shea, spitting contempt fueled fire, shouted back. Taking a syringe, he injected my arm with what I later discovered to be valium.

"Get me a stretcher!" I barely heard him call.

Unrecognizable sailors wrapped the canvas shipboard stretcher tightly around my body. They were able to lift me up the ladders, around tight corners and into sickbay with adrenaline induced ease. Being wrapped into the stretcher, made me feel like a giant burrito. The thought of being a human burrito should have made me laugh. The blow to my head must have caused my humor to leak out along with the rivulets of my blood. My thighs and my shoulders felt each foot step taken by the stretcher bearers. Mouths moved on the faces of those all around me, but I heard no sound.

They laid me on the exam table back in sickbay. The lights glared into my eyes. The smell of rubbing alcohol attacked my nose.

"Are you taking any drugs?" Chief Shea asked.

I didn't answer. I looked at him for a moment. I took a big breath and said, "No. The only drugs I have are the ones you gave me."

"Where do you keep your toiletries bag? In your locker?"

"Yes. It is right in the front, behind the door. You can't miss it."

I felt that this was a stroke of luck. I could feel a smile lift my eyelids. *If they want my toiletry bag*, I thought, *they must be calling for a helicopter to take me to the aircraft carrier. Maybe Freddy will be on the chopper that picks me up. Then I could tell him to warn the priest.* "Oh, No," I voiced, realizing that Freddy doesn't fly the choppers that transport sailors between ships.

"What's the matter?" Powell asked.

"You aren't going to fly me to the carrier are you?"

"Not very likely, even though I think you should be seen by a real doctor."

"Then why did Shea ask me for my toiletry bag?"

"Jaffe told him that you were probably taking drugs and that is why you ended up back here in sickbay."

His words slapped me so hard that I almost fell off of the exam table. Conflicting thoughts were making a whirlwind in my head, making it impossible to know what to feel. I felt relieved that I was not being taken off the ship and losing my chance to contact Freddy. At the same time, I felt angry that Jaffe backhandedly accused me of taking drugs. Tears flowed down my face and into my ears. I was caught in a nightmare from which I could not awaken.

Chief Shea returned and rummaged through some drawers in sickbay.

"I'll be honest with you. Jaffe and I went through your locker looking for dope. We didn't find any. So I'm not taking any chances on your condition. I'm going to insert an IV into you to get you stable and keep you from going into shock."

Even though he tried to find a vein by stabbing both of my arms several times, Shea was unsuccessful. Looking at Powell, as he threw the needle into the sharps container, he said, "You watch him until 20:00. I'll take over until midnight. Then you take over again. Come and get me if he gets any worse. I'm going to grab something to eat. Do you want me to bring you anything?"

"No thanks." Powell said, "His blood pressure is 160 over 90. It's coming down, but I want it closer to normal before I get a bite to eat."

Forty minutes later, my blood pressure dropped closer to normal; 132 over 92. Tapping me on the chest, Powell said, "Stay put while I go get us both something to eat. I'll be right back."

37 – MAKING AMENDS WITH FREDDY

"Hey, what's this bullshit about me owing you money?" Freddy yelled, as Powell nudged me awake.

It took a while for my eyes to focus. Freddy wore a frown. Powell's bottom lip bulged out under his mustache. I scowled at Powell. He lifted his palms up to his shoulders and tilted his head to the right.

"He insisted on knowing why I was bringing him down here," he said.

I clenched my teeth and continued scowling at Powell. I had asked him not to say anything to Freddy about the money. I had desperately needed to talk to Freddy before we bombed the church. Now that the killing had been done, I didn't want to see Freddy and explain the lie and my inability to stop the bombing. Freddy, knew nothing of this, of course.

Powell and Freddy stood by the side of my rack waiting for me to respond to Freddy's question. Freddy's lips were pursed, holding back word bayonets that were readying themselves to cut me for falsely accusing him of owing me money. I sat up slowly, careful not to bang my head on the pipes overhead above my rack. I felt like a vulture's prey wanting to die before being eaten alive.

"Powell, don't you have something to do?" I asked.

"Nope."

"I would like to talk to Freddy alone, if you don't mind."

"Ah, of course, I almost forgot. You need to make your dope deal," Powell said with a toothy grin. The wink of his eye punched me in the stomach, making me think that he may be serious. He walked away from us.

Freddy's mouth dropped as his eyes flew around the compartment, returning to the door that he had entered. I could see that he was mentally preparing an escape route.

Powell didn't get far. He stopped just outside the door.

"I thought you were leaving," I said.

Still grinning, he replied, "Freddy needs an escort."

The hair on my back stood up as my back muscles tensed. "I'll be his escort."

"You can't. You are not allowed to leave your rack."

"I'm out of here," Freddy said as he turned and headed toward the door. "I don't know what you two are up to, but I don't want any part of it."

"Freddy, wait." I pleaded. "There's something that I have to tell you and it has nothing to do with dope or money."

Powell's toothy grin teased me as he stood at the door. I didn't want him to hear what I needed to say to Freddy.

"Damn it, Powell. Can't you leave and come back in ten minutes?"

He crossed his arms and shook his head. "Nope."

I sighed and made him promise not to divulge anything he heard me tell Freddy. When I asked Powell if he had heard about the morning's bombing, he looked like he had bitten into a lemon.

"Yeah, Freddy just told me that we blew up a Catholic church."

Freddy rubbed his hand over his face. Looking up at me he said, "My guardian angel must be looking out for me."

"How so?" I asked.

"One of my buddies asked me if I wanted to go to mass at a

Catholic church in one of the villages. I didn't really want to go, but I said yes, anyway. When we asked the lieutenant for permission, he assigned us to a supply mission. The lieutenant must have known."

"Lucky for you," Powell said.

"Yeah, lucky for me," Freddy said, shaking his head and throwing his hands up. "But why blow up a Catholic church, especially during a Sunday mass? That's evil."

"Naval Intelligence told us that the Viet Cong were hiding ammo under the church," I said. "Our captain wanted a high body count. And yes, that is evil. It makes me want to puke."

"It makes me sick too," Powell said.

I asked Freddy how he found out about the church bombing. He told me that after making their supply run, they had been sent to the bombing site to assist in the cleanup, if necessary, and for a body count. He estimated 153 dead and said that there was no evidence of any ammunition hidden under the church.

"I hate doing body counts almost as much as I hate picking up our dead," he said. Freddy put his hand over his mouth and breathed in deeply. "The ants attacking their eyes always give me the willies."

"Just listening to you tell me about the ants gives me nightmares," I said.

"As we were finishing the body count, we caught fire from a sniper," Freddy said as his eyes looked inward, replaying the scene. "I saw him hiding in a tree."

"Did you get him?" Powell asked.

"Yeah, we got him good," Freddy said. "We took flight in our chopper, keeping our sights on him. When the other gunner shot him, he got his foot caught in a crook of a tree. He was hanging upside down trying to free himself."

"Did he get loose?" Powell asked.

"I helped the little bastard," Freddy said, laughing. "I shot his foot off with my machine gun."

He saw my eyes back peddle into my head.

"You have no room for complaint," he said. "You don't have to deal with the ants." Freddy's face relaxed as he turned his face up to look me in the eyes. "So what is it that you wanted to tell me?"

My palms glistened with moisture and beads of sweat stood look out on my forehead. I inhaled slowly, "I am really sorry that I got you caught up in all of this."

Freddy grabbed hold of a rack beneath me as the ship rolled over a swell. He hadn't earned his sea legs.

"What does that have to do with dope and lying about me owing you money?" he asked.

"Everything and nothing," I said.

"What do you mean?"

"Powell thought you and I were making a dope deal."

"It looked pretty suspicious," Powell said. "Especially with the way you've been acting since you got hit on the head."

"What's with the money you claim I owe you?" Freddy asked, glaring at me and punching his fist in his other hand.

"I wanted Powell to bring you down to see me when and if you landed your chopper. He said that he didn't have time. I needed your help, and I didn't trust Powell enough to let him know what I was really trying to do. So I made up a story about you owing me money."

"What were you trying to do?" Freddy asked.

"Don't you dare repeat what I'm going to say." I clenched my teeth. Heat flushed up to my face. I took a big breath and let it out slowly, my lips trembling. I turned to face Freddy and said, "I wanted to ask you to warn villagers about the Sunday morning bombing."

"What! I couldn't do that. Warning those Gooks is treason."

"I know that Freddy. Aren't you Catholic?"

"Yeah. So what?"

"You wouldn't kill people going to Sunday mass, would you?"

"Of course not," Freddy said.

"I was going to request that you ask the priest to hold mass somewhere other than in the church. That wouldn't be treason, would it?"

"Yes, it still would." He paused, rubbed his chin and let out a heavy sigh. "But, since you put it that way, I would've warned the priest."

Powell piped in telling us that he would have told Freddy himself, if I had asked him.

"I couldn't trust anyone," I said. "And now that you know,

you need to forget that this conversation ever took place. If anyone finds out that we tried to save the villagers, we could be tried and executed for treason."

36 - NO! NOT JEREMY!

I strolled along the water's edge, enjoying myself, kicking the cool and ultra-clear water onto the sand. The sea salt wafted in to my nostrils as the early morning sunshine warmed my cheeks. Looking up from the water, I saw a tall and very beautiful Vietnamese woman walking out of the jungle. She wore a shimmering green tunic with gold trim and matching pants. Three teenage boys, wearing only shorts, were laughing and talking to each other as they walked along a short distance behind her. I recognized them. My eyes grew wide. I began gulping for air. Those were the boys we killed on our first day.

"He was watching us. He let us die," one of the boys said to the Vietnamese woman as he pointed at me with his left hand. His words came out of his mouth like ship's ropes, wrapping around my stomach and squeezing all of the air out of my lungs.

The Vietnamese woman walked up to me, her gaze warm and caring. She asked, "That wasn't you. Was it?"

I knew that she knew that it was me. She wasn't trying to find out. She was addressing the man I was supposed to be. I wanted to say that I was sorry, but no sound came out of my mouth.

"Look how beautiful they are," she said as she turned and pointed to the boys. "They make their mothers proud. Why would anyone want to hurt them?"

The tone of her voice was firm yet nurturing, giving me the courage to say, "Yes, that was me watching. I am so sorry that I made their mothers cry." Moisture left my throat making is hard to swallow. "I didn't stop the killing."

"Look into their eyes," she said. "They do not hate you."

Trembling, I turned my head towards them. The boys came closer, becoming younger with each step, until they became toddlers. The Vietnamese woman took my hand and said, "See how beautiful they are."

The boys began running toward me, their arms outstretched and their faces aglow. As they ran closer to me, each of the boys looked exactly like my two-year-old son, Jeremy. I stood, mesmerized. Our five inch gun fired at them. I tried to stop them by putting my hands up and shouting, "Wait! Wait!"

The sound of my own voice echoed and raced back to our first day on the gun line. They didn't hear me. They kept running toward me. Sand dust, smoke, fire and body parts flew at me from the blast knocking me over. "Oh God, not Jeremy. Not my son! Noooooooooo!" I cried.

The Vietnamese woman wrapped one of her arms around my shoulder and the other around my head, pulling it into her bosom. She stroked my head, as tears slid down my cheeks and snot oozed out of my nose and over my mustache. Her hands were soft and warm, like my mother's hands.

"We must do what we must do," she said. I began to fall asleep in her arms. "We must do what we must do," she repeated, her voice fading. "We must do what we must do."

She jerked my arm and startled me awake, forcing my eyes to open. The bright overhead lights of sickbay made me squint.

"You must have been having a nightmare," Powell said, removing the blood pressure cuff from my arm. "You were putting your hands up and yelling, 'no.' Your blood pressure has gone back up. You're sweating and you feel clammy. How's your headache, on a scale of one to ten?"

I heaved a sigh of relief, realizing it was just a nightmare. "It hurts. It's about an eight," I said.

Powell spun around and opened a medicine cabinet. He pulled down a white plastic jar, read the label, opened it and shook one pill out into a tiny metal cup. "Sit up" he said, "I am giving you a Darvon for the pain."

Desperate to know, I asked, "When can I go back to my rack?

"It's only 18:30. We're going to keep you here all night for observation, so just relax. I brought some food and a glass of milk, if you feel up to it."

My head throbbed. I pushed my arm against the exam table and swung my legs over the side. The room swirled. When it came to a rest, I accepted the glass of milk. I poked the roast beef with my fork. I held it up to my mouth but when its stale aroma entered my nostrils, I put it down. I took another swallow of milk, and then put the glass down on the tray. My teeth clenched and a grimace flashed over my face as a stinging pain stabbed my head. Air rushed in between the spaces in my teeth. As the air left my nostrils, I turned my head to look at Powell and winced once again from the pain.

"Did you say that you are going to keep me all night?" I asked knowing that I had to get hold of Freddy to tell him to warn the priest that we were going to blow up the church the following morning.

"You are going to let me report for helo ops, right?" I asked.

"Helo ops?"

"Yes, the helicopter fire rescue team." I reminded him that I was the scene leader for the team, and the person in charge of that crew. I dared not tell him that I needed to ask Freddy to save the church.

Powell shook his head and rolled his eyes. "You must be really out of it. Did you forget that Shea pulled you off of all duty?"

I did not respond. I had been hoping that he had forgotten. I yawned and took another drink of milk, which helped clear the cobwebs from my mind.

"You look really agitated. Is your headache getting worse?"

"No, no." I lied. "I just need to be at helo ops."

"What's bugging you? Just relax. Someone has already taken your place."

My body sat still, while my eyes made laps around the sickbay bulkheads, as if they were lost and looking for anything familiar. The thought of the priest and the villagers getting blown up on Sunday morning was inciting me to find a way to get hold of Freddy.

"Have any of the helicopter crewmen ever come to see you in sickbay?"

"Funny that you should mention that. Last week, one of the crewmen came in asking for a bandage. He had cut the back of his hand as he jumped out of the chopper. He said that he knew you."

My eye brows stood at attention. "Was his name Freddy?"

"I really don't remember. Maybe."

Hearing this, my hope surged full speed ahead that I might be able to contact Freddy.

"How about doing me a favor when the next helicopter arrives?"

"What kind of favor?"

"If Freddy is on the next chopper, ask him to come down and see me."

"I don't have time for that, "he said.

His response reversed the screws on my hope. I opened the hold in my brain in hopes of finding a solution.

"Freddy owes me some money," I lied. "If he doesn't see me, he won't pay me."

"Do you want me to ask him for the money he owes you?"

"No, no. He won't pay you. He won't trust you."

"Are you doing a dope deal?"

His question side swiped me, even though he was grinning widely.

The Darvon slowed down the screws of my thinking. I felt as if wind had been taken out of my sails and I needed to find someone to ignite my boilers. The flashlight that Shea used to look at my eyes reminded me of the ship's signal light, which in turn reminded me of a flash on a camera.

I picked up my fork and looked down at the food tray, to avoid eye contact.

"Freddy wanted to buy a camera and he was short ten bucks," I hoped that I wouldn't screw up the lie I was making up. "Since I was the only one he knew on the ship, he asked me to lend him the money. I told him that he had to pay me, and only me."

"What's the matter, don't you trust your fellow shipmates?"

I could feel droplets of sweat creating canals down my back. His questions were irritating me. Why was he asking me all of these questions? Why couldn't he just say, OK? My head felt like it had run aground. I didn't want to try to make up plausible answers to his questions. I wanted to dock my brain, tie it to a pier, and take a nap.

"It's not my shipmates that I am worried about," I said, "I really don't know Freddy that well. I don't want to give him the opportunity to lie and say that he gave the money to someone on the ship to give to me."

"OK, I'll get Freddy for you, if I'm not busy."

"Thanks, and please don't tell him about the money he owes me."

"Why not?"

"I don't want him to make an excuse for not seeing me and therefore, not paying up."

All that thinking made me feel like a tugboat towing an overloaded tanker. I had run out of gas and needed to rest.

I handed Powell my food tray, telling him I was too tired to eat. I returned to a reclining position and put my left arm over my eyes. "Powell, can you turn down the lights, please."

"No problem. While you're taking a snooze, I'm going to step outside for some air." When he opened the door, he turned back to me, lowered his voice and added, "I still think you're doing a dope deal."

I shooed him away with my right hand, allowing the rolling of the ship to tow my consciousness away to other shores.

BOOM! My arms flailed, as I attempted to sit up. The safety belts retrained me from leaving the exam table. Opening my eyes, I realized that I was still lying in sick bay and I had been dreaming. I unbuckled the strap, sat up and stretched.

"I see that the rocket launch made you jump and woke you up."

"What? Did you say rocket?" His words stomped on my heart's accelerator. My eyes darted around the room in search of the clock. "What time is it?"

"It's a little past 08:00," Powell said, after he lit a Marlborough and blew out the smoke through his nostrils. "You had a rough night last night. When I took over for Shea this morning at 04:00 he told me that your blood pressure had been all over the place."

My ears buzzed and anchors pulled my heart down to my stomach. I found the clock and stared at it. *How long have I been lying here on the exam table? Is it Sunday morning?* The drugs cluttered my mind like a seaweed forest. *What was I trying to do? Oh yeah.* "Did Freddy show up?" I asked.

"Nope. No choppers last night. It rained pretty hard. Sorry you couldn't make your dope deal," he said, as he winked.

I rolled my eyes. "Do you know what the target was?" I asked and immediately wished I hadn't. I couldn't risk arousing suspicion that I was trying to warn the priest. I wouldn't put it past our captain to use me as an example of what happens to traitors. He'd have no qualms executing me before a firing squad on the helo deck. My mind created the scene; my hands handcuffed behind my back, blindfold over my eyes, and a row of my shipmates pointing their rifles at me. Powell's voice jerked me back into sickbay.

"We don't know what the target was. They don't divulge that kind of information to non-combatant hospital corpsman. But it must be something big for them to fire the rocket."

My shoulders sank. *I bet they blew up the church with the villagers attending Sunday service. All for a body count.* Tears overflowed their banks creating streams along the side of my nose. Embarrassment flushed my cheeks making them hot. I was grateful that Powell made no comment about my tears.

"After you eat some breakfast," he said, "I'll walk you back to your rack to make sure you get there."

As we strolled along the passageways, back to my berthing compartment, my mind conjured a Vietnamese priest holding up the bread and wine as the rocket crashed through the church walls bringing, screams, fire and death, in lieu of salvation.

"You're a Catholic, right?" I asked.

"Yeah, but where did that question come from?" His eyes narrowed. I couldn't tell if he was annoyed or concerned. "Your concussion has me worried, especially with the weird way you've been acting. Why do you want to know if I'm a Catholic?"

I wanted to tell Powell that the captain waited until the church was full of people before blowing it up. But I knew I shouldn't. "Will we go to hell if we kill people going to Sunday Mass? I mean if we do it on purpose?"

Powell stopped. His forehead wrinkled as he tapped his own head. "I don't think it's a good idea for you to fill your head with depressing thoughts." A smile came over his face. "Oh, you think that the rocket we fired hit a church, don'tcha? We don't know. The fire control technicians just set their computers with the coordinates that they are given, and then push the buttons to fire the rockets. No one tells them what they're bombing."

"But what if we did know, Powell? What if we blew up a church full of people on Sunday morning? Would God send us to hell?"

Powell rubbed the back of his head. "I doubt it. We'd have to know ahead of time. And we'd have to be able to stop it. Jesus, Mushroom, stop worrying about things you have no control over."

We continued on our way in silence. Arriving at the door to my berthing compartment, Powell said, "Stay in bed. We won't know what our rocket hit until the fly boys give us the body count. In the meantime, try thinking about the whores in Olongapo or your girlfriend back home. I'll come back in a little while to check on you. If your friend Freddy shows up, I'll bring him down here."

I pulled back the door latch and stepped over the threshold to my berthing compartment. My clothes were strewn across my rack and my locker door was still open. Jaffe and Shea didn't have the decency to put my things back the way they found them after they searched for drugs and came up empty.

I sat on the deck and cried. I didn't want to be there, aboard the USS Trippe. *How could I justify the bombing of a Catholic church, filled with people attending Sunday mass?* There simply was no justification. This was a grave sin requiring me to go to confession. I committed a sin of omission; a sin of not doing what I was supposed to do. Doing nothing to stop the bombing made me a coward. These thoughts bombarded me while I sat and cried. After what seemed like a long time, I looked at the ship's clock on the bulkhead. The dial showed 09:30. Putting my belongings back into my locker helped me pull myself back together.

I climbed up into the top of three racks, slid under the white bed sheet and laid my head on a towel that I had placed over my pillow to catch any blood that might ooze out of the dressing. *If the rocket didn't hit the church, what did it hit? Was I worrying for nothing?* My head throbbed. *Tomorrow I will find Matty to see what he knows.* I tried to push the thoughts of the church bombing out of my head by thinking of the ladies of the night in Olongapo. As I closed my eyes, memories of the previous night's dream; the Vietnamese woman and the three boys who turned into my son, replaced my thoughts of scantily clad girls, with the jolting awkwardness of ship's screws re-entering the water in high rough seas. I sank into a restless sleep.

38 – THREE DAYS OF SILENCE

Someone shook my shoulder to wake me up at 10:30 the following morning. Turning my head to see who was shaking me, I met Chief hospital corpsman Shea's eyes as he stood next to my top rack. He asked me to climb down and sit on the deck. After taking my blood pressure, he told me that I could go back on normal duty. He turned and walked through the compartment door.

I hadn't gotten off the deck, when I heard the clanking of footsteps coming down the ladder. Jaffe asked Shea, "When can I put that lazy Mexican back on watch?"

My cheeks flushed and my hands clenched.

Chief Jaffe wore a smug smile as he sauntered into the berthing compartment. "Your next sounding and security watch starts at noon. Get ready." He made an about face and left.

I removed my underwear, wrapped a towel around my waist and headed for the showers. As the warm water sprayed over face, pangs came from my stomach, reminding me to hurry and give myself time to eat. Drying myself off, I remember being taught in boot camp that the chiefs care for their men. Chief Jaffe, my chief, cared for the white sailors. He didn't bother to ask me how I was feeling. He only wanted to know when I could go back on watch.

My mind churned as I walked up to the mess decks to grab a bite to eat before I started my watch. My failure to warn the priest about the church bombing gnawed at my stomach. I felt as if I needed to see a priest and go to confession for my failure. Thinking about the priest brought back memories of my time studying for the priesthood. The seminary I went to conducted silent retreats every couple of months.

"Silence is a gift," Father Murphy would tell us. "This is your time with God. Use this time to think things out, to broaden your understanding, to connect with the divine."

I had failed to save the villagers from being bombed while they attended mass in the Catholic Church. The memory of their death was a demon haunting me, reminding me that I should've worked harder to save them, telling me that I had committed a mortal sin, worthy of the fires of hell. I needed the gift of silence to help me sort things out. But how could I go on a silent retreat when our ship spends its days bombing the shore, killing more people?

I sat alone, picking at the boring roast beef sandwich that we had every day, trying to find an alternative to a silent retreat. Who could I talk to that would understand? I remembered that Hospital corpsman Powell spent twelve years in Catholic school. We had many discussions about Catholicism and religion, in general. The U.S.S. Trippe's blowing up a Catholic church when it was full of people was repulsive to Powell. I assumed that he would be willing to help me out.

I felt guilty tossing half of my sandwich away as I got up to leave. Growing up, my mother made us eat everything on our plates. "There are children starving in China," she would say. Guilt slithered from my mind into my body and stole my appetite. I wobbled my way to sick bay and knocked on the door. Powell opened the top half of the Dutch door, leaned down, placing his elbows on the door's shelf. He was a big man, heavy set, a little over six feet tall with broad shoulders. He had a gentle face that usually made me feel that he had my best interest at heart. His eyes scrunched together and his lips pursed.

"Did I interrupt you, Doc? I need some advice." Powell liked being called "Doc." We had no real doctors on board. Being called Doc gave the hospital corpsmen a sense of status, a sign of respect. The ship only had two hospital corpsmen and he was the junior of the two.

His face relaxed, he smiled and asked, "What's on your mind?"

"I need a religious retreat where I can be in silence for a few days."

Stroking his chin he asked, "A silent religious retreat? Why?"

My left knee began to twitch. I knew that Powell couldn't give me a religious retreat on the ship. His questions made me clench my teeth. I needed him to help me. I wanted him to listen. I didn't answer him. I wasn't sure that I could word it so that he'd understand.

"You'll have to wait until we get back to Subic Bay to ask the base Chaplain if he's offering one. Do you know where the chapel is?"

"I can't wait 'til then. The devil's biting my ass and I need to sort things out. I need a religious retreat now."

"I can give you pills for headaches, I can sew up your scalp or set your bones, but there is no way in hell that I can give you a religious retreat."

"I have an idea that I want to bounce off of you."

"What makes you think that I can help?"

"You went to Catholic school, and you went on silent retreats, right?"

"Yes, but we did them in a church and the surrounding grounds. There's no church on board. Hell, we can't even get a chaplain to fly over here every once in a while. We have to wait until we get back to the Philippines to go to church."

"I am going to do my own silent retreat. I know I can do it. I want you to let me do it in sickbay when I'm not on watch."

"What? Sickbay is not a fuckin' church."

"I know. It's a place where I can hide and be alone without being disturbed."

Powell opened the bottom half of the Dutch door and let me in. He pointed to a chair and asked me to sit. He jumped up onto the exam table and looked down at me. "Why do you want to do this? Why now? Can't you wait until we get back to the Philippines?"

"The villagers won't let me sleep."

Powell paced the deck in front of me, stroking his chin. "Villagers?" He continued pacing, then bent down and whispered, "Are you talking about the villagers who we blew up on Sunday when they were going to church?"

"Yes. I can't stop thinking about them. It's making my headache worse."

Powell jumped down from the exam table. He looked at the medicine cabinet as if searching for a pill he could give me. I hoped he wouldn't do that. I didn't want a pill. I wanted time, alone.

"OK, I'll let you use sickbay, but Chief Shea won't like it if he finds you in here."

"If he does, I'll tell him that I came in to see you about my headache. If you aren't in here when he finds me, I'll tell him that you had to leave for a moment."

"But then you will be breaking your silence."

"I don't want to get you into trouble." I sighed. "I'll talk when I have no other option."

"How are you going to stand your sounding and security watch? You need to tell the bridge what is going on and what you find on your rounds. You'll be breaking your silence again."

"I could write what I need to say on a piece of paper and then show it to whoever needs to see it. That way I won't really be talking."

"That will only work, if nothing out of the ordinary happens. What about when your friends want to talk to you?"

"I'll have another note that says, 'I'm not talking because I don't want to.'"

"Why don't you just write that you are doing a silent religious retreat?"

"They won't understand and they'll insist that I explain it to them."

"And they won't expect you to explain that you're not talking because you don't want to?"

"They'll just think that I'm goofing around and they'll play along."

"You might have a point. But what if something happens that requires you to talk?"

"Like I said, I'll talk when there's no other option."

"You're crazy for trying. I understand, I think. When are you going to start your crazy ass religious retreat?"

"I'll start when I take over the sounding and security watch at noon."

He gave me an impish smile as he made the sign of the cross over me and said, "You have my blessing, my son."

I tore a sheet of paper from the sounding and security clipboard into a couple of pieces, about four inches long, when I took over the watch. Taking my time on the rolling seas to write legibly, I jotted, 'Sounding and security all secure, sir' on one piece, and 'I'm not talking because I don't want to.' on the other. The ink wasn't even dry when Norman came up and asked me to join him on the fantail. I handed him the piece of paper that said, 'I'm not talking because I don't want to.'

He looked at it and laughed. His eyes twinkled and the tone of his voice rose as he asked, "Will you talk if I make you a cinnamon roll?"

I shook my head, 'no.'

"How about if I roll you a joint?"

I burst out laughing.

"Isn't laughing like talking?" Norman asked.

Again I shook my head, 'no.' Looking at him, I pointed to the clipboard, turned my head forward and walked away to do my rounds.

Dear Jesus, Mary and Joseph, please help me on my retreat by keeping any more people from talking to me, I prayed silently. *Please help me sort this out.*

It seemed as if the saints listened to my prayers because no one talked to me during my watch.

Over and over I replayed the sequence of events in my head:

Matty telling me that we were going to blow up the church,

finding a solution,

the forward hatch falling on my head,

sneaking up to the helo deck,

waking up and finding out that the church had been blown

up. Why didn't God help me warn the priest? Was it because I didn't get on my knees and pray for help first? God wouldn't punish them because of what I didn't do, would he? Why would God let us blow them up?

When I completed my first cycle of soundings, I trudged up the ladder to the bridge. Wearing a nervous smile, I removed the note from the clipboard that said, 'Sounding & Security all secure, Sir' and handed it to the officer on deck. Nervousness oozed into my stomach as I waited. He held my little note with two hands, studied it and looked at me over his glasses. My hands began to sweat. I took another breath and forced a smile. He walked over to a shelf, pulled out a pencil and gave the note a check mark. Shaking his head and rolling his eyes, he handed the note back me. I could barely contain a laugh as I saluted him and walked out of the bridge. My note had eight check marks by the end of my watch.

I ran down to my berthing compartment, opened my locker and moved my clothes around hunting for a crucifix, a rosary, something religious. Surprised at not finding anything, I pulled out the last letter from home and read the last few words, 'We are praying for you.' Having nothing else, I folded the letter so it could fit easily into my back pocket. I put uniforms and everything else neatly away and trudged over to sickbay. I lifted my hand up to knock, when Chief Shea opened the door. My heart sank. Pretending to be just walking by, I continued on slowly. When Chief Shea passed me, I made an about face and returned to sickbay. Powell let me in when I knocked.

"I know you aren't talking. I'll be here working for two more hours, then you'll have to leave. I will only be gone for about a half hour. You can come back then, if you aren't at battle station."

I sat in the chair, while Powell, counted out pills and put them into small plastic amber bottles. Reaching into my back pocket, I pulled out the letter and made the sign of the cross. I put the letter back and closed my eyes. The chair slid to one side as the ship rolled. The sound of the ship's engine rumbled. I began to pray, 'Dear God, I am very sorry that I wasn't able to warn the priest to hold mass somewhere else. I am very sorry that I was too much of a coward to ask the captain not to blow up the church.' The ship's rocking and droning put me into a meditative trance. I saw myself knocking on the captain's door. I knocked and knocked. No one answered. I tried to turn the handle. "Captain, please open the door," I pleaded. "I need to talk to you. Please open the door."

Softly, barely audible, a woman's voice said, "No one can answer, if no one is there."

Although she spoke Vietnamese from behind the door, and I understood every word she said. Turning the handle, I opened the door and stepped over the threshold. Warm sand met my bare feet. I walked into the jungle and sat with my back against a tree. I wished I could turn back time so that I could warn the priest.

I did not turn when I felt the Vietnamese woman's hand hold mine. "You cannot go back to what no longer exists," she said.

Turning to face her, I realized that we were both nude. Shame did not come. This was a sacred moment. Warmth floated over my body, like a mother's comforting arms.

"I feel so guilty," I said. "I just wish there was something that I could do."

"There is. Look into your heart and you will find it."

"But won't God send me to hell for what I did? All those people in church are dead because I didn't warn the priest; I didn't ask the captain to stop."

"You create your own hell. God does not."

"I'm just an enlisted man. I have no power, no authority. What can I do?"

"All the power and authority you need is within you."

"Within me? Where? I'm just a coward."

"Be true to yourself and you will find it."

"How? I can't fight the Navy all by myself."

She wrapped her hand around my bicep and tightened her squeeze, saying, "When you put your intent out to the universe, it responds."

"149 over 100, and a pulse of 85," Powell said as he put away the blood pressure monitor. "Too high for my comfort. I don't know what you're meditating on, but when I saw how red your face got and saw you starting to sweat, I took your blood pressure. I have to go and you'll have to leave. Come back in a half hour, if you want."

I walked out of sickbay, dazed. My head throbbed as if a Viet Cong soldier were inside my head kicking from the inside out. As I climbed the ladder to the flying bridge, the wind blew a soothing breeze into my face. Looking out onto the water, I saw a fisherman sitting next to his toddler son in a boat. I wondered what I would say when my son asks me what I did in the war. I can't tell him that I helped kill innocent people who were going to church.

I wondered why the Vietnamese woman visited me again in my meditation. I expected Jesus, Mary or one of the saints. Who was this woman? Could she be an angel disguised as a Vietnamese woman? Why did she appear nude the last time I saw her? Would an angel do that?

The third day of my silent retreat started without incident until Chief Jaffe caught me in the passageway that led into the mess decks. The aroma of scrambled eggs, cinnamon rolls and roast beef blended with the ever present pungent odor of diesel fuel. Jaffe stood, legs apart, hands on his hips, blocking my way. "I heard that you aren't talking to anyone. How the hell are you doing your watch?"

I started to hand him my note, but he shooed it away with his hand. "I heard about your damn note and how the officer of the deck is letting you get away with your no talking shit. I don't give a shit if you don't talk to anyone else. But damn it, you're gonna talk to me. I'm giving you a direct order.

"OK, I'll talk to you. What do you want to talk about?"

"That's it?" Jaffe asked with a bewildered look on his face. "You're talking just because I gave you a direct order?"

"I'm not stupid, chief. If you need me to talk to you enough to give me a direct order, I'll talk."

"This is stupid," Jaffe said as he walked away.

"I win," I whispered.

He stopped, turned his face, glowered and said, "Don't you mess with me."

My retreat ended after three days. My only satisfaction was getting Jaffe's goat for the way he had been harassing me. I still had no answers, but somehow felt a little more at peace. Matty came by saying, "It's weird, that I haven't seen you for three days.

Norman told me that you weren't talking."

"I wasn't until Jaffe gave me a direct order to talk. So I am talking now."

"I can't believe he let you get away with it."

"He didn't. It took him three days to find out. That's when he gave me a direct order to talk."

"Three days?" Matty asked. "Your guardian angel must've been looking out for you."

Matty's face lit up like a kid who had a secret he wanted to tell. I took the bait and asked, "What's up?"

"Some sonar equipment broke," Matty said.

"That's scary, since we sail so close to shore," I said. "And there are mines hidden under the water."

Raising his eyebrows, Matty said, "We're heading for Subic Bay tomorrow morning."

"Good. That will give me a chance to get away from Jaffe for a little while."

"Don't be so sure," Matty said. "I hope your guardian angel watches over you in Subic Bay, too."

39 – DISPELLING THE LEGEND

I climbed the steel ladder to the flying bridge, stopping midway to admire the clouds soaring over the mast. They stopped and backed up, or so it seemed, at first glance. Laughing at myself, I realized that it was the ship's mast that moved as the ship rolled from side to side, not the clouds. The sky smiled happily, providing a blue stage for wispy clouds that looked like erotic dancers. Looking skyward while hanging on to the ladder's railing, I let my imagination create other sexual fantasies out of those clouds. Thoughts of Subic Bay and the ladies of the evening in Olongapo City, even for just a short break, awoke every sailor's sexual desires.

Reaching the flying bridge, I noticed the two newest crew members sitting cross legged on the deck with a signalman's manual between them. These two sailors had just arrived on the ship about two weeks earlier. I saw them come on board when they arrived by helicopter. They hadn't noticed me amid the fire rescue crew. Robby, the taller of the two, had pale white skin with a few freckles on his arms. His rust colored chest hair looked as if it were trying to climb out from his chest, over the collar of his t-shirt. Mike had jet black curly hair that accentuated his white skin. I overheard them talking about the Sunday morning bombing.

"I can't believe that they actually waited until Sunday morning to blow up a church," Mike said.

"Yeah, and it was a Catholic church," Robby said, "And I'm Catholic. Blowing up that church is just wrong."

Seeing me, Mike asked, "Hey, do you know why they blew up the church on Sunday when it was full of worshipers?"

"Our captain is into body counts. He has already killed too many innocent people and even some of our guys with what they call friendly fire. His numbers are on the negative body count side. He was hoping to move his body count into the positive number side when he blew up the church, full of people."

"That gives me the willies," Mike said.

"That's just plain crazy," Robby said.

As I started to leave and continue my Sounding and Security rounds, Robby turned to Mike and said, "Hey you know what else is crazy? You know that guy who we saw running around the ship's smokestack screaming last night, after we re-armed?

"I've never met him," Mike said.

I was about to introduce myself and thought that it might be more interesting to hear what Robby was going to say before they knew who I was. Robby's eyes sparkled as he talked to Mike. His arms moved about excitedly as he said, "That guy who screamed around the smokestack is called Mushroom. He was in a nightclub in Olongapo, lying on the dance floor with a dollar bill in his mouth. The dance girl danced around him, pulled off her panties and squatted on his face and picked up the dollar with her twat."

"No shit? You saw that?" Mike asked.

Robby did not look at Mike; he turned his head to look back at the Signalman's book in his lap. He coughed then added, "And you know what else?"

Mike's attention was fixed on every word that Robby let out of his mouth. When Mike responded with "What happened next?" Robby became animated again saying, "The dance girl told Mushroom that if he kissed her twat that she would give him two bucks. And he did."

"Oh wow!" Mike said. "Where was that? We'll definitely have to go to THAT night club when we go to Olongapo."

"Yeah, we should."

"Which night club was it?"

"Uh. I can't remember the name." Robby's eyes darted from side to side. "You know. After a few drinks they all look alike."

Stepping forward, I asked, "Really? And I suppose that after a few drinks your memory gets pretty distorted too."

"Well, yeah, a little," Robby said sheepishly while averting his eyes.

"I don't think that what you told Mike is exactly how it happened," I said.

Robby looked at Mike, then back at me. His shoulders came up, as his eyebrows came down. "How do you know? Were you there ... uh, too?"

"Yes, I was there. I'm Mushroom."

Robby's mouth dropped while Mike's eyes lit up. Mike blurted out, "You're Mushroom? That's cool!"

"Thanks," I said.

"What really happened?" Mike asked.

Robby turned his eyes downward and said, "Well, that's what I was told."

I was glad that the conversation shifted away from the church bombing to a subject that was actually fun. Since these two guys had only been on the ship two weeks, I did not know which crewmen they knew.

"If we all have liberty at the same time when we get to Subic, I will take you two to that nightclub." I said. "It's on Main Street. It's called, Kong's."

Those of us who did not have duty, were given liberty after the ship pulled into port and was moored to the dock. Barry and I left the ship with the two new crew members in tow.

I was happy that I didn't have to buy another pair of pants, like I did when we arrived in Subic Bay the first time. My weight had been dropping from the 180 pounds that I weighed when I left the States. After we crossed the river that divided the naval station from Olongapo City, Robby turned toward me and said, "That shit in that river is enough to make me gag."

"Just be glad that you don't have to earn your money by standing in that sewer river like those boys do," I said.

"Hey, Barry, I'd like you to be my counter," I said.

"Counter?" Barry asked. "Counter for what?"

"I want to see how many buns I could squeeze."

"Are you serious? This is gonna be fun. I'm also gonna count how many times you get slapped."

"I'll take my chances."

As we entered the first nightclub, a young barmaid came up and showed us to a table. I gently squeezed her buns as I sat down. She turned quickly, her frown changing to a smile, as she asked, "You buy me drink?"

"Only if you let me buy two drinks for myself and I choose which one I give you," I said.

She walked away, knowing that the bar maid's drinks are just colored water. If she drank every drink that the sailors bought for her, she would be a useless drunk barmaid before the night was half over. My hand reached out and squeezed every bun that walked by until the manager came by and told me to make up my mind and choose one girl and pay to take her to bed. I took that as my cue to move to the next nightclub. As we walked along the street I noticed the faces of the young boys who sold trinkets on the street and ran errands for the club owners. They reminded me of the Vietnamese boys that we killed. I continued squeezing buns the rest of the evening hoping to forget that we spent that last couple months killing babies and grandmothers, not just Viet Cong soldiers.

Mike, the black haired sailor, asked, "When are you going to take us to that night club that you talked about?"

Regaining my own smile, I said, "The next night club we'll get to is Kong's."

As we entered we saw a good looking girl doing a sexy dance. She smiled broadly while gyrating her butt and hips and wiggling her tits. She wore a shiny and tiny blue sequined miniskirt and halter top. Robby couldn't take his eyes off of her. She must have noticed because she danced over to our table. She took Robby by the hand and took him out on the dance floor. At first, Robby thought she was inviting him to dance. Boy was he surprised when she told him to lie on the dance floor. Robby looked like a puppy that just got yelled at. If Robby had dog ears, they would have hung down to the floor. The crowd started yelling, "Do it! Do it!" over and over again. When he saw us yelling the same thing, he shrugged his shoulders and laid his long lean body down. Since I had seen this act before, I pulled out a dollar bill and gave it to the girl.

Robby looked up at me, wondering if I had set him up. The girl took my dollar. She folded it neatly in half, lengthwise and placed it right over Robby's nose and mouth. She danced around Robby a couple of times and as she danced she pulled off her panties. The crowd hooted and hollered while they held up their bottles of San Miguel beer. The girl looked like she was really enjoying the reaction from the crowd. She was all smiles. Robby looked so funny because he just laid there with his hands by his side, almost like he was laying at attention. The girl danced from his shoes to his crotch forcing Robby to spread his legs apart. When she got to his crotch, she tickled his balls with her toes and gestured with her fingers showing a dick getting a hard on. The crowd went wild, yelling and hollering.

"I can't tell if he's squirming or enjoying it." I said.

"Probably both," Barry said.

The dance girl twirled her panties over her head and ran them over Robby's face. His face beamed bright red. When the crowd stopped hooting and hollering, she danced over his face and squatted down, picking up the dollar with her twat. The crowd roared again and applauded. She held out her hand and helped Robby stand up. For a finale, she stroked the dollar bill under Robby's nose. The guys laughed and cheered. The dancer helped Robby get to his feet. His white skin accentuated his red face.

"This is not too different from what the Admirals do to us," I said to Barry and Mike. "They entice us with words like honor and valor, then, when they have us on our backs, they shit on our faces, making us blind. As blind sailors, we join their war dance and kill and maim too many innocent people. When the dance is over, we realize that we were just cheap entertainment for the admirals. We, like Robby, end up feeling empty and cheated, not having reaped the "true" rewards."

I found myself yawning as we left Kong's. Barry had a young lady around his arm.

"I counted 48 bun squeezes and three slaps so far. Have one of these guys take over counting; I'm spending the rest of the night with this cutie."

Weariness and beer took their toll. I thanked Barry and said goodnight to Robby and Mike. I walked back to the ship alone. Ensign Denny stood at the end of the gangway. He told me that he had been looking over the sounding logs and noticed that two out of every three logs for the Sonar Equipment room shaft were always the same, day after day. He asked me to explain. I told him that the other two guys who stood the Sounding & Security were scared to go down into the sonar equipment room. They simply copied down the same figures that were there for the previous sounding.

"What are they afraid of?" he asked.

"Keegan, the first class boatswain's mate, told us that a welder fell down and died when they were building this ship. He got the guys really freaked out when he told us that the dead guy's ghost collects the ghosts of the Vietnamese that we kill and he brings them down into that hole."

"You don't believe that nonsense, do you?" Ensign Denny asked.

"Of course not. It's just spooky for them to go down there. And besides, there is no dancing girl down there willing to take off her panties to entice them to go down."

Shaking his head and rolling his eyes, he said, "Make sure that you take the soundings down there, tomorrow, when you're on watch. With all that shooting we did during general quarters when the MiGs were gunning for us, we might have taken a hit below the waterline. We can't afford to have the sonar equipment get wet and go off line when we go back out the Gulf of Tonkin, because you guys are afraid of ghosts. I want those logs to be accurate. If we are taking on water, we can fix it while we are here in Subic Bay."

I saluted ensign Denny, and made my way to my berthing compartment. I took off my civilian pants and looked at the tag showing the thirty four inch waist. The word, fat, blubbered around my head as I climbed into my rack. Laying my head on the pillow, I thought back to the beginning of our cruise and how I must have looked like a fat mafioso, from the movie, the

Godfather. After just 39 days in Viet Nam my pants were too loose to wear without a belt. I let sleep take over, hoping for dreams of squeezing 48 buns. I didn't want to think about being fat or of returning to the killing shores of Viet Nam.

40 – IT LURKS

I took heed of Ensign Denny's request when I started my watch and walked down the passageway to the hatch that led down to the sonar equipment room. Stopping at the alcove, I stared at the wheel that I needed to turn to open the hatch. My hands began to sweat as the hair on my back stood up. "There is nothing down there," I muttered under my breath, "I don't believe in ghosts. I don't care if a welder got killed when he fell down this hole. Ghosts aren't real."

I crouched down and turned the wheel, feeling an eerie resistance that made me slightly nauseous. Was someone or something on the other side trying to prevent me from going down there? This would be the perfect place for a Viet Cong to hide. My stomach muscles tightened involuntarily. Wiping my hands on my pants to dry them, I finished turning the wheel. My breathing sped up as I watched light seep out as I lifted the hatch. A rush of air blew passed my face, making my shoulder and back muscles shudder. Again, I told myself that there was nothing to be afraid of. I had been down that hatch hundreds of times and yet it still scared me. I secured the hatch in the open position and slowly peered over the edge, into the shaft, three levels down. The bottom seemed so far away as I stared down the narrow hole that was only as wide as a small shower stall. A single light, mounted near the top, illuminated the deep white hole that made me feel as if I were looking down into a very large gun barrel.

I unbuckled the holster and placed the gun, the sounding tape and clipboard adjacent to the opening, while I sat on the hatch's ledge. I felt for the ladder with my feet while squeezing my body through the small round opening, that was no bigger than the steering wheel on my car. I climbed down below until only my head was showing above the opening. Peering down, I wrapped one leg around the ladder for support. I was glad that we were in port and not in rough seas. As I climbed down the ladder, memories of how difficult it had been during our last storm occupied my mind. I remembered how the ship pitched and rolled. When I made it through the hatch, I braced myself then reached up and grabbed the gun. I waited for the ship to roll itself in the direction of the ladder. I had to hold on tightly before attempting to don the holster. I buckled the holster and reached up to grab the clipboard and sounding tape. "I don't know what I hate more," I said out loud to no one, "This rocking and rolling, or the story about the ghosts."

I took the sounding tape and clipboard in my right hand, I wrapped my wrist around one side of the ladder. Using my free hand to grip, I slowly worked my way down. The plumb bob on the sounding tape clanked against the metal treads, step after step. When I looked down, I said to myself, "If I fall, no will find me for days, since the other guys are afraid to come down here to take the required sounding." A hum from inside the sonar equipment room, made my stomach vibrate uncomfortably. It grew louder as I descended. The ship's creaking released thoughts of pirates and creepy crawlies. When I finally reached the bottom, I once again wiped the sweat from my hands. Looking up, the opening seemed as if it were a mile high. The eeriness did not dissipate as I unscrewed the top of the sounding tube and lowered the tape into it. When I pulled the tape back up, I half expected to see a dead Vietnamese soldier's head attached to the plumb bob. I saw liquid at the seven inch mark. I had to rub my eyes to convince myself that the liquid was not blood. I marked the level in the log and I saw that it rose a half inch from the last time I took a sounding. The ship had taken on a half inch more water. I took another big breath in preparation to enter the sonar equipment room.

The three inch porthole in the door only afforded me a view of the green, red and yellow lights on the surface of the tall gray, floor to ceiling computer boxes that deciphered the sounds that echoed back to the sonar bulb under the bow. Those boxes produced images on the sonarmen's screens, up in CIC. Slowly, I unlatched the dogs, those steel clamps that kept the sonar equipment room door watertight. I laughed at the thought that the dogs were keeping guard to make sure that the liquid intruder did not enter. I wondered if that is how those steel clamps got their name. The steel door creaked open as I lifted up the long steel handle. I cautiously put my arm inside, half expecting something to jump out and bite me. I wasn't sure why since we kept the Trippe so clean, we could eat off of the floors. There were no rats or spiders to worry about. Nevertheless, my stomach turned into a knot as I slid my hand along the bulkhead searching for the light switch. Click, the lights came on and I slowly lifted my foot over the threshold. My feet were sweating. I ran to the opposite side of the room and unscrewed the sounding tube as quickly as I could. I recorded seven inches of water in the bilge below the room. Reading the previous log entries, I noticed that the level had been the same since we arrived in the Gulf of Tonkin. No more water had seeped into that bilge.

After recording the level in the log, I hurried out of the room and secured the door. As I latched the dogs, I peered through the porthole and noticed that I had forgotten to turn off the lights. I didn't care. I wanted to get out of there as fast as I could. Putting the sounding tape and clipboard in one hand, I wrapped my wrist around the ladder and began my ascent. Looking up, the opening seemed much higher up than the distance I had come down. The sound of my boots hitting each rung echoed and reverberated eerily on the shaft's steel bulkheads as I worked my way up the ladder. During the last storm, the ship pitched forward knocking my face into the ladder. "I hate this shaft!" I said then.

I almost dropped the clipboard. When my head reached the

top, I placed the sounding tape and clipboard through the opening and onto the deck. I wrapped my left leg around the ladder, unbuckled the holster and lifted it up on top of the clipboard. I squeezed myself out of the opening and exhaled, glad to be out of there. I still felt like a tightly wound spring.

This descent to the sonar equipment room was uneventful and easy compared to when we have stormy weather. As I turned around to unlatch the hatch, Krack tapped me on the shoulder and startled me. I jumped up and kicked the clipboard all the way down the tube. Krack leaned over to look where the clipboard had fallen and said, "Oh, that's a bummer. Sorry."

I just glared at him.

His shoulders dropped as he put the palms of his hands up and said, "I just came by to ask you if you wanted to go to mid-rats. It's 23:30 and I'm hungry."

"That is a long way down and I hate going down there. Carrying all this stuff makes it a real pain in the ass."

"Sorry," he said again. "I'll hold your stuff while you go down and get the, what did I knock over, a clipboard?"

"Yeah, it's a clipboard." I said. I did not feel as fearful with Krack standing there offering to hold my things.

"I didn't mean to scare you," he said.

"It's OK. If you see anyone come by, please hide the gun. I don't want to get into trouble for not wearing it."

I secured the hatch in the upright position once more and descended back down the bowels of the ship. "What is hiding in here that scares us?"

"What did you say?" Krack asked as the aroma of cinnamon wafted down to me. I stopped my descent and looked up, I could see him licking sugar off of his lips.

"Nothing." I yelled up to him. "I feel like I'm a mortar being dropped into the barrel, to be blasted out."

"Let me know when you light your ass, so that I can get out of the way when you blast on by," Krack said.

"Do you always have to be a smart ass?" I asked as my boots clanked on each rung of the ladder. When I reached the bottom, I had to hunt for the pen which had come loose from the clipboard. When I found it behind a pipe, I began my ascent. I craned my neck upward. I could barely make out Krack's smile beaming down at me. I raced up the ladder as fast as my feet could carry me. I was out of breath by the time I reached the top.

Krack took the clipboard and said, "Man! You moved fast. Something must have lit your ass on fire." Not waiting for an answer, he added, "Do you know what Norman made for mid-rats? Cinnamon rolls. Hurry up! I want to get some more while they're still hot."

Just hearing about the cinnamon rolls made my mouth water and it took my mind away from the shaft that I had just climbed out of. Cinnamon rolls also made me yearn for home. As we walked to the galley, my thoughts returned to early spring when I took my two year old son to Winchell's Donuts to share a cinnamon roll and a glass of milk. He was so happy, smiling with a white milk mustache. I wondered where Vietnamese fathers took their young sons for a treat.

Krack opened the door for me. The aroma of cinnamon made me homesick for my son. I fought to suppress tears. I wanted so badly to be home and to take Jeremy to a donut shop. I could almost feel his little hand in mine as I walked into the galley. Sitting down at the table, Krack's face scrunched when he noticed my swollen eyes. "Are you alright?" he asked. "You look like you're gonna cry."

"I was just missing my son, that's all."

Krack motioned Norman over with his hands. Norman's smile beamed as he walked around the counter and handed me a roll. "Here, try one of these," he said. "They're still warm. I just pulled them out of the oven."

I took one and bit into it. "Mmmm. It does taste good," I mumbled with a mouthful of warm cinnamon roll. Our conversation moved to the rocket launching that we did just before we left to come to Subic Bay. No one else in the galley, eating mid-rats, had heard what our target had been.

"Matty probably knows. Anyone know where he is?" Norman asked.

"Either asleep in his rack or he's on watch," I said.

"I hope the target was Hanoi," Krack said.

"Why can't we just bomb Hanoi, invade the North and be done with it?" Norman asked.

"Because we don't want the Chinese or Russians to enter the

war," I said.

"Fuck em. Fuck em all to hell," Krack blurted out. "You can't win a football game if you don't go past the fifty yard line. Fuck Hanoi. Bomb the shit out of it and we get a touchdown. We win and go home."

"Why do we have to bomb anyone?" I asked. "Why can't we just invite them for a game of volleyball?"

Norman slapped me on the shoulder as he said, "Volleyball? And you didn't even take a single hit off of our joint. I think that you're more stoned than we were."

Krack, who was sitting at the table across from Norman and me, motioned with his eyes that he saw someone enter the galley. We turned around and stood at attention as Ensign Denny entered.

"As you were," he said as he sat down at our table. Addressing me, he asked, "Did you get an accurate sounding in the sonar equipment room?"

"Yes sir. But there were no girls down there, not even one in a Playboy centerfold."

Rolling his eyes he said, "I just got word you will have a meeting with a couple of officers from NIS. They will fly in from the carrier in a couple of weeks"

"NIS? Naval Investigative Service? Why do they want to see me?"

"I don't know. I only know that they want to talk to you, privately."

Getting up to leave he said, "Carry on." He grabbed a cinnamon roll as he walked out. When he passed through the door, we heard him, say, "Hey, this tastes good!"

Krack and Norman both looked at me with furrowed eyebrows. "What's that all about?" Norman asked.

"Beats me. But if NIS wants to talk to me, it must be important," I said.

"You don't suppose they found out that you were trying to warn the priest that we were going to blow up his church do you?" Norman asked.

"I hope not. Maybe it's about my getting hit on the head. I wrote my parents and asked them to help. But I don't know why NIS would get involved with my head injury."

Krack his eyes and said, "I wouldn't be surprised if your chief called them in hopes of getting rid of you."

41 – PHONING HOME

Norman and I walked down the ship's gangplank and halfway across the Navy base to the Subic Bay telephone exchange. The mugginess of the night air oozed drops of sweat down my back. My heart ached in anticipation of hearing my two year old son's voice. As we walked under a grove of tall trees, I leaned over toward Norman and asked, "Are you going to call your parents or your girlfriend?"

His eyebrows shot up as he replied, "Linda, of course. I know you're calling home."

"You bet I am. I want to talk to my son."

"Will he recognize your voice? You've been away for a long time in that kid's life."

Norman's words stung. I hadn't seen my son since I came on board, five months ago, nor spoken to him since we set out to sea, 3 months ago. The little one story, white stucco telephone exchange with its red clay tile roof reminded me of the Spanish style houses back home, making me more homesick than ever. Cigarette smoke billowed out of the entry to the telephone exchange. It seemed as if everyone waiting to make a phone call puffed on a cigarette. I walked up to the operator and handed her my parent's phone number. Since I didn't smoke, I took a seat near the open door. While we waited for a phone booth to become available, we overheard half the conversation from the phone booth closest to us.

"Hi Mom. How are you? I'm fine." A huge smile lit up the sailor's face as he talked on the phone. "No. The food isn't as good as yours, but it's healthy enough. Yes, they give us fresh milk." His eyes brows scrunched together. His mother must have told him something he didn't want to hear. Tilting his head into the phone, he blew cigarette smoke slowly while holding his cigarette next to his temple. "I can't tell you that over the phone. I don't know how long we'll be here. Thanks. I appreciate that." Rolling his eyes, he said, "Yes, mom, I pray every night ... "

Norman tapped me on the shoulder, pointed to the sailor that we were eavesdropping on and said, "Sometimes it seems as if every mother has the same script that they say on the phone. I betcha that if I called home, that I would be saying that same exact thing to my mom."

"You've got to admit, Norman, that our being out here scares the hell out of our parents. Hell, it scares me."

"Yeah, that's for shua." Norman said with his Boston accent. "But what bugs me most is that we've got to be careful not to say anything over the phone that the censors won't like."

"I want so badly to tell my dad about blowing up the church," I said. "Maybe he'd have an idea about what to do?"

Norman grabbed my arm, pulled me closer to him and whispered, "Don't even think about opening your mouth about that. The censors will cut your call and throw your ass in the brig so fast; you'll think that you started to make your call in the brig. You're better off talking to your dad about the whores in Olongapo."

"I won't talk to my dad about whores, my brother maybe. I bet the censors will be getting horny listening to you talk to your girlfriend," I said.

"Fuck 'em. Let 'em beat their meat while they listen, I don't give a fuck."

I heard the operator say, "Montoya to booth number four, Montoya to booth number four."

When I reached the phone booth and picked up the receiver, the operator's voice said, "We connected you with the phone exchange in California. You will be charged the long distance cost from San Francisco to Long Beach. The charges will start when I reconnect you."

"Thanks," I said. I heard a double click.

"Hi Mom. How are you?"

"We're fine," she said. "Your Jeremy is getting so big. It's hard to believe that he is two and a half already."

Hearing my mother's voice brought an overwhelming feeling of homesickness.

"Please send me some photos of him, OK? Can I talk to him?"

"He's asleep. It's five in the morning," she said. "I just finished making breakfast for your dad. Where are you and what time is it there?"

I clenched my teeth and hit the side of the phone booth.

"I'm in the Philippines and it is eight at night. I'm sorry that I'm calling you this early, but I can only get to the phone exchange in the evenings. Is there any way that you can wake him?"

"Even if I tried, he's such a sound sleeper that he probably won't talk. Can you call back around eight, our time?"

"This place closes in an hour, Mom. I can't." I hit the phone booth again.

"How long will you be there before you go back to Viet Nam?"

"I can't give you details because the phone calls are monitored. We'll only be here for a few more days, just long enough to make some repairs."

I heard a couple of clicks on the phone, letting me know that the censors were listening.

"Repairs? Did your ship get attacked?"

"No, Mom. We didn't get attacked. We're safe, really. Please don't worry about us. The ship's main engine needed some maintenance."

"Are you telling me the truth?"

"Yes, Mom. Please don't worry."

"Are you eating well?"

"Yes, Mom. The food on the ship is better than I get at home."

"That's good. You know that I never liked the kitchen. When I was little, I worked with the animals while your aunt Lucy did the cooking."

"Thanks Mom, your poor cooking makes the navy chow taste good."

"Don't be mean. If it weren't for my bad cooking, you wouldn't have learned how to cook for yourself. Have you seen a real doctor about your head injury? We wrote a letter to Senator Montoya asking him to help. Did you get my letter about that?"

"Yeah, I did. Thanks."

"I have the whole church praying for your safety."

"Thanks, Mom."

"Are you going to church on Sundays?"

"Mom, there's no church on the ship; there is not even room for a chapel."

"I know that. But aren't you in the Philippines? I know they have a church there. It's a Catholic country."

"OK, Mom. If I'm here on Sunday. Did you get my last letter? I included a photo of me in the ship's repair shop. It's for Jeremy. What was his reaction when you gave it to him?"

"*Cochino*! I can't give that to him."

"Why not?" I asked, "Why are you calling me *cochino*?"

"Your picture shows you sitting in front of posters of naked ladies. *Cochino*! I can't give that photo to your baby."

"Mom, I didn't se ... " I stopped talking. My face got hot as I remembered where we shot that photo.

My mother was laughing. She had a way of setting me up to tease me. She did it again.

"I'll cut out the naked ladies and give him the picture," she said. "*Cochino*!" She laughed again.

Click, click, "Excuse me, this is your one minute warning." Click, click.

"The operator just cut in telling me that my time is up. I gotta go. Love you, Mom. Tell everyone I love 'em."

"I love you, too. *Cochino*! Go to mass on Sunday." Click, click.

Her laughter was the last thing I heard before the line went dead.

Norman finished his call to this girlfriend at the same time. As soon as we stepped outside the door he lit up a cigarette.

"I think you're right about mothers all having the same script, Norman."

"I think girlfriends have the same script too. Did you get to talk to your son?"

"I was so bummed out that he was still asleep. My dad was getting ready for work. All my brothers and my sister were still asleep. I only got to talk to my mom."

"Lucky for me, Linda was up and getting ready for work."

"Did she tell you what she wasn't wearing yet?"

"Fuck you. That's for me to know and for you to mind your own business. What did you tell your mom?"

"She asked me if I had seen a real doctor. I told her that the doc didn't even look at my head."

"That's 'cause the navy docs are all quacks," Norman said.

The street lights cast long shadows as we walked past them. A shore patrol car whizzed by us, going in the opposite direction.

"I purposely didn't tell her that he spent most of his time asking me if I was taking illegal drugs."

"I bet that if you were an officer that you would've been flown to the carrier to see a real doctor as soon as you got injured, and no one would have suggested that you were doing drugs, no matter how weird you were acting. And, you've got to admit that you were acting pretty damn weird."

I stopped walking and turned to Norman. Throwing my hands in the air I said, "Hell, killing people is weird."

"But we'ah at wah," Norman said.

"And what about blowing up churches on Sunday? That's weird," I said as I put my hands on my hips. "Getting hit on the head gives me a legitimate reason for acting weird."

Norman rolled his eyes, started walking and said, "Linda says, hi. She asked me how close we get to the shore. I told her that I couldn't tell her."

"Why did you say that? You're just going to scare her," I said. "When I talked to my mom, I lied to her. I made no mention of how close to shore we were. I didn't even tell her we were in the Gulf of Tonkin. Doing that would only have made her worry about me even more."

Norman threw the butt of his cigarette on the ground and stepped on it. "Well, at least I didn't tell Linda that we are heading back there tomorrow morning."

"I don't think that omitting that little detail helped her worry any less, Norman. You might as well have said, 'Sweetheart, tomorrow morning we're headed back to the killing shores of Viet Nam. And we'll be so close to shore that we'll be able to count the sea shells on the beach.'"

42 - NIS COMES CALLING

My mouth opened into a big yawn as I handed the sounding log, the sounding tape and the fifty caliber pistol over to my replacement. Having completed the midnight to 0:400 watch, my bones felt rubbery after walking all around the ship for the last four hours. I rubbed my dry eyes and wobbled my way down to my berthing compartment. Worrisome thoughts floated up to the surface and shot questions into my vibrating head. I could only guess what NIS wanted to talk to me about.

Matty caught up with me as I walked down the forward passage way. "Hey! Wait up," he said. "What's this I heard about NIS coming to see you?"

"I wish I knew, Matty. Ensign Denny told me to get some sleep before I talked to them. He said that he was going to talk to Jaffe, so that I won't get into any trouble for sleeping passed 06:00." I opened my mouth wide for another big yawn as I said, "I am soooooo tired."

Matty's eyes grew small as worry plowed furrows into his forehead. "You don't think that they heard that you were trying to warn the priest about our bombing the church, do you?" he asked.

"I hope not, Matty. I wrote to my parents and asked them to ask Senator Montoya for help. He's a distant cousin."

"You have a cousin that is a US Senator? Wow! That's cool." He said as his furrowed brow relaxed a bit.

"My parents wrote to him and asked him to help. I don't know if the senator asked NIS to investigate."

"Investigate? Investigate what?"

"My head."

"You're head? Ha! You need a psychiatrist for that, not the NIS."

"Shut up! Matty. Actually, I was hoping that you could shed some light on the subject. You radiomen always get the skinny on what is going on before anyone else does."

"Nah. The only transmission we got is that NIS is coming to see you. The message didn't say why. Do you think they are coming to investigate your head?"

As we walked toward my berthing compartment, the constant buzz from the engines grew annoyingly louder. "I am so tired, Matty, I can't think straight. And with NIS coming to see me, I can't help but get the jitters."

Matty grabbed my shoulder to stop me before I opened the door into the next passageway. He had the same facial expression that my little brother got whenever he got into trouble at school and wanted me to talk to mom, before mom yelled at him. Matty's expression squeezed a longing into me to be home with my little brother, almost making me want to cry.

Matty said, "They wouldn't fly NIS over here to talk to you, unless it was really important. I still think that they might've found out about our attempt to warn the priest. We could all be in a world of shit. We could all be tried for treason and shot."

"Matty, let's get real," I said in an effort to calm down my eighteen year old buddy. "I don't think that they are coming for that. Remember all the shit I went through when I got hit on the head?"

"Are you talking about when Chief Jaffe and the other chiefs ganged up on you in the shower?"

"Yeah! I wrote to my parents asking them to get me some

help so that I could see a medical doctor. I wanted a real doctor to show that I had a concussion and that I was not taking drugs. That is the only way I can get Jaffe off my back."

"He's such an asshole." Matty said.

"You can say that again! I am hoping that the Senator received my parents' letter and that NIS is here at his request."

"I wouldn't put too much faith in that. It would easier just to fly you to the carrier to see a doc."

"That is why I am so freaked out about NIS wanting to talk to me. It doesn't make sense. But I keep thinking that it might be about my attempt to warn the priest. I just don't know."

"Good luck," Matty said as he left and I turned to go down to my berthing compartment. I tried to sort out the questions as I undressed and climbed onto my rack. The ship's rocking lulled me to sleep.

"Wake up, they're waiting for you." said a sailor who I could not see in the dark. "There is no time for you to get dressed. Hurry, follow me."

I ran after him, wearing only my underwear. He opened the door and pushed me through. I found myself standing in a Catholic church. Vietnamese people filled the pews. The Vietnamese woman who appeared in previous dreams stood in front of the altar. Her green native dress shimmered. Four Navy officers stood on either side of her. One of the Officers called out, "Attention!" Everyone in the church stood up.

I wanted to run, to hide, to find something to cover my near nakedness. The Vietnamese woman held out her hand and spoke softly. "Come here, and take a seat."

My knees shook involuntarily. I could taste blood in my mouth. One of the officers said, "You are accused of killing all those people who were attending church. How do you plead?"

I tried to speak. My mouth filled with blood and I began to choke. The congregation pointed their fingers at me.

The Vietnamese woman asked, "Why didn't you help them, they are all dead. It is their blood that you drink."

I tried to get up and run but I was tied to the chair. One of the officers took the chalice from the altar and poured the blood into my mouth as he said, "This is the blood of a new and everlasting covenant; this is the blood of the people who didn't help."

I pulled my shoulders back and forth trying to get my arms loose. I tried to yell.

"Mushroom, wake up, wake up," someone said as I struggled to get loose. "You're having a nightmare." Dawson's voice boomed at the end of the long arm that shook me.

My own saliva made me cough as I struggled to untangle myself from my blanket. The back of my head and the back of my knees dripped with sweat.

"What time is it?" I asked.

"About 05:30. They won't start serving breakfast until 06:00. You can go back to sleep."

I didn't want to go back to sleep. That nightmare seemed too real. I climbed down from my rack, removed my white Jockey briefs, wrapped a towel around my waist and walked to the showers. I wanted to wash the nightmare away. A deck ape stood in the shower compartment, holding a stop watch.

"One of the boilers is acting up," he said. "We're rationing the water until we get it fixed."

"How long of a shower can I take?"

"You only get three minutes. If you turn off the water after you soap up, I'll stop the clock and won't start it again until you rinse off."

The shower was too short to offer relief. I could still taste the blood in my mouth. I ambled out to the fantail and sat with the aft winch blocking the wind. I hoped that a good meditation would shoot the nightmare back to the Vietnamese shore from whence it came. I took several slow and deep breaths telling myself to relax with each breath. I began my mantra and eased into a meditative state. I found myself on the Vietnamese shore that I had sent my nightmare to.

The Vietnamese woman, who had appeared in my previous meditations, took hold of my hand. She wore an iridescent green ao dai tunic and pointed straw hat. I turned toward her and started to tell her about my nightmare but she put her index finger to my lips, stopping me. Her eyes were blacker than I had ever seen. I stared at them, unable to look away. The bodies of the My Lai massacre victims I saw in the magazine article were lying next to the bodies of the people we killed in the church. I stopped breathing.

"You have difficulty forgiving yourself because you think that you are only inside your skin."

"Where else would I be?" I heard myself say, almost as if I were someone else.

"Everywhere and in everything," she said.

I wanted to tell her that I didn't understand. But the softness and gentleness of her hand distracted me. "There was nothing I could do to stop the killing of those people," I said.

"You are those people. They are other aspects of your greater self," she said.

"How can that be? They are dead and I am here talking to you." I turned, looked at the trees, then the sand, then back to her. "Greater self?" I asked.

"You are connected with everything here," she said, stretching her arms out toward the trees and hills.

"But I've never been here, not before this war."

"You are connected to everything here," she said, pointing to the Tonkin Gulf, to the sky, then to the hills behind her.

I wracked my brain trying to figure out what she meant. I inhaled and exhaled a few time before I said, "I'm connected because I am blowing them up."

She smiled at me the way my boot camp drill instructor did, when he listened patiently while I tried to explain what treason meant. The Vietnamese woman let go of my hand and patted me on my chest. "Your brain cannot answer for the heart."

The sing song character of her voice, the warm softness of her hand, the accepting smile on her face stopped the continuous rumbling of my stomach.

"Inhale deeply," she said. "Close your eyes. Let your heart show you your greater self."

I shut my eyes and waited.

"Breathe in the answer you seek. Listen with your heart."

I opened my eyes, looked at the beach and saw my son playing with the three boys that we had killed. Jeremy turned and ran with his arms outstretched toward me. His face changed into mine as he drew closer.

"Can you see that your son is part of your greater self?" she asked.

I nodded. "He's my son," I said. "So he is part of me."

"You're almost there," she said. "Look deeper with your heart. Look again."

Jeremy, along with the three boys, stood at my feet looking up at me. All four of their faces changed into the same face, mine. I bent down to get a better look. Warmth radiated from the area below my navel. I stopped breathing when I saw my adult self looking down at us. I was the boys.

I sat down and looked at the sand between my legs. She sat down beside me and leaned her body against my arm. We gazed at the water, not saying anything. A voice and the smell of diesel fumes intruded into my meditation. I fought to maintain my meditation. When I turned to ask her how that happened, she was gone.

"I thought I'd find you here," Ensign Denny said as I opened my eyes. "The helicopter, bringing the NIS officers, will be here in about ten minutes. I'll meet you in the helo hangar when they arrive."

I dashed to the mess decks where the cook plopped some powdered eggs into my tray. Before I finished eating, "Chopper incoming," came over the loudspeaker. I sprinted out of the mess decks taking my place as fire scene leader on the helo deck. When the chopper rotors stopped turning, I saw two officers disembark. My heart raced as my feet became sweaty. Ensign Denny walked out to greet them. I told my crew to put things away, because the NIS officers would stay for a couple of hours. My stomach muscles tightened. I wanted to run away. Walking into the hangar, I saw the ensign talking with the two NIS officers. He called me over and introduced me to them. They were younger than I expected. They looked like they might be in their early twenties, no older than I. The ensign asked us to follow him to his own quarters where we could speak privately. One of the NIS officers entered the room with me, while the other left with the ensign. I tasted blood in the back of my throat.

I sat in a chair, while the NIS officer sat on Ensign Denny's bed. "Do you know why we are here?" he asked.

"No, sir."

"We are here to comply with a congressional request."

"Is that request from Senator Montoya?"

"Then you do know why we are here."

"Not really. I asked my parents for help. I assume that they got hold of Senator Montoya. I got hit on the head with a steel door and I went sort of crazy. I want to see a real doctor, but my chief won't let me."

"We talked with your chief. He says you're doing drugs."

"When did you talk to him?"

"That is none of your concern."

I felt blindsided. Hearing that made me want to punch chief Jaffe.

"We're here to get your side of the story so that we can respond to the congressional request."

"Where is the other NIS officer?" I asked.

"He is asking other people to verify your story."

"Good. Make sure that he talks to corpsman Powell. He knows what's going on."

The Officer asked me to explain how I got injured. In great detail, I relayed what had happened starting with Dawson and me fixing the door hatch. I explained how I received the concussion and how Chief Jaffe came to sick bay, not concerned for my welfare; rather he asked if I would be able to stand watch. I described the physical sensations and how painful the headaches were. He took notes on a green military issue notebook.

"So what kind of drugs were you taking?" the officer asked when I had finished telling my story.

My eyebrows jumped on top of my forehead. Wasn't he listening to what I had just told him?

"Drugs? The only drugs I took were the ones that the corpsmen gave me."

"The chief corpsman told us that he thinks that you were taking drugs."

"That's because Chief Jaffe wants me out of the Navy. He convinced the chief hospital corpsman that I was taking drugs. I asked the chief corpsman to send me to the carrier and have me checked out, if he thought I was taking drugs. He said that it wasn't necessary."

"Why do you think Chief Jaffe wants you out of the Navy?"

"He's my boss. His is racist and harasses the minorities on the ship. He's gung ho Navy and I am not. I hate this war. It's immoral. We aren't killing communists. We are killing farmers and babies. And because he knows how I feel, he'll do anything to get me out of the Navy." I groaned inaudibly as I worried if I had said too much.

"How do we know you weren't taking drugs? The chief said you were acting irrationally."

"I was acting irrationally. The head injury scared me. My body and my mind were going haywire. There were no illegal drugs in my body. It was the concussion that made me act irrationally."

"If you'd just fess up to taking drugs, we could probably get you out of the Navy on a general discharge. It would not be a problem."

"What!?" My neck muscles tightened. Looking into the officers blue eyes, I searched to see if he was really listening. I wanted to shake some sense into him. I didn't want a less than honorable discharge. My whole life would be ruined. I wouldn't be able to get a decent job. How could I convince this young officer, who was probably the same age as me, that I needed his help, not his accusations?

"Look here, Sir I have some college. I want to be a school teacher when I get out."

"That's a noble profession," he said.

"Exactly!" I said. Seeing that his eyes were now focused on mine, I realized that I needed to stay calm, even though I wanted to stand up and scream at this young NIS officer. "I want to be a school teacher. I am not going to jeopardize my entire future for a moment's pleasure. When that door hit me on the head, my whole world fell apart. And now, I am talking to an officer who I had hoped was here to get the truth instead of acquiescing to chief Jaffe's wish to get me kicked out of the Navy."

"Don't get angry. We are here to get to the truth."

"The truth? Honestly?"

"Of course," he said.

"The truth is that I have a concussion. Plain and simple! I didn't take any illegal drugs. I'll prove that if you send me to the carrier and have the real doctors check me out."

"I'll see what I can do. Remember, I can still offer you a general discharge."

My shoulders sank along with my heart. His last remark made

me realize that he only wanted to investigate the drug accusations.

Boom! The Officer jumped up. His eyes flashed and his complexion turned white. "What was that?"

"We could be under attack. Are you through with me? I have to get to my battle station."

"What should I do?" the officer asked.

"Stay in here. Someone will come and get you when it is safe." I lied.

No way was I going to be nice to this arrogant Boy Scout. A mixture of relief and disgust enveloped me. I suspected that he had never been near any action. I assumed that the blast came from the five-inch gun. Going outside, I saw that the ship had sailed closer to shore. The five-inch gun pointed toward the beach. Looking at my watch, I made my way to my battle station. Bam! Another shot. I smiled knowing that the NIS officer would be in Ensign Denny's quarters for a few hours worrying about getting killed.

43 – FIRE DRILL

At 14:30 the Trippe pulled away from bombing the Viet Nam shoreline to rendezvous with the ammo ship. I needed to conduct our monthly fire drill and decided to use the opportunity to test our portable fire pumps. We had approximately one hour to hold our drill, before the men would assemble on the deck to heave the lines that would transport our pallets of ammo to our ship. I asked Otis and Dawson to help me carry two fire pumps from the repair locker to the fantail.

"We won't be needing any gas, these pumps are full," Otis said.

"When the deck apes get here," I said, "you two show them how to attach the fire and water supply hoses. When you're done, roll the hoses back up for the drill."

When everyone assembled and had been shown how the hoses are attached to the fire pumps, I checked my watch. "This is going to be a timed drill," I said. "When I give the word, attach the hoses and drop the hard black water supply hose over the side. Make sure the end is all the way in the water before you pull the cord to start the pump."

"Can I man the nozzle this time?" Dawson asked. "I got soaked the last time because that dumb fuck couldn't control it," he said pointing to the deck ape walking toward us.

Otis let out a belly laugh. "He did it on purpose, you dip shit."

"I'll let you," I said with a wink. "As long as you don't retaliate."

Dawson rolled his eyes and nodded in agreement. When the deck ape in question grinned, Dawson flipped him off.

"Fire in the hole! Fire in the hole!" I yelled and looked at my watch to time them.

The team attached the hoses and pulled the cords to fire up the pumps. A puff of smoke belched out of one of the pumps.

"Where's the fire?" Dawson asked.

"Look at the sign on the trash can that Mushroom tied up," the deck ape said. "Jeez, Dawson, get your head outta' your ass."

Dawson glared at the deck ape and turned on the nozzle, dowsing the trash can.

"We did good time, guys," I said to the team. "It only took 90 seconds to connect to the pump and turn on the nozzle."

We repeated trash can fire simulation until all seven guys had their turn at the nozzle.

"What happens if we get torpedoed under the waterline?" one of the team asked.

"The difference is that we will put the water supply hose on the floor of the compartment that is leaking and put the nozzle over the side," I said. "We'll use as many pumps as necessary to keep the ship from sinking."

When I dismissed the team, Otis brought over a bucket of fresh water and said, "I'll flush out the salt water so that our pumps will be battle ready in case our ship gets torpedoed or runs into a mine."

After we put the equipment away, I went down to the repair ship to log the fire drill and the testing of the portable water pumps in the Planned Maintenance book. Bruce jerked his welding helmet down and struck an electric arc. The dusty acrid odor of melting metal filled the shop as he practiced his welding technique by laying a bead onto a set of barbells that he had been making for himself. I stared at the Playboy centerfolds mounted on the bulkhead and then noticed the second hand ticking its way around the brass clock.

"You have ten minutes before battle station, Bruce," I said. We were both on the blue team. The gold team would take over in five hours. The teams alternated standing at battle station for five hour intervals.

I grabbed my helmet and followed Bruce out of the repair shop. Thoughts of a torpedo blowing a hole in the side of the ship sloshed around in my head. My helmet was a tactile reminder that catastrophe lay in wait just outside of the bulkhead, right under the waterline. Memories of our war simulations in Damage Control school flooded my mind. I hoped that we had conducted enough fire drills to be able to save the ship from sinking in case of a direct hit.

When we reached the area above the forward repair locker, Bruce pointed to the hatch. He looked around as if he were about to sneak into a place he wasn't permitted to be in. I chuckled, seeing Bruce act out of character. He normally took being a sailor seriously. He turned the wheel to open the hatch and climbed down the ladder. When I heard his feet hit the deck, I squeezed myself through the eighteen inch round opening and pulled the hatch down, turning the wheel tight to ensure that it would be watertight. We walked to the repair locker and took our positions on the floor next to the open repair locker door.

Yawning, I pulled my knees up to my chest and stretched them out again.

"Don't ya go falling asleep on watch. The Chief will have ya ass for that." Bruce said.

"I am so tired I could go to sleep standing up and not care if I fall over when the ship rolls. I'd just finished my sounding and security watch when I walked into the repair shop and I didn't even have time to yawn before the chief sent me to unclog a stinking pipe."

My knees felt as if grit had been injected behind my knee caps and sand had been sprinkled into my eyes. It had been nearly 24 hours since the last time I had gotten four hours of unbroken sleep.

Matty walked down the passageway, passed Bruce then sat on the other side of me.

Bruce smiled at Matty, leaned over to me and asked, "Who's he?"

"That's Matty. He's from New York."

"What's he do?"

"You know him, don't ya? Matty is a radioman."

"Now ah rememba. Hi Matty."

Matty nodded and turned toward me and asked me when I would be free.

"Meet me on the helo deck when your watch is over," he said. His eyes darted back and forth. He held his hands together close to his chest as if he held an awful secret within them. "It's important."

When Matty noticed Bruce crane his neck to hear, he added, a little louder than necessary, "I want to talk to you about my girlfriend, back home."

Bruce rolled his eyes and shook his head in obvious disbelief. He slouched against the bulkhead, feigning that he was ignoring us.

Matty leaned over to me and whispered, "I got a transmission about one of our ships getting hit. I'll tell you more, later."

As Matty struggled to stand up against the rocking of the ship, Bruce said, "He ain't gonna talk about his girlfriend. He musta heard something on the ship's radio."

44 - USS WARRINGTON DD 843

"Wait, Matty," I called as he began walking away. "You might as well tell both of us what you heard over the radio. If one of our ships got hit, we're all going to hear about it any way."

My words lassoed Matty, bringing his feet to an abrupt stop, as his head bobbed forward. Standing in the middle of the passageway, he scratched the back of his head, as though trying to decide whether or not he should turn around or continue on his way. Matty did an about face, and marched back to us.

"You're right. I got so carried away with the news that I forgot that the chief said that we would give an all hands briefing about it."

Sitting down next to me, on the deck, he crossed his legs and leaned forward to look at Bruce. "Before I start, Bruce has got to promise that he won't tell anyone that I told him about what happened." Turning his face to me he added, "I know you won't tell."

Bruce blinked both of his eyes as he said, "Shuah. It's no sweat off ma back. What'd ya heah?"

"We got a transmission a little while ago. One of our ships got hit."

"Which one?" Bruce asked.

"The USS Warrington DD843."

Bruce jumped up, his arms waving, his eyes opened wide. His Massachusetts accent getting heavier, he said, "No Shit? The Wahington? Hey! She's from our home port in Newport, Rhode Island."

"Do you know anyone on the Warrington, Bruce?" I asked.

"Yeah. I got a couple of good friends on that ship from Woosta (Worscester), Mass.," he said. "Fuck! I hope they're OK."

Bruce paced the three foot wide passageway, flicking his hands as if trying to rid them of water. "Oh shit! Oh shit!" he repeated over and over.

"Sit down! Bruce," I yelled. We sat cross legged to get closer. Bruce and I turned to face Matty.

"Did anyone get killed?" I asked.

"They don't know yet," Matty replied. "The report said that there might be casualties, but it didn't say how many or how badly they were hurt."

My stomach tightened, knowing that we could be next. I could feel my head getting hot under my helmet.

"Where were they?" I asked.

"Just a few miles north of us."

"Did they get into a fight with a Viet Cong ship?"

"No. The report said that the Warrington came under rapid and heavy fire from the shore."

My mind began calculating the distance that the Warrington needed to be in order to get hit from the Viet Cong artillery that was on shore. "How close were they? What were they doing?"

"The report did not give much detail. It said that the Warrington was on Linebacker duty."

"Linebacker duty?" I asked. "Linebacker duty, linebacker duty, what the heck is Linebacker duty? I can't remember."

Bruce piped in saying, "Yeah, Linebacka duty is above the DMZ. Those ships ah trying to blockade any supplies from the Chinese into Hanoi and Hai Phong harbor."

"If the Warrington's doing Linebacker duty and she's only a

few miles ahead of us, what the fuck are we doing this far north?" Matty asked. "We aren't part of that mission."

Bruce threw his hands up in the air. "Our butt fuck of a captain is probably trying to be a cock sucking hero."

Matty told us that there had been torpedo boats in the area but they weren't sure what hit them. It could have been mines.

"Where did the Warrington get hit?" I asked.

"The report said that she got hit on the port side, behind the engine room and in the control room," Matty said.

Bruce said, "If she got hit twice, on the same side, she musta got hit bah torpedoes."

"Yeah, she had been under fire from the shore, so that makes sense." I said, "And besides, the sonarmen would have seen mines on their scopes before she would've run into them.

"What else did you hear, Matty?"

"The last thing in the report was that she asked for a tow from the USS Robinson?"

"If she's being towed, she musta been hurt pretty bad," Bruce piped in.

Matty stood up and said, "Now I really gotta go." Reaching down to give me a hand, he winked and whispered, "I'll see you on the helo deck later and tell you what else I heard."

45 – BATTLE STATION GRUNT

Bruce and I sat quiet for a while. I couldn't get comfortable sitting on the deck. The bulkhead felt harder than usual against my back. I couldn't keep my legs still. My eyes were drying in the bright passageway lights. I wanted to leave my station and find Matty. I wanted to know what else he found out and if there was any more news about the Warrington.

Bruce distracted me by emitting a noise that mimicked an animal. Facing forward, he grunted again, this time louder. Could Bruce be playing, I wondered? Taking the cue, I cleared my throat, twice. I did not turn my head because doing so would seem to violate an unwritten rule. After sucking in a lung full of air, he rolled a long low grunt. Looking at the lights overhead, I uttered a guttural noise, as if asking a question.

Bruce's eyes grew wide with worry as he turned his head slowly toward me. Dropping his shoulders, he gurgled with his mouth closed, the air escaping between his lips. Putting my hands on the deck, I inched away from Bruce. I muttered a fast mumble of gravely sounds before turning my head toward the overhead light fixture. Playing was such a welcome relief.

Bruce and I carried on with our wordless conversation for about an hour. Neither of us uttered an intelligent word to each other. We bonded, as friends for the first time. I was grateful for the distraction away from worrying about the USS Warrington, away from worrying about the war.

Bruce stood up to stretch his legs. He walked into the repair locker and brought out a huge pipe wrench that was about 3 feet long. "This is humongous! Did ya use one of these in Damage Control school?" he asked.

Getting up off the deck and taking the wrench, I said, "Yeah, we did. I'm sure glad that the handle is made out of aluminum. Otherwise it would be too heavy to lift."

"Too heavy for a pussy like you maybe," he said as he winked. "Jesus! This is big. Did you go to DC school at Great Lakes Naval Station?"

"Nah. I went to Damage Control school on Treasure Island, near San Francisco. How about you?"

"Ah went to shipfitter school at Great Lakes Naval Station," he said. "So tell me. What did ya do with a wrench this big?"

"When I was in Damage Control school, they put us into a simulation chamber that looked like we were below decks on a ship, kind of like we are here, with pipes, ductwork, and wiring. They sounded the general quarters alarm and yelled out that we had been torpedoed. Freezing cold water began pouring in from everywhere."

"What did ya do?"

"I grabbed a wrench like this one, found the valve that I hoped would shut off the water and tried turning it. It was stuck. Water was spraying everywhere. I had to find someone to help me with the wrench."

"How deep was the wahta?"

"The water rose up to my chest in a matter of seconds. That made finding the valve under water almost impossible. In the meantime, several other sailors started wrapping a ruptured pipe with sheets of tin and wire. We had to move quickly because the water was rising too fast."

"Were ya scared?"

"Hell, yeah. Even though we knew it was a simulation, it felt very real." I said as I wondered how the USS Warrington had actually taken its hit. Continuing with my story, I said, "The water was so cold, my feet and hands went numb. I froze my balls off."

"Is that why your dick is so small?"

"Shut Up!"

"How many times did ya have to go through that exercise?"

"We practiced in the simulation chamber several times. The instructors kept yelling that we were too slow and that the ship was sinking. The water rose so fast, we believed them. By the end of the week, we plugged up the leaks fast enough to pass the course."

I wondered if the Warrington's damage control team had been fast enough to keep the ship from sinking.

"That sounds like fun."

"It was fun, like an amusement park ride that is supposed to scare the hell out of you. And it did, every time." I knew that the Warrington's damage control team must have been scared. I hoped that everyone was OK. Looking at my watch, I wanted it to move faster so that I could leave my battle station and find Matty.

Bruce took the wrench from me and walked back into the repair locker. Returning with a green satchel, he opened it and asked, "What's in heah?"

"Drugs."

"No man, Ah am serious."

"So am I. Those are the drugs I will administer if we get attacked with chemical or biological warfare agents."

"No shit?"

Pulling out a small white box, he asked, "What's in heah?"

"Atropine."

"Atro what?"

"Atropine. If we get hit with nerve gas, I will open that box, take out a vile of atropine and inject myself with it. Then I will inject you and everyone else I find."

"Let me see what that looks like?"

Opening the box, I wondered if the Warrington had been hit with nerve gas or any other chemical agent. I pulled out a vile with the needle attached. The vile looked like a small tube of toothpaste. Bruce's eyes grew as he said, "Holy shit. That is the fattest needle I eva saw. That theya needle is bigga than a ten penny nail. Ah could neva shove that needle into myself."

"That's why they trained me to do it."

"What was training like?"

"After the instructor told us about nerve gas and showed us a movie about it, he made us stand in front of the class, one at a time and slam that needle into our thighs."

"That must've hurt."

"I don't remember if it hurt. I was so scared. The instructor told me to drop my drawers. Then he handed me a vile, and told me to make a fist with the needle pointing down away from my pinkie finger. He told me to slam my thigh hard with my fist then squeeze the atropine out."

"Did anyone in class not do it?"

"We all did it. One guy almost got himself in the nuts. He closed his eyes just before he slammed his thigh. He got himself in the left groin, barely missing his nuts."

"Nah, Ah couldn't've done that. Ah'm glad Ah went to ship fitters school."

"That's because you're the one who's a pussy," I said.

As Bruce smiled and flipped me off, we heard our five-inch gun firing, putting an abrupt stop to our reminiscing.

"Damn guns. Ah hope that the sonarmen are awake and not as sleepy as you. Ah want them to see any fucking mines so we don't run into em."

46 - GREED

I scurried up the ladders to the helo deck as soon as my battle station watch had ended, in hopes of finding Matty. Opening the door onto the starboard side of the helo deck, I stepped outside into total blackness. I stood against the bulkhead, next to the door waiting for my eyes to adjust. The ship's engines rumbled. The sea breeze combed my beard. The smell of the jungle wafted on the wings of the wind, mixing with the salt air. My lungs expanded making me feel renewed.

"Follow me," I heard Matty say.

"Wait, Matty! I'm blind as a bat."

"Just walk straight forward and grab the lifeline. Then walk towards the corner."

"Listen, Matty do you hear the helicopters?"

"Yeah, they are on the port side. They'll have another battle tonight."

My eyes adjusted to the darkness, allowing us to walk across to the port side of the helo deck to get a better look of the activity on shore. Gun fire broke out on shore. A white stream shot skyward terminating in a blast. A brilliant white flare danced its slow descent, illuminating the forest below.

"The tracers make it look like the helicopters are shooting with ray guns, doesn't it?" Matty said.

"Yeah it does. I know you didn't ask me up here to show me the nightly battle. What did you want to tell me?"

"The Captain is volunteering us for a dangerous mission."

"What kind of mission?" I asked.

"I don't know exactly. I overheard my chief talking to one of the other chiefs."

"What did they say?"

"They mostly talked about the captain. He wants to be hero so that he can earn the rank of captain."

"We all know that, Matty. That's old news."

"I know, I know. They were saying that he's a greedy bastard. That he wants all of the glory for himself. They said something about the captain volunteering to sail into Hai Phong Harbor."

"That is totally insane, Matty. We'd be too close to Hanoi. Hell. We're too close now."

"I know that. He made a request that we take over the Linebacker mission that the Warrington was doing. And I was the one who sent it. It made me sick."

"What?" The hair on my arms stood straight up. "If the Warrington took a couple of hits, what makes him think that we won't get hit?"

"The chiefs are really pissed off," he said. "They think that the captain is nuts and that he'll do anything to make rank. He doesn't care who gets killed, as long as he becomes a captain. He said that if he or any of us got a purple heart, that he could make captain."

"The chiefs are right," I said. "The captain is nuts."

"I also got another transmission just before my watch ended. It said that we will be taking on part of the Warrington crew."

"Holy cow! That's scary, Matty."

"You bet. It scares the hell out of me, too."

"I bet they accepted his request," I said.

"They didn't say that, exactly. We're taking on part of her crew, I read that for sure."

"Well, wouldn't that mean that we're going to take her place?"

I asked. "Somebody has to."

"Yes, but I didn't see anything in the transmission that said we were taking her place on Linebacker."

My head began to pound and my breathing began to race. I didn't want to die or get injured just so that Commander Reardon could earn the rank of captain.

"I hope you're right, Matty. But I have a bad feeling about this." I said. "Keep your ears peeled. I start my underway watch in a hour and I'll be through with that in four hours. Where will you be?"

"In five hours? Hmm? I'll be getting off my next watch. I can meet you in the helo deck and tell you if I hear any more news about the Warrington."

"Wait for me outside, I don't want the chiefs to spot us."

47 – REARDON''S PLEA

My eyes were riveted to the battle in front of me as the U.S.S. Trippe patrolled the North Vietnamese shoreline. White flares, imitating ballerinas, danced below their gossamer parachutes, illuminating the night blanketed jungle beneath them. The Viet Cong, now exposed, ran for cover into the bushes and behind tree trunks. Helicopters flew after them, like swarming wasps in hot pursuit. Their machine guns fired on all those who were exposed by the dancing white flares. Every fifth bullet, flying red hot, illuminated its pathway.

A Viet Cong sniper's gun shot at the helicopters from high up in a tree, his red hot tracers exposing his position. Mesmerized, I stood on the deck watching the counter attack. Pulsating light beams, reminding me of science fiction ray guns, carried death on the backs of machine gun bullets and delivered it to the tree climbing sniper. I jumped when Matty tapped me on the shoulder.

"What the hell! Don't sneak up on me like that!" I yelled.

"Sorry." Matty said.

"If I'd been on watch, I might have pulled out my pistol and shot your sorry ass. What took you so long to get here? I've been waiting here for a long time."

"Damn, you're in a foul mood tonight," he said.

Matty read my mood as easily as if I'd a worn a reflective vest with the words, "Fuck Off" boldly written across the front. My mood smoldered with hate filled embers waiting for the slightest wind to help them burst back into flame. I was still very angry at Chief Jaffe, for his accusation that my weird behavior had been induced by illicit drugs, rather than the after effects from the blow to my head. My headaches made me feel as if the sniper had shot me in the head.

"I'm sorry, Matty, my head is killing me and the pills the corpsman gave me don't do much. Did you get any more news about the Warrington?"

"Yeah, we did. A transmission came in when my watch ended and I couldn't leave until I relayed it to the chief."

"What did it say?"

"The transmission said that we were taking the place of the Warrington."

"Shit! Shit! I knew it!" I yelled. "The captain got his way and we're all going to get killed."

"Hold on, hold on," he said. "That's not what's happening."

"You just said that we're taking over the Warrington's place. We're gonna get killed!"

"No we're not. You can't tell anyone, but we're getting out of here," he said.

"That is not a funny joke, Matty. Getting killed is not my idea of how I want to get out of here."

"It's no joke."

"Matty, the Warrington is patrolling as far North as possible. Taking her place is not getting out of here. That is jumping from the frying pan into the fire."

Matty put his hand over my mouth and said, "Will you shut up. I'm trying to tell you that the Warrington is part of a three ship flotilla that's on an around the world goodwill tour. And they are from our home port in Newport, Rhode Island."

"Bombing villages is not a goodwill activity," I said.

"Jesus, can you just be quiet for a minute and let me finish?"

"All right," I said. "What else did you hear?"

Even though it was pitch black outside, I could see Matty's eyes sparkle when he said, "The Warrington is scheduled to leave in less than a month for Singapore. We're going around the world!"

"Look out there, Matty," I said, pointing to another white flare that floated slowly above the jungle. We could hear the gun fire and see the helicopters flying back and forth. "There is a battle going on over there. This ship is needed here. I can't imagine that they are going to let us leave. We've only been here a few months."

Matty and I leaned against the base of the rear rocket launcher, watching the battle. When the floating ballerinas extinguished their white flares on the jungle floor, and blackness once again blanketed the jungle, only the invisible whop, whop, whop of the helicopters gave evidence that death lurked just a few hundred yards from where we sat. A streak of yellowish light painted a quickly disappearing white line skyward. Poof. The white flared ballerina began her dance again, exposing the trees, the bushes, and anyone who had not already been hidden by the underbrush. Pulsating beams of light created the roadways upon which the bullets traveled.

When the ship turned around, taking away our view of the battle, Matty said, "I'm not supposed to tell you this."

I interrupted him saying, "Matty, you aren't allowed to tell me anything you hear or read, and I know that. So stop stating the obvious."

"We received a transmission telling us that we are taking the Warrington's place. My chief said that it was because our negative body count was too high."

"That is great news," I said. "But I'm not going to get too excited until we get to Singapore. The captain isn't going to take that news lying down. Knowing him, he will try to figure out a way to keep us here. If he leaves Viet Nam, he can kiss his chances of becoming a real captain goodbye."

No sooner had the ship turned away from the shore; I heard the announcement for helo ops, telling me to take my position on the helo deck. A few moments later I heard the whop, whop, whop of the helicopter blades. I didn't like doing helo ops at night. I felt that we were more vulnerable. We were within striking range from the big gun that we were trying to find and expose. If it fired on us at night, we would have a hard time locating it.

The darkness made it hard to see who was aboard the helicopter. Hearing Freddy's voice after he jumped out of the chopper, I walked up to him. "Do you have a minute, Freddy?" I asked.

"Yeah, I got something to tell you, too," he said.

I lead him down to the fantail, to a place where I knew no one could hear us talking. "I'll let you go first," I said.

"I heard that your ship is leaving in about a month."

"How did you hear that?" I asked, "That is what I was going to tell you."

"You're captain is a loose cannon. He's become a liability to the Navy with his high negative body count. Our colonel made a request to headquarters to get rid of you guys. I guess the Navy listened."

"I hope you're right and the Navy doesn't change its mind," I said.

"If it does, I will have more time to frag your captain. I already have it figured out. And I could do it without getting caught."

"That's crazy, Freddy. You wouldn't really kill him, would you?"

"Oh yeah! In a heart beat. We were called in to pick up two wounded in this morning's mission. We landed in a clearing, between a rice paddy and the road. I about shit in my fuckin pants when I got down to help put them in the chopper."

"What happened?" I asked.

"As I lifted the second man in to the chopper, I saw one of our guys stabbing a gook over and over. At first I thought they were fighting. But the fight was over. He cut off the fucking gook's head, picked it by the jaw and carried it back toward the village. I was hoping that he wasn't going to put it on a post."

"Did he?"

"No. He put it on his jeep, like a hood ornament.

"That's sick," I said.

Venom spewed from Freddy's voice as he said, "No sicker

than your captain blowing up a village and killing one of our guys, just for fucking body count. I swear, if I see his ass as we're landing, I'm going to kill that cock sucker."

"You can't do that, Freddy."

"The hell I can't. He won't even know what fucking hit him."

When the helicopter left, I headed back inside to stand my underway watch. Putting on the .45 caliber pistol, I wondered if Freddy really would shoot the captain. Knowing Freddy for only a short time, I couldn't rule that out. He was so upset when he found out that we blew up a whole village and killed one of his guys in one of our last bombings. I put my hand on my pistol and thought, if I had been in Freddy's shoes, I could be angry enough to kill the captain, especially if it had been one of my buddies who got killed.

After a couple of hours on my watch, I saw Matty go into the radio room. Noticing that the radio room door stayed open, I peeked in to see if he were alone. He wasn't. I pulled back to stay out of site, but stayed close enough to hear.

I heard another deeper voice, probably his chief's, say, "The captain just brought this message for you to send out."

"Did you read this message?" Matty asked.

"I don't care what it says, just send it out," the chief said.

Matty's voice went up, "It says that the crew is requesting that we stay in Viet Nam. The captain is asking headquarters to send another ship to take the Warrington's place.

"That is none of your business. Just send the message as you were told."

"Do I really have to since you ... " Matty's voice faltered, "and I both know it's a lie?"

"It doesn't matter if you think it's a lie," the chief said.

"But he's asking me to break a regulation. We aren't allowed to send a deliberate false statement."

The chief's voice grew louder and raspy as he said, "You have no authority to determine if it is a false statement. Just send it."

Having heard the dialogue, I tightened my hand in to a fist and clenched my teeth. I wanted to punch some sense into the chief. Hearing no more conversation, I left to continue my rounds. When I reached the helo deck, about an hour later, I saw Matty leaning against the hangar bulkhead. His hair looked like it had been in its own battle with hair pointing in all directions. Matty said, "I came out for some fresh air. It didn't help."

"What's up, Matty?" I asked.

"You were right. The captain is trying to keep us here. And I'm in a world of shit."

"If he succeeds, we all are."

"That is not what I am talking about," Matty said. "I added something to the captain's transmission."

48 – DEATH IN THE FAMILY

My battle station watch crawled across the last hour to its termination. "Sometimes I think I'm going to die right here just waiting for battle station to end," I said to Bruce.

"I certainly don't want to die like Ivan did, hitting his head on the table. That's just dumb," he said. "There's nothing heroic about that."

"Screw that! There is nothing heroic about killing people going to church."

"Why do you always have to bring that up?"

"Because it's killing me. We're going to hell because of that!"

"We aren't going to hell, we're already there," he said, getting up to leave.

I walked out onto the bow, letting the wind slide across my face. Looking west, I realized that we were leaving the shoreline. I caught a whiff of the diesel fumes accosting the ocean's salt air as we sailed out to the safety of the open sea in the late afternoon. Off our starboard side I saw the ammo ship turning toward the west allowing us to approach her port side. Once the two ships were sailing at the same speed and the ropes were secure, the transfer of ammo and supplies began. Boatswains mates from both ships worked quickly, but cautiously pulling the ropes that were attached to the pulleys that suspended our ammo. As I watched the hills disappear in the west, Matty found me.

"Have you ever wondered what would happen if a rogue wave knocked the two ships into each other?" Matty asked. "Would the ammo that they're transferring explode and blow us all to smithereens?"

"Yes, Matty. Let's pray that those boatswains mates know what they're doing. We have enough to worry about."

I hadn't received any mail for a couple of weeks. The discussion about death brought thoughts of my son that patrolled the perimeter of my mind, dropping homesick bombs into the pit of my stomach.

"They'll be transferring some mail from the ammo ship," Matty said. "I heard our chief talking to the lieutenant commander."

My ears perked up. I prayed that current photos of Jeremy that I had been asking for would be arriving at mail call tonight. The postman took about an hour to sort the mail. By the time he finished, a line of anxious sailors waited outside of his door, but standing watch prevented me from waiting.

Krack sat at a table, his shoulder hunched over, reading a letter, as I passed through the mess decks.

"I see that you got a letter. What's it say?" I asked.

Krack's eyes were gray, his cheeks hanging low. "It's a letter from my mom. She says that my grandmother's in the hospital." Putting the palm of his hand up to tell me to wait, he read on. "My mom says that my grandmother probably won't last more than a couple of weeks." Looking up at me he added, "She's had cancer for a while and she's really been going downhill for the past year." Picking up the envelope he said, "It was postmarked two weeks ago."

"I'm sorry Krack. Will you be going home for the funeral?

"I don't know if she's dead yet. And yes. By the way, can I borrow your back pack? I only have my naval duffel bag and that's way too big."

"Sure," I said. "If everything goes as planned, we will be headed back to the Philippines in a couple of days."

"I sure hope so," he said. "I love my grandma. Maybe I can catch a hop back to the states once we're back in Subic Bay. Are your grandparents still alive?"

"I only have my grandmother on my mother's side. My grandfather died last year."

"That's too bad. I still have all of mine."

Krack explained that his grandmother had been suffering for quite a while and his family hoped that death would end her suffering. "I wished that the last chapter in my grandmother's life would have been a happy one. But instead she's in a hospital hooked to a bunch of tubes and machines."

"When I die, I want to be ancient and die of a heart attack while making love," I said.

A smile revealed his teeth. "If you're an old fart, your dick won't get hard enough for you to make love. You'll die holding your wet noodle."

"What about you? How are you going to close the book on your life?" I asked.

Before he answered me, an announcement came over the intercom: "We're cutting our current tour short and heading for the Philippines. We'll be in Subic Bay in two days."

A loud cheer rose from those that were in the galley. Krack raised one eyebrow and said, "Big deal. We would have been there in three days anyway."

"Do you really think that we're leaving Viet Nam?" I asked.

"When I fly back to the ship and it's in Singapore, then I'll know we really are leaving."

"But if they fly you back to Subic Bay, you'll know that the captain got his way."

"And that he will continue to raise his body count," he added.

"You never answered my question, Krack. How do you want to die?"

"Let's go get your back pack and I will tell you."

Before he could answer, the supply officer came up to Krack, with a note in his hand.

"It is a message from the Red Cross for you," he said. "It says that your grandmother died. I'm really sorry. We'll do whatever it takes to get you home once we get to Subic Bay."

A tear dripped down Krack's cheek. I put my arm around his shoulder as we walked to my berthing compartment.

"I wish I could go with you, Krack."

"Yeah, you and the entire ship. You guys had better not be here when I fly back to the ship. I don't want to die in Viet Nam."

"Where then?"

"At home, surrounded by my family, when I am old, but not too old to still have a stiff one."

He smiled, and then broke into tears.

49 – THOUGHTS OF HOME

I had just finished my Sounding and Security watch at 04:00. The early morning air, blowing over the Trippe's bow, put me at ease. I lay down on the deck and leaned my head over the side mesmerized by Keegan's sea fairies, the phosphorescence that made the ocean glow as we cut through the water. Lying there, the vibration of the ship's engines gently released the tension of war and let my muscles go limp.

Thoughts of Krack flying back to the states were laced with envy. Flying back for a funeral would not be fun, but it sure beats being a sitting duck in the Gulf of Tonkin. The ship sailed northward as the moon went into hiding beyond the western horizon. The stars poked holes in night's velvet blanket shifting my thoughts away from Krack to my son back home.

"Would ya be enjoying me sea fairies, eh laddy?" Keegan asked as he came up and sat on the deck next to me. I could smell a hint of whiskey on his breath. Keegan only talked to me in a friendly manner when he had been stealing away a little alcohol.

"Hello Keegan, I am. And I certainly see why you call them sea fairies. They're beautiful."

"Aye, that they be, laddy. Ye wouldn't be screaming around the smokestack tonight, would ye?"

"I did that after dinner. If we really leave Viet Nam and all this killing, I won't need to scream anymore."

"Aye, we are leaving. That's for sure. Would ye be thinking that maybe now, Chief Jaffe, would leave ye be?"

"I hope so. He's been on my ass ever since ... "

"Ever since ye started yer bloody screaming. But if that be over now, ye can enjoy me sea fairies without the worry of guns and bombs and such. I love me sea fairies."

I hung my head over the side watching the ship glide through the water. Turning to Keegan, I said, "I wish my son could be out at sea with me and see this."

"Would ye be having a son, now? How old be the wee one?"

"He's two and a half, Keegan. And I'm not there to be with him, like I should be."

"Aye, laddy, a wee one should be with his father."

"Do you have any kids, Keegan?"

"Aye, I have a bonnie lass and I …."

Silence, like a fog, made all the words invisible.

"You only have one daughter?"

"No, no. I had a son, too. Aye, it breaks my heart just to mention his name."

"May I ask what happened to your son?"

Keegan heaved a long slow sigh. "T'was his heart that gave out. T'was a shock to all of us. He was playing soccer and he just fell, without even kickin' the fucking ball. He just fell, right there in the middle of the field. We rushed him to the hospital. But the doctors couldn't save him."

"Why did he fall, Keegan?"

"They don't rightly know. They said that he had a bad heart all along, but he gave us no warning. If I really believed in banshees, I'd be blaming them for giving me boy a bloody curse. But there aren't no banshees to blame. That's why I stayed in the Navy and took to drinking too much."

"I'm sorry Keegan."

"Aye, Don't be giving me none of your pity. That's the last

thing I need."

"Sorry, I didn't mean it that way."

"Forget it laddy. Would your son be playing soccer, now?"

"Like I said, Keegan. He's only two and a half. Not yet old enough to play sports. As I was looking at your sea fairies and wishing I could show them to him, I started thinking about how glad I am that we will be leaving Viet Nam. The longer we are here, the greater chance there is for my son to be an orphan."

"Don't even let yer mind wander into those dark places, laddy. Ask the sea fairies to take away those evil thoughts."

"I can't help it, Keegan. Don't you worry about what would happen to your daughter if you died?"

"Aye. But I did die, laddy. I died when me son died. Died a thousand times, I did."

"I can't imagine losing my son, Jeremy."

"Jeremy, is it? That be a fine name for a lad."

"What was your son's name?"

"Conan, 'tis Irish for wolf. I wish he'd be having a wolf's heart. He might still be here if he did. Would yer Jeremy be strong and healthy?"

"Yes, Keegan. He is a strong little guy."

"Good, good. Would yer son and wife be living in Navy housing? I didn't even know you were married."

"My son is living with my parents."

"And not yer wife?"

"Not with my ex-wife. We were only married for eighteen months, Keegan."

"Now you've gone and made me confused. Shouldn't yer ex-wife be taking care of your son, or at least her parents?"

"I tricked her so that I could get permanent custody. But it backfired. When we got divorced, I became draft eligible because I no longer had two dependents. I rejoined the Navy and that's why I'm in Viet Nam with you. That's why my parents are taking care of my son."

"That's still confusing, laddy. At least he's in good hands for now. Would ye be taking care of him when we get back to the states?"

"Yes, and I can't wait."

"Aye, you'd be making a good father to the lad."

"Thank you, Keegan. I want to be a good father. I just hope that we really do take the Warrington's place on their around the world tour."

"Didn't ye hear the news? Would ye be having wax in yer ears, laddy. We are going to Singapore."

"Yes, I did hear. But the captain ... "

"Fuck the bloody captain," Keegan interrupted. "The My Lai massacre is a bloody wound on the America's flag. The Navy ain't going to put another wound on it, if it can help it. The Navy prides itself on being better than the army or marines. They'll not let it happen again."

"I can't help but worry about it," I said. "Our captain is nuts. I'm afraid that he'll figure out a way to get us back in the battle."

"Aye, our captain is fuckin nuts. I won't doubt you that, laddy. But he ain't no fuckin good and the Navy knows that. Go to bed, and if ye be lucky, the sea fairies will bring you some sweet dreams of you playing soccer with yer son, go on with ye now."

I left Keegan, and walked to my berthing compartment, wishing that I could believe that what he said was true.

50 – SHE HAD MY EYES

My boots clunked on each rung of the ladder as I made my way to the helo deck. The rumbling of the ship's engines vibrated my hands and made a buzzing sound whenever my watch touched the ladder's railing. The salt air filled my nostrils in a failed attempt to blow out the odor of diesel smoke. The bright morning sun erased the lemon and apricot hues that the dawn had painted on the clouds just moments ago. "Look up dayer," Matty said, pointing to the clouds. "That one looks like a mother holding a baby on her lap, almost like a Madonna and child."

"It sure does, Matty," I said. "It reminds me of my ex-wife holding our baby son." Knowing that I was missing out on my son's early years, I fought back the tears that were trying to pry open the flood gates of my eyes.

The sound of Matty's voice abated my tears when I heard him say, "Oh! Oh! Look next to it. It's an eyeball looking down at them and it even has a pupil. Ha! We don't have clouds with pupils in New York."

"Look! Matty," I said, "That pupil is moving towards us. I bet it's a helicopter." Hearing the intercom announce its arrival, I said, "You're going to have to leave, Matty. They just called for helo ops. My fire rescue crew will be here any minute and I've got to get them ready."

"Can I stay and watch the helicopter land?" Matty pleaded. "Since my duty stations are inside, I never get to see."

"You're not allowed up here when the chopper is landing. It's not safe."

"I won't be any trouble. I'll be here in the corner." Matty said.

"Matty, if I let you stay, I'll be the one who gets in trouble. If there's an incident, you will be in the way." I started to send him away, but his puppy dog eyes reminded me so much of my little brother that I ended up saying, "OK, but if the chief shows up, you'd better get out of site and duck into the hanger."

"I will, I promise," Matty replied, his eyes sparkling with glee.

Whop, whop, whop, came the helicopter. As it slowly descended, I caught sight of the chief walking on the lower passageway toward us. Getting Matty's attention, I placed my hands over my eyes, as if they were binoculars, and pointed down to where the chief could be seen. Matty, mimicked my hand binoculars, looked below, gave me the thumbs up and skulked into the hangar.

Freddy jumped down from his helicopter and strutted over to me. Without his usual smile, he asked, "Can we get away from here? I need to talk."

"How about running down the mess decks for a bite?" I asked.

"No. It's personal."

I led Freddy up to the flying bridge where we would be protected from the wind and still be aware if anyone approached. Scanning the location I picked, Freddy said, "This will do." We sat on the deck with our backs against the bulkhead. He folded his arms, but didn't say anything. Looking into his eyes, I saw him gazing inward, hunting for the words he needed to release.

"She had my eyes," Freddy said. "The baby girl had my eyes."

His eyes took flight somewhere beyond the ship. I fidgeted with the keys in my pocket waiting for Freddy to continue as the ship rolled over the swells. I drew in the salt air through my nose and let it out slowly. *Whoever this baby is must be really important or something happened that really freaked him out.* I hoped that it wasn't going to be another horror story with our guys chopping off heads and hanging them on posts.

"She cradled the baby in her arms," Freddy said. "The chopper had room for both of them. We were there to rescue the wounded."

I could hear gunfire on the shore. Each second inched slowly as I waited for him to continue. "Her mom's eyes were so swollen and red that she looked as if she had been punched in the face. At first, I thought she was just another village girl."

"Who, Freddy?"

He did not respond to my question. His eyes had not yet come out to confront the world. They remained across the water, in a village that I could not see.

"When I got about twenty yards from her, I recognized her and ran, calling her name. She sat against a tree, not moving. Tears flowed down her cheeks."

"You know her? Who, Freddy?"

"Yes." Freddy's voice hobbled off his tongue and dragged sorrow into my ears. "I knelt down beside her and when our eyes met, she grabbed my hand and whispered, 'Our baby's dead.'"

"What? Did you say, 'Our baby?' Oh God, Freddy, that was your girlfriend and your baby?"

"Yes." Freddy's eyelids were swollen; his eyes looked gray, unable to contain the nightmare inside his head. "I didn't know she was pregnant."

"Holy Shit! You didn't know? Then, how do you know the baby is yours?" I asked.

"Oh, she was mine alright, there was no denying that. The baby looked exactly like my little sister when she was a baby. She had my eyes."

We sat in silence with the sound of the ship engines rumbling beneath us muffling the sounds of the shelling in the distance.

"What happened?" I asked.

"There was a fire fight outside her village," he said. "The fucking grunts asked for artillery support."

"From our ship?" I asked.

"Yeah, from your fuckin ship," he said. "When they called in the coordinates, your ship hit the target, which is what they wanted."

"Good!" I said,

"Fuck no! Why did your ship shell the village? The fuckin Viet Cong were not in the village. No one asked for that."

My shoulders weighed me down. Early yesterday morning, our five-inch gun blasted an unseen target and its neighboring village. I had wondered which village we had hit. The officers never told us the names of the villages, only the coordinates. They wanted to make sure that we only saw them as targets, not as real villages with real people. Searching for an answer to his question, I said, "It's for the bod ... "

"Body count," he interrupted, "I remember. Your fucking captain's god damn body count."

Part of me wanted to run away. Being a member of the Captain's crew made me feel dirty and partially responsible. Listening to Freddy, made me wonder what kind of man would kill mothers and their babies for a body count. Did the captain sit up in his quarters, counting the numbers on his body count list, like Scrooge counting his money? Did he have no heart at all? Couldn't he see that those numbers represented the killing of mothers with their babies, grandmothers, little girls and boys and not just the enemy?

"Oh God, Freddy, my captain's a monster."

"Monster? Hell, he's a fucking Hitler," he said. Freddy's shoulders sagged, his face losing its color as he said, "The baby and her mom got hit with shrapnel."

"Is the mom OK?"

Liquid sorrow overflowed the banks of Freddy's eye lids, creating rivulets running down his cheeks. Taking a handkerchief out of his pocket, he wiped his tears and turned his face from view. "I was so stunned looking at my baby girl that I didn't see the blood oozing out of her side."

"The baby's side?" I asked.

"No. My girlfriend's side. She was bleeding badly. But I didn't notice. Staring at the baby's eyes, I couldn't move. I just stared."

Freddy wiped his face with his handkerchief once more.

"The baby was dead. I knew it. But she looked so much alive. Her eyes were open. I could've sworn that her stomach moved."

"What did you do? Did you call for a corpsman?"

"No. I didn't see the medic anywhere. I was thinking that I could carry them to the chopper. My girlfriend was sitting against a tree holding the baby on her lap. Carrying them would be easy."

"So you got them to the chopper?" I asked.

"No. I froze. I couldn't pull my eyes away from the baby, until her mom fell over on her side, dropping the baby on the ground. When I leaned over to pick them up, my girlfriend's eyes were quiet, too quiet. I picked the baby up and almost dropped her when I saw that she really was dead. I rubbed the dirt off of her and placed our baby girl in my girlfriend's lap. There was nothing else I could do."

"I'm so sorry, Freddy,"

Freddy's stomach moved in and out, slowly keeping time with air flowing in and out of his nose. Looking into my eyes, he put his hand on my shoulder, and shook his head.

"When I first got here," he said, "she was working in a makeshift restaurant just outside of our post. I got to know her and one thing lead to another. It wasn't just the sex that I liked. My heart fell for her. I imagined taking her home with me when my tour of duty ended. But she disappeared."

"Where did she go?"

"I was fuckin pissed off. Nobody would tell me shit. They told me that they didn't know where she was, or if she'd come back. Finally, one of the other girls who worked there told me that they fired her and that she went back to her village."

"Did you look for her?"

"Yeah. But it didn't do any fuckin good. No one knew the name of her village. Whenever the chopper landed at any of the villages near our base, I asked if anyone knew her. Looking back, I think that they did know. They must've sent her home when they found out she was pregnant. I hadn't seen her, until today."

Hearing the shelling in the distance, I stood up and grabbed the binoculars. Peering across the water, to the jungle beyond the shore, I saw a sparkle, the sun's reflection on glass. I wondered if a pair of enemy eyes was staring back at us through their own pair of binoculars.

I sat back down. Freddy squinted his eyes as his thoughts returned to his last mission. "When the shelling stopped," he said, "we flew in to support the ground troops. After the area was secured, we landed to pick up any wounded and to do a body count. That's when I found her holding our baby."

My son's face came into my mind's eye. I put my hand on Freddy's shoulder and said, "My god, Freddy, I don't know what I would do if I found my wife and son dead. If I found out who did it, I'd kill him."

"What's so fucking weird is that for a few moments I was a dad, a real dad and I found my girlfriend. We were together, a family. Can you imagine that? A family. But your fuckin captain blew my family to bits. And for what? God damn numbers. Fuck!" He kicked the bulkhead with his boot.

I sat there, listening to Freddy, wanting to fix what had happened, feeling hopeless. I wanted to do something, say anything that could erase the story that Freddy was telling. All I could do was sit and listen.

Freddy shook his head, saying, "When I turned in the body count, I made sure these two and everyone else who got killed in the village were on the negative side, the one that shows that your ship killed innocent people."

The sound of the helicopter's engine, warming up, brought an end to our conversation. Freddy jumped up saying, "I gotta go. Thanks for listening to me. I can't tell anyone else. I'd get in big trouble for getting a native pregnant."

"I'm sorry about the baby and your girlfriend, Freddy."

Freddy turned his gaze skyward, as he repeated, "She had my eyes. My eyes."

Returning my own gaze to the clouds, I saw that the Madonna and child were fading away.

Freddy climbed down from the flying bridge, waited for me at the bottom of the ladder and said, "Thanks for listening." He gave me a long, tight hug and whispered, "If I get the chance, I'm going to frag your fucking captain. He's dead meat."

51 – WOULD FREDDY REALLY SHOOT HIM?

Thoughts of Freddy's dead baby and girlfriend bombarded the darkness around my rack and prevented me from falling easily to sleep even though I had been awake for the last twenty hours. I tossed and turned in my rack, telling myself to relax and go to sleep because I needed to get up in four hours for my next battle station watch.

"Whop whop whop," the blades announced the arrival of the helicopter as it flew in from the shore. I stood ready with the fire rescue team, in the shadow of the hangar. Looking forward, I saw the captain approaching the life boat as he plodded along toward the helo deck. I hated the captain. I hated the fact that he was making me an accomplice to his murderous deeds, to his killing Freddy's baby and girlfriend, to his blowing up the church full of Catholics going to pray. I wished that Freddy would frag him.

I saw the captain turn his head from side to side as if he were looking for something or someone. I wondered why he was out there. Seeing him away from the bridge and Command Information Central (CIC) was very unusual. He usually sent his steward or one of the sailors to get things or people that he wanted.

I wondered if it were possible for a machine gunner, hovering overhead in his helicopter to see the insignia on the captain's clothing. Could Freddy identify the captain? He had seen him in the mess decks. Would Freddy really shoot him?

The chopper flew slowly around the ship. I thought that was quite odd because I had not seen a chopper do that before. It seemed as if the pilot were searching for a target. Looking inside the chopper, as it flew by, I thought I saw someone's fingers on the trigger of the machine gun. This, too, seemed odd. The gunners were usually relaxed, as they flew in to land on the helo deck. Out here, on the water, they were safe, not needing to be on guard with their hands on the trigger. But when I looked up, I could clearly see Freddy's fingers on the machine gun's trigger. He sat on his helmet, his eyes searching for the killer of his baby girl. Freddy's eyes opened wide. His lips parted, as he yelled to the pilot. The whop, whop, whop chopped away the words, preventing me from hearing what Freddy was saying. The chopper flew around our ship again.

The captain appeared from behind the lifeboat. I tried to yell at the captain to go back. But the blades blew away my words. I slid down the ladder on my hands, throwing my feet forward. The ship rolled and I fell to the deck and rolled over on my side. I saw the captain running toward me. I threw my hands ups waving back and forth for him to stay away. The chopper came around the bow. In a matter of seconds, the captain would be in full sight of the chopper. I struggled, trying to get up as quickly as possible. The Captain stood in the open space between the lifeboat and the ladder.

"Are you alright?" he asked.

He was an easy target. Looking up at the chopper I saw Freddy, his fingers on the trigger, his eyes fixed on the captain. My heart beat to the whop, whop, whop of the blades. I jumped to my feet and rushed toward the captain. For as much as I fantasized having the captain killed, I didn't want his blood on my hands. I didn't really want Freddy to shoot him.

"Bam!" I heard one shot. My head began to burn. I tasted the iron seasoning of my own blood. Looking down at the deck, the toes of my boots were covered with red droplets. Did the bullet graze my head before it hit the captain? The captain lay face down, on the deck. As I stood over him, I saw blood dripping onto the back of his shirt. My blood. I knelt down next to the captain. My head burned as the blood continued to drip, one drop at a time, onto the captain's clean and perfectly pressed khaki shirt. I leaned over the captain, and grabbed his shoulder, turning him over onto his back. I recoiled and jumped back against the lifeboat. Ants were crawling out of the captain's eyes.

I inhaled big gulps of air. But I still couldn't catch my breath. I turned around and hurried back up the ladder, to get help from the rescue team. When I reached the top of the ladder, no one was there. "Where are they?" I asked. "Didn't they just see what happened?"

I dashed to the front of the hangar. Although the chopper had landed, the flight crew remained inside. I walked up to the chopper and looked inside. Freddy was talking to someone, the pilot I thought. I jumped into the chopper. Freddy stood up and walked forward. I followed him, taking several steps before we reached the cockpit. The helicopter seemed so much bigger than I had imagined. Freddy didn't say anything to me. He just pointed to the pilot's seat. When the pilot turned around, an invisible fist punched all the air out of me. In the pilot's seat sat the Vietnamese lady I had seen in my dreams.

"Control your hatred for the captain. He, too, is your brother," she said in her soft and gentle Vietnamese voice.

"How can you say that when he wantonly kills innocent people, your people, just for a body count?" I asked.

"He is still a child of Mother Earth. He is confused. Your hatred will only add to his confusion," she said.

"He's evil. I hate him. My not hating him isn't going to make him change."

"When you direct hatred toward your brother," she said, "you create powerful negative energy that feeds his own negative tendencies. Your hatred fuels his confusion and his own hatred."

"Am I just supposed to do nothing?"

"Direct love and compassion toward your captain."

"That's lunacy. I can't do that. How can I love a person who kills mothers and their babies?"

"Direct your love to the person, not to his actions. Your love will bring healing to his soul. When his soul is healed, he will not ….."

Bam! A loud blast, just on the other side of the bulkhead from my rack, jolted me from my nightmare. Lifting my head off my pillow, I felt my head. Sweat drenched my hair. The stitches in my head, still tender, burned.

"Go back to sleep," Dawson said, "It's just the captain playing with his percussion grenades again. Damn! I wish someone would frag that bastard."

The dream seemed too real. I wondered if the Vietnamese lady would return and finish her conversation. Tossing and turning in my rack, I eventually fell back to sleep.

Dawson woke me up, "Hey man, the captain's percussion grenades must have given you a nightmare last night. Well, it can't be any worse than this nightmare of a war."

"You can say that again," I said.

I had only been asleep about 3 hours. Cobwebs cluttered my ability to think. I needed to hurry and get dressed if I wanted to grab a bite to eat before my next battle station watch began. Grabbing a tray and utensils, I stood in the chow line behind hospital corpsman Powell. He turned around and asked how my head was doing.

"It hurts like hell most of the time, and I'm so cranky I want to punch somebody," I said.

"You have a concussion, you know."

"You bet I know," I said as my jaw clenched. "I've been having weird dreams."

"I'm not surprised. That is pretty typical. The cut on your head was not easy for me to sew up. You had a big lump and you bled quite a bit. I'm sure you cracked your skull. You should see a real doctor when we get back to the Philippines."

"I already tried that," I said as my jaw tightened. "The doc only wanted to know if I was taking illegal drugs. No exam. No x-rays."

"He was probably briefed by your boss."

"He told me that Chief Shea's notes were all he needed."

"What a lazy ass, that doc is," Powell said, as he shook his head.

"This headache has gone on too long. Why can't they fly me to the carrier to see a real doctor?"

"That takes resources that they don't want to take away from the war effort."

"That is nothing but bullshit and you know it. The supply officer had a toothache and they flew him to the carrier to see the dentist. A blow to the head needing several stitches seems a lot more serious than a tooth ache. Oh, I get it. The supply officer is a white man."

"Man oh man, you are cranky," Powell said, as he wagged his head. "Did you take the pain meds I gave you?"

"I ran out."

"Why didn't you come and ask for more?"

"Jaffe has been giving me hell and accused me of doing drugs."

"Fuck Jaffe. Since we put you back on duty status, you need to be able to think clearly. If we get hit, we need you to save our ass. And you can't do that if you have a severe headache. Come to sickbay after breakfast and I will give you something for the pain."

John Denver sang, *'Take Me Home, Country Road,'* over the loudspeaker as we sat down in the mess decks with our trays of reconstituted scrambled eggs and bacon. I had taken my first bite when the music went silent and the words, "Chopper incoming" came over the loudspeaker. I stood up. "The pain meds will have to wait until the chopper leaves," I said.

"Aren't you going to finish your breakfast?" the corpsman asked.

"No time," I said. "It doesn't look that appetizing, anyway."

I gulped down half a glass of milk and ran to join the helicopter rescue team. I stood in the shadow of the helo hangar, relieved that the Vietnamese lady in my dreams was a symptom of the concussion. Turning my attention to the task at hand, I could see the helicopter flying in from shore. The chopper flew in slowly, working its way around the ship rather than hovering over the helo deck, as it normally did. Getting a closer look at the chopper, as it flew past me, I saw someone's fingers on the trigger of the machine gun.

The hair on my head stood up. When I looked toward the

bow and saw the captain approaching the life boat as he plodded along toward the helo deck. This was unfolding just like in my dream. My stomach tightened into a knot.

"Oh shit! I'll be right back," I yelled to the crewman standing next to me.

I stood at the top of the ladder, yelling at the Captain to stay away, but the helicopter blades blew away my words. My dream was replaying itself right in front of me. Because my hands became sweaty, I slid down the ladder with my hands on the railing faster than I expected. The ship rolled. I lost my footing, fell, head first, into the railing and sprawled, face down, on the deck. Everything went black for a second. I opened my eyes. The captain was running toward me. I gasped. I scrambled to get up on my knees. I threw my hands up, waving back and forth for him to stay away. The whop, whop, whop of the chopper vibrated in my chest. Casting my eyes skyward, I saw the chopper come around the bow.

"Oh my god!" In a matter of seconds, the captain would be killed. As I struggled to stand up, I looked down at the deck; the toes of my boots were covered with red droplets. My head began to burn. I tasted the iron seasoning of my own blood as it slid down the back of my throat. I turned back toward the captain. His body lay face down, on the deck.

"Oh god! How could this happen?" I ran and knelt down beside the captain. "I didn't even hear the shot."

My own blood dripped, one drop at a time, onto the back of the captain's clean and perfectly pressed khaki shirt. My breathing accelerated. I was terrified of seeing the ants. I reluctantly reached down to grab his shoulder to turn him over. But, he got up.

"That was stupid," he said, dusting himself off. "When I saw you fall, I ran to help you and lost my footing."

I remained kneeling, stunned that he got up on his own.

"Your nose is bleeding," he said. "You'd better take care of that."

My knees began to shake as soon as I stood up. I pinched my nose, turned around and, without saying a word to the captain, headed for the bathroom. By the time I entered, my legs had regained their stability. My shoulders relaxed as I let the air out of my lungs. I walked over to the sink, pulled on the paper towel dispenser with my left hand, while pinching my nose with my right. I was relieved that the dream did not replay itself exactly..

"God damn it, I tore a hole in my pants," the captain said, as he walked into the head.

He washed his hands, shook them and dried them on a paper towel. He looked as if he were going to ask me a question, then he turned and walked out.

I wondered about the Vietnamese lady's words. If she was merely a symptom of my concussion, why did her words make so much sense? As I pondered that question, I washed my face and looked into the sink to see if my nose had stopped bleeding. Seeing no blood dripping when I removed my fingers from my nose, I looked into the mirror.

"Oh my god!" I yelled as I jumped back, my hair standing on end. The Vietnamese lady stood behind me. My stomach heaved in an out as I inhaled and exhaled deeply. I turned around slowly, but she was not there. I returned to the faucet, soaked a paper towel under the water and held it on my face as I tried to make sense of what had just happened.

I jumped when someone tapped me on the shoulder. I quickly removed the paper towel from my face.

"Are you alright?" the corpsman asked. "You're as white as a sheet. I was bringing some pain meds for you when I saw the captain in the passageway. He sent me in here to check on you. He said that he wanted everybody to be ready for our next mission."

"What mission?" I asked.

"He didn't exactly say. He mumbled something about volunteering to find out where the torpedoes came from that damaged the Warrington."

"Shit! That's too close to Hanoi," I said. "The captain's going to get us all killed. We'll be the next ones listed on his damn body count."

52 – THE DECISION

No gunfire, no violence, no helicopters disturbed the smooth waters of the Gulf this morning. I've been sitting at the bow of the U.S.S. Trippe listening to the rumble of her engines for nearly an hour, waiting for the sunrise. Sitting up here prevents the diesel exhaust from contaminating the musty smell of the jungle, just a short distance off our port side. I like this time of the predawn morning. I can only see the stars on the eastern horizon because clouds float overhead. In a few minutes, the Lord of the Dawn will get out his paint brush and dazzle me as he colors the clouds. I can pretend that we are not at war. I love the sunrise.

I can't believe that we've only been here in the Gulf of Tonkin for nearly three months. It seems like a year already. Who knows how much longer the Trippe will be here? And why here? Here where it is so beautiful, with the hills covered in trees that sway in the breeze. Those shoreline hills hide young boys who I know don't really want to fight. Why would they? I don't want to fight. They really aren't communists. They are just boys, like most of us on the ship.

Not even three months? But long enough to blow paradise to bits. Enough to make too many mothers cry for their dead sons. I should be praying for the dead. I should be praying for all those grieving mothers. I wonder if anyone every prayed for Mary, Jesus's mother when he died. I haven't said a single prayer since we got here, other than my nightly request: Please dear God, let me wake up tomorrow morning, back in my own bed in Long Beach and let this all be a nightmare.

It's a nightmare from which I cannot awaken. When I scream in a dream, it wakes me up. I screamed around that smokestack every evening that we were on the gun line. But my screaming doesn't wake me up from this nightmare.

Is God punishing me? What did I do? Did I die and not know it? Is this hell or purgatory? Am I here because I got married in a Methodist church and not a Catholic church? That's stupid. Why would God even care? Jesus wasn't a Catholic or a Methodist. Hell, he wasn't even a Christian. He never stopped being a Jew. He was a better Jew than Chief Jaffe, that's for sure. Does God even care? Does he even know that I am here; killing people whose only crime is that they were born here?

Oh wow, look at those clouds. Who would've ever thought that gray and pink went together so well? I can see the horizon barely lightening up into a yellowish hue. It's the forward color guard announcing the arrival of the sun in a few minutes. Why couldn't we be here to film the sunrise? God, why are we here blowing up paradise, while you paint the clouds? Are you toying with me? What lesson are you trying to teach me?

The bombing of the church haunts me. Is that why you keep entering my mind? I tried to warn the priest. You know I did. What more could I have done? Why don't you do something? You're God. Shit! Oops. Sorry. I guess I'm not supposed to say, "Shit" to God. I guess I could write a letter to the newspaper back home telling them what we did. It would be like going to confession. But I'd be confessing to the whole world, not just to a priest. And I would be getting the whole ship in trouble. The captain would say that I'm playing into the hands of the enemy.

I can't do nothing. I feel guilty as it is. If I do nothing, then aren't I an accomplice? No. How could I be? No one asked me if we could blow up the church. I have no authority to make any decisions. I'm required to follow orders. But isn't that what the Nazi soldiers did? Did God send them to hell for all eternity because they didn't speak up?

God, this isn't fair!

Hopefully, we will be in the Philippines in a couple of days. I could call my parents from the base and tell them what happened. No. That will take too long. The operator won't give me enough time on the phone. The censors would probably cut me off before I could tell them anything important, anyway. It's probably better if I write a letter home and ask Dad to send the letter to the newspaper. But what if the censors get it? They won't let it go and then I'll be in trouble. How can I get around the censors?

The clouds are exchanging their gray coats for their party regalia of gold and orange and a sliver of the sun is peeking out of the water, at the horizon. It's looking to see if the coast is clear, across the water to the western shore. That's it! I will sneak out across the bridge to Olongapo City and send the letter from there. The censors will never know. OK, OK. That's what I'll do. I'll get Norman and Krack and maybe Matty to look over the letter before I send it. Maybe not Matty. He's pretty young and he worries too much about getting caught.

But what am I going to write? I can't start off by telling them that I tried to warn the villagers through the priest. That would still be treason. They'd shoot me or send me to the brig for the rest of my life. They'll want to know how I found out. If I tell them that Matty told me, he'd get in trouble, too. Being a radioman, he's not allowed to divulge any information to unauthorized personnel. A hull maintenance technician, like me, is not authorized to know anything.

That sail on that Vietnamese fishing boat out there is pink and orange. I should've brought my camera. Look at those birds creating a silhouette against the orange clouds. I like seeing birds so much more than seeing helicopters. Helicopters.

I'll write that the guys on the choppers told me about blowing up the church on Sunday morning. But I will need to tell them that we were ordered to blow it up on Friday night. How could I tell them that I knew? I have to think about this. How would I know that we were supposed to blow it up on Friday night unless

Matty told me? How do I tell them without implicating Matty?

I'll write that the gunners mate told me. I'll tell them that the gunner received orders to blow up the church on Friday night. When Friday came, he told me that the orders were postponed until Sunday morning. Wait. That won't work. Will it? The fire control techs launched the rocket attack, not the gunner. But the gunner knew about it. The gunners and the fire control techs work together. Damn, the gunners mate who killed those boys on our first day gave me the willies the way he relished telling me about blowing up the church. Yeah. That'll work.

Here comes the rain. Ha. I never had orange clouds rain on me before. I'd better get out of here before I'm soaked. I need to find a place to write the letter before I change my mind.

53 – LETTER T FOR TRUTH IS TREASON

I ran through the passageways and slid on my hands down the handrails to my berthing compartment. Bruce and a couple of guys were talking. The forward repair locker would be a safer place to write the letter. I grabbed some stationery and my favorite purple felt pen and left the berthing compartment. I wanted to get some fresh air before I started writing.

The sun had descended, and the stars twinkled overhead. The smell of dead fish mixed with the diesel fumes squelched my desire for fresh air. Two hours had passed since we finished re-arming for tomorrow's bombing. I had an hour before taking over the sounding and security watch at 20:00. I walked down to the next level and unlocked the repair locker door. Looking around to make sure that no one would see me enter, I reached my hand inside, turned on the light, stepped over the threshold and closed the door behind me. The shelves of repair tools and safety equipment would provide a place to hide the letter I was about to write. My knees started to shake. I spotted a box of gas masks and pulled it down. The box would be a makeshift desk for me. I sat on a pile of coiled fire hoses and pulled out a letter that I started to write to my brother. I put it under the blank paper, just in case someone came in while I was writing this letter. I didn't want my mother or my younger brothers to read this letter. I decided to enlist my friend Kathy and ask her to help.

****

Hi Kath,

I need you to do me a big favor. It could mean legal trouble if this letter gets into the wrong hands. So please, please don't show this to anyone but my dad. Make sure my mom doesn't see it. She would worry herself to death. Well, maybe not to death, but you know what I mean.

I can't risk sending it through normal channels because the censors will stop it. And if they get it, I could spend time in the brig for writing it. That's if they don't shoot me for treason first.

Here's hoping that this letter actually gets to you. I am sending it from the town across the river from the Subic Bay Navy Base. Remember when I wrote to you about ladies of the night in Olongapo City? That is where I am sending this letter from. Oh no. Please don't show this part to my dad, just give him the attached letter. I can't have dad know about the ladies of the night.

We are supposed to be leaving Viet Nam soon and taking the place of the USS Warrington. It got hit and we're taking over the remainder of its around-the-world cruise. Yeah!!! I hope. Our captain is still trying to find a way to have another ship take the Warrington's place so that we can stay and he can advance in rank. I couldn't tell you this stuff before because the Navy's censors would've stopped it.

Thanks for your help, Kath,

Love Mushroom

****

Beads of sweat slid down my temples, passed my ears and into my beard while Trippe's engine vibrated my butt. The repair locker had no air conditioning. The odor of rubber gas masks, cardboard and fire hoses filled my nostrils. The ship creaked as it sailed over a swell. Footsteps clanked down the passageway making me jump up. My left foot had fallen asleep and began to prickle as it awoke. My breathing stopped when whoever it was stopped in front of the repair locker. My heart pounded. The footsteps continued down the passageway and were gone. I breathed a heavy sigh and started the letter to my dad.

****

Hi Dad,

I have a moral issue that I'm hoping you can help me with. I need to do what is right, even if it means taking a big risk.

You were in the Navy in WWII. I remember you telling me stories that you heard about with the Japanese and the Nazi soldiers. But you never talked about the good Nazi soldiers or the good Japanese soldiers. You never told me about the ones that didn't want to do what they were ordered to do. When I was in high school, I read about a Nazi soldier who helped the Jews escape from the concentration camps. He got caught and was executed. If I get caught sending this letter, I could be tried for treason. But if I don't send this letter, then I am no better than the Nazi and Japanese soldiers who saw terrible things happen and did nothing.

I'm sorry if this letter is confusing. I'll start with Captain Reardon. He is only a commander. Do you remember what that is? It's equivalent to a lieutenant colonel and a Navy captain is equal to a full colonel. He wants to earn the rank of Navy captain while we are in here in Viet Nam. Weren't you on a destroyer? The U.S.S. O'Brien, right?

Our captain has a negative body count. That's when we kill our own people or civilians. Did they have those in WWII? The captain is afraid that if his positive body count isn't far higher than his negative body count that he won't get promoted. He keeps doing things that I feel are wrong and immoral, and

310

probably illegal. But, being a low ranking enlisted man, I don't have any authority and no way to contact higher ups at headquarters. I'm hoping you can help.

Do you remember reading about the Mai Lai massacre, and how Lt. Calley and his crew got in trouble for killing all those civilians? Our captain is doing the same thing. He's killing anybody on shore in hopes of increasing his positive body count. But it only gets worse. The gunner on our ship told me that we were ordered to blow up a Catholic church. Can you believe that, Dad? A Catholic Church. Intelligence told us that the Viet Cong were hiding their ammo under the floor boards of the church. We were ordered to blow it up on a Friday night. And that still would have bothered me, because it was a Catholic church, after all. And since we're Catholics, I don't think that God wants us to blow up churches, certainly not Catholic churches.

I don't know why this is so hard to write. My hands are getting all sweaty and the ink on this paper is starting to smear. Can you still read it? My ears are peeled in case anyone opens this repair locker and catches me writing this letter. When I finish, I'm going to have to hide it. I will mail it from a Philippine post office so that the censors don't see it. Wish me luck. That's dumb. If you get this letter, I won't need luck anymore.

It was bad enough that we were ordered to blow up a church on a Friday night when no one would be in church. But our crazy captain ordered the bombing to take place on Sunday morning when the church was full of

 I had to stop. A couple of guys are talking outside the repair locker. I'm holding my breath. I'm putting the old letter on top, in case they open the door.

They're gone. Oh, I didn't finish what I was telling you: He thought that if he blew up the church that was full of people that his positive body count would go up. Oh, my God, our captain is evil. No one in their right mind would expect Viet Cong communists to go to church on Sunday morning. It was full of Vietnamese Catholics going to mass. I feel so sick about that.

I had a plan to warn the people not to go to church that Sunday. It didn't work out because I got hit on the head with the forward hatch. I already wrote to you about that and asked you to help so that I could be seen by a real doctor. I couldn't tell you about our blowing up the church because the censors would have stopped it and I would have gotten in big trouble. They can still throw me in the brig forever, if they find this letter, so I need to hurry and finish. But I can't write too fast or you won't be able to read my handwriting. My hand is shaking as it is. You and mom should have made me take hand writing lessons. I am writing this slowly so that you can read it. But it's making me real nervous. I'm hiding in a repair locker right now. When I get done, I'll hide it in a gas mask.

Here is what I want you to do: Please find a newspaper reporter who can get this story out. He will probably need to verify the dates and location. We are in the Tonkin Gulf. We blew up the church on August 13th. Unfortunately, I don't know the name of the Vietnamese town where the church is. I couldn't pronounce it and now I can't remember. But a good reporter should be able the find the name and get more details. There can't be more than one Catholic Church that got blown up on Sunday, August 13th, a few miles off shore from the Tonkin Gulf.

Ok. There I wrote it. I hope I don't get caught before this gets to you. Pray for me.

I hear more footsteps. Gotta' go.

Love ya,
Mushroom, Jeremy's Father

54 – ANOTHER PAIR OF PANTS

Barry and I had been watching the sunset from the helo deck as we were leaving Viet Nam on our way to make repairs to the U.S.S. Trippe in Subic Bay naval shipyard. I left him to go down and check my civilian clothes that were required for anyone wanting to leave the naval station. I sat on the berthing compartment deck wearing only my underwear. I held the last pair of civilian pants that I bought in Subic Bay in my left hand. In my right hand, I held my dungarees. Barry slid down the ladder on his palms, bounded into the berthing compartment and came over and sat beside me on the deck.

"I saw you doing this exact same thing the day before we arrived in Subic Bay, not even three months ago," he said. "Are you going to do this little ritual every time we are about to pull into port?"

"It's not the same, Barry." My annoyance squished into a pout.

"It is the same, only different. This time you aren't the fat mother fucker you were when you first got here. As a matter of fact, now that I see you in your white Jockey underwear, you're down right skinny."

"This war has blown my appetite to smithereens, Barry. The chow hasn't been very appetizing since we arrived in Viet Nam."

"You were a chunky fucker when we arrived," Barry said. "I can't believe how skinny you are now. How fat were you when we first got to Viet Nam?"

"I was a disgusting 180 pounds."

"Is that why the ship listed to whatever side you were on?"

"Up yours," I said as I flipped him off.

"How much do you weigh now?"

"A whopping 125 pounds. I weighed more when I was a senior in high school."

"Jesus! That's a fifty-five pound loss," Barry said.

I was shocked when I heard Barry say that I had lost fifty-five pounds. How did that happen without my noticing until now? We had been fighting in Viet Nam for three months. Worrying daily about getting killed, and being sleep deprived, were appetite suppressants. Trying to warn the village priest that his church was going to get bombed when it was full of worshipers and then failing to do so made me feel responsible for their deaths. All the while worrying about getting caught and being court martialed for treason were enough to give me ulcers. The steel hatch falling on my head gave me a concussion, and made me feel as if I were going crazy. It's no wonder I didn't notice.

As I pondered my drastic weight loss, I remembered the night before we pulled into Subic Bay three months ago, on our way to join the gun line off the shores of Viet Nam. I put on my Navy issue dungarees and struggled to get the button into the hole. I quickly unbuttoned my pants and took them off. Reopening my locker, I pulled out the only pair of civilian pants that I had left; a pair of bell bottom dress slacks, gray ones with a hint of blue. Their subtle stripes would have been invisible were it not for the ultra thin bark blue pin stripes that revealed their presence. Girls had given me so many compliments on them that these became my favorite pair of pants, even though they had no back pockets. When I inserted my left leg into my favorite pants, I felt the fabric slide all the way up my thigh. It reminded me of my ex-wife pulling on her pantyhose. Grabbing the top of my pants and exhaling, I struggled to close the gap between the button and its button hole. Sweat beaded up on my forehead. I took a big breath of air and blew it all out. Again, I sucked in my stomach and tried to reach the button hole. No luck. Sliding my slacks down my legs, I tried to remember how long it had been since I had worn them. Five months had elapsed since I wore them, bar hopping in Newport, Rhode Island.

The first time Barry saw me sitting on the deck, holding two pairs of pants in my hands, he irritated me. He told me that I couldn't leave the base in my Navy uniform. I'd have to buy a larger pair of pants before leaving the base. I didn't want to do that for two reasons: (one) pants were cheaper and more stylish in Olongapo City and (two) buying a larger pair of pants would signal defeat in my personal war against fat. I wasn't about to give up my favorite pair of pants. And now the opposite was happening. I needed to buy a smaller pair of pants before I would be allowed to leave the base.

"The whole crew is looking forward to shedding our Navy dungarees and wearing civilian clothes when we get into Subic Bay tomorrow," I said.

"It's not about clothes," Barry said. "We're a bunch of horny bastards, wanting to get laid." A smile lit Barry's face as he put his hand on my shoulder. Donning an air of authority, he said, "Son, I'm not surprised that this unfortunate consequence has befallen you."

I burst out laughing. "That's exactly how you said it the first time, Barry."

Lowering his voice and looking me straight in the eyes, he said, "When we first got here, you were a five foot eight inch tub of lard."

"I guess I was," I said as I squinted and lost my smile. "Hard to believe that was only three months ago."

Barry eyes scrunched to match mine as he asked, "Did I upset you?"

"No, no, Barry. I just realized something. And you're right, this was an unfortunate consequence."

"So? What did you just realize?"

I told him that my first payday made me fat.

"You got fat because of a payday? Let's go to the mess decks to eat dinner," Barry said. "I gotta hear this."

Barry stood, turned around and reached down to give me a hand. Lifting me off the deck, he said, "God, I was expecting to pick up a fat fucker."

"Used to be, Barry. Used to be."

Standing in the chow line, I stared at the food behind the counter. I couldn't decide what to eat because nothing looked appetizing. Barry filled his tray with the same boring roast beef, mashed potatoes and canned green beans that they had been serving us for the past month. I put a small slice of roast beef and three green beans in my tray. Sitting at the table, I stabbed one green bean with my fork and ate it. It tasted metallic and old. I put my fork down and proceeded to tell Barry how a payday made me fat.

I told him that when I attended damage control school, I stood at the front of the pay line to receive my first pay. I stared at the dollar amount next to my name on the pay list. The disbursing officer handed me a slip of paper showing my pay with deductions. I couldn't believe the amount on the list nor on that piece of paper. Looking at the disbursing officer, I asked, "Is this really all I get for a whole month's pay? $270 dollars?"

The disbursing officer looked at me as if I were an idiot as he pointed to his log book showing me that I got $386.00. I said, "But I can't spend $386.00 because you took out 30 percent for taxes and things."

"They're not going to give it to you tax free," the disbursing officer said.

I inhaled loudly though my clenched teeth. I could feel my face getting hot. I'm sure the disbursing officer saw how upset I was getting. When I told him that I made more than $386.00 every two weeks at my last job, making beer cans, he stood up and said, "Look at it this way, you don't have to pay for an apartment or food. The Navy takes care of that for you."

The disbursing officer's answer made me mad enough to want to pull my hair out, if I'd had any hair long enough to pull. I bent down to look him in the eyes and said, "But I have to share my apartment, as you call it, with twenty one other guys and I can't choose who my roommates are."

He tired of my whining and told me to sign for my cash.

Turning around slowly, I headed for the exit. My cheeks sagged, making my eyes feel heavy. I took my sweet time getting back to the barracks. Recounting the money in my hand over and over, I wished that more would magically appear. When I got to my room, my shoulders drooped as I slumped into my chair.

Rick, my roommate from Missouri, came in smiling like a little kid who got free ice cream. Taking the cash out of his wallet, he waved it at me and asked, "Have you picked up your pay yet?"

His happy smile irritated me. In a low voice, I dragged the words out of my mouth, "Yeah, but the amount is so small. And I have a kid to support back home."

When he asked me how much I got paid, I said, "Only $270.00."

Hey, what're you bitching about?" Rick asked. "That is more than what I got. And we don't have to pay for an apartment or buy food."

I jumped out of my chair, as the hair on the back of my neck stood up. I wanted to slap some sense into Rick's smiling face. I said, "Rick, did you hear what you just said? Who told you that bullshit? Did you talk to the same disbursing officer I did or did they feed you that garbage in boot camp?"

Rick stood in front of me with his mouth open, staring at me. After a moment, he put his cash into his wallet as if he were feeding it. A glimmer in Rick's eyes kick-started his smile again as he said, "If it means that much to you, eat it."

"Eat it? Eat what, Rick?"

"Make up the difference with chow."

"Rick, there is no way I can eat enough food to make up the difference."

"Ha, ha. That would be fucking A," he said. "The chow ain't bad. I'd like to see you try to eat the money that you say you're losing."

"OK, Rick, the challenge is on. I'm going to make the Navy pay for my lost wages with food."

Putting my hand on Barry's shoulder, I said, "And that, Barry is how a payday made me fat."

"That was then," Barry said. Pointing to my newest civilian pants, he said, "Before we get back to the Philippines, you're going to have to go back to eating like a pig, if you want to get off base in those big pants."

"Fat chance of that happening. We'll be in Subic Bay by tomorrow."

"I didn't even notice how skinny you've gotten, with you wearing your baggy dungarees and growing your beard. I'd see the doc about that, if I were you. Losing that much weight, in less than three months, can't be healthy."

"The corpsmen already made an appointment for me."

"About your weight loss?"

"No. To have my head checked out."

"Why bother? We already know that you're crazy," he said as he punched me in the arm.

"The doctor, in Subic Bay, is going to going to give me a check up to see if there is a residual damage from my getting hit on the head when the hatch fell on it."

"You'd better watch out for those docs. They could have you committed to some psych ward or worse."

"What are you talking about, Barry?"

"The docs are officers. Most are gung ho Navy. They don't always have your best interest in mind when they're asked to check you out. Did Corpsman Shea let you read what he wrote on his referral? You might want to check that out."

55 – MATTY'S REVELATION

I walked into the bridge at 20:00 at the completion of my sounding and security watch. The bridge was dark, except for its tiny red and green lights that elicited an eerie appearance. We were still in battle station mode. Barry chatted with the helmsman. I gave my report to the officer on deck and handed the gun, clipboard and sounding tape over to Barry.

"I've been dreaming about the girls in Olongapo," Barry said as he grabbed his crotch.

"I can't think about them with all this bombing and killing that we're doing here," I said.

"Thinking about those girls is the only thing that's keeping me from going crazy. Remember that chic in Kong's nightclub? The one with the mini skirt who took you to her room? She was hot. It's thinking about girls like her that'll keep your mind off this fucking war and back on your dick where it belongs." He laughed and slapped me on the back.

I walked out of the bridge and meandered along the weather decks to the fantail. We sailed toward Subic Bay, Philippines, as a bright full moon rose above the horizon. My nose caught the scent of the salt spray, untainted with the smell of gun powder. I inhaled deeply, feeling refreshed. The U.S.S. Trippe slithered across the water, sailing eastward, away from Viet Nam, away from the killing, away from the climbing body count.

I sat on the deck, hung my legs over the side, and watched the ships wake. The breeze reinvigorated my soul as the stars twinkled above. A smile came over my face as I realized that I wouldn't need to go to my battle station watch in an hour. I would get my first full eight hours of sleep in nearly thirty-eight days.

Footsteps clicked on the deck behind me. I turned to see Matty come and sit next to me.

"Do you ever think about God?" he asked as he let out a puff of cigarette smoke.

"What are you getting at, Matty?"

"I've been doing a lot of thinking, especially after the church bombing. I wish that I could do something to stop the captain from killing any more Catholics. I'm a Catholic, like you, and I feel so sinful and dirty about killing those people going to church. I bet God's going to send me and the rest of us to hell because of what we did."

"Matty, where do you think we've been? This is hell."

Matty rolled his eyes and shook his head. "Yeah, and I suppose he sent us here for spanking our monkeys too often."

"Now you're starting to talk like Barry," I said.

"Do you mean talking shit or doubting our fuckin purpose in the universe?"

"Both."

Matty's lips curled. "I bet our fuckin' captain has the five-inch gun tattooed on his dick and he slaps his monkey while he reads the goddamn body count." The embers from his cigarette glowed as he took a hard drag. "God's going to send us all to hell because our asshole captain gets his rocks off blowing up churches."

"I've already had a conversation about God and hell," I said.

"You have? With who?"

"Myself. I've been doing a lot of thinking. I have to do something. I can't just say that we were following orders and therefore have no responsibility for what happened. Otherwise, we're just like the Nazis."

"I know. I feel the same way," Matty said as he flicked his cigarette butt over the side. "I wanted to obey the rules, to do the right thing. But how can I when I hear the transmissions and record the body count? We aren't here to fight communism. We are just killing, killing and killing. That makes me and you killers too."

The ship slid over a swell, the screws rumbled and vibrated the ship and my butt. I appreciated the brief distraction.

"Yes, the Navy has turned us into killers," I said. "But I can't do nothing. I wasn't going to tell you this because I didn't want to get you into trouble. Now it's me asking you not to repeat what you hear. I wrote a letter to my dad asking him to help me."

"How can your daddy help? He doesn't work at the Pentagon. He isn't a congressman."

"No. He's just a mailman."

"How the fuck is a mailman going to do anything?"

"He isn't. I asked him to send my story to the newspaper and get it published."

Matty squinted, scratched his head, and pulled out another cigarette. He lit it and looked out at stars. The embers on his cigarette glowed as he inhaled. I was glad that I was upwind.

"What did you say in that letter of yours?" he asked. "Did you write that I told you about the church bombing?"

"No, Matty. I was careful. I said that the gunners mate told me."

We stared out at the water watching it ripple the moon's reflection.

Matty broke the silence. "How is a reporter going to stop any more slaughters from happening?"

"If a reporter had not exposed Calley, the world would not have known about the My Lai massacre and many more massacres would be happening right now. The church bombing is another senseless mass killing. We have to do whatever we can to keep our captain from doing it again."

"The captain's fuckin' evil," Matty said in a low voice. "I bet a lot of other captains are just as fucked up. Do you really think that a news story will stop it?"

"Maybe not completely," I said. "When the spotlight is on the military, those in charge behave a little better for a while."

"Let me see your letter before you send it? Wait! You can't do that from the ship without the censors reading it and stopping you."

"I know that," I said "When we get back to Olongapo City, I'll have one of the New Haven Club girls put it in a girly envelope and send it for me. By the way, Matty, what did you write at the end of the captain's request?"

Matty looked around to make sure that we were alone and out of anyone's hearing range. Keeping one eye looking behind us, he said, "I couldn't let the transmission go with the captain's lies about how the whole crew wanted to stay in Viet Nam. So, at the end of his request, I wrote: *The crew of the USS Trippe ...* "

Bam! We jumped. A blast up against the ship was the last thing we expected, being so close to the Philippines. We turned forward toward the sound of the blast. The moonlight exposed a silhouette of man tossing something over side. Bam! I held my hands to my ears.

"It's our fucking captain, throwing over the last of his grenades," Matty said.

I shook my head and let out a long sigh. "I hope that is the last blast we hear, Matty. What were you saying before the captain threw his grenades?"

"I sent out the captain's transmission like the chief ordered me to," he said. He pulled out a piece of paper out of his back pocket and unfolded it. "Before I finished, I made sure no one was watching me and I added this." He pointed to the piece paper in his hand. It was too dark see the words, even in the light of the full moon. He pulled out his lighter, lit it and held it under the paper for just a couple of seconds. He read it at almost a whisper,

"The crew of the USS Trippe is almost at the point of mutiny over what the captain is making us do in an attempt to turn around his negative body count."

"What!" I turned and stared at him. "Matty, they're going to hang your ass for that."

"There's more," he said, as he fired up his lighter once more.

'The crew has really freaked out since we blew up a church on that Sunday morning. I know that I will get in trouble for adding this to the captain's transmission, but I felt that you needed to know the truth.'

That's what I added. Then I tore off this last part of our copy so I wouldn't get caught"

"Wow, you've got bigger balls than I thought," I said.

"Hell no! It's got nothing to do with having balls. I'm scared shitless. For me, it's a damned if I do, damned if I don't situation."

Matty's eyes darted fore and aft. I put my hand on his shoulder and moved close enough to his face to smell the cigarette smoke on his breath. His eyes stopped and locked onto mine.

"That took courage," I said slowly and deliberately keeping my eyes fixed on his. "You didn't have that courage three months ago. None of us did."

Matty's breathing slowed, his shoulders relaxed. He started to say something but didn't.

"You've become a man," I said. "You put yourself on the line to save us from going back, knowing full well that you will pay a heavy price. You could've kept your mouth shut. No one would've been the wiser."

"Maybe you have a point,' Matty said. "The captain's negative body has wrecked not only his reputation; it's damaging the Navy's as well. There is a fair chance that Fleet Command will deny his request, even without what I added."

He sucked in air through his teeth and let it out between his lips.

"For me, the damage is done and I can't undo it. If we go on the around the world cruise, I might get off easy," he said. "If they grant the captain's request to go back to Viet Nam, he'll find out what I did, and he'll hang my ass, for sure."

He tore the copy in his hands into little pieces and tossed them overboard. We watched then float down and disappear in the ship's wake. I suggested that he learn to meditate and try not to think about it until we leave Subic Bay.

"Are you still going to do that meditating thing, even though we ain't fighting anymore?" Matty asked.

"That and screaming are the only things that have kept me

from going completely insane," I said. "In fact, I'm looking for a quiet place to meditate, now."

I made my way to the fantail and looked past the back of the ship at the water. The bubbling, churning water melted my back and neck muscles. I sat on the deck with my back against the winch, crossed my legs, and closed my eyes. My breathing slowed, opening a doorway to another world.

"You ain't gonna believe what I heard," Otis said as he came over and sat on the deck, next to me.

"So much for meditating." I said as I crossed my arms and frowned.

"Oh, were you gonna do that meditation shit?" he asked. "Sorry."

"What did you hear, Otis?"

"I was gonna tell ya that right before sunset, when the quartermaster and I were shooting the shit on the weather deck behind the bridge, we overheard the XO (Executive Officer) talking to that new lieutenant who flew in on the chopper a couple of days ago." Otis took a big drag on his cigarette and let the smoke out slowly. His smile expanded. "They were talking about you."

"About me?"

"Yeah. They were standing next to me looking down at you running around the smokestack, screaming your head off, like you do every night. The lieutenant scratched his head and said, "Look at that guy. He must be crazy."

"Why is that a big deal? Everyone thinks I'm crazy for doing that."

"Wait, you didn't let me finish. When the lieutenant said that you were crazy, the XO shook his head and said, 'No. He's not crazy. He's the only sane person on this ship.'"

Otis beamed a huge smile and exclaimed, "Ain't that wild?"

"That is wild," I said. "I'm surprised that the XO thinks that."

"You can go back to your meditating shit, if you want to," Otis said. "I gotta go. I have the next sounding and security watch."

I closed my eyes and tried to relax but I kept thinking that if I had let Freddy shoot the captain, Matty wouldn't have needed to add his note to the captain's transmission and get himself in trouble. We'd be leaving Viet Nam, without question. I inhaled and imagined an open gate. I let the air out slowly through my mouth as I imagined my concerns escaping through the gate. I breathed in and out slowly. I watched the thought 'I can't let Freddy shoot the captain, no matter how much I want to leave Viet Nam' evaporate beyond the gate. I imagined myself passing through the gate.

My meditation drifted to the shoreline we had just left. The beautiful Vietnamese woman who had appeared in my dreams and meditation sessions, stood at the water's edge, her arms outstretched. Dressed in her traditional Vietnamese pants and tunic, she shimmered in the sunshine. Her voice cajoled me into believing that I could stand up and walk over to her.

"1972 is long gone. This new day is only a thought away, only a glance away, only a gunshot memory away," she said. "Viet Nam beckons you to return. Viet Nam is at peace now."

Soft, salty tears flowed over my lip and into my mouth. My breathing accelerated and grew shallow. My face flushed, awaking an embarrassed smile as I continued listening to her.

"I forgive you," she said in a melodic voice. "I will help you forgive yourself and help you regain your soul. Come, I await your return to how you should have come in the first place. Come, I have forgiven you."

I remembered those words that she had spoken to me before. Again, tears rolled down my cheeks, as she said, "I forgive you. I will help you forgive yourself and help you regain your soul." Standing in her shimmering green tunic with the water lapping at her feet, she extended her hand to me and whispered. "Come with me to how you should have come in the first place. Come, I have forgiven you."

"What's you be doing there?" someone asked.

She evaporated. I opened my eyes slowly. Keegan stood over me with his hands on his hips.

"We're about to pull into the bay," he said. "We be needing this here winch." He squinted his eyes and held out his hand to give me a lift. With a voice barely audible over the rumbling of the ship's engine he said, "Get a grip o' yerself, laddy. Wipe yer face."

I pulled my tee shirt out of my pants and wiped my tears.

Sucking in a big breath, I accepted his hand. He lifted me off the deck and patted me on the shoulder.

"The guys will be up here soon. You'll be fine, laddy."

I tromped off to the helo deck, where I could get a better view as we sailed into Subic Bay. Looking west, I spotted Grande Island, a little island in the middle of the bay, not quite a half mile across that is owned by the Navy for what it calls, rest and relaxation. I made a mental note to make sure I got out there after we tied up to the dock.

Matty tapped my shoulder. He forced a smile that looked more like a grimace. "What's on that island, Mushroom? It looks like a fun place to go."

I looked at him, wondering why his smile looked forced. "That's Grande Island. It has beaches, a restaurant, and a small hotel, which is more like my high school dormitory with several beds to a room. And, for the price of thirty-five cents, you can't complain.

"Are you going there?"

"Most of the Trippe's crew will make a bee line for Olongapo City to hit the bars and brothels. I need to go for a swim and wash the war off my body. Only Grande Island could afford me that opportunity. You ought to come with me. It will wipe that frown off your face."

"I can't. They stuck me with the first watch while we're in port. I wonder if the captain found out what I added to his transmission."

56 – JAFFE'S RESCUE

R-Gang was always the last of the ship's crew to leave the ship when we came to a port. We needed to connect its electrical, water and steam lines to the utilities on the dock. We finished a little before noon. The Captain granted everyone who wasn't on duty an early liberty. I debated whether or not I should eat lunch before heading out. Hauling the water and steam lines to the dock's hook ups took a lot of effort and made me hungry. I gobbled up a fast sandwich that I made with roast beef and two slices of bread. I gulped down a glass of cold milk and rushed to my berthing compartment to change into my civilian pants. As I tightened my belt to hold up my now too big pants, I overheard Chief Jaffe talking to our Filipino machinist mate through the open repair shop door.

"With all due respect, Chief, you're not being fair," said the machinist mate.

I took a couple of steps back from my rack to get a clear view of those two, being careful not to appear that I was snooping.

Chief Jaffe put his hands on his hips and jutted out his chin, saying, "Why should I treat you any differently? You can have free leave when we get back to fucking Rhode Island, just like everybody else."

"My family is here, in the Philippines, not in Rhode Island. You're the only chief who's not allowing Filipinos to visit their families without taking leave."

"You are the only god damn Filipino I have working for me. What the other chiefs do with their own Filipinos is none of my fucking concern. I don't give a shit if I am the only one. If you want more liberty, fill out a fucking leave request."

I felt sorry for the machinist mate. Why does the Chief have to be so sadistic, so mean to the non-Whites? I hurried out of the berthing compartment as quickly as I could, before Jaffe saw me. I didn't want to give him an opportunity to find a reason to deny me liberty and besides, I had an appointment with a real doctor in twenty minutes.

The Officer of the Deck returned my salute as I turned and loped down the gang plank. Relearning how to walk on solid ground without swaying from side to side, proved to be a challenge.

I looked at the base map and located the clinic. I entered and handed the receptionist my paperwork.

"We've been expecting you," he said. "Thanks for being on time."

I didn't wait long to be called into the doctor's office. He sat behind his wooden desk. He asked me to sit in a chair instead of the exam table. He put his head down as he flipped through my medical chart.

"Have you had any thoughts about suicide?" he asked.

"No. Are you going to X-ray my head?"

"That won't be necessary; your hospital corpsmen did a pretty thorough job in your chart."

He had me stand up, touch my nose with each hand and turn around in both directions.

"Are you still getting headaches?"

"Yes," I said. I started to tell him about the strange physical sensations I'd been experiencing, but he but his hand up to stop me.

"I'm writing a prescription for Darvon. I'll give it to the nurse to fill for you. It will help with your headaches."

He stood up walked out of the exam room without saying another word. The nurse came in with a small bottle of pills telling me take no more than 4 a day and that I could leave. I was stunned. I finally got to see a real doctor and he didn't want to be bothered. I left the clinic and made my way to the Grande Island boat launch. When it came within my sight, I picked up my pace trying to outrun my disappointment. As I got close, the WWII landing craft that would've transported me to the island was already pulling away. My head dropped. Barry surprised me with a slap on the back as he came running up behind me.

"Didn't you hear me?" he asked, breathing heavily. "I called you."

I turned to look at him, but did not answer.

"Why so glum?" he asked.

"You were right about the Navy doctors. I just left the doctor's office. He was supposed to check out my head. He didn't even look at it. No physical exam, no x-ray. What a waste of time."

"I'm sorry it didn't work out," Barry said. "He probably read what was in your chart and since you walked in on your own two feet, figured that you were fine. Where are you headed now?"

"I missed the damn boat to Grande Island. The next one won't be for another two hours, according to the schedule."

"Join me, then," he said. "We'll go into town and have a few beers while we wait for the next boat. I need a beer or two or three after 38 fucking days out at sea. With a little luck, maybe I can get a little pussy. Damn, just being on solid ground is already making my pecker hard."

I really didn't want to go into town. I wanted to get away from the Navy, even if it was only an illusion. Grande Island could do that, whereas Olongapo City would be full of bar hopping sailors, getting rowdy and drunk.

"Well, are you coming or not?" Barry asked. "You've got plenty of time; two hours to kill. I'll buy you a San Miguel. A little beer will do you good. And you could buy yourself a better fitting pair of pants. The one's you're wearing are huge. Come on."

I acquiesced. I really did need a smaller pair of pants. As we crossed the river that separated the base from Olongapo City, well tanned boys stood in chest high water yelling, "Hey, body! Throw me coin." The way they mispronounced buddy as body made me think that the word, body, was more accurate than buddy.

"How can they fucking stand the smell of that shit in the water, much less, swim in it?" Barry asked.

We held our breath as we walked across the bridge. The boys continued pleading, "Hey body, throw me coin."

One of the boys standing in the brown fecal smelling river looked like he could be one of my little cousins. Reaching in my pocket, I tossed a couple of dimes to him. He caught one and dove into the shit brown water to hunt for the one that bounced out of his hand.

"Oh, fuck!" No way could I do that," Barry blurted. "I swear, my grandfather's fucking outhouse smells better than that shitty river."

"Thank God, Barry, we didn't grow up here, having to swim in that sewer of a river just for a few coins."

"Let's get the fuck outta here. My nose hairs are starting to fuckin singe," he said as we sped the rest of the way across the bridge.

Olongapo City had a carnival atmosphere. The aroma of skewered beef cooking on a small black grill was a welcome relief from the putrid smell of the river.

"That's probably monkey meat." Barry said, "It tastes good. You ought to try it."

I rolled my eyes, "Get real, Barry. When is the last time you saw a monkey in Subic Bay?"

"This morning. He's your fuckin boss."

"Jaffe is more gorilla than monkey," I said.

A boy of about twelve, in shorts and tee shirt with a photo of Marvel Comics', The Hulk, interrupted our conversation. He held out corn on the cob that he was roasting on skewers over an open fire in a fifty five gallon drum. The smell of beer and cigarettes, along with the sound of Three Dog Night's '*Joy to the World*,' billowed out from the bar we were passing. Converted old Jeeps, called Jeepnees, decorated in neon orange, yellow, red and green, honked as they rolled down the street carrying sailors who were too lazy or already too intoxicated to walk. A couple of young women, wearing blue and yellow miniskirts and tight fitting blouses, stood in a night club doorway. Waggling their fingers with their highly polished long fingernails, they beckoned us to join them saying, "Hey sailor. You want fucky, fucky? I give you good price." Barry and I smiled at them as we meandered our way around sailors and street vendors crowding the sidewalk. Passing an alley, marijuana smoke tickled our noses while Brewer and Shipley's 'One Toke Over The Line' played from a portable cassette player next to a man hawking records and music cassettes. Barry gave me a shit eating grin as we headed for the New Haven Club at the end of the block.

We walked up well worn wooden stairs through a tunnel of dust covered stucco walls and a wooden slanted roof. The music of Janis Joplin's 'Me And Bobby McGee' grew louder as we reached the top. The odors of cheap perfume and beer colored the air. Out of the dark belly of the bar, a young woman, in pink hot pants and a nearly see through matching pink tank top, jumped up wrapping her arms and legs around Barry. She grabbed his head, rubbing her braless breasts into his face.

"I knew you'd come back to me," she squealed.

Barry's eyes sparkled as he carried her to the table. He ordered a round of beers for the three of us. Responding to our query about where I could buy a pair of pants, she gave me directions to a men's clothing store around the corner. When I finished my San Miguel beer, Barry winked and said, "Go buy your pants. Don't wait up for me. Rosita and I are spending the night together."

She blew me a kiss. "Tell Jose, in the men's store, he better give you good price or I no sneak him free beers no more."

I didn't like spending what little money I made on another pair of pants. My waist had shrunk from 34 inches to 29 inches since my last pair. My body was as lean as the boys' in the river. My watch indicated that I still had an hour to kill before the next boat for Grande Island. I left the men's shop wearing my new pants and holding my old ones in a plastic bag. I tossed my old pants into an empty box outside the Elephant bar. The cool air flowing out of the bar lured me in, out of the day's heat. When I passed by the fake elephant tusks at the entry to the nightclub, I remembered having come here with a group of African

Americans from my ship the last time we were in port. Marvin Gaye's, '*What's Going On*' blared through the large speakers set by the door. As my eyes labored to adjust to the dim bar room light, I recognized some of the African Americans from our ship. My stomach tightened when I heard them yelling at someone in the middle of their circle. I couldn't see who.

"You honky son of a bitch!" the Black sailor in front of me shouted, his saliva glistening in the bar room lights. "We're gonna fuck you up one side and down the other!"

"You cock sucking asshole!" another screamed.

Their screaming that they were going to kill him made the hair on my arms stand up. With my heart thumping, I joined the circle to see who they were yelling at. My Black shipmates made an opening for me, as if I were expected. A stocky white man, wearing a Hawaiian shirt held his head down and his hands out in defense. When he backed up, someone thrust him back into the circle.

A man with a big afro leaned forward, his face inches from the white man's, in a loud and low tone, he said, "You ain't going nowhere, you mutha fuckin honky cunt!"

The white man lifted his head. I gasped. What was our racist chief doing in a Black nightclub without any of his White cronies? Trying to make some sense out of it, I looked again. Was that really Jaffe?

When he saw me, he broke down and cried, "They don't understand."

"We understand, loud and clear," one man yelled. "You're a mutha fuckin racist son of a bitch. You fuckin treat the minorities under you worse than anyone on the ship, and you treat the rest of us like shit."

One of the men pushed Jaffe in the chest. "You're not so high and mighty now; you white ass pile of shit! We're fuckin tired of you treating us like your personal niggas'."

Another said, "Yeah, especially the minorities stuck working for you! I ought to make you suck my big black dick right here! See how you like it!"

As they tightened the circle around him, one of them turned to me.

"We'll gladly beat the shit out of your fuckin boss,

Mushroom."

Jaffe whimpered, his lower lip shaking, "No, no. I'm not really that way." The barroom lights reflected off of his bald head. The front of his shirt was soaked with sweat.

My breathing stopped as I saw the hate in the Black faces surrounding Jaffe. *I could make this racist bastard pay for all the shit he's put me through.* I thought. *Here's my chance to beat the crap out of him.* I imagined my fist smashing into his face, blood spurting from his mouth.

The circle coiled tighter. One of the guys lifted his fist, ready to crush Jaffe's nose. He waited, looking at me to give him the go ahead. Jaffe's been the devil personified, making my life hell. *Why should I become his guardian angel, showing up in the nick of time to rescue him? Is this what four years studying for the priesthood has done to me?*

There were so many of them, they could easily kill him, without intending to. Heaven knows he deserves whatever they'd do to him.

"No, leave him alone." I heard myself saying. "If we hurt him, we'll give him more reasons to hate minorities. And he'll find ways to get us all in deep shit."

I must have been the voice of reason because they moved apart, creating an opening for him. Jaffe cowered and slinked toward the door. A tall, muscle bound sailor, walked beside him, putting his mouth next to Jaffe's ear, saying, "You'd better hang your fuckin tail between your legs, or we're gonna fuck you like a bitch."

Jaffe kept his head down and didn't look back. When he reached the door he quickly looked both ways and bolted to the right. I told the man standing next to me, "The Golden Rule; 'Do unto others as you would want them to do to you,' turned on him"

"Bit the cock sucker like a fuckin rabid dog, it did," he said. "You should've let us beat the bird turd shit out of him. I wanted to punch his fuckin' face so bad, I could taste it. I hate that mutha' fucka."

The look of terror in Jaffe's eyes surprised me and showed me how vulnerable this man, we called the Hulk, really was. I followed him, without his seeing me. I'm not sure why. I was curious to know if he'd run back to the safety of the ship.

Crossing the bridge, I tossed a couple more coins to the boys in the shit river. I made sure that they caught the coins easily so that they wouldn't have to dive into that fecal smelling muck after the coins. When I reached the Grande Island boat launch I stopped and watched a shaken Chief Jaffe continue his return to his safe haven. I surprised myself that I didn't let them beat him. Either this event would soften his attitude toward the minorities or make it worse.

57 – BLUE DAMSELS

I climbed down into the WWII landing craft that would transport me to Grande Island. I hadn't noticed Norman and Krack sitting with their backs against the rear bulkhead until I looked for a place to sit.

"Hey, Krack, I thought you were flying back to the states for your grandmother's funeral?"

"I can't get a flight out until the day after tomorrow. It looks like I'm stuck with you two."

"Are you guys spending the night?" I asked.

"Ya betcha," Norman said. "I need to sleep on solid ground without rocking and rolling and the constant hum of the ship's engines. How about you?"

"I intend to have the sun wake me up," I said. Smiling widely I sat on the bare deck next to him. "Riding in this landing craft feels like were floating in a shoe box."

"We are!" Krack said.

When we landed, we walked into the little restaurant that protruded from the hotel. I asked the old wrinkled faced lady who worked there for an ice cream cone.

"You sit," she commanded, with a frown on her face.

Norman smiled at me and turned his palms up as he tilted his head. "Can you make that two?" he asked the grumpy lady.

She scowled at him and pointed to the table. We obeyed.

"I was hoping to get pistachio ice cream," I said to Norman.

"Fat chance," Krack said, "They probably only have one flavor, otherwise she would've asked you what you wanted."

She had disappeared into the kitchen as the three of us waited for what seemed like a very long time. We chatted excitedly about joining the two other ships on an around the world cruise.

When she came out, she said, "Fifteen cent."

We dug into our pockets. I pulled out a dollar and handed it to her.

She looked up at me and said, "No change. Fifteen cent." while holding out her hand.

Norman and Krack both only had dollars. I handed the dollar back to her and told her it was for all three and that she could keep the change. Maintaining her scowl, she took the dollar and gave us our chocolate ice cream cones.

"I'll be glad when we leave this place for Singapore and we don't have to look at her frowny face again," Norman said. "Hey let's hurry and get up to the golf course, and to golf tee number seven, on the top of the hill so we can watch the sun set."

"What's so special about golf tee number seven?" I asked.

"It has a gazebo and will keep us dry if it rains," Norman said.

Across the bay from our hill top vantage point we could see two storms forming over the hills across the bay. The sun illuminated the clouds from behind, painting them an orange and yellow hue. Opposing storm clouds collided, lightening and thunder announcing a celestial battle.

"Wow!" I shouted, "That was awesome! Did you see how the clouds on the right looked like a Roman warrior with a shield and spear who bent down to kiss a girl holding a dog?"

Norman laughed as he said, "Yeah, but I thought it was a football player kissing a girl with a cat."

Krack laughed and said, "I don't know what you two were smoking, but you should have let me have some too."

When I pulled out a bag of M&M chocolate covered peanuts

out of my pocket, an envelope fell out. Norman bent down and picked it up.

"What's ya got heah?" he asked in his Bostonian accent.

"It's a letter I want to send home that I hope my parents will send to the press," I said.

Krack, who had been sitting on the other side of Norman stood up across from us and asked, "What would you possibly want to send to the press?"

Handing Krack the bag of candy, I said, "It's a letter about the church that we blew up and how we tried to warn the priest."

"Norman turned quickly to face me. "Are you out of your fucking mind? No one can know about that?"

"The families of all those people we killed in that church, they all know about that," I said.

"I know. I know. But they don't know we tried to help. And it's better that way. Remember, what we tried to do is treason."

"How can it be treason when what we tried to prevent is so wrong, so immoral."

"Fuck that shit, Mushroom. You can't send that letter without getting us all in trouble. And Krack and I are already in big trouble for our refusal to fire the rockets. This is all the Navy needs to hang our asses."

"He's right," Krack piped in. "And Matty will lose his rate because they will know that he had to have been the source of information. If they don't shoot us, we'll all spend time in the brig. Forget that fucking letter, tear it up."

"I hear what you guys are saying, but how else are we going to stop this kind of senseless killing. It's just another My Lai massacre, only this one, we're keeping secret."

"You got that right. No one here is arguing that point. We just don't want to go to jail," Norman said.

"If you send that letter it won't have any effect on stopping the senseless killing," Krack said. "All war is senseless. Did those graphic newspaper and TV stories of the My Lai massacre stop the captain from purposely waiting to bomb the church when it was full of people? Don't be a cock sucking idiot."

"But if I don't do something, I will regret it for the rest of my life."

"If you send that letter, we will all regret being involved for the rest of our lives," Norman said.

I let out a heavy sigh, took the letter out of its envelope and read down to where I started discussing the church bombing. I folded the letter at that line and tore off what I had written above. I handed the letter to Norman.

"I'm keeping the personal part to send home in my next letter. You can tear up the part about the bombing. I don't have the heart to do it."

"We know you want to do the right thing," Norman said as he padded me on the shoulder. "This just isn't the way to do it."

We turned our attention back to the sky where we watched the celestial battle evaporate, in much the same way as my attempt to send the letter evaporated. Night came with her blanket of stars hiding our way back down the hill.

"I didn't bring a flashlight," Krack said. "So we better hurry before it gets any darker."

We meandered our way following the trail down to the hotel. When we reached our destination, the security guard told us that there was a storm coming and that we should have left on the last boat. Everyone left the island and he thought that he was the only one left. When I asked him if we could stay in the hotel, he held out his hand and said, "Thirty five cents, please." Norman pulled out a dollar and told him it was for all three of us. The guard led us up stairs to a dorm with about ten beds. He pointed to the first three, next to the door. As soon as he left, we jumped into the beds next to the window. I made sure that the blinds were open. Krack turned out the lights. Sleep came quickly to all of us.

The sun caressed my face as it gently woke me up. Opening my eyes, I immediately knew that I could not be on a ship. Navy ships have no windows in berthing compartments. I felt happy. I pulled the white sheet back and put my feet on the cool linoleum floor. Both Krack and Norman were awake, lying on their beds, enjoying the morning sunshine as well.

"I'm going for a swim before breakfast," I said.

"How?" Norman asked. "I didn't see you bring anything with you. Do you have swimming trunks in your back pocket?"

"Heck no," I said. "We don't need any stinking swimming trunks. Right now, we're the only people on the island, except for the security guard. I'm going skinny dipping."

We headed for the beach on the South side of the island, away from the dock, since we knew that people would eventually arrive. I stripped off my clothes and laid them in a pile on a rock. Donning the face mask and snorkel that we found at the hotel, I went into the water first. It was crystal clear and warm. I hadn't gotten very far when I saw a large school of blue damsels, little bright blue fish with yellow tails. They swam around me giving me the illusion that I was swimming in a huge aquarium with no glass boundaries. The fish were free to come and go as they wished. Envy crept into my thoughts as I watched the fish. I heard Norman calling me, telling me that he wanted to use the mask and snorkel, too.

I stood up in water that was only chest level deep. "Give me five minutes," I said.

My body slid back into the water. I started thinking that life would have been so much better if we had gone to Viet Nam to snorkel instead of fight. Guilt swam around me as I remembered my failed attempt to save the villagers from getting blown up in church. When I turned around to swim back to shore, I saw the Vietnamese lady who appeared in my dreams, swim under water toward me. She wore the traditional Vietnamese pants and tunic. But they were made of thousands of live blue damsel fish.

I froze.

"Good bye, be sure to come back," She said with a smile and waved her hand. "I forgive you. I will help you forgive yourself and help you regain your soul." she said. "I await your return to how you should have come in the first place."

I stood up as fast as I could, my breathing raced to catch up with my heart beat. I put my face back in the water but the Vietnamese lady was gone. I swam back to shore hoping that our ship would not return to Viet Nam.

58 – THE FINAL DECISION

"Now hear this, now hear this. All hands on deck," blared on the ship's intercom. The last few members of the "R" gang took their places in formation on the helo deck for morning muster. A light musty breeze fanned my face as the sun beamed its warm glow, casting long shadows on the deck. Chief Jaffe made the usual announcements telling us what our specific jobs were for the day. He stopped, moved his head from side to side to look at each one of us.

He feigned a frown and said, "I'm saddened to tell you that we won't be returning to Viet Nam." He couldn't sustain his scowl. His face and ours erupted into broad smiles when he added, "The U.S.S. Trippe will depart for Singapore tomorrow morning. Get the ship ready to sail. Dismissed."

He walked up to me and ordered me to stay put. My shoulders slumped along with my smile. As he walked around the helo deck, I wondered what he wanted and why it looked like he was making sure that we were alone and out of earshot.

"I have a question to ask you," he said with a soft voice. "Why didn't you join them?"

"Join who?" I asked. He knitted his eyebrows. His whole body stiffened.

He forced a whisper, "Those Negros, I mean Blacks in the Elephant Bar. They were going to kill me. Why did you stop them? Why didn't you take the first punch at me when you had the chance? I would've, if I had been in your shoes."

"I'm sure you would've, Chief," I said as I looked directly into his eyes. Part of me had an urge to tell him just how much I had wanted to punch him, but the memory of the Vietnamese Lady brought out the best in me.

"Let me ask you something," I said. A loud patrol boat sped passed the dock where our ship was tied up forcing me to hold my question until it passed.

The chief stood with his arms crossed, his face turned at three quarters waiting for my question.

"Do you remember the comment you wrote on my annual performance evaluation?" I asked.

He pursed his lips, cast his eyes down, and said, "Oh. That." He breathed in deeply through his nose. "Yes, I wrote that you were a peacenik. I guess I can't call you a hypocrite." He shuffled his feet and turned to leave. "Thanks," he said as he walked away.

The clacking of my leather soles followed me down the ladder to the repair shop.

* * * * * * *

Three years after the USS Trippe left Viet Nam; the clacking of my heels followed me down the corridor to the hearing room. I was now in the Long Beach Naval Station Administration building, room 202, for my discharge hearing as a conscientious objector. The old off white walls of the hearing room had a four foot tall mahogany wainscot. I sat in a lone wooden chair on one side of a long highly polished mahogany table across from three hearing officers who sat in leather and wood chairs. A chief yeoman sat at the end of the table taking notes. My spouse and my parents were seated in wooden chairs behind me. The Officer who sat in the middle chair pulled out a manila folder from a large envelope and opened it.

"I see here that your chief, on the U.S.S. Trippe, wrote that you were peace loving on your first mid-year performance evaluation."

"Yes, Sir. It was a known fact that I was against the war. I made no attempt to hide it."

The officer to his left held a page of my discharge request in his hand. He used a Mont Blanc pen to scroll down the page. His pen stopped in the middle.

"I find what you wrote here offensive," he said as he tapped his pen against the page.

I froze in my seat. I couldn't think of what I had written that would be offensive? I held my breath.

He continued, "You state that being a mafia hit man is on a higher moral ground than being a United States Marine?" His face had formed a deep frown. "My father was a marine who survived the death march on Bataan."

He glared across the table at me. The room was so quiet I could hear my father breathing behind me. I remembered my father telling me about the seventy six thousand American and Filipino soldiers who were captured by the Japanese and forced to march eighty miles without food or water. His best friend was among them.

"Would you care to explain that?" he asked, leaning his body toward me.

My explanation was right in front of him. Worry ropes tightened around my stomach. What else could I add to what he had in front of him? Hadn't he already read the entire request?

My mouth felt like it had been wiped dry with cotton balls. I took a breath and said, "I have the deepest respect for what your father must have endured at the hands of the Japanese on the Bataan death march. With all due respect, Sir, what we did in My Lai was just a bad. All war is tragic." All three officers and the yeoman were looking at me, waiting for me to answer the question. I could hear the clock ticking on the wall. I breathed in through my nose and said, "Allow me to explain. When a mafia hit man is ordered to kill someone, he is careful. He makes sure that there is no collateral damage."

I took another big breath of air and let it out slowly. I knew he wasn't going to like what I was going to say next.

"A marine, by contrast, doesn't go after only enemy soldiers; he'll blow up a whole village, with women and children, if that is what he thinks it will take to get his enemy."

The officer wrote something down then looked up at me with a frown. "I disagree with your answer, but I will let it stand."

I heard my spouse whispering to my parents behind me. My palms became sweaty.

"You state that killing is wrong," the officer said. "Would you kill someone who was attacking your family?"

"With all due respect, Sir, I'm not stupid. Of course I would kill someone who was trying to kill me or my family. But I wouldn't shoot mortars into his neighborhood, in an attempt to get him."

The center officer nodded to the officer on the right, indicating that he would field the next question.

"Let's say that you are at home and that an enemy army is just over a hill ready to attack the next morning. There is no place for you to run away to," he said and squinted his eyes. "What are you going to do?"

The scenario was unrealistic. I knew the question was a trap and how I answered it would determine whether or not they granted my request.

I looked at the three officers. Swallowing with difficulty, I took a big breath. "I would sneak over the hill to see where their weapons were. I would blow them up or disable them. If they have no weapons, they can't fight. I would kill, only as a last resort."

The center officer wrote something down and asked me and my parents to wait in the corridor until they called us back in.

My knees were shaking. I stood up and put my chest out. I didn't want the officers to know how scared I was. The chief opened the door for us to pass through and then closed it behind us. My mother took hold of my arm, turned me around and gave me a big hug.

"No matter what they decide in there," she said with a big smile. "I am proud of you."

"I wasn't too sure about the wisdom of doing this," my father said. "But I have to agree with your mom." He gave me a good tight hug. "I am proud of you, too."

I paced the deck, glancing at the door then looking at my watch. Denise took my hand. "What you did in there took courage. You showed them what you're made of. They have to grant you the discharge."

"Relax *mijo*," my mother said. "We asked the whole church to pray for you. God will answer our prayers."

I wished that he had answered my prayers to save the people in the church we blew up. The look of confidence on my mother's face was in direct contrast with my father's and mine.

The door to the hearing room opened and the chief asked us to come back inside. The three offices sat in their chairs, their faces expressionless.

My chair had been removed. The Chief told me to stand in front where my chair had been.

The officer in the middle stood up and said. "Your request to be discharged as a conscientious objector has been reviewed and accepted."

My heart raced, the palms of my hands were wet. I hadn't noticed that I had been holding my breath until I heard his words.

"Don't get me wrong," he added. "But if you and I were in combat, I would want you on my team."

He leaned across the table, shook my hand, and then handed me the manila envelope that held their decision. The chief held the door open for us to leave.

"It's over," Denise said as we walked out the door. "You won't have to kill anymore."

She grabbed my hand and said, "He tried to insult you."

"I know he meant it as a compliment," I said. "It's a military man's compliment."

My mother took my other hand, gave me an impish smile and said, "I was almost expecting him to say, 'Good bye, be sure to come back.'"

Her words shot me back to the summer of 1972, to the last time I swam in the water behind Grande Island.

I had been skinny dipping in the early morning with fins, snorkel and a mask. As I swam away from shore, I started thinking that life would have been so much better if we had gone to Viet Nam to snorkel instead of fight. I should have been there helping them build a church, not blowing it up and killing everyone inside for a body count. When I turned around to swim back, I saw the Vietnamese lady, who appeared in my dreams, swim under water toward me. She wore the traditional Vietnamese pants and tunic. But they were made of thousands of live blue and yellow damsel fish.

I froze.

"Good bye, be sure to come back," she said with a smile. "I forgive you. I will help you forgive yourself and help you regain your soul. I await your return to how you should have come in the first place."

I stood up as fast as I could, my breathing raced to catch up with my heart beat. I put my face back in the water but the Vietnamese lady was gone.

EPILOGUE

I submitted the following to PBS (Public Broadcasting Service) in response to my visit to the Viet Nam Memorial in Washington DC:

To The Parents of the Young Men That We Killed in Vietnam

by Mushroom Montoya |
December 11, 1996

I still keep a letter that I wrote to my brother, John on his 17th birthday under my keyboard as a "momento" of my loss of innocence. I wrote to him on my first day on the gun line. On our first strike and our first of too many "targets" too high a body count. The letter starts of innocently enough, "Happy Birthday, John! Your being 17 makes me feel old. The USS Trippe killed her first VC today. Somebody's mother's child is dead and, unfortunately, I was part of that. It makes me sick just to think about it. ... I can't tell you much though 'cause Mom's ears and eyes would hurt ... Take care of yourself, Mushroom"

What I couldn't let my mother's eyes read is that on our very first strike, our very first shot, I watched three young men running on the beach carrying a wooden box. We fired! Screams, blood, body parts! Two of the young men got up and started running. Bam! Shot number two. No screams, just body parts. I was looking through the Big Eyes (huge binoculars).

The gunner jumped down from the gun ecstatic over the news of his "better than perfect" score. I stood there, still in shock over what I had just witnessed. I looked him in the eye, and yelled, "How can you be happy? You just killed three guys! and you don't know for sure who they really were. You just killed THREE guys!"

His eyes went wild as he screamed back, "Damn you, Mushroom! They are NOT people! They are just targets! If they were people, I couldn't do my job? F ... You! Why did you have to go and spoil a perfect hit on a moving target?"

Too many "targets", too high a body count. Now my first born son is dead. "And somebody's father's child is dead." He died in uniform, returning from lunch to the reserve center in

348

Albuquerque, New Mexico. I wonder if those three boys were returning from lunch so many years ago on the shores of Vietnam. Now I have a glimpse of the pain we caused to the mothers and fathers of those young boys that we killed in Vietnam.

Every night, in Vietnam, I used to pray and ask God to let me wake up from this nightmare and be back home. This HAD to be a nightmare, it couldn't possibly be real. But each time I woke up, the "nightmare" was still going on. Later, in 1978, while watching the fireworks, someone shot off white flares. For a small eternity, I was back in Vietnam. I was terrified that night. I was afraid that 1978 was a dream and that I would wake up on the ship and it would still be 1972.

Too many "targets" too high a body count. I was unable to watch and enjoy fireworks without the weight and fear associated with the war until I went to the Vietnam Memorial in 1992. The Memorial caused a healing through many tears. I had my younger son take a photo of me pointing at the place where my name should have been. Part of me died in Vietnam. Part of all of us who were there died.

We lost our innocence. We lost our sanity. We are plagued with ghosts that haunt us. We are all wounded too deeply from too many "targets" too high a body count. Mushroom Montoya HTFN USS Trippe DE1075 Rdiv.

After my second tour in Vietnam, I was granted a 6 month early out as a conscientious objector. War is not healthy for children, parents and other living things.

Viet Nam Body Count

ABOUT THE AUTHOR

Mushroom Montoya circumnavigated the globe after killing soldiers, women and children in Viet Nam.
Now, as a shaman, he heals the planet one person at a time.

He served two tours in Viet Nam aboard the USS Trippe DE1075 and the USS Truxton DLGN 35.

IF YOU ENJOYED THIS BOOK
Your comments under *Customer Reviews*
Viet Nam Body Count by Mushroom Montoya
at Amazon.com would be appreciated

353

CPSIA information can be obtained at www.ICGtesting.com
Printed in the USA
LVOW12s1635110514

385319LV00018B/1382/P